This book is for my parents:
Norman Keith McEwan
(1918–1990)
and
Iris Genevieve Puett Dunn McEwan
(1921–1997)
Who would have ignored the dirty parts
and loved it anyway.
And for
Barry Humphries
Who makes me laugh very hard,
for very long, very often!
—Douglas McEwan

My ghostwriter seems to have hijacked my dedication page!
Let me assure you that I dedicate this book to all the
little people sitting out there in the dark, watching me,
and touching themselves. Drink up, darlings!
—Tallulah

CONTENTS

A Note From Miss Morehead's Ghostwriter

No live organism can continue for long to exist sanely under conditions of absolute reality; even larks and katydids are supposed, by some, to dream. Morehead Heights, not sane, stands by itself astride mighty Tumescent Tor, holding darkness, and Miss Tallulah, within. It has stood so for eighty years, and might stand for eighty more. Within, walls continue upright, bricks meet neatly, floors are firm, and doors are sensibly shut. Silence lies steadily against the pressboard and linoleum of Morehead Heights, and whoever comes there, comes alone.

Miss Tallulah Morehead is a True Legend, and by "True Legend" I mean a legend as Paul Bunyan was a legend, and, like Paul Bunyan, she is a towering figure generally accompanied by a lot of bull. (All right, Bunyan's "Babe" was an ox, not a bull. Cut me some slack. I'm making a point here. Besides, Babe was a *blue* ox, and when Miss Tallulah starts spreading the bull, she talks a blue streak.) And I mean "True" in the same sense that Bill Clinton does when he says, "This is true." In any event, during the time I spent with Miss Morehead in her world-famous mansion, Morehead Heights, compiling these reminiscences, she showed me just how frighteningly real she can be.

As anyone who knows her intimately can tell you, Miss Tallulah Morehead is an ardent believer in, and adept practitioner of, the Grand Oral Traditions that have made our country what it is today. Which is to say that Miss Morehead related her story to me orally, without reference to notes, diaries, or memoirs of any kind, relying solely on her celebrated powers of recall. "Never make evidence, darling," has been her motto throughout her unparalleled career, and who can argue with that level of success?

However, Miss Tallulah has also been known to imbibe just a whisper. That is to say, she drinks . . . frequently, and with awe-inspiring skill, and truly fervent enthusiasm. Consequently, there are a few inconsistencies, contradictions, vagaries, implausibilities, and downright lies, along with some glaring omissions and yawning gaps scattered throughout the narrative. Miss Tallulah's recollections of any given event may vary widely from day to day, sometimes from hour to hour, at times even sentence to sentence. One afternoon Miss Tallulah held me spellbound for two hours with a tale of her rise in the theater until I realized that she was actually relating the plot of *All About Eve* retold from Eve's point of view.

All of which is to say that you may find that the various parts of this story don't add up, don't make sense, or are just plain impossible. Some parts may contradict other parts, and some of the most basic bits of information are just plain missing. I know. For example, how many husbands has she had? Even she no longer knows. You won't find a tidy reckoning, or even a tidy room, in this book. You are best advised to just accept that now. It will only save you heartache later. As Miss Morehead herself says, "It is not a lady's function to fill her own gaps, except in prison, of course."

Occasionally the names of real and famous personalities will pop up on these pages, although with Miss Morehead doing the talking, it's a fairly safe bet that they have been used fictionally—which, as Tallulah always says, is better than never being used at all. Besides, my lawyers assure me that it's legally impossible to libel the dead, no matter how hard Tallulah tries. And if one or two famous folk mentioned within aren't quite as dead as my lawyers would like, then they've been used "satirically"—yeah, that's it, just like Jerry Falwell in *The People v. Larry Flynt*. It's all a joke. I mean, honestly, the Forward is by *John Barrymore,* for Christ's sake, who died long before I was born! Get a clue. Besides, unlike Larry Flynt, this book will not be accusing any real-life personalities of having had sex with their mothers in outhouses, even if they did! So let's just all drop the summonses, relax, and have a good time, okay?

Thus, I present Miss Tallulah's story to you exactly as she told it to me, only you'll have to provide your own cocktails. So hurry on down to the Liquor Barn, stock up and settle in, because what a story it is: the films, the costars, the scandals, the Trial, the husbands, the sex, the drinking, all the awards and accolades she's nearly received. What is a "Tallulah Law"? You'll find out in Chapter 2. Merely mentioning a few of the titles of her more than eighty films sends shivers down the spines of cinema lovers: *Heat Crazed!, Damaged Cargo, Amok!, The Revenge of Cleopatra, The Mailman Always Comes Twice, The Godawful Truth, Single Indemnity,* her Dinosaur Trilogy: *1,000,000 Years Ago, When Dinosaurs Ruled the Block, Jurassic Tart,* and *Wet, Wild and Willing* (with **Elvis!**), *Boot Camp Bitches, HER!, Tarzan's Secret Shame,* the delightful morale-building wartime musical *Privates on Display* and its peacetime sequel *Privates in Public,* her Bob Hope and Bing Crosby classic, *The Road to Hell,* and the list goes on. But perhaps no other facet of her fame is more illustrious than her world-renowned home.

At the northwesternmost corner of Los Angeles County the ocean spends its passions crashing against the mighty twin rocks at the root of monumental Tumescent Tor, which, with priapic magnificence, thrusts insistently skyward, rising to a lofty, magisterial peak; and mounted firmly astride its formidable, muscular, intimidating, yet strangely inviting head sits Morehead Heights, Miss Tallulah Morehead's celebrated Movie Star Mansion. It was at Morehead Heights where Joan Crawford learned to nurture, where Boris Karloff faced his greatest personal terror, where Cecil B. DeMille bared his "B," where, for over forty years, more than usually revealing and deeply probing auditions for the role of Tarzan were held weekly whether the part was being cast or not. Intrigued? Well, all those stories and many more besides, which I listened to right there in the very rooms where so many of them happened, if they happened, lie ahead. My advice is just go with the flow, because with Miss Tallulah, there's always plenty flowing.

I'd also here like to thank Maestro Bryan Miller, Miss Tallulah's longtime accompanist and "straight man," who composed the score for this book.

—Douglas McEwan

FOREWORD

The Morehead, The Merrier!
by
John Barrymore

I was born and raised, as every truly cultured American knows, in the waning decades of the nineteenth century, in the great city of Philadelphia, to a family that was "theatrical" back when that meant "works in the theater" rather than "lives with the costume designer." I grew up in the house of my grandmother, Mrs. John Drew, nationally renowned for her Mrs. Malaprop opposite Joseph Jefferson, and the actress-manager of the celebrated Arch Street Theater. It was common for us, as I was maturing, to have the greatest stars of the day staying with us in our home while they appeared in Grandmama's theater, performing the great works of Shaw, Sheridan, and the Divine Shakespeare. Can you imagine what it meant to a budding superstar like myself, listening to Edwin Booth reciting sonnets over the dinner table, Edmund Kean thundering out Lear's mad scene at tea, and Joseph Jefferson clowning with Molière while I was trying to undress for bed? My boyhood was one long train of unforgettable experiences, though in the case of the Jefferson anecdote I have put it as far from my mind as I could.

But even with all those as common daily occurrences, it was still a time of rare, of extraordinary excitement that one week, when I was but a lad of fourteen springs, when the already legendary Miss Tallulah Morehead came to appear at Grandmama's Arch Street Theater in her national comeback tour of *Ten Nights in a Barroom,* and to stay in our own home.

Certainly it was an education in acting to watch Tallulah bring an unprecedented authenticity to that beloved melodrama. The fashion in acting in those days was a heavily stylized performance of broad gesture and declamatory speech. Not so Miss Tallulah, whose naturalistic delivery often rendered her unintelligible in the front rows and inaudible in the rear stalls, whilst her minimalist approach to gesture sometimes led to severe doubts in the minds of some audience and cast members as to whether she was even fully conscious. But the *realism* of her approach was truly breathtaking. Never have I seen alcoholism portrayed on the stage with such ferocious honesty! You could literally *smell* the fumes of demon rum, even in the second balcony. In fact, after her most intense performances you could still smell the fumes in the theater the next morning! And this is all the more impressive when I tell you that in the play Tallulah was playing the alcoholic's *wife!*

But my fondest and most vivid memory of Miss Tallulah on that long ago summer was of a *private* performance she gave on a languid afternoon in my grandam's cozy attic for an enraptured audience of one. Need I say that that ardent suppliant there to learn from the mistress all she had to teach was myself? And it was then and there that Miss Tallulah Morehead, out of her great generosity of spirit and her love of youth, took this trembling boy and gently, caringly, gave him his first tender introduction to Life's Greatest Pleasure.

I was nervous, a little afraid, but eager when Tallulah, noticing that the other adults were out, said so lovingly, "Where's that scamp Lionel? He's out, too? Well then, you'll have to do, sonny. Don't be afraid. Come upstairs with Tallulah and tell me your name. I'll give you something you've never had before."

My heart was racing as I silently followed the great star up the stairs to our attic hideaway. Tallulah, ever thoughtful, kept my mind from becoming too preoccupied with her constant stream of witty banter: "So, John-boy, that big sister of yours, Ethel, what's the skinny on her? Is she by any chance a daughter of Lesbos? Does she slake her thirst in the Well of Loneliness?" I had no idea what Tallulah meant, but smiled to show I was still agog.

"Is she a frequent guest at Radcliffe Hall? Answer me, boy, does Ethel yodel in the canyon? You have no notion of what I'm talking about, do you, darling? As far as you know, the maid is the only woman around here to, ah, *shampoo the carpet.* Well, never mind. Come have a look at what Auntie Tallulah has to show you."

And then she revealed to me the glories she had hidden within her blouse. My breath was taken away. I was near to fainting when I first put my quivering lips there. Tallulah, ever caring, said, "Whoa, slow down, young man. Make it last. Savor its sweetness. Because if you like that, you're going to love *this!*"

Afterwards, my head spinning, I lay in her arms, knowing at last how a man feels, as Tallulah said, "Don't pass out on me, boy. That was just the first one. I want another. Pass me my cocktail shaker."

Yes, it was Miss Tallulah Morehead on that long ago June afternoon who gave this innocent lad his very first vodka martini! I will always be grateful to her for commencing my lifelong love affair with booze!

Then afterwards we had sex, of course. I was an old hand at love-making, having lost my virginity months earlier, in that same attic, with my stepmother.* Alcohol isn't everything.

So cheers to Miss Tallulah; long may she reign!

—John Barrymore

---

*Before you start calling in attorneys concerning this bit about losing my virginity to my stepmother, thinking it a violation of the promise not to portray real people having sex with their mothers in outhouses, I just want to point out that this episode doesn't qualify under the Jerry Falwell ruling for three reasons:

1. It occurred not in an outhouse but in an attic.
2. She was my *step*mother, not my birth mother.
3. It's not a joke. It really happened. Read my *Biographies*. Skoal! –J.B.

INTRODUCTION

Rye Memories

There's a moment in the movie *HER!,* which I starred in for Merian C. Cooper during a memorable loanout to RKO back in the thirties, when the intrepid jungle explorers led by C. Aubrey Smith, who was *all man,* if you take my meaning, and adorable Charles Farrell, who was more like forty-percent man on a good day, come across the ancient fifty-foot statue of me supposedly erected by my native worshippers in the dim and distant eons of the past.* (You'll recall that the immortal temptress/goddess I played in *HER!* was supposed to be over three thousand years old. Bosley Crowther of *The New York Times* called it "perfect typecasting.") As the awestruck adventurers gaze up at the enormous idol, C. Aubrey speaks for all when he says, "Good God! I think it's . . . a *woman!*"

Well, darlings, that describes me to a tee. Let no one doubt. I am . . . a *woman!* Oh yes. I have witnesses. *But,* I am *more* than a woman, much more. I am a *Star!*

I have been a *Star* since the forgotten days of Silent Television. I have worked in every medium known to man, and in a few that aren't. I've been married more times than I remember. I've known the great, the near-great, the not-so-great, and the downright awful, most of them in a biblical sense.

Shakespeare said some are born great, some achieve greatness, and

---

*Cooper gave Tallulah this statue when the picture was completed. It was used again twenty years later when she appeared in the semi-sequel *Abbott & Costello Meet She Who Must Be Obeyed* at Universal. Today the statue adorns the garden here at Morehead Heights.–Douglas.

some have greatness thrust within them. Well, in my case, two out of three ain't bad.

But the thought of putting all this down on paper was daunting. I've always been orally oriented. Even in silent movies, my mouth was legendary.

Why even attempt it, you ask? Well, there were two reasons. But it all began with my number one fan, Gilmore.

I should explain about Gilmore. If you are a private citizen, what we in the business call "nonentities," and you have someone like Gilmore in your life, you call him a stalker and you take out a restraining order. But when you are a *Star* like myself, you call Gilmore a fan and you encourage him to reproduce, albeit asexually, which in Gilmore's case is a pretty safe bet.

Gilmore, quite simply, is obsessed with me and my career, despite the fact that I haven't made a film since before he was born. When other boys his age were becoming fascinated by *Star Trek* or sports, Gilmore was watching my old movies over and over until he knew the dialogue far better than I ever did.

When I first met Gilmore he told me that I was plastered all over his apartment. This sounded quite plausible to me as I have been plastered all across this great nation of ours, and, frankly, I don't always remember with whom. It turned out that Gilmore also had pictures and posters from my greatest films all over his walls, the sound track from my popular, morale-building World War II service musical, *Privates on Display,* booming from his CD player, and my dolls, action figures, Tallulah swizzle sticks, and other Tallulah-related merchandising items crowding his curio shelves, as well as a complete library of all my surviving films on videotape, including a rare Japanese bootleg copy of my never-released-in-the-USA Oriental musical, *A World of Woozy Song.* The centerpiece of his collection was the authentic zebra-striped sarong I wore as Melanoma, the simple island princess ("Kiss, what means this word kiss?") that I played in *Sudan Sunset,* which Gilmore had had altered to fit him, though it might have made more sense to alter *him* to fit *it.* I know it *is* the actual costume because I not only recognize the stains on the lining, but could put a name to them without recourse to DNA tests, which is more than I can say for the outfit I'm wearing today.

Since our first meeting Gilmore has been to every one of my openings. Indeed, he says he can sniff out one of my openings from a mile away, and has, in fact, publicly demonstrated this unique talent, once in front of a paying audience, though I soon put a stop to that.

One evening Gilmore escorted me to a local West Hollywood cabaret called *What a Drag,* where the entertainment consisted entirely of Tallulah Morehead impersonators. You could have knocked me over with a tire iron when I learned, to my amazement, that all the performers were, at least biologically, males! These strapping young men had spent many days scouring the malls for duplicates of my famous ensembles.* The results these boys achieved were astounding! Some of them looked damn good! I was actually kissing one of them before I realized that he *wasn't* Ida Lupino.† Needless to say, I retrieved my tongue in a hurry.

Once Gilmore and I had convinced the performers that not only was I a real female (which required the most vivid and incontrovertible evidence! Those boys were *skeptical!* They wouldn't take "yes" for an answer), but that I was the *actual* Miss Tallulah Morehead herself, we had a lovely evening as I regaled the boys with tales of my life and career while they competed for the honor of paying my bar tab. (Sadly, the winner lost his car as a result.)

Gilmore pointed out to me that if there were people willing to pay to see men *pretending* to be me, how much more would they pay to see what's left of the *real* me? There was a certain logic to that, and I've never been averse to money. My liquor bills don't pay themselves.

Shortly after that, Gilmore became my personal assistant and introduced me to Bryan Miller and Douglas McEwan, and with their help I put together my cabaret show, *Rye Memories,* which had a remarkable success.††

Eventually Gilmore pointed out that I could reach still larger numbers of people with a book. I noted that during the wars I entertained

---

*By the way, have you noticed that some of our malls *need* scouring? Pitch in and help. It's fun! Why, only yesterday I went down on Beverly's Center, where I spent an hour on my knees polishing Sam's Goody! Just seeing it gleam was reward enough! –Tallulah

†A lovely lady, but frankly, I've always suspected that she was the merest whisper of a lesbian. You didn't think Howard Duff was really a man, did you? Well, you didn't hear it from me.–Tallulah

††Oddly, we found that in San Francisco and West Hollywood we had better attendance if we led the audience to believe that Tallulah was a male impersonator. One happy upshot of Tallulah's cabaret career was that Bryan and Gilmore, after spending many long, steamy, sweaty afternoons bent over a hot piano, as well as working out Tallulah's music, ended up sharing a house and are now raising pets together. –Douglas

thousands of servicemen one at a time with no complaints.* Still, the argument had merit. So the first reason for writing this book was to please Gilmore.

The other reason was the money, of course. And so, with Douglas's editorial assistance, the project was launched.

Mine is a strange story, rich in glamor, heartache, sex, and cocktails. It's a tale of Hollywood at its grandest and its seediest, and of the wonderful personalities who populated it throughout this fabulous century. Join me in looking back as we enter My Second Millennium.

Good God! My glass is empty! While I refill why don't you turn the page and embark, darling?

—Tallulah Morehead
Morehead Heights, 2000

---

*I *believe* they were all *American* servicemen, but it's so hard to tell when they're out of uniform. In the dark all cats are gay.–Tallulah

PART ONE

Enter Tallulah!
1896–1915

1

Born in a Drunk

I was born in a trunk in the Princess Theater in Pocahotass, Idaho. It was during a matinee on Friday, and my mother used a cocktail napkin for my didy. When I first saw the light it was pink and amber, shining on a crystal martini glass. But I'm getting ahead of my story.

I never knew my father. He died before I was born. Unfortunately, I can't say the same about my mother, who deliberately survived well into my adulthood just to annoy me. I'd tell you her name, but that's just what she'd want, and it's bad enough I have to mention her at all.

My mother was born in one of those *other* countries that make up what cartographers refer to as "foreign markets." I used to ask Mother what country she was from, but getting a sober answer from her was never easy at the best of times. She didn't like talking about her past much, though it was certainly obvious that she had one. "If I'd wanted my past catching up with me, I'd have left a forwarding address," she used to say. All she'd ever tell me of her life before marrying my father was that under no circumstances was I ever to reveal her whereabouts to anyone named Angelo.

Mother was an "actress," which, for some reason, she always insisted be spelt with the quotation marks. She said that when she met my father she was "working the streets" of her native city. When I asked her how an "actress" could be working on streets, she explained that it was "Street Theater." In any event, my father must have been impressed by Mother's performance, because they had a whirlwind courtship. In fact, they married on the very day they met, like that cute couple on that lesbian TV sitcom *Dharma & Grace*.

My mother always said my father's name was "Sam or Fred or Bill. Something like that, anyway. He didn't talk much."

"But didn't you talk to him?" I asked her when still just a little girl.

"Tallulah, child," Mother slurred, "if I've told you once, I've told you a hundred times: it's rude to talk when your mouth's full."

Father was a soldier. Mother was certain of that, she said, because his uniform fit him. The war was raging and Daddy was due to ship out the next day, hence the hasty marriage. Fortunately, one of Daddy's pals—"John or Slim or Alfie or something. I wasn't taking notes, child"—was some sort of "lay minister," so they were able to throw together a quick wedding right in Mother's flat. Mother's "costar" (quotation marks Mother's) Trixie was maid of honor, and Daddy's other pal—"Bruce, I'm *sure* his name was Bruce!"—was best man. Then, when Mother and Daddy were wed, they took over maid-of-honor and best-man roles while Bruce married Trixie. The five of them then threw themselves a "reception," which in this case was three soldiers and two "actresses" killing a couple of fifths of vodka and dancing to the Victrola until that magic time when my mother, a nervous, blushing bride, and her shy new husband retired to Mother's bedroom for their blissful wedding night, while Bruce, Trixie, and Reverend John-or-Slim-or-Alfie retired to Trixie's room for theirs.

"Were you a virgin on your wedding night?" I once asked my mother when I was too young to know the obvious answer.

"Of course I was, Tallulah child," Mother replied. "I was born a virgin and I'll die a virgin."

At one point during my parents' one night of joy it occurred to Mother that she didn't yet know what her new last name was. She lifted her head, looked up into her new husband's eyes, and said, "My love, what's your last name?"

Daddy gently placed a caressing hand on the back of Mother's head. With his eyes rolling in bliss he gave Mother's head a firm shove as he grunted out the single word, "Morehead."

"Mrs. Morehead," Mother repeated, silently, so as not to be rude.

Daddy, Bruce, and Reverend John-or-Slim-or-Alfie had to be up early the next morning to ship out to the front. Mother woke just in time to see Daddy depositing a handful of crumpled singles on Mother's dresser, apparently all the cash the poor private had to leave his new bride as he went off to face the enemy. She struggled to her feet, never her easiest accomplishment. Mother, like most "actresses" before the advent of film, was unaccustomed to arising before noon, and at any time was steadier with her feet above rather than beneath her. She staggered out to the living room just in time to see Trixie kissing Bruce and Reverend John-or-Slim-or-Alfie good-bye. (The Very Reverend J-or-S-or-A had apparently chaperoned Bruce and Trixie throughout their wedding night, probably to safeguard the Blessed Sanctity of their union.)

Watching these brave, satiated young men leaving the Heavenly Haven of their marriage beds to face the Horrors of Battle brought a tear to Trixie's eye. "Do you think," she asked around her wake-up cigarette, "that we'll ever see those privates again?"

"Trixie, honey," my mother, ever practical, replied, "if Life has taught me anything, it's that we'll both go on seeing privates as long as we live!"

"That's nice," said Trixie, much relieved. "Say, you want a shot?"

"I'm awake, aren't I?" was Mother's witty retort.

In the months that followed, Mother, now known professionally as Mrs. Morehead, did her part to honor her husband's war effort by organizing Trixie, herself, and a few other "actresses" into a sort of informal, unofficial USO-type performing troop called the "Morehead Ladies," entertaining hundreds of battle-weary privates, unit by unit. How many privates, on their last evening of freedom, penetrated my mother's threshold to "Shoot the moon," which was Mother's unique method for remaining "faithful" to her absent husband? No one, least of all Mother, could say, even under oath.

But at last there came a day, a few months after Father's departure, when Mother found she no longer fit into the "costumes" she occasionally wore. Needless to say, Mother's Little Weight Problem was me. Mother compromised with my added weight by going on a liquid diet consisting entirely of a patent medicine then popular that, apart from trace amounts of uric acid, was chemically identical to scotch.

"Did your obstetrician actually prescribe that tonic?" I once innocently asked Mother.

"Did my *what* do *what*? We're in America now, Tallulah. Speak English, and mix me another gimlet," was her always waggish reply.

But, even as Mother prepared to welcome Sam-or-Fred-or-Bill Morehead's young heir into the world, she received *The Letter,* the one that seven out of every ten war wives dread. Though the original, written on official army stationery, has been lost in the sands of time, one paragraph was sufficiently burned into Mother's memory to still exist in mine:

It is with great sorrow and tremendous regret that I inform you that I was killed in battle two days ago. It will, I hope, be some consolation to you to know that I died bravely, defending a whole lot of other guys, yeah, and some women and children, too. I'll probably get a posthumous medal; though, if you never receive it, it's because it got lost in the mail. Also, I was blown into such tiny smithereens that there isn't enough of my body left to ship home, so you won't be burdened with a funeral or burial or anything, though if you'd like to hold a private memorial service, feel free. My sincerest condolences to you on my loss. Rest assured that my last thoughts were trying to recall you. Oh yeah, and Bruce would like you to tell Trixie that he's dead, too.

Can you imagine the shroud of grief that descended on that once happy household? Tears came to my mother's eyes, and a howl almost indistinguishable from one of rage tore from the depths of her notoriously deep throat as she crumpled the tear-stained letter and tore it into shreds. Trixie was equally shattered once Mother had reminded her of who Bruce was.

"Oh yeah," Trixie said after Mother managed to pierce her amnesia, "I remember those boys. What a double act they were. That's too bad. Is the phony priest dead, too?"

"The letter doesn't say," Mother replied.

"Oh, I hope not. Frankly, he was by far the, ah, *bigger* man. Ya get me?"

"Why do you say a 'phony' priest?" Mother asked, nervous lest any aspersions be cast on the legitimacy of her marriage and her Little Weight Problem.

"Well, I'm sure I don't know," said Trixie, who tended to turn defensive when cross-examined. "All I can say is, he wasn't no celibate, not unless they've changed the rules drastically since I was expelled from Our Lady of Eternal Torment Boarding School for Girls, though he was certainly catholic in his tastes."

Mother faced up to her bereavement in our family's traditional manner: lots of vodka, set off by occasional rounds of gin. A few days later, when Mother regained consciousness, she decided to put her grief and her brief married life behind her and emigrate to the USA.

Unfortunately, Mother had neglected at the time of her wedding to obtain the necessary documents to prove her marital status to the passport bureau or the immigration officials. Nor had the army sent her any official papers certifying her Gold Star Widowhood either. After a few weeks of horsefeathers and runaround Mother decided to cut through the red tape. She bought an extremely large steamer trunk, drilled a few holes in it, packed it with her few garments, her leopard-skin fur, and plenty of vodka, selected a city at random from a map of the United

States, and had herself shipped to the Princess Theater in Pocahotass, Idaho, labeled as "Wardrobe."

When the trunk finally arrived at the theater it was making one hell of a racket. A Friday matinee of *Charlie's Aunt* was in progress on the stage, and it must have sounded to the audience as though a particularly uninhibited production of *The Trojan Women* was being rehearsed in the wings. A very distraught elderly stage manager, hearing what sounded like the screams of the damned emanating from the trunk, grabbed a crowbar to pry open the locked trunk, in a state of panicked confusion since no shipment of theatrical costumes had ever before arrived shrieking.

When he got the trunk open he saw within my besotted mother holding in her arms a squalling newborn infant girl, Yours Truly, upstaging the actors on stage with my very first breaths. "Don't just stand there, you dolt, slack-jawed and agape!" burbled Mother, always in command. "Can't you see I'm out of vodka? Get me a cocktail immediately! Then summon the wardrobe mistress to get this hideous placenta out of my fur! Oh, and a bottle of diluted gin with a nipple, too. Can't you see my baby Tallulah is hungry?"

2

Just a Spoonful of Vodka

Shortly after giving birth to me, like many women throughout the world, my mother suffered a bout of postpartum depression, although in Mother's case, it was to last over forty years! Being essentially a generous woman, Mother bountifully shared her depression with everyone she knew.

I don't know how much I can tell you about my childhood as, quite frankly, I have only the haziest memories of it. It was, after all, the better part of a century ago or so.[*] Good Lord, I barely remember last week! Who won the Oscars this year? Did they finally nominate Greer Garson[†]?

When I was an infant, Mother couldn't bear to be parted from me, though, fortunately, she eventually got over this, after she married my stepfather. Mother and I toured in vaudeville for the first few years of my life. The first year our act was billed as "Bertha Morehead, Baby Juggler." It was a hell of an act. Mother would toss me about in an amazing manner, at one point spinning me on the end of a pole! (I still have an indentation in my back that I *think* came from that pole, or some pole anyway.) At the climax, Mother was juggling me, a watermelon, and a machete, all at once; on the last pass, Mother would grab the machete and split the watermelon in midair and then catch me, at least at the performances where she got it right.

I was, quite simply, a *sensation* on stage right from the start! Aud-

---

[*]Near as I can figure out, Tallulah was born sometime in May or June of 1897. –Douglas

[†]A great lady, but what a gasbag! And frankly, I suspect she may have been just the merest whisper of a lesbian, but you didn't hear it from me.–Tallulah

iences would gasp and scream at my high-flying antics, but around my first birthday, Mother decided that it was time for a new act, as my weight was now more than twice that of the watermelon and was causing Mother to become seriously unbalanced, and *not* for the last time, I might add. This was a courageous decision when you consider how successful this act had been. Mother and I were "in demand," as they say; in fact, Mother was officially "wanted" in seventeen states. *Variety* had stated, "Child-abuse has never been so thrilling!" And to this day I am proud to know that it was *my* stage debut that inspired new, stricter children-in-show-business labor laws all across our great land! In the decades since, many a fortunate child has been ripped from its mother's arms thanks to the "Tallulah Laws."

Many were quick to criticize Bertha Morehead as a Bad Mother, little realizing that "Bertha" was just a stage name, taken on a lawyer's advice so that arrest warrants would always be taken out against a fictional person. But no mother could have been more concerned with her child's health; after all, a sick baby couldn't go on stage. "Ever try to juggle a baby dripping snot?" Mother would ask in her refined way. "God knows she's slippery enough as it is." Mother was always shoveling various patent medicines and remedies down my tiny throat. She had a little saying: "Just a spoonful of vodka helps the medicine go down," and right she was.

I was six, and we were doing a ventriloquist act, which had the simple advantage over our old act that the authorities didn't know there was a child in it, when Mother met Maxie, the man who became my stepfather. Maxie was a manager who took over booking our act. Once he and Mother became "more than just friends," if you know what I mean (and if you don't you're probably still trying to figure out Chapter 1), Maxie became concerned for my education. Maxie and Mother would come home late and find me in their bed. "Christ, why isn't that floor rat in school?" Maxie would bellow endearingly as he undressed. "Here, Tallulah, here's a *whole* dollar. Why don't you go see a show? Your mom and me need some privacy." I was so dazzled having an entire dollar, a *fortune* in those days, that it never occurred to me to point out, as Maxie shoved me out the front door, that there weren't really all that many shows a six-year-old could go see at two in the morning.

It was Maxie who arranged for the beginning of my formal education when he had me shipped off to Major Barbara's Military Boarding School for Girls. Mother was opposed at first, but Maxie convinced her that the vaudeville circuit was no place to raise a child, that I needed a steady home and a bed of my own, one I didn't share with them.

Mother became further alarmed when I wrote to tell her that drinking alcohol was strictly forbidden for Major Barbara's cadettes. Mother came tearing out to the academy and taught Major Barbara a thing or two about warfare. "My child was suckled on whisky!" Mother lectured. "She takes her medicine with a spoonful of vodka. For Heaven's sake, milk is Mother's gin to her!" By the time Mother was finished I was the only cadette in the history of the academy allowed alcohol, which made me *very* popular.

Major Barbara was an amazing woman. During the previous war, when told that women weren't allowed in combat, she'd simply masqueraded as a man and enlisted. Fortunately, male impersonation was second nature to her; it was *female* impersonation where she was less than convincing. She had fought valiantly and had received many decorations, including three Purple Hearts and the Congressional Medal of Honor, all without anyone ever suspecting her actual gender.

After mustering out, she had opened her military academy, training young girls in the precepts in which she believed. To her I will always be grateful for the grounding she gave me in literature, history, and hand-to-hand combat. I may not look it, but I know fourteen ways to kill a man unarmed, knowledge that has proved endlessly valuable in Hollywood.

My years with Major Barbara were happy ones, learning the enriching values of female comradeship from my bunkmates. I excelled at sports, biology, and, of course, drama; and the "chemistry experiments" I performed back in our barracks made me a legend. The early rising at reveille was good training for the hours I would later have to endure as a Screen Star.

One day, a little less than a year after I enrolled, I received a letter from Mother. She and Maxie had married. This time Mother made sure everything was signed and legal and performed in front of sober witnesses, never Mother's best audience. Mother said she had wanted me at the ceremony but that Maxie had recommended not interrupting my education.

I gave no thought to my future in those carefree days. I had no career goals in mind. My life was a busy round of classes, exercise, forced marches, war games, homework, wilderness survival training, and gossip with the other cadettes.

Major Barbara took a special interest in me right from the start. She could sense in me that magical spark that would later be recognized as Star Quality. She took me to her bosom and treated me like an incredibly intimate member of the family.

Mother, meanwhile, was still touring, doing an animal act that was very popular, but eventually, when I was around nine, the donkey died in an accident that also left Mother with a broken hip. Her act was washed up. That was when Maxie got *The Idea*. "Tallulah's been sponging off of us long enough. It's time she carried some of the load."

I was yanked out of Major Barbara's Military Academy the night before we were to commence our annual "All-Out War" with Colonel Ripper's Military School for Boys with a pre-dawn sneak attack, for which I had prepared the stink bombs myself. I was deeply upset. "All-Out War" was our favorite event. Not only did we get to handle live ammunition, but Major Barbara's (or "Major Babs," as I alone was privileged to call her, and only in private) take-no-prisoners policy left us free to enjoy the boys we captured in any way we chose before disposing of "the evidence." We *always* won. Major Babs repeatedly said, "Defeat is *not* an option," and also, "To win one must have the will to do what is necessary to win," a motto that came in damned handy in Hollywood. And, of course, afterwards, during our victory celebration, there was the friendly competition for the new beds left vacant by the girls who wouldn't be coming back. Sadly, this time my bed would be up for grabs as well, and not for the last time. I remember Major Babs's tearful farewell at the train station, the major telling herself to "suck it up. Take it like a man" (another of her oft-repeated mottos).

Thus I came for the first time to the little bungalow Mother and Maxie had bought out on Long Island. There the plans were laid for me to relaunch my theatrical career. I was to return to vaudeville as Baby Tallulah!

3

Drink Up, Tallulah

And so it was that at the tender age of nine, I made my first Show Business Comeback. Audiences, however, were completely unaware of the "return" nature of my act, since we decided not to publicize that I had been Baby Morehead as there were warrants still out in some states. This was to be a whole new start, and I was to court stardom as "Baby Tallulah."

Mother was laid up with her broken hip, and Maxie had a booking office in Manhattan where he worked every day, so neither of them could go out on the road with me. A combination escort, stage manager, and chaperone had been found to accompany me on the road, handling all the details and seeing to it that all the money was sent home. A woman had been found who was considered ideal for the job as she asserted that no man had ever touched her, and there seemed no reason whatever to doubt her word on that score. Certainly in the time I spent with her, thrown together twenty-four hours a day for five years, I never saw a man touch her. In fact, I never saw a man voluntarily come within ten feet of her. Children, dogs, cats, and birds all avoided her as well.

My chaperone's name was Mildred Puett, and there's a special word in the English language that was coined just to describe her: *drab.* Mildred possessed Anti-Glamor; if she ever touched a glamorous person they would annihilate each other, and the resulting explosion could level a city.*

---

*I hear you out there asking, "But, Miss Tallulah, you are Glamor Personified. How did you survive Mildred, the Anti-Glamor?" Ah, but hard as it may be to believe at nine years old, after three years in a girl's academy, I was not yet the incredibly alluring beauty I am now.–Tallulah

There was still the little matter of what was I to do onstage. Adorable as I was (and am), none of us really believed that an audience would pay to just stare at me standing still. Even in my recent years, when I returned to the cabaret stage I found that just standing there was not enough (although standing is a far greater accomplishment for me now than it was then); it was still necessary to speak to the audience and even to sing.

But what to do? I had talent, of course, big greasy gobs of it, but I had no training. Major Barbara had schooled us in *martial* arts, not *theater* arts. What could I do? I didn't know how to sing; I didn't know how to act; I didn't know how to dance or tell jokes. What could I do? What special skill did I possess? These were the questions I asked my mother.

"Well, you make a mean martini," Mother replied, although I didn't yet see how that would help.

"That's true, and her screwdrivers are pretty good, too," added Maxie. "And so are her gimlets and her manhattans. Too bad she can't just mix drinks onstage."

This was true, my "chemistry experiments" at school had made me one hell of a junior mixologist. It took a few more moments, but finally the penny dropped.

And so was born "Baby Tallulah, the World's Youngest Bartender." A chorus of young men would come marching out on stage wheeling a short, but fully stocked wet bar, singing:

Ladies and Gentlemen, good evening to you.
We've got a very special lady here, it's true.
We know that she's young, but if you're on a bender,
You'll never go wrong with our favorite bartender.
So prepare to drink up and make your report,
She can make you a tall one even though she is short.
[Spoken] Ladies and Gentlemen, presenting,
That five foot one, ninety-eight pound,
Spirited mixer of spirits,
The one who brings sunshine to our moonshine.
The World's Youngest Bartender,
Baby Tallulah!

At which point I leapt out through a paper hoop, dressed in a German barmaid costume, heavy on the frills, pirouetted twice, sank down in the splits and hollered out in my shrill little voice, "Hello everybody, My name's Tallulah. Who the hell are you?"

I would coax a gentleman up from the audience, ask him what his favorite mixed cocktail was, and then make it for him. Then it was requests from the audience, which always evolved into "Stump Tallulah" as the audience shouted out increasingly obscure concoctions, but I always whipped them up. Rarely was I stumped, and I was never stumped with the same drink twice.

I was nervous when I picked up the first drink on stage that first night. Did I have *Star Quality?* I hesitated for what seemed like an eternity with that drink at my lips, until I heard my mother's voice, bellowing supportively from her wheelchair in the stage box, "Drink up, Tallulah!" What nine-year-old girl hasn't wanted to hear those words? I closed my eyes and swallowed. As it always would be in the future, it was heaven.

As I grew more at ease onstage I began to chat with the audience as I made drinks, developing the conversational style with which I was to hold audiences spellbound decades later in my twilight cabaret years.

By the end of my act most of the audience was feeling no pain. I was a crowd pleaser. I was quickly moved to a headlining "closer" position because, quite simply, no one wanted to follow me, claiming that when I got through with them, the audience was in no condition to appreciate anyone else.

I played every state in the union except, for some reason, Utah, where they never seemed to appreciate my special form of entertainment. Talk about rare praise: W. C. Fields always said of Baby Tallulah that mine was the only child act he'd ever enjoyed.

I was one of the first stars to be thoroughly merchandised. Maxie set up a whole division of his business just licensing my likeness on Baby Tallulah dolls, dresses, games, books, swizzle sticks, cocktail shakers, and our biggest seller, "Baby Tallulah's My First Wet Bar."

Throughout all the Baby Tallulah years Mildred Puett never left my side, no matter how often I begged her to. Mildred rehearsed the men in the chorus while seeing to it that none of them ever came within yards of me offstage, kept the "props" stocked, handled the money, the train tickets, and the accommodations, and enforced my curfew with a strictness that made Major Babs look like a Rastafarian.

The only times Mildred lightened up was whenever we played Chicago. Mildred had a friend there, Minerva Thatcher, a lady even less attractive and less fun than Mildred, hard as that is to imagine. Next to Minerva, Margaret Hamilton was a glamorpuss. For that matter, Mildred made Marjorie Main* look like Rita Hayworth. Minerva was a

---

*Terribly nice lady, but what a *nympho!*–Tallulah

librarian who disapproved of reading, as it tended to give people "ideas." When we played Chicago, Mildred would go to see Minerva, and I would actually get time alone.

The first time Mildred returned from an overnighter at Minerva's (they called them "slumber parties," although I strongly suspect that there was never more than just the two of them there), I didn't even recognize her at first. It took several minutes to figure out that the reason Mildred looked so alien was because she was smiling.

One time, when we were playing Chicago—I must have been twelve—knowing that Mildred would be at Minerva's, I decided to try a little nightlife myself. After my last show I made myself up to look as old as possible (I based the look on Mother, who was *not* aging gracefully), dressed up in my most adult ensemble, and asked one of the young men in the chorus, a fellow named Kevin, to take me out to a real nightclub.

Talk about glamor; I was agog. The fine ladies in their furs and feathers, the men in their shiny tuxedos. I longed to shout, "Hello everybody, my name's Baby Tallulah. Who the hell are you?" but as I was far too young to be there, I had to avoid drawing attention to myself, something I've always found difficult.

The only disappointments were the drinks. I'd always mixed my own cocktails before, so I didn't know that the sinister practice of *watering down drinks* existed! When I tasted the first martini they brought me I involuntarily spat it back out, most of it on the waiter. "What the hell do you call this slop?" I raved. "I've had higher proof milk! My cat pees a better drink than this! Take this soft drink back and bring me a vodka tonic, *heavy* on the vodka, just the merest *whisper* of tonic! Do you get me, boy?" Needless to say, after that they brought me more respectable cocktails.

My memories of the evening begin growing hazy at this point. I recall dancing with Kevin to the Big Band playing. And I remember Kevin and me in a room somewhere later, and my asking him if he had any tattoos.

The next thing I remember after that is waking up to the glaring face of Mildred Puett. "Well, Tallulah," Mildred roared, "what have you to say for yourself?"

Her voice shot through my brain like a flaming sword. I could barely make out the sense of her words through the agonizing pain of hearing them. "I'm sorry, Mildred. What's wrong?" I asked.

"Don't you know where you are? Look around you," Mildred said with a terrible politeness.

I looked about me, but the bare, comfortless room was utterly unfamiliar. "Where am I, Mildred?" I asked, growing a little alarmed.

"Where are you, Tallulah?" Mildred pursed out the words stingily. "Why, you're in jail, Tallulah."

"In jail?"

"Yes, in jail," Mildred answered, her anger mixed with an odd form of satisfaction. "In jail . . . in Tijuana!"

"In Tijuana!" I gasped. "How is that possible? I was in Chicago last night! You'd need to invent some sort of flying machine to get from Chicago to Tijuana in one night, and everyone knows that's impossible."*

"Last night, Tallulah? Last night? The last time you performed your act in Chicago was *five months ago!* Would you care to explain where you've been and what you've been doing for the last five months? I have twenty irate theater managers who want to know why you never showed up for your engagements!"

"Five months! But, where's Kevin? What's happened to Kevin?"

"Don't trouble yourself over that little child molester. I've discharged him. He's in another cell here and he'll probably never get out. Statutory rape, contributing to the delinquency of a minor! Disgusting!"

It was true. Five months had passed. Fortunately for Kevin, we were arrested in Mexico, and my birthday had come during those five months so that I was thirteen when apprehended. In Mexico this meant I was an adult, practically a grandmother, so the charges against Kevin were dismissed. I was dragged off to finish a split week in Albuquerque.

A medical examination confirmed what I already felt somehow sure of; sometime during those missing months I had *misplaced* my virginity, I assume with Kevin, who was, after all, a professional dancer and thus quite a well-set-up young man. I felt like sending him a postcard: "Had a wonderful time. Wish I'd been there." But Mildred absolutely forbade any further contact between myself and him. Oh, Kevin, a woman always carries a special feeling for her first man, even if she can't remember it. I hope it was good for you. For that matter, I hope it was good for me, too.

When I rejoined the Baby Tallulah company, which Mildred now referred to in private as "Slutty Tallulah," I found Mildred had taken further steps. All the heterosexual chorus boys had been sacked and replaced by boys who were as light in their loafers as they were on their feet.

Later I received a cable from Mother. It read:

---

*Tallulah was wrong about that. The Wright brothers had invented flight several years earlier, but apparently she hadn't heard about it.–Douglas

TALLULAH STOP WHAT WERE YOU THINKING STOP
DON'T DO IT AGAIN STOP LOVE STOP MOTHER STOP
P.S. YOUR STEPFATHER IS A BASTARD ALSO STOP
MEN STOP

This was the beginning of the end for Baby Tallulah. For one thing, during those five months I had entered the wonderful world of puberty and had shot up several inches, so no one really bought the "Baby Tallulah" title anymore. Also five months of missed engagements had seriously hurt my reputation in the business, so prime bookings were harder to come by.

We tried a year of "Dainty Tallu," but the bookings weren't coming, and the merchandise sales dropped off. The gravy train was over. Finally I was summoned home. The good part of the end of the act was that I got to say good-bye to Mildred Puett, who moved to Chicago to set up shop with Minerva Thatcher, publishing anthologies of obscure lady poets. They sent me a copy of the first one, *My Fertile Crescent, Women on Wombs,* and it was the merest whisper of an anthology.

But as for me, it was all over. I was washed up.

4

School Haze

I was only fourteen and already a has-been for the *second* time. I thought then that my show business career was over forever, that all that lay ahead for me was the drab, boring, inconsequential life of an anonymous nonentity. You know, like *your* life! How wrong I was, thank God! The best lay ahead in a form that was not yet even imaginable. There was a flickering novelty sweeping the nation; they called it the nickelodeon. I paid it no mind. Destiny had other plans.

I returned to the bungalow Mother shared with Maxie out on Long Island and enrolled as a freshman at Lillian Roth High School. Maxie's business was doing well, having expanded upon booking with merchandising. Mother's hip had, of course, long since healed, but by then she was disinclined to go back on the stage, having instead embraced a career as a full-time housedrunk. She had also put on a few pounds during her years of inactivity; she had, in fact, nearly doubled in size. Vaudeville no longer seemed to be the ideal medium for her, though, had she the energy, she might have fit in well in the circus. But any sort of labor would have seriously interfered with her drinking schedule.

I suppose I should comment here on the subject of alcohol. I'm only going to say this once and then I shall drop the entire subject, never to be mentioned again. Don't think for one moment that I don't know about the ugly, nasty, utterly *untrue* rumors that circulate about *my* consumption of alcohol. Certainly it is true that I am no stranger to fermented refreshment. As a result, certain jealous people in some quarters have accused me of being a souse, an inebriate, a lush, a problem drinker. One very famous public figure, who was well known to envy my beauty and style, once called me "a besotted, piss-happy, bag of a dipsomaniac" to my face! I maintained my dignity, refusing to rise to her level, or my feet, and merely said, "Let history decide between us, Mrs. Roosevelt," as I crawled from the East Room unassisted.*

Let me make this clear, once and for all: I am strictly a *social drinker!* I will occasionally imbibe the merest whisper of alcohol simply to lubricate the social gears. And I've always said, just because you're alone is no reason to be antisocial. Indeed, the term "high society" was coined in reference to me and my grand Hollywood social whirl.

My mother, on the other hand, was a *DRUNK!* A filthy, smelly, sloshed wreck of a woman, who was forbidden by federal law from breast-feeding until the repeal of Prohibition!

I once asked my stepfather if I should be looking forward to a little brother or sister. Maxie just cast a loathing eye over mother's bloated form, snoring thunderously on the living room sofa as usual, and said, "Not unless we've got blind burglars." We both shared a good laugh over that one.

At school I was very popular. My natural vivacity and wit, combined with my high spirits, and my thermos, made me many friends. Naturally I excelled in drama, and was the president of our drama club both my junior and senior years. I wanted to join the glee club as well, but Mr. Haynes, the choral director, told me that I had "more of a solo-type voice, which, I'm afraid, the rest of the choir can't really *blend* with." This was but the first of the many unique compliments my singing has brought me over the years.

Then, of course, there were boys. Now every once in a while my intimate friendships with other women have given rise to rumors concerning *my* sexual preference. Basically my sexual preference has always been, "Yes, please." But when I hear ridiculous rumors about *me* being a *lesbian,* I have to choke back a laugh. Talk about an offensive mouthful. What sort of person goes about spreading specious rumors about perfectly normal women being lesbians? That is something *I* have never been guilty of!

I brought this very problem up with friends just the other day. I was at kd lang's home during a birthday party for Melissa Etheridge, playing twister with Lily Tomlin, when I brought up the manner in which I have been so long slandered. "Tallulah, darling," said Sandra Bernhard, who was playing Pin the Tail on Madonna, "you've got to lick these rumors, and lick them hard."

She's certainly right. Basically, rumors of homosexuality plague all

---

*This one incident aside, when she was probably the worse for liquor, in general Eleanor Roosevelt was a terribly nice lesbian, but *so* full of herself.–Tallulah

celebrities. Why? It's always been so in Hollywood. Everyone from Claudette Colbert to Marlene Dietrich has been a victim of these baseless rumors. Even dainty little Babs Stanwyck has been prodded by the finger of suspicion.

And it's even worse for men. Look at poor little Richard Simmons, a womanizing beast who loves 'em and leaves 'em begging for more, yet the most incomprehensible slurs on his unmistakable virility continue to dog his step classes. From William Haines to Rock Hudson, careers have been jeopardized by the foundationless gossip of know-nothings. I remember once relaxing poolside with Liberace, after one of our frequent frantic bouts of Hot Monkey Sex, when I asked Lee, as he tongued the last of the chocolate from my navel, how he thought such rumors got started.

"It's a mystery, Tallulah," Lee replied, a sadness crossing his face, for, believe it or not, such rumors had even been spread about *him!** "One day you're marrying Judy Garland, the next, people think you're smoking sausage. I don't understand it. You know yesterday somebody tried to tell me Paul Lynde was gay!"

"No!" I replied, deeply shocked. "How idiotic! My God, is there a woman left in Los Angeles that Paul hasn't ravished?"

"Oh, I know," replied Liberace. "I just wish I could score with a fraction of his leftovers."

Part of the problem in my case may have arisen from the fact that most of the many men I have married never remarried. Is it *my* fault that I spoil them for other women? Yet the silly story that all my husbands were gay still persists, to the point that at my last wedding the band played *Here Comes the Beard*.

Well, let me just state here for the record that I like men as much as the next guy.†

With adolescence my face took on the contours and planes that the camera was to come to love, but before the camera loved it, there was many a boy who got there first, and many another boy who didn't complain to have sloppy seconds.

At the beginning of my senior year Maxie informed me that there was no money for college, nor, as far as he was concerned, any point to higher education for a girl, a common attitude at the time. I was going

---

*I'm not joking!–Tallulah
†Well, maybe not quite as much. Sitting here at Morehead Heights, relating these stories to Douglas, I realize that this makes Douglas the next guy, and I don't think *anyone* likes men as much as he does.–Tallulah

to need either a career, a husband, or a scholarship. I decided to apply myself. I was on the honor roll, so a scholarship didn't seem out of the question. Drama, chemistry, and biology were my best subjects.

Then one day Billy, another senior, asked me for help studying for his biology class. He had an exam coming up the next day on the female reproductive system, and he just didn't have any firsthand acquaintance with one. I agreed to help him cram on the subject for the exam.

We got together at my house as Maxie often overnighted in Manhattan near his office in those days, and Mother could be counted on to be passed out on her sofa, so apart from the snoring and the smell, it was like living alone.

Like most boys, Billy just wanted to start cramming immediately, but I decided to start slower, in order to uncover his strengths, and see where his soft spots were, which would require more concentration. We had a couple of cocktails to loosen up our intellects, and then I gave him an oral pop exam, a challenge to which he rose quite impressively. There was no denying his penetrating interest in the subject at hand. Getting more deeply involved, I guided him through the primary features of the female reproductive system, and, as he warmed to my subject, he probed more deeply, obviously needing to stretch the subject to its limits. Soon he was cramming away for all he was worth, a very hard worker, willing to sweat over his subject all night if need be, certainly willing to give his all. I, for my part, had a feeling of fulfillment such as I never remembered feeling before. Could it be I had found my calling? Could this be the career I sought? Could it be that I was destined to be a biology tutor?

At lunch the next day Billy came up to me with his friend Mark, a taller, handsome boy, who, even at seventeen, already had a liberal coating of curly black chest hair. Billy said that Mark was also in his biology class, and could I possibly cram with both boys that night, as I had been such a help to Billy the night before. I said I thought the exam had been today, but Billy explained that it was a two-part exam, today the true/false questions, tomorrow the multiple-choice. This seemed reasonable to me, so I agreed to help Billy and his well-set-up friend Mark that evening.

After tiptoeing past Mother's comatose form in the living room, back into my bedroom, we had a few cocktails, broke out our study aids and got to work. Rather than the crowded chaos of having two boys trying to cram with me at once, we developed an alternating system whereby I would administer an oral exam to one boy while the other one would do the hard-core cramming. Then, when the crammer had spent himself and needed a study break, the boys would switch positions with the other boy doing the hard cramming while I would orally exam the spent boy until I'd brought his interest in the subject springing back up again. In this way we kept at it, studying our brains out until the dawn took us by surprise.

The next day at lunch Billy and Mark came up to me, all smiles, bringing a third boy, Russell, with them. Russell was on the varsity wrestling team and had a burly, muscular build that I had noticed and admired many times about the schoolyard. They explained that Russell was also in their biology class and could also use some help cramming for the exam. "But wasn't the exam over?" I asked.

"No," they replied. "It was a *three*-part exam." They had done the true/false and the multiple-choice questions, but they still had to do the essay questions, and these would be the hardest of all.

One look at their youthful, knowledge-hungry faces melted whatever resistance I might have had. And to tell the truth, tutoring these boys had been the most rewarding and fulfilling work I had ever done. It seemed as though the empty places in me were being filled with things warm and loving.

Still, cramming three boys at once; could I do it? It almost seemed like more than I could handle, but I checked my schedule and saw that I *did* have enough openings to handle all the boys, provided that each one of them was willing to take a back seat part of the time. That evening I mixed the cocktails especially strong.

Thank heaven it was a Friday night as by the time Saturday morning rolled around I was barely able to stand and was certainly in no shape for school. Never before had studying been so exhausting or so rewarding. I was weak from fatigue, but I'd never felt better in my life. I felt so great I didn't even want a drink! I began to believe that, yes, I *had* found my calling. I was born to be a biology tutor.

Monday at lunch, up came Russell with the rest of the varsity wrestling team, six more strong, burly boys, and asked if I could help coach the whole team in female biology. I said I didn't realize the entire team was taking biology, but Russell explained they weren't. They wanted to cram for biology for extra credit. Well, who could turn down seven well-set-up young men who merely wanted to better themselves?

There were simply too many boys to have over to our house. Fortunately, one of the boys came from a fairly wealthy family and actually had his own private "clubhouse" on his family estate, far from prying eyes. Not only was it private, but it had a bedroom, a bathroom, and, best of all, a fully stocked barroom. When the team and I, along with Billy and Mark, arrived, I mixed up several pitchers of martinis, made some drinks for the boys as well (although many of them were more than content with just beer), then took the boys, in groups of two, into the other room for their cramming sessions.

Well, the session was a success for all concerned and quickly evolved into a regular Friday night event. It was amazing the number of boys interested in learning about biology. At midterms and finals as many as fifteen boys would show up for their study sessions. I was a little worried about cramming in so many pupils but, fortunately, two or three boys could always be counted on to be what we in the theater call "quick studies." At the other extreme were boys like Mark and Russell, boys who put the "stud" in "student," boys who put grueling hours of effort into their studies and were always delivering rich rewards, the cream of my crop. These boys always brought me the ecstasy only a teacher knows.

The only odd thing was that after our sessions became a regular thing, Orlando, the boy who owned the clubhouse where we met, renamed it "The Train Station." I felt "The Little Schoolhouse" would have been more appropriate.

The one time our schedule changed was during the run of the senior play. That year the play was an original entitled *The Lost Recess,* and, not surprisingly, Mrs. Stevens, our drama teacher, cast me in the lead, as a young girl whose virtue is imperiled by her addiction to demon rum. I based my characterization on Mother, and devoted every spare moment to researching my role. So insistent was I on realism that I used only real alcohol in the drinking scenes on stage. The result was a sensation. The local critics wrote about us, and people came from as far as Manhattan to see our unusual show.

But we performed Thursday, Friday, and Saturday nights for two weeks, which meant my tutoring sessions had to move for those two weeks to Sunday evenings. The boys responded by studying religiously.

It was at about that time that I met Antoine. Antoine was not a student. He was a full-grown, striking-looking gentleman of a dusky complexion who dressed in a manner that could conservatively be called "colorful." Antoine approached me on the street one day as I was walking home from school. "Miss Morehead, please," he called out, "I have a proposition for you." Mother had always cautioned me to avoid gentlemen of color, but, knowing the value of Mother's advice, I always went out of my way to be friendly and accommodating to my dark brothers, and was often rewarded in return by discovering them to possess enormous Hidden Talents, sometimes so enormous I don't know how they kept them hidden.

As it happened, Antoine not only already knew my name, but a good deal more about me as well. It seemed that my extracurricular educational activities had come to his attention. Antoine ran a little night school that catered both to the high school boys and to "adult education," *very* adult, as it turned out. I had been recommended to Antoine as a possible teacher for his institute. This was like a gift from heaven. In less than a month I would be graduating from high school and would need a job, and here was Antoine with a firm position for me. He invited me to come and visit his place of business any evening to see for myself if I wanted to find a home there.

I protested that I would have only a high school diploma, no teaching credentials to seek such a position with, but Antoine explained that this was no problem. He could himself issue me an "Antoine G.E.D." after personally administering an intensive examination to determine if I was qualified to teach at his school.

I came out the following evening to Antoine's, and what a lovely place it was. The premises didn't even suggest a school: there were no desks or blackboards, but rather Antoine had adopted a milieu not unlike the one I had endeavored to create in my tutoring sessions. There was a full-service bar in the lushly appointed common room, where the student body could mingle with the faculty before going off to one of the many lovely classrooms.

The students were all male, of every age. This was not unusual. As I've pointed out, in those days higher education for women was considered a waste. Women were just going to be wives anyway. Certainly the men at Antoine's didn't have marriage on their minds. The faculty was mostly female, although Antoine did maintain a few male instructors as well. Antoine's philosophy was "we don't judge; we just try to meet each student's special needs."

Classes were one-on-one unless the student requested otherwise. Sometimes a class would consist of one student and two or even three teachers. What intensive coaching those lucky men received.

I had only coached boys in biology, but at Antoine's, although there was still a strong emphasis on biology, other subjects were taught as well. I visited the most amazing history classes, for instance, in which the teacher and the students actually dressed up in historical costumes and learned about historical events by reenacting them. In one classroom a scene from the Spanish Inquisition was being enacted in which a female inquisitor was punishing a naughty male heretic. (Antoine told me that in this class, which was surprisingly popular, the student had the option to enact either role.) In another classroom the rape of the Sabine Women was being reenacted with a wild abandon.

In addition to history Antoine maintained a sort of campus ROTC-type unit that taught discipline. Mistress Evelyn ran these classes with an iron fist in a leather glove. You never saw such polite, respectful students.

It was in Mistress Evelyn's class that I had the shock of my life. I didn't actually enter the room, Antoine showed the class to me through a one-way mirror, apparently installed in all the classrooms to allow proctoring. In Mistress Evelyn's class one of her students, or "slaves" as she affectionately called them, was being punished for some infraction of the rules. The student had been tied over a barrel naked and Mistress Evelyn was whipping his cheeks with a cat-o'-nine-tails, which seemed to me a rather severe schoolroom punishment. The student, however, when finally released, crawled over to Mistress Evelyn, expressing over and over his deepest gratitude. But when he turned his face toward the one-way mirror (on Mistress Evelyn's order to "look at your filthy face, worthless scum!"), my heart nearly leapt into my throat. It was my stepfather, Maxie! Seeing Maxie's own real enthusiasm for adult education, I began to think that maybe there would be money for college after all. Certainly Mistress Evelyn was teaching him a lesson.

After my tour of the facility, Antoine sat down and explained to me about the noble history of teaching. "When the first caveman showed the second caveman how to do something he had learned, teaching was born. You see, Tallulah, teaching is the World's Oldest Profession."

I told him I had to think it over. This was a big decision. Antoine understood. I pointed out that my stepfather might object, and as he was a regular enrollee, it would be difficult to hide it from him. But Antoine said that my joining the staff would qualify Maxie for a Family's Member Discount, which would undoubtedly soften his attitude, as it was a substantial savings. A full course at Antoine's could be quite pricey.

Antoine suggested that he conduct his personal examination of me right then, so I could be certified and could, if I so chose, start work immediately upon graduation. I agreed that this was sensible, and Antoine then conducted the most thorough and deeply probing examination I had ever been given. Antoine certainly gave me a rigorous workout, but when it was over he was pleased to tell me I had passed.

So now the balls were in my court. Graduation was coming up, and I had a big decision to make.

5

Plucked from Obscurity

As graduation grew closer I found myself sipping an old-fashioned while I contemplated a career in the World's Oldest Profession. What I didn't know was that destiny was about to offer me another path, and that destiny would come in the guise of a short, plump, balding immigrant named Louie B. Thalberg, the head of Pari-Mutual Studios, better known to movie fans the world over as PMS.

Louie B. Thalberg was born Herkamer B. Minkowitz in Eastern Europe. He emigrated to the United States with his parents and worked in his parents' Old Country Foods Store, where the homesick immigrant could purchase goat's bladders, sheep's eyes, haggis, and any other stomach-churning favorite they'd developed a taste for in the old country while their aristocracy hogged all the palatable food. Why eat filet mignon or linguini when you could eat raccoon gizzards fried in goat intestines, with a side of boiled okra? The store did a thriving business on the Lower East Side, populated by tired, poor, huddled masses bred for generations to have no taste.

When Louie was twenty-one his parents died in a freak accident; during a family celebration the inferior construction of their ceiling gave way, and the roof collapsed. Louie's parents were crushed to death under a plummeting fiddler. Louie inherited the store.

The nickelodeon craze came just as the immigrants' children were discovering that good food tasted better than bad food, and that in America you could have appetizing food in your home without cossacks coming and stealing it and burning down your hovel. Business at the Minkowitz store was dipping, but there was no danger of their going out of business entirely. The older generations of immigrants still refused to eat decent food, and they all tended to live to be two hundred or so, and even longer if they had a disagreeable disposition. Still, to help goose business, Louie installed a nickelodeon in the back, where the fresh ox lungs used to be.

The nickelodeon was such a success that in one year Louie owned three full-size movie theaters, and in five years he sold the store to his cousin Herschel, changed his name, and opened Pari-Mutual Studios in Astoria. By the time we met, Louie had become one of the biggest moguls in the movie business, with studios on both coasts.

Unbeknownst to me, Louie had been in Schwab's Long Island Bar one afternoon that May when he'd spotted a strikingly pretty young woman in a tight zebra-striped sweater sipping an old-fashioned. Of course, it was I.

Intrigued, Louie followed me back to Lillian Roth High School. There he saw a sign posted advertising *The Lost Recess*. The sign had my picture on it and contained several of my glowing reviews. Even more intrigued, Louie decided to attend a performance, incognito, since all hell generally broke loose whenever it got out that he was in the audience of any kind of amateur theatrical performance.

Louie was quite overwhelmed by my performance. Of course, he already knew I had beauty (he had eyes, after all), and certainly it was obvious I had talent. Most of the boys in the senior class could have told him of my talents by then, but my skill as an actress was far beyond anything he'd ever seen in any teenager. Few adult actresses had ever played alcoholism with the stunning, odiferous verisimilitude I brought to it, as I gleefully portrayed my mother onstage. Louie knew that this was not just an actress, but a *Star* in vitro. He resolved to offer me a position at PMS, and, if that worked out, a job.

Meanwhile, I knew nothing of this. Following my very educational evening at Antoine's night school, I decided to have a chat with Maxie on the subject of higher education. One evening over dinner, as Mother's musical snore wafted in from the living room, I said to Maxie, "You know, stepdaddy, I'm graduating next week, and I'm going to need money for college."

"I told you before, Tallulah," Maxie growled endearingly, "I ain't giving you another cent. You haven't brought a penny into this household in four years, and as far as I'm concerned, this is it. I'd have tossed you out on the street entirely on your eighteenth birthday, but your mother would have noticed eventually, and, unfortunately, she owns half of my business. But there's no more money for you here."

"That's odd," I replied, as enigmatically as possible. "You certainly seemed to have enough money for Antoine."

Maxie spat a chunk of lasagna across the room before replying: *"WHAT?"*

"Wipe your filthy face, worthless scum, as Mistress Evelyn would say," I replied.

"What do you know about Antoine's?" sputtered Maxie in a rage.

"I know that you've spent two thousand dollars there in the last year, so let's not have any more crap about no money for me!" I replied in a loving tone.

"Why you little . . ." Maxie unwisely began.

"Or would you rather I told this to Mother. I believe I can sober her up enough to understand."

"She'll never believe you."

"Oh, I'm afraid Antoine gave me all the proof I'll need." Maxie had no reply to that, but just sat there with his mouth hanging open, dangling lasagna shards. I'm afraid I had to laugh.

The next day I was coming out of the bank, having just deposited two thousand dollars in my "College Fund," when a short, funny little man approached me on the sidewalk. "Miss Morehead, please . . ." he began, in his adorable accent.

"Yes," I replied, approachable then as now.

"I had the distinct pleasure of seeing your most unusual performance in *The Lost Recess* last week. I was most impressed."

"Why, thank you, darling," I replied, always gracious with my public, especially when they're dressed in a suit as expensive as his.

"Allow me to present my card," he said, handing me a minute piece of cardboard with lettering and the world-famous PMS logo on it. "I am Louie B. Thalberg, president and founder of Pari-Mutual Studios, and I believe your future is as an actress."

"You don't say, Mr. Thalberg," I replied, now recognizing his face from newspaper photos, "Well, why don't we discuss this over cocktails."

"Certainly, my dear," he replied. And so was born one of the great film business partnerships of all time as little Louie B. Thalberg plucked me from obscurity. Oh God, how he plucked me!

The day after my high school graduation I reported to PMS's Astoria Studios for my screen test. Louie B. Thalberg was wasting no time in plucking me from obscurity; indeed, the very afternoon we met, after discussing my career goals over cocktails in his hotel bar, we went up to his room so I could read some scenes, and Louie pretty much plucked my brains out.

For my screen test I had to take a bubble bath and then play a torrid love scene opposite Gilbert Rolaids, one of the leading Latin lovers of the silent screen. Knowing me to be a neophyte before the cameras, Gilbert gallantly took me back to his dressing room to rehearse our scene privately so that I would be at ease before the lens. Dialogue, of course, was unimportant in the silent cinema. In the finished scene Gilbert and I are actually discussing his new car as we make passionate love, but the emotions and the movements must be perfect every time. Gilbert wanted to make sure I could express for the camera all the emotions of a woman making love to a hot-blooded Spanish man, so we rehearsed the scene in tremendous depth, far greater depth than the scene as written called for. Gilbert explained that to suggest more on the screen than we could show we had to feel as though we had gone all the way and really made love. Well, by the time we emerged from his dressing room, redid my makeup and hair, and shot the scene, I not only felt as though I had really made love to Gilbert, but as though he had turned me every which way but loose.

From Gilbert I learned the enormous difference between boys, even ones as gifted and endowed as Mark and Russell, and *men!* Gilbert was all man—in fact, he was more like a man and a half! He taught me so much about screen acting, and he introduced me to Spain's greatest contribution to civilization: tequila.

My screen test was universally declared to be a sensation, and a debut feature was rushed into production for me. Louie, knowing that I was going to be a major *Star* attraction, decided that no expense was to be spared in presenting me to my soon-to-be-adoring public. At eighteen years of age I was to be romantically paired opposite dashing Gilbert Rolaids, the studio's number one leading man, with Cyril Von Millstone, the nation's greatest film director, behind the camera in my debut movie *Heat Crazed!,* the movie that made me what I am today.

PART TWO

A Coming Sensation!
1915–1928

6

Heat Crazed!

Most film fans familiar with *Heat Crazed!* today, are actually aware only of the sound remake I made some years later, with its popular tango title song, which became my personal theme song, like *Thanks for the Memory* was for that youngster Bob Hope, *Over the Rainbow* was for sweet little Judy Garland, and *I'll Kill You, Bitch* for that lovely little rapper person, Snoop Doggy Dick, or whatever his name is. But my first *Heat Crazed!* was a silent movie spectacular shot at PMS's New York Astoria Studios when I was but a lass of eighteen.

The plot of *Heat Crazed!* was simple yet profound. I played Gloria Swansong, a man-eating temptress who dances at The Casbah in some country where it's terribly hot. A married man, played by Gilbert Rolaids, falls madly in love with me when I vamp him. I promise to surrender to him if he kills his mousy little wife, Tansy, played by the effervescent Lillian Gush, whom I hate for being a "Spring" when I am an "Autumn." Gilbert can't bring himself to kill her and gets more and more disturbed as I continue vamping him relentlessly. I tease and tempt him, bringing him to the brink again and again by doing the Dance of the Six and a Half Veils, but always without surrendering that last half-veil. However, every time he tries to kill Tansy, her shining, simple, virginal purity prevents him. I eventually kill the little simp myself, while laughing insanely, for I am Heat Crazed, and then I wait for Gilbert in his home.

Unfortunately, by the time Gilbert gets home, he too has gotten Heat Crazed, and, in his insanity, he thinks *I* am Tansy! (He *had* to be insane. We look nothing alike! Lillian was a sallow little thing while I am glamor incarnate!) Paying no heed to my cries that I am Gloria, Gilbert strangles me to death, bellowing aloud once I am dead, "Now at last

Gloria will be mine!" When he tosses my lifeless form to the ground, Lillian's corpse falls out of the closet, where I stowed it, onto the floor beside me. Seeing the two dead women lying side by side, Gilbert utters the most succinct and powerful title card in all of silent cinema: "Oops!" The sight of Gilbert's face, looking severely nonplussed, ends the film, at least in America. In the now lost, original, much more ironic ending that was only released in more sophisticated Europe, Gilbert, truly heat crazed, at last gets his desire slaked and makes mad passionate love to me when I'm too dead to enjoy it.

The making of *Heat Crazed!* was a joy all around. Gilbert and I were enhancing our onscreen chemistry by having a torrid offscreen affair. Lillian was a complete delight, always full of fun and gossip, and Cyril taught me everything about acting for the camera, literally creating the famous "Tallulah Magic" look on the set as we went. I would arrive on the set, fully made-up and partially costumed, at eight every morning for cocktails with the director and my costars while we discussed the day's shooting schedule.

Bubbly Lillian Gush was having an affair with Cyril Von Millstone that I felt might have adversely affected how I was shot, so I took the further precaution of having a slight little side affair with James Dong Lowe, our cinematographer. Nothing major enough to threaten my relationship with Gilbert, just enough raw animal sex to ensure that I was brilliantly lighted and breathtakingly photographed. Fortunately, Lowe was of Japanese descent, so it was not a big deal.

Additionally, Lillian had just married the beloved silent comedian Billy Bowlegs, and he was a constant visitor to the set—and when he wasn't there, his private detectives were. How I envied him his world-famous legs. That man's knees were farther apart than Joan Crawford's at a fraternity mixer. His zany antics kept us in stitches all day long. He was always surprising Cyril with goofy slapstick gags from his wacky films: pies in the face, sawing through the legs of his director's chair so it collapsed when he sat on it, dropping anvils on him from the catwalks, wiring his car ignition to explode,* shooting at his house with a high-powered rifle, telling the FBI that Cyril was a child molester; the jokes never stopped. We were splitting our sides every day.

After taking the streetcar in from Mother and Maxie's house to the studio each morning for a week, I rented a spacious apartment nearer the studio at a place called The Big Astoria, where I had more privacy. I was worried that Maxie wouldn't want me to leave, as that would leave

*That poor chauffeur! We had to laugh, but not in his hospital room.–Tallulah

him alone with the tasks of seeing to it that Mother ate something occasionally, hosing her down at least once a week, and goading her into changing her clothes once in a while, but Maxie was nothing but pleased by my sudden success and actually encouraged me to get my own place, weeping tears of joy as I moved out that weekend.

In the lovely days of silent cinema there was no tiresome dialogue to learn. We didn't need *words;* we had *title cards!* Since we had no lines to memorize for the next day, once we had finished the day's shooting around five and watched the "dailies" from the day before over cocktails in the screening room, we were free to party all night. The Big Astoria became Fun Central for the hardworking, hard-drinking *Heat Crazed!* unit. From there it was off nightclubbing in Manhattan (this was before **THE GREAT EVIL**[*] so we could still drink in public), Broadway theaters, more parties, more cocktails, then back to my place for still more cocktails, this time with sex, a quick bout of beauty sleep, and then back to the studio for the next day's shoot, catching catnaps between setups. It was busy but it was fun.

On the last day of shooting we were all sad; after all, no one knew if I was going to catch on with the public or not. This might have been my last day ever before a camera. If *Heat Crazed!* tanked at the box office, I could have been teaching at Antoine's by Christmas.

As it happened, my most difficult scene had been saved for last: the original, European ending, where Gilbert makes very mad passionate love to my lifeless carcass. In essence, all I had to do was play dead while Gilbert did all the work, but, never having been married, I was unaccustomed to merely lying inert under an active man, even more so since Gilbert insisted, for reasons of emotional reality, in taking a more hard-core approach to the lovemaking than would show up on camera, which held on a tight two-shot of our faces and shoulders. You try looking dead while a hot-blooded Latin man drills your brains out sometime.[†] As I had in high school, I called upon memories of my mother to capture the reality of a lump of dead meat. So convincing was I as the corpse that they were actually calling in paramedics when Cyril yelled, "Cut! Print! That's a wrap!" and Gilbert yelled back, "No! I'm not done yet!" Everyone was relieved when I sprang back to life after the shot. *Heat Crazed!* was in the can, and, moments later, so was I.

We had a lively wrap party, but it ended early. An end-of-shoot gift

---

[*]**THE GREAT EVIL** is Miss Tallulah's term for Prohibition. She still refuses to use the word itself.–Douglas
[†]I mean it! Try it! You'll like it!–Tallulah

arrived for Cyril, and when I noticed that the address label was made out in Billy Bowlegs's handwriting, I suggested to everyone else that we let Cyril open his gift in private. We all tiptoed out to continue festivities at my place, although that turned out to be one shoot that really ended with a bang.

With no sound track to record and mix, the gap between production and release, while the film was being edited, was much shorter in those days, though a no less busy period for the professional actress. I embarked on an endless round of interviews and publicity shoots. The publicity campaign for *Heat Crazed!* ballyhooed me as "A Coming Sensation," something I have always striven to induce in people of all genders.

Having now studied the art of cinema, I knew I still had work to do to ensure that my performance came off well in the finished film. To that end, I embarked upon a brief but incredibly intense affair with the editor. No task was beneath me in fine-tuning each and every scene, and I worked my fingers to his bone making certain every shot was perfect. By the time the film was ready to open, my performance in the finished product was polished to a bright sheen, and my name was on America's lips.

My first world premiere took place on Halloween at the Colossal White Elephant Theater, which the studio owned on Sixth Avenue in midtown Manhattan, a gorgeous theater decorated throughout with hundreds of white marble elephants, twenty of them life-size! Gilbert Rolaids couldn't publicly escort me to the show as he was still technically married to the glamorous actress Delores Delgado, at least according to the pope, so Louie escorted me. Gilbert and Delores, who was unreasonably rude to me at all times, came together.* Lillian came with Billy. Cyril didn't come at all as he was still recuperating from the flash burns. Mother and Maxie came also. Mother hadn't been out of the house since my freshman year, when she had found a liquor store that delivered, so this was really a major event.

The film's reception was simply thrilling! By the end of the screening there wasn't a dry seat in the house. Seeing myself projected on the gigantic screen (the Colossal White Elephant Theater was the IMAX of its day) for the first time was overwhelming! The camera didn't simply love me, it was like an obsessed paramour, stalking me, going through my garbage, and opening my mail. When I was presented to the crowd after the screening, their ovation left no doubts; I was a major star.

---

*Always a rarity in their relationship, according to Gilbert.–Tallulah

At the party afterward it seemed that everyone wanted a piece of me, and, as Gilbert was lumbered with the pretty but hopelessly common Delores, it was not entirely out of the question. Louie had thoughtlessly invited Maxie and Mother to the soiree under the insane delusion that this would please me.

I soon found out that Maxie was going around telling people that *he* was *my manager!* The nerve! I took him aside and politely informed him that if he continued to tell people this, pictures of Mistress Evelyn teaching him the meaning of "squeal like a pig" would be sent to every paper in town. That shut him up fast. Mother behaved in a far less embarrassing manner. She simply took a seat at the bar and began seriously drinking, occasionally telling people foolish enough to sit next to her that "Tallulah wasn't so lah-de-dah back when I was juggling her in vaudeville. So now she's too big for her diapers." Usually, by that time the person whose ear was being bent had fled, and Mother had to begin again with her next victim.

I realized that I was going to need real representation. I was going to need an agent. Fate was ready for me again. That very night, at that very party, I met the man who was to become my agent and my first husband, F. Emmett Knight.

7

F. Emmett Knight

I have been married and married and married. Everyone should have a hobby. There's no trick to spotting a man with good husband potential. Given the slightest encouragement, the best ones will stick out a mile. Certainly, with my first glimpse of F. Emmett Knight, I noticed his qualification. At first glance I wanted to give him a glancing blow.

What can I say about F. Emmett Knight? Actually, Bryan Miller, my musical director, reminds me of F. Emmett quite a lot: tall, handsome, charming, talented, debonair, and just the merest whisper of a homosexual, but, when we met, that was for him to know and me to find out. I knew on the spot that we were fated to wed. True, I was having a torrid affair with Gilbert Rolaids, but Gilbert was still technically married, at least in the eyes of his wife, and besides, I've always felt that being in love should never prevent one from marrying.

I still remember the first words I heard F. Emmett speak. I was wolfing down some shrimp at the *Heat Crazed!* post-premiere party when I heard a voice say, "Oh Miss Morehead, *puh-leeze!* I was completely *bewitched* by your *magnificent* performance! You were *absolutely fabulous!* You are not just some actress, you are a *goddess!*" Something in his subtle tone and simple honesty lured my attention away from the shrimp, who was finished anyway. I turned to see a handsome young man in a gorgeous crushed velvet suit with a bright violet ruffled shirt hopping from foot to foot in the excitement of meeting me.

"Oh, Louie knew *exactly* what he was doing when he cast *you!* You could make any man *Heat Crazed!*" Now, if there's anything I hate, it's mindless flattery, brown-nosing adulation, and apple-polishing toadying.

The quickest way to my bad side* is to inundate me with compliments and honeyed words. But F. Emmett Knight's direct, *brutal* frankness, his willingness to tell me his true opinion, consequences be damned, won my heart at once.

He presented me with his card: F. EMMETT KNIGHT, THEATRICAL AGENT. "Are you really an agent, Mr. Knight?" I asked.

"Miss Morehead, please! Call me F. And yes, guilty as charged."

"How fortuitous. It so happens that I am seeking representation."

"Are you? How *fabulous!* I would be *honored* to represent you! After tonight's triumph you'll certainly need to renegotiate your PMS contract. I would love to handle the talks! I'd make PMS bleed!"

"Would you?"

"Oh yes, I'd make them bleed green money right into your veins."

"F, my darling, I like the cut of your jib. Perhaps we could get together tomorrow and discuss matters over cocktails."

"Oh, Miss Morehead!"

"Please, Tallulah."

"Tallulah, I'd be delighted!"

The next afternoon I met F. Emmett and his business partner, Milton Mare, at their favorite Manhattan brasserie, a lovely little place, remarkably dark for mid-afternoon, with the charming name of The Manhole. As it happened, I was the only woman in the place at that hour. F. Emmett was all charm. Showing himself to be an astute acting critic, he went over my performance as Gloria Swansong in minute detail, describing with brusque candor the many extraordinary choices I had made, daring to enumerate all the moments where I'd gone beyond wonderful and into the realm of *Magic!* That he had the courage to call me a genius to my face impressed me even more. By the end of the afternoon I'd signed the contracts. F. Emmett Knight and the Knight-Mare Agency were now my official representation.

A celebration was in order, so F. Emmett took me out that evening on a tour of his favorite watering holes: lively, fun places, full of men who were bursting with gaiety, places with names like Mineshaft, Daddy's Den, The Corral, and The Spear. I little suspected that this would be the last time I would be able to barhop anonymously.

The following week *Heat Crazed!* opened nationwide, and my anonymity was at an end. Our reviews were a bit mixed, but the critics have never held any sway over my core audience. (Some of the nastier

---

*That is, my left side.–Tallulah

reviewers have claimed that this was because my audience couldn't read. What libel! If they were illiterate how could they have read the title cards, I ask you? Certainly you, loyal reader, aren't illiterate, or you couldn't be reading this. I rest my case.) The *New York Times* certainly felt the intense heat bubbling up in our film when they called it a "potboiler par excellence."

Louie wanted to rush Gilbert and me right back into another film at once, but F. Emmett insisted that property selection be written into my new, remarkably remunerative contract. Louie tried to hold out, but *Heat Crazed!* was a massive hit, and the money was rolling in. He knew he needed me tied up exclusively to PMS, or other moguls would come sniffing, and Louie hadn't plucked me for them. "Let them go pluck themselves." was his motto. In the end I signed a huge contract, giving me refusal rights on scripts, costars, and directors, and one hell of a lot of money!

While my new vehicle was being written, I embarked on a nationwide publicity tour. F. Emmett accompanied me, along with Pete Moss, a studio publicity flack, who set up all my interviews and arranged for the massive spontaneous receptions that greeted the "Tallulah Express" at each major city.

F. Emmett, I should state right now, was a complete gentleman at all times. Other men, alone with me on the train or in hotels night after night for seven weeks, might have pressed their advantage, especially when I was clawing at their door, begging them to, but F. Emmett Knight would have none of it. "No, Tallulah," he tiresomely repeated again and again, "I respect you too much to treat you like some whore."

"It's all right, honest," I told him.

"Tallulah, please," he replied, "I'm not worthy of a goddess like you."

"Of course you're not, darling," I modestly agreed. "No one is! But that doesn't matter. Let me lower myself to your level. Let us wallow together."

"No, Tallulah, it's not right. We'd only regret it later. My mother taught me that sex with women before marriage is wrong!"

How could I argue further? This was the first time any man had mentioned marriage to me. The more he withheld himself, the more I fell in love with him. In the meantime, well, there were always *ardent* fans wherever we went, and, in a desperate pinch, there was always Pete Moss, although the man was certainly no Gilbert Rolaids, and always smelt of fertilizer.

One fan who showed up in Chicago was my old school chum and tutoring pupil Mark, who was attending Northwestern University. He said he'd been to see my film five times and thought I was a great actress.

"Boy, Tallulah," he said, his new college maturity making him even more maddeningly attractive, "you were great! The way you kept teasing that guy but would never go all the way with him—that's *acting!* If I didn't know better I'd have completely believed you." What did reviews matter next to compliments like that?

Mark took me to a party at his fraternity house. To my surprise there were no other girls present. Just what kind of perverted frat house was this, I wondered? Had Mark joined the *Boys in the Band* since I'd seen him last? It didn't seem likely. Mark wasn't the least bit musical, but stranger things have married me. My fears turned out to be groundless, of course. Mark explained, "What drab little college girl could compare with you, Tallulah? You're a *Star!*" Well, there was no arguing with that logic. And what woman could complain of having a whole fraternity full of handsome boys all to herself? Not this girl. Frankly, it was like old times back at my tutoring sessions all over again. It was almost enough to make me wish I'd gone to college. But then I remembered the terms of my new contract, in which, over the next year, I would be making more money than these boys would pay out over four years for their educations, and I mean all of them added together.

Another remarkable thing about F. Emmett Knight was that I could talk to him about anything. For instance, after my night with Mark and his fraternity brothers, I was able to tell F. Emmett all about it without his being the least bit jealous. If anything, he seemed a mite envious. I could never have told Gilbert about things like that. His hot-blooded Spanish nature would have boiled over and there would have been violence, and poor Pete Moss would be stuck inventing cover stories for the press. But F. Emmett just sat there, with his legs tightly crossed, asking me to repeat certain parts in more vivid detail.

By the time we returned to New York I was Heat Crazed. F. Emmett's relentless refusal to surrender to me had won my heart. Before him, I didn't know there were men who ever said "no." But the more I couldn't have him, the more I wanted him. I guess I've always hungered for "Forbidden Fruit."

In my absence Louie had put together a new film for me, the now lost classic *The Human Woman.* I was to be romantically reteamed with Gilbert; and Cyril Von Millstone, whose eyesight had returned by then, was again to direct.

At this point I'll be damned if I remember the plot of *The Human*

Woman, and, like many of my silent pictures, no print is known to still exist, so I can't refresh my aging memory by watching it. I played the title role, of that I'm *certain!* It was another hit! I was no flash in the pan. I was a true *Star,* and I was in love.

It was at the party following the premiere of *The Human Woman* that I proposed to F. Emmett. At first he didn't believe I was serious, but when I made it clear that I was, he was delirious with joy. "Oh, Tallulah," he cried sweeping me up in his arms, "you've made my mother the happiest woman in the world!"

I wanted to elope immediately—what woman wouldn't?—using the promotional tour for *The Human Woman* as a honeymoon. However, Louie got wind of the engagement, probably from F. Emmett's hollering his joyful acceptance over the canapé table. Louie insisted on a long, well-publicized engagement. To my disappointment F. Emmett agreed with Louie. He seemed to feel that, as long as we were getting married anyway, we should exploit it as much, and for as long as possible. In fact, F. Emmett suggested an engagement of five years! So much for the impetuousness of youth! I refused to consider an engagement of longer than a few months.

Pete Moss finally came up with a compromise. We would wed when my next movie, *Bluebeard's Daughter,* opened, so the publicity would do some good for the studio. Since Louie wanted to avoid overexposing me* he was limiting me at that time to one film a year. This meant at least a nine-month engagement! In a normal relationship this would be almost long enough to make marriage pointless, but sadly, not in this case. In fact, F. Emmett absolutely refused to consider making a woman of me until after the wedding. "Tallulah, my love," he lisped, "if I just give you the cream for free, you'll never buy the bull." Oh, I was buying his bull all right.

In order to avoid any appearance, or chance, of premarital impropriety, F. Emmett took his longtime roommate, Effingwell Lovett, along on this promotional tour. Frankly, I didn't care much for Effingwell, or "that Effing person," as I usually referred to him, nor did he even attempt to conceal his dislike of me. If it wasn't an absurd conjecture, I'd almost think Effing was jealous of our forthcoming marriage. He'd merely been distant to me prior to our engagement, though not so distant that he was above occasionally asking to borrow some of my more glam-

---

*Not that you could tell that from the way she was costumed, or semi-costumed, in his films, generally appearing in ensembles that left no doubt that she was a *Human Woman!*–Douglas

orous outfits for "Special Events," but once our pen
announced he became openly hostile to me. "Why di
your Effing roommate along, F?" I asked my belove
seen *The Human Woman*. He said the title was so s
leave the theater."

"Oh. That's just his little joke," F. Emmett repli
feelings before mine yet again. "If only you knew him better, Tallulah,
he's so funny. And he thinks the world of you."

"He called me a drunken slut!"

"He didn't mean it. He was just joshing you. A little private joke."

"He said it to Alexander Woolcott!"

"They're chums. He thought it would make him giggle."

"Woolcott quoted him on his radio show!"

"Is it Effing's fault if Woolcott was indiscreet?"

"You're damned right it's his Effing fault!"

"He was shocked Woolcott used it."

"He stole PMS letterhead stationery from Pete Moss and sent out a
fake press release to every paper in New York. 'For immediate release:
Miss Tallulah Morehead is a drunken slut who's bedded every man in
New York,' which isn't even true!"

"It was a prank. He thought they'd realize that. After all, only three
of them published it."

"One of the ones that did was *The New York Times!*"

"Pete Moss sent 'round a refutation."

"He sent 'round a release that said 'Miss Tallulah Morehead has *not*
slept with every man in New York yet!'"

"There you are."

Sometimes arguing with F. Emmett was like being beaten with pil-
lows. This looked to be a very long tour, between my fiancé, who
intended to be a virgin on our wedding night, and his Effing roommate.
Fortunately, Gilbert also came along this time, sans the overrated Delores
Delgado, so at least I had something to do evenings. After making appearances at whichever theater in town was playing our movie, we'd return to our hotel, I'd kiss my husband-to-be good night, then he'd retire
with his roommate while I retired with my lover. F. Emmett said we
ought to write it up for a screenplay and call it *Design for Touring*.

Gilbert didn't actually approve of my matrimonial intentions, either,
but, as he was still technically married, at least according to the papers
Delores had served me with, he was in no position to officially object.
F. Emmett Knight just wasn't his idea of a man. F. Emmett wasn't athletic; he didn't hunt or box or beat up homosexuals. He'd never even

his own dinner. Gilbert didn't feel a man was a man until he'd
wn blood in his first duel.

But F. Emmett had other skills that Gilbert lacked. True, he'd never
killed his own meal, but he was one hell of a cook. God, how that man
could bake! He could turn out pastries that were so light and daintily
flaky that eating them was pure heaven. He could dance, and not just
ballroom either. The man could toe dance like a prima ballerina. He had
a gift for matching colors. He knitted beautiful sweaters. And there was
nothing he didn't know about opera.

And, when it came to contract negotiations, F. Emmett could go toe
to toe with Louie B. Thalberg and never flinch. Talk about combat!
What Gilbert never knew was that, thanks to F. Emmett, by our third
film together, I was making more money than he was.

When the tour reached Chicago I found myself half hoping that my
old school chum Mark would be waiting on the platform. F. Emmett
was still relentlessly saving himself for marriage, though I didn't really
feel that a small advance deposit would leave him completely spent, and
while Gilbert was one hell of a man, he was, after all, quite a bit older
than I. I longed for a little companionship my own age, someone who
wouldn't need a nap afterward, or worse, as in Louie's case, during.
When I looked out on the platform I had a horrible shock; not only was
Mark not there, but far, far worse, Mildred Puett and Minerva Thatcher
were!

They were gushing with enthusiasm. They had seen *The Human
Woman* and loved it for its title and subject matter.* They didn't care
much for Gilbert Rolaids and, in fact, completely ignored him when I
tried to introduce them. After their freezing rudeness to him, I felt
Gilbert was fully justified in frostily telling them, "If you dear ladies are
here in Chicago, then Holland must be flooded."

They were kinder to F. Emmett and his Effing roommate when I introduced them. Mildred said, "Well, Tallulah, you're in the public eye,
so I suppose you *have* to marry. But if you must marry, then these are
just the right sort of men for you." F. Emmett just beamed at this unexpected praise (it *was* the nicest thing I'd ever heard Mildred say about a
man) while Effing sidled up to Minerva, asking her where she had gotten her *stunning* black leather jacket.

When Mark didn't try to get in touch, I inquired after him at

---

*I just wish I could remember what that subject matter was. The title gives no
clue.–Tallulah

Northwestern University only to learn he'd been expelled from school for some picky morals infraction and that, in fact, his entire fraternity had been disbanded. No one had any idea where he was now. I was very disappointed. Of all my pupils in those now far-off days, Mark and his wrestler friend Russell were by far the best looking, best equipped, and most talented, showing the most promise for the future. I'd hoped to keep a tab on them as they grew into men, to measure their growth, but now that seemed unlikely—they were scattered to the four winds. I made a mental note to be certain to attend my high school reunions when they came along, just in case reunion became a possibility.

Somehow the tour finally finished. We returned to New York, my tail between *my* legs for once. Gilbert went back to the poorly aging Delores, F. Emmett and Effingwell went back to their stunningly decorated apartment in Greenwich Village, I returned to The Big Astoria, and to the studio for fittings and script meetings over *Bluebeard's Daughter,* a film that would be called an erotic thriller today. I was to play a black widow type character who married and murdered man after man, and, in the mood I was in, that was fine with me.

I had to take F. Emmett to dinner with Mother and Maxie one evening. There was simply no avoiding it, though I managed to get them to meet us at a restaurant and thus avoid bringing F. Emmett to the house, which, with me gone now more than a year and a half, had developed an insufferable odor that seemed to have seeped directly from Mother's pores right into the woodwork.

Dinner was uncomfortable, to say the least. F. Emmett tried to make conversation by describing his plans for my career. Mother sat silently glaring at him all evening. Maxie, on the other hand, was in a remarkably jovial mood. Something about my man just amused the hell out of him. Every time F. Emmett said anything, especially if his sentence contained many 'S's, Maxie just broke out in bellowing laughter.

After dinner, while F. Emmett was in the petite boys room, Maxie told me, "He's just the man I would have picked out for you, Tallulah." And then brayed out another rollicking roar of laughter.

Mother, as usual, was completely contrary, asking me, "Are you certain that *that* is what you want to marry?"

"Of course I'm certain, Mother. I'm in love!"

"Wouldn't you rather have a real man? What about that dashing Gilbert Rolaids? I thought you were falling for him."

"Mother, he's still technically married, as you well know. Besides, I love F. He's handsome and gentle and sensitive."

"I'll bet he is!" Maxie bellowed, nearly doubled over with his snide sniggering, "I'll bet he's a prime specimen of *Homo* sapiens, and I do mean sapiens."

"Oh, what the hell does it matter?" muttered Mother into her drink. *"All* men are bastards, so what does it matter which one she marries?"

"Have another drink, dear," said a now obviously annoyed Maxie. "Your liver's still functioning."

At which point F. Emmett returned and suggested, "Let's order dessert. I think a chocolate fondue would be fun for all." That was my man, always able to turn any social disaster into a party.

Dinner with F. Emmett's mother was a pleasanter experience, except for the food. Fanny Knight insisted on preparing us a home-cooked meal herself in her little fourteenth floor walkup, and she wasn't the cook her son was. I'd never had Gingersnap Stew before, or since, for that matter. It was a beef dish with a sauce made from gingersnaps, and it tasted just like it sounds. Fanny must have invented it herself while delirious, probably to encourage little F. Emmett to eat beef by flavoring it like cookies, although in all the years I knew him, he never needed encouragement to stuff meat in his mouth.

Fanny was very sweet, and was crazy about me. Every time she looked at me she burst into tears, crying, "I'd given up all hope! Oh, Tallulah, at last my boy's found a woman who isn't blinded by those glamorous sheik-type boys and who sees F for the rugged he-man he is." F. Emmett blushed at this, nearly as purple as the suit he was wearing, which, incidentally, he'd made himself, as, in fact, he made most of his own clothes.

As we left I slipped my arm through F. Emmett's and whispered in his ear: "Darling, don't even *think* of moving her in with us."

I began feeling better during the shooting of *Bluebeard's Daughter.* Perhaps it was because of my wedding day drawing closer. Perhaps it was the hostilities I was working out as I murdered my string of cinema spouses. I don't know. I *do* know that the day I slit Gilbert's throat was an especially satisfying afternoon. I remember thinking, "Only a Mormon would say you're still married *now!"*

This was truly a *Star* vehicle for me. Instead of one leading man, I had eight, each of whom I dispatched in different gruesome ways, except for the last one, the spoilsport who found me out by opening the door I'd told him never to open, in which I kept the souvenirs I'd snipped off and pickled from each of my victims. In the original Bluebeard story the serial-killing polygamist keeps the heads of his wives in jars in the locked room. In my version, I'd hung onto the only portions of my husband's anatomies worth having in the first place. The prop department had outdone themselves preparing for this shocking scene. When filming was completed, I asked for and was given the seven bottles with their amazingly lifelike contents. They sit today in a special cupboard upstairs here in Morehead Heights, where they remain a source of beauty and inspiration. Sadly, my special cupboard is the only place they have ever been seen. Although *Bluebeard's Daughter* was produced long before the Hays Office or the motion picture production code, no one was prepared at that time to distribute or exhibit the film with that one shocking shot intact, not even in Europe. Audiences were left to imagine for themselves what adorable little Norman Talmadge was shrieking at.

The plan now was to marry at the premiere* and then honeymoon in Europe. We would sail to France and appear at the film's opening in Paris, then on to Berlin, Venice, and Rome. Louie planned on moving all production to his newer, West Coast studios in Hollywood, so when we returned we'd be taking up residence in California, three thousand glorious miles away from the in-laws.

Unfortunately, as the end of shooting approached, when I glanced in the newspaper to start planning our trip, I noticed that some sort of war thing was going on. It seemed that Germany and France and England were all very annoyed with one another and were killing each other in large numbers. How rude! In France they had established something they called a "No Man's Land," and that didn't sound like any fun at all. It began to look as though I was going to have to suffer the humiliation of a *domestic* honeymoon! This so-called World War One was becoming severely inconvenient!

But, just when things look blackest, something wonderful seems to happen. Every silver lining has a cloud. In this instance, just as I'd given up all hope of a European honeymoon, America entered the war! Louie pointed out that we could go to London on a troopship and honeymoon there while entertaining American troops facing death and English cooking. Not only would I see London, but the publicity would be great for the studio. It would be a dangerous crossing, of course, and I was afraid F. Emmett wouldn't want to go. He wasn't the boldest man on the planet, but when I explained to him that we would have to cross the

*Given the film's portrayal of marriage as one murder after another, this was perhaps not the most appropriate idea Pete Moss ever had.–Douglas

Atlantic on a troopship with thousands of "doughboys" F. Emmett couldn't have been more enthusiastic. "Oh Tallulah," he cried, "it's *exactly* the honeymoon I've always *dreamed* of! How *absolutely fabulous!*"

"That's the brave, patriotic man I fell in love with," I replied, trying to throw myself into his elusive arms, "Really, darling, I wish you'd keep your hands to myself."

And so, before an audience that had just spent ninety minutes watching me marry and kill,* I wed F. Emmett Knight in the Colossal White Elephant Theater. Effingwell Lovett was best man, and Lillian Gush was my maid of honor. Maxie gave me away. I wore white, although that Effing person had suggested beige.

Mildred Puett and Minerva Thatcher came from Chicago to attend the screening/wedding. (That Effing person invited them. *Typical!*) If Mildred and Minerva had liked *The Human Woman,* they LOVED *Bluebeard's Daughter,* which Mildred said was the finest and most honest depiction of male-female relations ever put on film. They insisted on my sitting with them during the screening, when I should have been backstage being sewn into my wedding gown and flying harness; and every time I killed a man on screen Mildred would painfully clutch my thigh while cheering aloud, "That's the way to show the bastards! Go, Tallulah, go!" It was a trifle embarrassing, especially when I slit Gilbert's throat and Mildred turned around in her seat to snarl at Gilbert behind her: "That'll teach you, Rolaids, old boy!"

The wedding was a modest and tasteful affair. Pete Moss had basically functioned as wedding arranger; as a result, the Colossal Philharmonic Orchestra, under the baton of Leopold Stokowski, played me down the aisle (the *right* aisle, as it happened, since the Colossal White Elephant Theater had no center aisle), which I rode down on an actual live elephant that had been painted white for the occasion. F. Emmett, in an astonishing multicolored, sequin-covered tuxedo he had made himself that was louder than the orchestra, was carried down the left aisle on a litter by four spectacularly muscular oiled black men wearing miniscule loincloths and nothing else. (This was F. Emmett's own idea, and he'd spent weeks extensively auditioning and costuming the bearers at his office.)

Pete had invited the pope to come to America, at PMS's expense, I might add, not that the pope couldn't afford it out of his own silk-lined pocket, to perform the ceremony, but the pontiff couldn't be bothered,

*Pete Moss came up with an inspired slogan for the film: "When Tullulah Kills, you'll envy the dead!"–Douglas

offering some transparently lame excuses about F. Emmett and me not being Catholics and it being Easter weekend and so on, blah, blah, blah. Apparently Mr. Oh-So-Holy Pope was *too good* to perform the Wedding of the Century! Finally, Milo O'Donegal, a fine PMS stock character actor who specialized in playing priests, was cast to perform the ceremony. Pete Moss found a nearly-Christian sect centered in Harlem willing to ordain him so the marriage would be legal.

Louie B. Thalberg's World Famous Bathing Beauties were my brides-maids, while F. Emmett had got the chorus line from a musical show called *Boys on Top* that was playing somewhere down in the Village to be the ushers. Eugene O'Neill wrote our vows, which were projected on the screen as title cards while we just mimed them below. Victor Herbert wrote and Florenz Ziegfeld staged the finale, a fifteen-minute produc-tion number with forty singer/dancers, climaxing with F. Emmett and me on wires being flown (by Foy, of course) together up to Matrimonial Heaven. Alexander Woolcott said that if we were willing to perform it nightly, our "boffo" wedding would run longer than the marriage.

There was only one sad note; near the end of the ceremony the ele-phant collapsed on the brass section of the orchestra and died, evidently suffocating in the paint like Shirley Eaton in *Goldfinger.*

F. Emmett and I had our reception and spent our wedding night at the Ritz Hotel, knowing that, like my father had the morning after he married Mother, we would be shipping out to war the next day.

But first, there in the vast bedroom of the Ritz Presidential Bridal Suite, alone with my husband, I learned just what every nervous bride is afraid of: that F. Emmett Knight didn't approve of sex with women *after* the wedding either!

8

I Lick the Kaiser!

As wedding nights go, my first one was pretty much a bust. I'd bought the bull, oh boy, had I, but I still wasn't getting any cream! Finally, after F. Emmett had locked himself in the bathroom sobbing, I wandered back downstairs to the reception, where our wedding celebration was still going, although in my case it was more of a celibation.

As it happened, the four black bearers who had carried my reluctant husband to the altar were still there, though they had changed into less revealing outfits. We took a couple of fifths of vodka back to their room and had a proper improper party.

Early the next morning I returned to our bridal chamber in a much better mood than when I had left. When I entered the bedroom I saw my new husband lying in our marital bed fast asleep. He looked so angelic, so peaceful, so handsome. To my disappointment he was wearing monogrammed silk pajamas (which he'd made himself), but they buttoned up the front. There were a couple of brown hairs curling over the top button, seeming to beckon me toward the tantalizing mystery within. I laid down gently next to him, slipping quietly beneath the sheet. My fingers strayed slowly to that first button, seemingly of their own accord. Ever so softly they slipped that first button through its accompanying slit. F. Emmett's pajama top opened an itty bit more, revealing another inch and a half of his curly golden brown fur. I could almost hear it calling to me. Ever so languidly, my fingers strolled down to the next button.

Ten minutes later F. Emmett was locked in the bathroom sobbing again. I could see that marriage was going to be entirely different than I had dreamed. For one thing, twin bathrooms were obviously a necessity.

We set sail for England several hours later on the *U.S.S. Esprit de*

Corps. Pete Moss had arranged a small spontaneous send-off. His crowd of well-wishers (actually, extras with PMS) bidding me good-bye for the cameras of the press filled the pier, crowding the families of the departing soldiers back into the dock house, where they were in no danger of sunburn. Although neither Maxie nor Mother was there, I did see Mildred and Minerva waving a frantic good-bye, and also that Effing person, crying his eyes out. At least I'd seen the last of him for a while. (F. Emmett had actually tried to argue for bringing him along as a wardrobe assistant, but I put my foot down, my spiked heel, causing that Effing person to limp for three days.)

Being at sea with the men seemed to lighten F. Emmett's mood. I, for my part, was delighted to discover on our second day out that my missing old school chum Mark was on board, now just another doughboy, a private first class. Given how disappointing my honeymoon was turning out to be, Mark was a godsend. I saw no reason to wait until we arrived in England to begin entertaining the troops. These boys were tense and frightened. We could be attacked and sunk at any time. Each day might have been our last. Mark was able to arrange, privately and secretly, for me to begin entertaining our boys when off duty.

Space limitations dictated that I entertain the boys individually, which was fine with me, and with them, as it enabled me to personalize each performance to the needs and tastes of the individual. In this manner I perfected an act that was to delight and relieve the anxious young soldiers and sailors of two world wars. Most Hollywood performers providing military entertainment—that boyish scamp Bob Hope is a prime example—would put on shows where pretty girls were exhibited to hundreds, even thousands of troops, all at once, where they could only titillate and frustrate the poor soldiers more. My more personal approach, taken in memory of my late father, may have taken longer, but it raised the boys' morale much higher, and I never left a young man about to risk his life for his country unsatisfied and seething with frustration. With each one I silently thought, "This one's for you, Daddy."

I introduced Mark to my husband, and F. Emmett immediately took a shine to the likable young man. After some quiet, private "man talk," Mark said that employment might be found on shipboard for F. Emmett as well. It seems there were always a few soldiers whose tastes in entertainment differed from the norm, but neither Mark nor F. Emmett felt they should be excluded from the fun for that. Frankly, I didn't see what he could do for the men that I couldn't, but Mark assured me that some people simply preferred bananas to donuts. I had no idea what he meant by that! I've always eaten both, but I raised no objections. Soon

F. Emmett was entertaining his own small following while I was handling the rest of the crew.

The third day out I was in the middle of a specialty number I had perfected that was tremendously popular with the boys when the captain burst into the room. He was furious for some reason, stopping the basket in mid-twirl and yanking me out of it. I couldn't quite understand what he was so upset about, but I spoke to him alone for about half an hour, and by the time I was wiping down the basket again, the captain had decided to turn a blind eye to my performances.

London, even under the austere conditions imposed by the irksome war, was a gay, mad metropolis. We were staying at the Savoy, which was luxurious beyond the dreams of Maxie. Although I had never studied it, I found I picked up the language quite quickly and could understand what was being said to me, and make myself understood, in just a few weeks.

We had a "Royal Command" premiere for *Bluebeard's Daughter* at the Colossal London Palooza Theatre in Leicester Square, though we would have held a premiere even without orders from the high and mighty Royal Family, the print having traveled over with us. I guess ordering performers around keeps the British Royals from feeling *utterly* powerless. My films were very popular in England, where I was known as "*Lady* Tallulah Morehead." There were no cultural barriers in the silent cinema. Overacting is the same in any language, and the title cards had all been translated by a skilled and cunning linguist at the studio.

The picture went over big in London. Sadly, the rest of the country had to wait, as we had only brought the one print, but *Heat Crazed!* and *The Human Woman* were both still in wide release in England. Even the normally chilly English critics warmed to *Bluebeard's Daughter*. Simon Coldpeter in the *London Tribune* wrote, "Tallulah has never been more terrifying," and the usually terminally snooty Havelock Beeton-Oft wrote in the *London Times,* "Lady Morehead's latest film is murder from beginning to end," which I felt revealed too much of the plot. Darling Joey Bingewell in the *Bloomsbury Poofter* wrote, "With each new murder you'll want to scream at the screen, 'Tallulah, *stop!*' "

At the reception after the Royal Command Premiere, Duke Something-or-Other asked me if I wanted to meet a queen. "Please," I replied, "I gave at home. You must not have met my husband."

"But Lady Morehead," retorted Duke Something-or-Other, "she's here with the Queen Mother. They're both dying to meet you."

"A queen and his mother," I riposted. "Sounds like dinner at my mother-in-law's. Let's just save the gingersnaps, shall we? I need another scotch."

"Lady Morehead, please," beseeched Duke Something-or-Other, like all men *far* more attractive when begging, "I was asked to present you to the queen."

"You're *way* too late for that, darling," I answered. "I was given as a present to a queen *weeks* ago. The damned problem is, he hasn't even unwrapped me yet!"

Back at the hotel that night, F. Emmett was still protecting his virtue with an insulting vigor. I asked him what he had expected from marriage, and he replied, "I certainly didn't expect my wife to treat me like a big piece of meat!"

"How big?"

"Tallulah!"

"Hey, *you* brought it up!"

"I did not bring it up!"

"Well, why don't you bring it up and I'll show you what it's used for."

Needless to say, F. Emmett was locked in the bathroom sobbing in short order, and I was wandering the West End wondering what kind of uncivilized primitives close the pubs at eleven o'clock. By now I regretted not having taken up Duke Something-or-Other's offer to introduce me to his queen friends. They're usually fun, and would know where a lady could get a drink. I was crossing Covent Garden when I heard an extremely cultured voice say, "Pray excuse the liberty, miss, but have I the honor of addressing Lady Tallulah Morehead, the great American cinema actress?"

I turned and saw a tall, handsome man, graying slightly at the temples, with a pencil-thin mustache, exquisitely dressed in an expensive formal suit and top hat, eyeing me through a monocle. "Yes," I said, intrigued by this dapper stranger, who seemed to exude class, breeding, and refinement, unlike that terribly common Duke Something-or-Other. "But you have the advantage on me, sir."

"Of course, dear miss. Please allow me to present my card." He slipped me a silken card on which was embossed in golden letters: EDWARD FELCHER, LORD SEXCRIME, EARL OF INCESTSHIRE.

"Lord Sexcrime," I exclaimed. "What a pleasure. Tell me, your Lordship, do you have any idea where a gal can get a drink at this hour?"

"Indeed I do," responded Lord Sexcrime. "Just come with me."

Say what you will about Lord Sexcrime, whatever his faults, and, as it turned out, he had several, he knew how to show a girl a good time. When I staggered back into our hotel room I was in such a good mood I didn't even try to molest my husband, who always looked his sexiest when unconscious.

With the studio business out of the way and my honeymoon a pathetic fizzle, I threw myself into entertaining our troops. I traveled around England from American base to American base, leaving F. Emmett's behind in London. I would set up "camp" just outside the base, and for three or four nights running entertain the troops in my usual fashion, raising their spirits one by one.

Lord Sexcrime was able to arrange for me to visit British military camps as well, and I found the language was no barrier to giving these boys what they wanted most. Besides, by this time I spoke the language so well you'd think I'd been speaking it all my life. (Certainly I was proud to find I was bilingual.) I like a satiated audience. "Always leave them wanting less" is my motto when it comes to showing our fighting men a good time. I guess it's because of my father's noble sacrifice, but all my life I've loved a man out of uniform.

These camp forays took place during the week, but I always weekended in London. Lord Sexcrime was introducing me to the cream of London society. F. Emmett seldom accompanied me as he had found a few little places in Soho and in Earl's Court where he felt more at home. Frankly, F. Emmett never really mastered the British tongue as I had, and I think he was embarrassed to visit posh Mayfair homes when he was as incomprehensible as a Frenchman. He preferred to socialize with others like himself at expatriate pubs like Bozie's and The Leather Riding Crop.

As visiting American cinema royalty, I naturally expected an invitation to Buckingham Palace for tea with the Royal Family, or, even better, to Windsor Castle for a weekend, but no such invitation came, even though I'd done their blasted Command Performance. I cannot for a moment imagine why these people snubbed me. Perhaps they feared— mousy, drab things that they were—that they would be outshined by my already legendary glamor and beauty, fears far from groundless.

Fortunately, Lord Sexcrime's friends were more welcoming. Eddie, as I called him, took me around town to see all the fabulous sights: the Tower of London, Nelson's Column,* Tower Bridge; I particularly re-

---

*I'd never realized Nelson Eddy *had* such impressive dimensions! Lucky Jeanette!–Tallulah

member the evening he introduced me to Big Ben, who more than lived up to his name.

The pesky old war made the return crossing too dangerous to attempt and, thanks to my contract, the studio was paying our Savoy bill (my husband could certainly screw *Louie,* at least), so there was no hurry to leave and we just stayed on and on in London.

For months Lord Sexcrime had been taking me about London, introducing me to his posh cronies and allowing me to participate in their refined games of pleasure. During all this time he had dropped hints about his club, a private organization for men of a certain class, where they indulged in mutual genteel pastimes. Unluckily, like most London men's clubs, women were strictly forbidden. Finally Lord Sexcrime agreed to try to sneak me into the club, even though this would put his membership at risk. I had to disguise myself as a man, and I wasn't to tell anyone where I was going or with whom. I agreed to these conditions and, two nights later, in a short wig and crepe mustache and wearing one of F. Emmett's suits, I accompanied Lord Sexcrime to his private club, an establishment with the delightfully charming old-world name of The Hellfire Club.

Once inside we changed from our street clothes into the club uniform, a large black robe with a pointed hood. Then we went down several flights of stone stairs that looked to me to be hundreds of years old until we were well below street level and came into the club playroom, a large stone den with an altar-like device at one end. After assuring me that the room was utterly soundproof, he said that they were planning to enact some ancient rites that evening and I was to play the role of the virgin sacrifice. Well, hell, I was an actress, I could play anything, even a virgin!

Twenty minutes later I was strapped to the altar-like device, naked and spread-eagled, though I'd pointed out to Lord Sexcrime that this would sort of give the game away as regards my male impersonation. Eddie said that that no longer mattered and asked me again if I'd told anyone at all where I was going or with whom. I assured him that I'd told no one. He smiled.

The other revelers then filed in. They were all wearing the robes and hoods, though on a cue from Eddie, they shed their robes and all stood about me stark, staring naked, each one, I might add, at attention, so to speak. "Who says you English are repressed?" I asked, as the altar I was on was lowered and turned so I was lying flat on my back, feet in the air. "You boys look ready to party." Eddie then held a goblet to my lips. I slurped up the odd-tasting wine as best I could in that rather awkward position. Then, as the first reveler, Lord Sexcrime himself, mounted the altar, I began feeling drowsy. Improbable as it sounds, a gang bang, after all, being anything but boring, I quickly fell deeply asleep. Maybe it was the monotonous chanting of the others. All I can say is, Satan himself could have been at that party* and I'd never have known. I was out cold.

When I regained consciousness I was no longer naked, although the cheap clothes I was wearing I wouldn't have been caught dead in. I was tied up, gagged, and blindfolded. I heard a voice with a heavy German accent speaking: "Ach! Your precious little cargo is vaking up, Mein Herr."

Then a second voice spoke, unmistakably that of Lord Sexcrime: "I can give her another shot if you're not ready for her yet." Eddie's voice had a timbre I'd never heard in it before, hard and cruel. I found it quite arousing, especially the part about giving me a "shot." Frankly, I was parched.

"Nein, nein, Mein Herr," said the first voice. "Ve vill let zee little Fräulein vake up. After all, ve must inspect zee goods before ve make final payment."

"Fine. Fine. Just get on with it," said Lord Sexcrime impatiently.

The gag was taken from my mouth and the blindfold pulled off my eyes, and, as the world swam into focus, I found myself looking into the fat, sideburned and mustachioed face of an enormous middle-aged man in a strange-looking uniform and wearing a silly-looking helmet with a spike sticking out of the top. His face was only a couple inches from mine, and he was examining my face intently.

"Hello, darling," I said in as chipper a manner as I could manage under the bizarre circumstances. "I say, I'm dryer than Mormon pornography. How about a cocktail, and then maybe untying me? Hard to drink with no hands, you know."

"Ya, ya, you are right, Mein Herr," the burly gentleman said, as though my simple, civilized request had been unspoken. "It *is* zee American film goddess. You are an honest scoundrel. Schultz, give zee man vhat he deserves."

A much smaller man in a similar uniform stepped out from behind the fat guy, said something that sounded like "Ya vole!" and shot Lord Sexcrime through the forehead with a small pistol. The late Edward

*He was, but left early.–Douglas

Felcher, Lord Sexcrime, Earl of Incestshire, slammed back against the wall and slithered to the ground in a heap.

"Good God, darling," I exclaimed, "that was certainly gratuitous! Now I could *really* use a drink. How about a vodka tonic, *heavy* on the vodka, just the merest *whisper* of tonic?"

"Schultz," barked the large man, without taking his eyes from my face, "drag zat English schweinhunt's carcass out of here unt feed it to my Dobermans."

"And on your way back, Schultz darling," I added, "could you possibly bring me a martini? Shaken or stirred. I'm not particular."

"He vill not respond to your requests, Mein Frauline Morehead," the burly bully went on. "I suppose I should introduce myself to you and explain zee facts of your new life to you. I am Kaiser Wilhelm. You've heard of me, of course."

"Not actually, darling. Are you an actor? You look like someone I've seen in the movies. Have you worked for Griffith or DeMille or that pig Von Stroheim?"

"Nein! Nein! I am not some *actor!*" The man was sputtering with rage. "I am zee kaiser of all Germany, vhat you vould call zee king! I am zee ruler of Germany, soon zee ruler of zee entire German Empire, including France unt England."

"Well, darling, that must keep you busy. Now, if we're really in Germany, how about some schnapps?" I then added, remembering the sudden demise of Lord Sexcrime, "We could do shooters!"

"Mein Frauline Morehead, *bitte,* listen closely. I am zee most powerful man in zee vorld! I am making var on mein enemies, unt you, my proud beauty, are my prisoner."

"All right, I'm your prisoner. So when do the prisoners get cocktails?"

"Mein Frauline Morehead, let me make myself plainer still. I haf seen your films *Deranged vith Sweat* unt *Zee Human Herren,* unt I have become obsessed vith your beauty."

"Good God, darling, you're Heat Crazed! Let's celebrate with a frosty stein of lager!"

"Ya, deranged vith lust, like zat Spanish schwein in zee movie. Vhen I heard you vere in London, zo near yet zo far, I knew I *must* possess you! I haf many agents in London; I am, after all, a member of zee British Royal Family. Do my foolish English cousins really zink changing zeir name to Vindsor vill fool anyone? I had one of my agents bribe zat idiot Lord Sexcrime to abduct you and deliver you to me here in

Berlin! You are now a prisoner of love, what you might call my personal sex slave! What do you think of zat, Mein Frauline?"

"I think that calls for a drink. Don't you have any alcohol in this empire?"

The kaiser just grinned in an unpleasant manner. "I zink, mein beautiful Tallulah, zat it is time for you to learn just vhat you are here for." The kaiser then stood up a few feet away from me and began to disrobe. In a few moments he was standing there completely naked and I realized why he found it necessary to have silly-looking phallic spikes sticking out of his hats. These days the word would be "overcompensation."

I know that, on the face of it, being abducted on your honeymoon and held against your will, friendless and alone, in a foreign country where everyone gabbles in what sounds like guttural gibberish, as a personal sex slave to a morbidly obese Hessian dictator who was hung like a "Ken" doll, *sounds* like a nightmare, but it had its pleasant aspects, and once I'd gotten the old gasbag to install a wet bar I could reach, the life was actually not all that bad. Compared to sharing a vaudeville bill with Sonja Henie and a dog act, it was heaven. As the weeks stretched into months I grew accustomed to his face. It almost made my day begin, usually by bellowing in my face, "Vake up, mein frauline Tallulah, I vant some hot loving now!" although his approach wasn't always so subtle, and sometimes he dispensed with verbal warnings altogether.

I was kept in a large, beautifully appointed bedroom with an enormous bed, as indeed it had to be to accommodate the kaiser's bulk, before a huge mirror. There was also a wet bar and a bathroom. I had a closet full of negligees, which were all I wore, aside from a fur-lined manacle around my ankle connected by a chain to the bed. The chain was long enough to allow me to get to the closet, the bathroom, and the wet bar. My only duty was pleasing the kaiser, which didn't require a lot of effort. His tastes were simple and unimaginative, his equipment miniscule, and his energy flagging. Frankly, I don't think his circulation was very good, and his alertness was below par, too. He sometimes fell asleep right in mid-act, which was fine with me as long as he wasn't on top. He certainly paid more attention to me than my husband had.

I assumed that my disappearance couldn't have gone unnoticed long. Once word reached President Wilson that America's Sweetheart, Miss Tallulah Morehead, was a prisoner of the Hun, I could be certain that all of America's resources would be expended on one aim alone, my rescue. I had never quite understood just what we were doing in this awkward war in the first place. To the best of my knowledge no Germans had invaded New Jersey, but now, with me a prisoner of Hessian lubricity, America's gallant fighting men had a real motivation for kicking some serious Hun bun!

Nor was I disappointed. It was soon obvious that something was depressing Wilhelm, and it wasn't hard to figure out that he was losing the war. The renewed vigor that my abduction had given the American doughboy had turned the tide of battle.

Wilhelm wasn't quite the only person I ever saw. Sergeant Schultz brought me my meals and restocked the bar, and, if Wilhelm was away, would sometimes stop in for a quickie. He may have been the underling, but he was by far the more impressive man, if you take my meaning.

One day I was lying about idly, experimenting with new alcoholic combinations, when the door opened and a man I'd never seen before slipped into the room. He was maybe forty, handsome in a rugged way, and wearing a German uniform, though when he spoke he had no accent, and there was something familiar deep within the voice.

"Miss Morehead, are you all right?"

"All right? Darling, I'm a *legend!* Do you think homicidal, power-mad, despotic heads of state kidnap just *anybody?* So who are you, my dear, and do you want ice in yours?"

"I'm Illinois Smith. I'm here to rescue you."

"You're here to rescue me? Good God, darling, did President Wilson and my husband send you?"

"Indirectly. Have you been hurt?"

"Hurt? Of course I've been hurt! My husband doesn't want to make love to me! Wouldn't that hurt any woman?"

"No, I meant has the kaiser or his goons hurt you?"

"Oh. No, but they've annoyed the hell out of me. Frankly, if you've ever seen the kaiser naked, well, he'd have a hard time *hurting* anyone. I think of him as *Moby Dickless!* But the liquor here is definitely substandard. I mean, I know there's a war on, but is that any excuse for this Scotch? And who the hell do you have to invade to get a decent vodka, for Christ's sake? Really, taste this swill. Go on, taste it! Isn't there some sort of Geneva Convention against serving bilge like this to a helpless prisoner? Thank God the beer's good. Basically there are two things the Germans do well: mass murder and beer, in that order."

"There's a Geneva Convention against rape!"

" 'Rape'? That's a little strong. I don't know that we should bandy words like that about when the man's not here to defend himself. Anyway, in Wilhelm's case, it's more like forcible prodding. But shouldn't we be escaping?"

"Not yet."

"Not yet? You mean you're here to *schedule* a rescue? Well, let me get my book and see when I can pencil you in."

"It will be tonight."

"Tonight? No. That's no good for me. I have a coerced violation tonight. I need more notice. I have to coordinate accessories. How's next Thursday for you?"

"Here," he said, pressing a small vial into my hand. "Slip this into the kaiser's drink tonight. I'll be back at midnight."

"You want me to kill Wilhelm? I think you're confusing me with the character I brilliantly play in my latest PMS extravaganza, *Bluebeard's Daughter.* How's that doing by the way? You don't happen to have the grosses on you, by any chance?"

"This won't kill him. It'll just knock him out for a few days. I'll see you at midnight."

"But wait, let's drink a toast to our success. The champagne's acceptable."

"No time, my sweet one. I must go before I'm found out. Until tonight." And with that he swept me up in his massive arms and kissed me like I'd never been kissed before. Even Gilbert could learn a thing or two from Illinois Smith about smooching. Then, as quickly as he'd come, he was gone. *What a man!*

When Wilhelm came staggering in that evening he was already the worse for drink, so it was no trick to spike his schnapps with the potion Illinois Smith had given me. I had had a light dinner, only three fingers. When Illinois arrived Wilhelm was snoring in a manner even Mother would have envied. My hero's entrance was presaged by a commotion in the hallway that proved to be Illinois subduing the guards.

When he burst into the room he was carrying a large bag and a ring of keys. He unlocked my chains, and I was a free woman for the first time in months. In my rush of gratitude, I cried out, "My hero!" and ran to the bar. "Let's celebrate with cocktails."

"There's no time. At any moment we could be discovered. You must put these on and we must leave at once!" He handed me a German uniform that he took from the bag.

"There's always time for cocktails."

"Not now, Tallulah, my dearest."

"Why, Illinois, you're so passionate! All right. I'll play dress-up if you like. Be a lamb and make me a martini while I do."

Five minutes later we were creeping down the hallway, both dressed as German officers, one carrying a martini. It was a male disguise that had gotten me into this mess in the first place, thanks to the late, unlamented Lord Sexcrime, more recently the Duke of Dogfood. Now it was another, far more unfashionable male disguise that was getting me out of it.

Or was it? We came to the top of a staircase only to see a squad of soldiers on their way up. We quickly retreated back into my room, dragging the bodies of the sentries with us. Once we'd stacked the bodies in the room, we slipped out into the hall and pretended to be the sentries while the squad marched by. Then Illinois said, "We'll never get out that way. Maybe there's another exit in the bedroom."

We went back into the bedroom and I mixed us some cocktails while Illinois pounded on the walls. To my amazement a secret door opened up beside the big mirror. We slipped in there as I tried to give Illinois his drink. "No, I need a clear head," he said senselessly. I was forced to drink for both of us. Someone had to be muddleheaded enough to find our way out of there. Fortunately, I'd had the sense to stick a few liquor bottles into my pockets before leaving. Who knew what lay ahead?

Behind the mirror, to my shock, we found a movie camera setup. Apparently it was a one-way mirror, and that ratbag the kaiser had been filming our sessions together. Deciding that this was footage that shouldn't be left in enemy hands (I was, after all, under *exclusive* contract to PMS), I loaded all the film cans into a carton lying there and took them with us.

In the back of the secret room we found a staircase leading down to a secret tunnel. We followed along in the tunnel, which seemed to go on for several miles, finally exiting at an airfield outside Berlin. The quaint biplanes of the day were sitting on the darkened tarmac. We tiptoed up to one of the planes. Illinois checked to see that its fuel tank was full, then we loaded the film cans aboard, I climbed in. Illinois started the prop and then climbed into the pilot seat.

Just then a truckload of German soldiers came wheeling up, shouting and shooting. Our escape had been discovered! The chase was on!

We taxied down the runway with the Germans right behind us, shooting at us. Soon we were up in the air and away from the pursuing Hun. Fortunately, none of the bullets tearing through the plane, which seemed to be made of balsa-wood and cheesecloth, had hit the liquor bottles.

Just when I thought we were safe, we heard the buzz of other motors. Six German planes were in hot pursuit! That rapscallion Wilhelm! He really wanted me back! Well, who could blame him?

Illinois went into all kinds of crazy flying maneuvers trying to elude the other planes, making it damned hard to pour and consume a cocktail. I was finally forced to stop attempting to mix drinks altogether and just down straight vodka directly from the bottle! This damned war had reduced me to the level of a barbarian! What would be next? Brandy without a snifter? Don't kid yourself, war is *hell!*

We managed to elude our would-be re-captors and landed in France near Boulogne. Friends of Illinois were waiting and took us in. Finally, after an exhausting day and night, I was alone with my hero in a bedroom in a simple French farmhouse. We would be crossing the channel back to England the next day. The alcohol I'd stolen from Wilhelm was used up, but this was France, there was wine aplenty, and now Illinois would finally share a drink with me.

"Illinois Smith, my darling," I said. "The world shall know of your bravery. Take your rightful reward now, with me, my hero. Take me!"

"Ah, Tallulah, my sweet, dear one," said Illinois, suddenly turning shy. "There's something I must tell you first."

"Hush, my brave champion," I said, putting my fingers on his lips. "Not another word. I don't care if you're married. *I'm* married. Whatever your secret is, it can wait for morning. All that matters now is that you're a man and I'm a woman. Make love to me as you deserve to."

"Well . . ."

"Don't you want me?"

"Oh yes, yes, my darling, yes."

"Then have me."

"All right, but put out the light first. I want to do it in the dark."

While not terribly flattering to me, I had no objection. We made love in the dark, long and slow, and his tender fingers and tongue brought me to a rapture such as no other man had ever brought me, while not requiring, or even wanting, it seemed, several of my most male-pleasing specialties. *What a man!*

In the morning a tremendous shock was waiting for me at first light. I started to open my eyes when a hand clamped down over my face. At first I thought we'd been retaken by the Germans, but then I heard Illinois's strangely familiar voice saying, "Just a moment, Tallulah. Remember, you made me wait to tell you my secret. I do love you. I came all the way from America just to rescue you, but . . ."

"But what, darling?"

"Just, don't hate me."

Then Illinois took his hand away and my breath went with it. For lying on the bed beside me was none other than my old military school teacher Major Barbara! I *knew* that voice sounded familiar!

After my escape, the last of the kaiser's will to win went out of him. Within a week of my rescue Germany had surrendered and the war was over! "Illinois Smith," a.k.a. Major Babs, and I had won the war for the allies! That Major Babs, one hell of a woman, but *what a man!*

Fourteen hours after Major Barbara's shocking revelation, I was back in London. Of course, I had discarded the German uniform. Hardly the sort of thing to wear while strolling round Piccadilly Circus, but, as a lark, I'd had Major Babs fit me out in one of her numerous male drags, complete with mustache and muttonchops. I sauntered into Bozie's in my resplendent manly attire. Sure enough, there sat F. Emmett Knight at the bar, near a sampler on which had been embroidered one of Oscar Wilde's less amusing epigrams: "All women become like their mothers; that's their tragedy. No man does; that's his."* I rambled up to F. Emmett, lowered my voice to its deepest register, and said, "Hello, handsome. Can I buy you a drink, stud?"

An hour later we were back in our room at the Savoy. As F. Emmett did a slow strip in front of me, as per my request, I said, "I thought I recognized you. You're married to that incredibly glamorous movie sensation, Lady Tallulah Morehead."

"Yeah," he sighed, as he revealed his bare chest to me for the first time, and worth waiting for, it was, "I am, but don't worry, hot stuff; it's in name only. Besides, she's off entertaining soldiers or shopping or something. I haven't set eyes on her in weeks."

Forty-five minutes later F. Emmett was locked in the bathroom sobbing again, but I was snoozing with a grin. I'd finally consummated my marriage!

---

*I can tell you from personal experience, that when Oscar penned that fatuous homily, he definitely had his head up his butt, among other things.–Tallulah

9

Morehead Heights

With the war over, F. Emmett and I were able to return to America. Louie was very annoyed with my having been away for the better part of a year, and he didn't seem to feel that my being abducted and held as a sex slave by an obese, power-mad, thimble-pricked dictator was any kind of excuse for my not reporting back to work on time for my next film. It seems that my loving husband, F. Emmett Knight, Jerk Extraordinaire, never even noticed my absence all the months I was gone, and so had never reported me missing! If Major Barbara, in London as a "doughboy," her school now closed due to some sordid scandal that I never asked about,* hadn't tried to look me up and discovered that no one had seen me in weeks, and then gone undercover to find me, I might never have escaped. *What a man!*

As for Louie, he was placated when I presented him with all the footage the kaiser had secretly filmed of me. Even though much of the footage had to be scrapped as too pornographic for general release, there was still enough usable footage that with just a week's worth of additional shooting we were able to cut together a releasable film titled *Grand Delusion,* the credits claiming that Kaiser Wilhelm was a nonexistent actor named Emil Schoos. The film, obviously a tale of erotic enslavement, did rather well. No one in the general public ever suspected that the man playing opposite me in those hair-raisingly sadomasochistic bedroom scenes didn't just resemble, but actually *was* Kaiser Wil-

---

*Though Tallulah didn't inquire, others did. According to legend, Lillian Hellman later based *The Children's Hour* on this scandal.–Douglas

helm himself! This is the first time the story of my abduction and captivity has ever been told to the public.*

Once the additional shooting needed to make *Grand Delusion* releasable was completed, Louie closed down PMS's Astoria studio and moved all operations to the gleaming new lot in Hollywood, California. I had to pull up stakes and head west immediately to begin work on my next film, a biblical epic based on Genesis and set in the Garden of Eden in which I was to play the Mother of Them All, Eve, in a picture called *Adam's Bone.*

F. Emmett Knight had to stay behind in New York to close out his East Coast office and prepare to move the Knight-Mare Agency to Los Angeles. Strangely, given that we were newlyweds, F. Emmett didn't seem the least bit upset by this new separation. I had hoped that once we'd consummated our marriage it would draw us closer together, but F. Emmett was as distant as ever and certainly displayed no desire whatever to make love to me again, even when I offered to dress up in my male drag once more. "Please, Tallulah," he said when I'd press him on the point, "respect my wishes."

"What about *my* wishes? You made love to me once!"

"Don't remind me!"

"Look at this womanly body. Doesn't it arouse you?"

"God, you're making me sick!"

"The most powerful man in the world desired me so much he risked his empire to steal me!"

"He was a psychotic madman!"

"There's no need to name-call. Why not just close your eyes and pretend I'm Ramon Novarro?"

"Oh *yuck!* Tallulah, I've *had* Ramon Novarro. Trust me, you're no Ramon Novarro!"

What *did* upset my husband was the fact that while we were gone his Effing roommate had met someone else (*there's* a huge shock!) and had moved out, taking everything in the apartment with him, allowing the landlord to rent it to someone else, and leaving no forwarding address. F. Emmett started to whine about how he had no place to live and would wind up on a park bench until I pointed out that, as my husband, he was *supposed* to live with *me.*

---

*Incidentally, concurrent with the publication of this book, PMS Video is releasing a new, "fully restored" print of this always popular film, with *all* the kaiser's pornographic footage included. Look for *Grand Delusion, The Dictator's Cut* at your local video outlet. It's available in VHS and DVD.–Douglas

"I guess," he said. "But, if you try anything, remember, I can always go back to the park bench."

Shortly thereafter, leaving F. Emmett's behind at The Big Astoria, where it would have plenty with which to occupy itself, I was off to Hollywood to shoot *Adam's Bone,* a picture in which I wore little beyond my long, luxurious platinum tresses and a few well-placed mink fig leaves.

I moved into The Garden of Kali, an adorable residential motel in the heart of what is now West Hollywood, where everyone who was anyone was staying, while I looked for a house or a place to build one.

Gilbert Rolaids wasn't even considered for Adam in my new film. He was too much older than I, and he wasn't really going to look all that great in a fig leaf. Those sashes he wore in his traditional Spanish ensembles really functioned as a corset, cinching in his rather ample tequila gut. He was a lot of man, but, in the minimalist costumes we would be wearing in the film, he was *too much* man. Although Gilbert could not be cast as Adam, I did throw my wholehearted support behind his so-called "wife," Delores Delgado, being awarded the role of the snake. But Louie insisted that the serpent was a male role. Frankly, my relationship with Gilbert Rolaids had cooled off during my time in Europe and we never really rekindled it once I got back. Although we would go on to make four more films together, our off-screen romance was ended, not that that placated the unending wrath and petty jealousy of Delores, who showed no gratitude at all for my selfless efforts to get her a role in my film, something a lesser actress like herself would never have done. Frankly, I hate to call any woman a bitch, but then I don't really consider Delores a woman.

A new leading man, closer to my own age, who would look good in just a fig leaf, had to be found, and fast. When I told F. Emmett in a letter of the casting search for a muscular new leading man for me, my husband, loyal if nothing else, volunteered to come west long enough to help out with the talent search. Whatever my private differences with F. Emmett were, even I had to admit he had an eye for masculine pulchritude. The man knew the taste of talent. However, Louie didn't want to wait, and felt that our casting director, Bruce Camellia, who certainly had an eye, and other organs as well, for male talent, was up for the task. I can say, from personal observation, that Bruce was not only "up" *for* the task, but *throughout* the task as well.

Since I had refusal rights on costars, thanks to F. Emmett, who was very satisfying *outside* the bedroom, I also participated in the talent search, and not in a passive role either. My coworkers will tell you that when there's work to be done, especially when a leading man has to be cast, I'm the first one to roll up my legs and get my hands wet.

Bruce and I went through the photo submissions from agents together. Because the actor chosen would be playing Adam and physical build was all-important, we requested bare-chested shots only. Any time Bruce and I started to argue over who got to keep the picture, we realized that this was someone to call in. Bruce would interview them, and then I would take the candidate back to my dressing room for an audition scene with me to see if we had "chemistry." I had chosen the scene in which Adam and Eve commit sin back when it was original.

After about a hundred candidates we came across a truly outstanding young man. (Actually *I* came across him. Bruce merely interviewed him.) The actor in question was named Sherman Oakley, and he was one impressively well-set-up young man. If you've seen *Adam's Bone,* or any of Sherm's other movies, you know what a breathtakingly gorgeous man he was: black, rich, lustrous hair, eyes so dark they looked black too, the squarest jaw since Dick Tracy, a noble roman nose, full lips, clearer skin than mine, shoulders broad enough to seat four, a chest that would have had Michelangelo scouring the quarries for a worthy chunk of marble, a perfect bubbled behind that had me doing some scouring of my own, a pair of legs that would make Victor Mature look spindly, and between them an asset that would force the costumers to grow him an extra-large fig leaf! Just walking down the street he could make women run home and shoot their husbands. And on top of all that, he had talent!

After interviewing him, Bruce Camellia told me, before leaving for the emergency room, that he felt Sherman Oakley was the perfect casting for Adam. (During the interview Bruce had dislocated his jaw. I told you this boy was *impressive!*) I took Sherman to my dressing room for his audition and started to explain to him about my costar refusal rights. Before I got too far he stopped me. "Miss Morehead, please, you don't have to explain," he said in his deep, dreamy baritone, as he began stripping off his clothes, "I understand how things work in Hollywood."

"Please," I said, reclining on my casting sofa and hiking up my expectations, "Call me Tallulah. Oh my *God!*" One glance at his talent and I was damper than a Venetian jaywalker.

Of course, Louie still had to pass on Oakley before he was officially cast. We sent him up to Louie's office in Ozymandias Tower with both Bruce's and my highest possible recommendations. To no one's surprise, Louie quickly plucked him. Louie knew talent when it was brandished in his face.

For the role of the serpent who tempts Eve into sampling apple cider, Louie made the peculiar, casting-against-type choice of using a *real* snake! I tried to exercise my costar approval clause only to discover that it applied only to *human* costars! I was going to have to work with a slimy reptile, and not for the last time, I might add.

If Shirley the boa constrictor* was a literal nightmare to work with, Sherman was a dream. I felt that as long as my husband was three thousand miles away, Sherman and I should spend as much time together as possible, to really get the chemistry of the Parents of the Human Race going, so I moved him into my cabaña in The Garden of Kali.

Sherman Oakley was the most agreeable man on the planet. He was willing to spend long hours working on the love scenes, slaving over a hot costar. If Pete Moss needed him for press interviews, fine. If Lance Analvice, the costumer, misplaced his inseam measurement and needed to take it *yet again,* no complaints. If Bruce Camellia needed more time, Sherman was happy to cooperate. "No" didn't seem to be in his vocabulary. Sherman was a people-pleaser.

One Saturday afternoon Sherman was pleasing this person on a deserted stretch of beach near the northwest corner of Los Angeles County when, during a rare lull, a shadow crept across my face. I opened my eyes and beheld the most awe-inspiring sight I had ever seen. It towered over my face, eclipsing the afternoon sun: a massive, priapic column seeming to reach for the sky. "Good God," I gasped, "Sherman, my darling, what is it?"

"I believe it's what they call a promontory," Sherman replied.

This was my first glimpse of mighty Tumescent Tor. It is a magnificent shard of land. Rising haughtily from between a pair of gargantuan boulders at its base, against which the breakers churn ceaselessly, high tide or low, it juts out high above the sea, tipped with a broad verdant, fertile head. There was something about it more inviting than any landscape I'd ever seen. I had to find out if it was owned or not. All I knew was that I wanted to live my life mounted astride that glorious headland.

As luck would have it, it was for sale, and I snatched it up. Then I began planning my home, the now world-famous mansion Morehead Heights. Now that I had the land, I next needed the perfect architectural genius to design it.

The English genius Winchester Buttress had first risen to prominence

---

*So much for Louie's insistence that the serpent be played by a *male,* though the real snake was certainly more attractive than Delores Delgado!–Tallulah

some twenty or thirty years before when he designed a truly stunning mansion named Hill House for a Hugh Crain in Maine. He'd done the overall plans for the breathtaking Overlook Hotel in Colorado. He'd designed several wings of Sarah Winchester's mansion in Santa Cruz, California, and the Bates Mansion near Fairvale. He had designed a number of brilliant manor houses back in his native England, homes with names like Bly, Edbrook, Thanatopsis Manor, The Belasco House (a.k.a. Hell House), Despair Cottage, Bleak House, Hideous Heights, and Gloom Lodge. The surviving residents of these homes often referred to them as "too haunting to inhabit!" or something like that.

His work on Morehead Heights so impressed Louie that he hired him as a production designer, where he contrived sets for nearly all of my PMS pictures and, indeed, was central to giving them their trademark "haunted" quality, remarked on by so many critics over the years. He retired in 1942 and moved out to Amityville, Long Island, where he remained active, designing the occasional residence or cemetery, almost as a hobby. Though long dead now, he lives on in the houses he created, as their sporadic residents will attest.

I had met Buttress, or Winnie, as I called him, in London, where we had been introduced by Lord Sexcrime, late of England, currently roasting in hell. In fact, Winnie had redesigned the interiors of The Hellfire Club, the building itself being hundreds of years old. Though a member, Winnie swore he wasn't there the night of my abduction. When the time came to design my unique residence on this exhilarating site, I knew Winnie was the only man who could build me the house I deserved.

He quickly drew up a set of plans for a modest forty-room mansion with wet bars—some mini, some maxi—in every room. There would be a pool, a sauna, even a distillery in case of emergencies or very long weekends. Sadly, there wouldn't be room for Mother or Maxie to live there, or even visit, though my idiot husband did give them my mailing address without clearing it with me first. *Typical!*

The style was "Hollywood Gothic," the usual everyday blend of Mediterranean-Tudor-Japanese-Victorian-Bauhaus-neo-Georgian styles sort of tossed in a blender and rimmed with salt. Winnie was as excited by the site as I was, and strove to create a "union" between the house and the land, as though they were joined in a perfect coupling, conceiving a new form of domicile.

Meanwhile, back at the studio, except for a rather severe case of sunburn, the shooting of *Adam's Bone* was pure, adulterated pleasure. The knowledge that instead of the usual sensational, titillating blend of sex and violence aimed at the audience's basest prurient instincts, we were making an inspirational, profound, religious biblical epic about the birth of mankind and man's relationship to his Creator made the constant nudity and abundant sex a joyful duty. As gloriously beautiful Sherman Oakley and I made love again and again and again, utterly naked, in every conceivable position and in a variety of majestically ravishing locations, occasionally even on camera, we had the comfort of knowing that we were doing God's Work. It wasn't smut! It was Holy!

The building of Morehead Heights, which was happening simultaneously, was more trouble-plagued. First off, it turned out that Tumescent Tor *wasn't* an ancient Indian burial ground. Winnie liked to build on burial grounds. He felt it gave a house Roots and History, so a couple of Native American cemeteries had to be raided in the middle of the night to exhume a collection of sufficiently ancient mummies to bury under the building site before Winnie would start construction. Winnie, Sherman, and I ended up doing this ourselves as there was a noticeable lack of available, reliable body snatchers in Los Angeles in those days.

Once the framework started up, the construction workers began to have problems with some of Winnie's more outré concepts. For instance, to "reflect Tallulah's unique personal style" Winnie had dispensed with right angles, perpendicular walls, level floors, and other "architectural cliches," as he called them. The idea was to create a distorted space that to a sober person looks like a drunk's world, while to a social drinker like myself it would appear normal. I felt this was *genius,* but it was hard on workers used to building less imaginative homes.

Then there were the workers' silly complaints about a headless Indian brave haunting the site and picking off the men one by one. Just ridiculous! From the brink of Tumescent Tor was a thousand-foot drop to the boulders, reefs, and churning sea below, and the winds up there get fierce. Surely we don't need an avenging revenant to account for the occasional disappearance of a clumsy-footed worker. I have lived in Morehead Heights now for over eighty years, and in all that time the headless Indian brave has never been anything but a gentleman!

At the time *Adam's Bone* wrapped shooting, Morehead Heights was nowhere near ready for habitation, so Sherman and I stayed on at The Garden of Kali. One afternoon Sherm happened to bring in the mail. Glancing through it, he said, "Tallulah dear, here's a letter for you from F. Emmett Knight."

"Who?" I asked.

"F. Emmett Knight. You know, your . . ."

"My . . . what? Oh. Of course! My agent. Where's my mind these days?"

"Your agent and your husband."

"My husband? Are you sure? I don't think . . . Good God, darling, you're right! I *am* married to the little twerp. Isn't that funny? I'd completely flushed him from my mind. Somehow, I think of you as . . ."

"Hold it right there, Tallulah," Sherm snapped, the first time I'd ever heard him speak sharply. "I'm crazy about you, and I love what we do together. But we are *not* married! More to the point, *I* am not married! And I never intend to be married."

"All right, darling. No need to get churlish. Give me F's letter. I better see what the little pissant wants. Oh my God! He's finished up his business in New York and is moving out here to live with me! He expects to arrive in time for the premiere of *Adam's Bone!* Oh God!"

"Well, won't we be a fun little triad?"

I looked at Sherman Oakley for a moment, trying to see him as F. Emmett would. I immediately saw that, through F. Emmett's eyes, Sherm would look exactly the same as he looked to me: the Most Desirable Man on Earth. The three of us living together? Design for disaster! F. Emmett would be insanely jealous, and of the wrong person!

Then an even worse possibility occurred to me. True, Sherm and I had been going at it like Spaniard castaways since about four minutes after we met, but I'd never actually heard Sherm say "no" to anyone. I thought about Bruce's dislocated jaw, Lance Analvice's constant refittings for a single-leaf ensemble, and how even Louie B. Thalberg, who as far as I knew was reasonably straight—at least it always straightened out around me—had plucked the hell out of Sherman Oakley. If Sherm was so ravishing that not even straight men could resist him, and he just didn't have it in him to rebuff people in the buff, what would happen if he was under the same roof with F. Emmett Knight for more than, say, twenty seconds? I'd end up playing solitaire for the rest of my life, that's what. I was beside myself with worry, which, incidentally, is my favorite position. I had to think of something, and fast.

The next day I visited Morehead Heights. The primary structure was complete, the interiors were being finished, and outside the pool was being gunnited. I always enjoyed watching the brawny construction men working up a sweat. I stepped out to the pool area and heard a familiar male voice cry out, "Tallulah? Tallulah Morehead? Tallulah, how the hell are you?" When I looked around I saw the man doing the gunniting waving at me and grinning. He was a burly, well-muscled man who looked strong as an ox. He was wearing goggles, and his face and hair were whitened with a coating of gunnite dust. I confess I did not recognize him. He put down his gunnite hose and ambled over to me saying, "Don't you know me, Tallulah? Oh, of course. How could you? Here." And, as he neared me he removed the goggles. Suddenly I did recognize him. He was older and beefier and coated with gunnite, but, if anything, the years had only made him more attractive. It was my old Female Biology pupil Russell, the pride of the Lillian Roth High School wrestling squad, now grown into a real man.

"Russell, my darling, is that really you?" I asked, delighted to see my very favorite pupil, even more of a favorite than Mark, again after so long.

"You bet, Tallulah!" he shouted, literally sweeping me up off my feet in his robust, powerful arms, larger and stronger even than they had been in high school. "God damn, I'm glad to see you!"

"Russell, darling," I replied as best I could when placed back on my shaky feet, "how wonderful to see you gunniting my new swimming pool."

"This is *your* house? Hot damn, woman! You know I've seen every one of your movies, Tallulah. I'm just real proud of your success. My wife can't believe I actually knew you. You're her absolute favorite."

"You're married, darling?" I said, disappointment crushing me.

"Sure am. So are you. I saw that in the newspapers. Married your agent, it said. He must be one hell of a stud to nail you down to one man! I remember how back in high school the whole wrestling team couldn't wear you out."

"How sweet of you to remember. Yes, my husband is one hell of a stud, with the emphasis on 'hell.' But this calls for a drink. Can I lure you away from my work for a few minutes?"

"Tallulah, you could tempt Atlas into dropping the world. Besides, you're the boss. Hey Sid, take over here. The boss lady wants a conference with me."

"Sure thing, Russell," replied a short homely fellow, also in goggles, as he picked up Russell's hose.

"There, Tallulah, I'm all yours."

"If only you were." I said, leading him into the house. Since I visited the site nearly every day, I'd had the bar in what would become the master bedroom stocked. There was no furniture yet, the floors were raw wood, but there was booze in the bar. Here I led Russell for a cocktail and a reminisce.

"So you're in the gunniting business now?" I said, awkwardly trying to reinitiate the conversation, once the drinks were poured.

"Yeah, well, Talia, that's my wife, her dad owns the business. Actually, it's concrete, cement, gunnite, blacktop, all kinds of paving and construction. He gets lots of very important contracts. He's *connected*, you understand?"

"He knows people?"

"Exactly. Important people. Wiseguys."

"Smart alecks?"

"No, Tallulah, you know, mobsters. My father-in-law is Don Lorenzo Damfino, the godfather of the Damfino crime family. You don't know this. I didn't tell you."

"You mean the Mafia is putting in my swimming pool? How melodramatic. Have you deposited any bodies in the gunnite? My architect would be delighted. He feels building on corpses gives a house, or in this case a pool, character."

"Nah, Tallulah," Russell replied, actually blushing, "I'm not in the illegal end of the business. I'm strictly legit. All you're getting out there is a pool."

"And is that all I'm getting in here?"

"What do you mean?"

"I mean," I said, shrugging off my mink coat and then lying down on the heap it made, "are you too married for a, ah, refresher course?"

A lovely smile of pure lust spread charmingly across his sensual face. "Tallulah, babe," he said, slipping his overalls to his ankles with a practiced ease, "no man is *that* married."

An hour later, during what Russell called his "union break," I told him about the little problem I was having with F. Emmett and Sherman. "Good grief, Tallulah," Russell said. "Imagine you, of all people, married to a fruit. What a waste!"

"Well, I'm not exactly drying on the vine."

"Oh, you're plenty moist all right. You got your cutie costar. But you think your husband coming here is going to mess things up."

"Let's just say his imminent arrival is *inconvenient*. If only he could disappear for a while."

"I hear you. Tallulah, you're an okay broad. Maybe I can help you out. I mean, I'm connected now, and making people disappear is a sideline of the family business."

"You really think you could help? Would you?"

"Sure. You've always been great to me, Tallulah, and I haven't nailed that many movie stars. I'd be glad to speak to my father-in-law on your behalf."

"I wouldn't want anything *permanent* to happen to F. Emmett. He's a *very* good agent! I just need him out of the way for a few months, long enough to finish the house and get a divorce on grounds of desertion."

"Say no more. Russell will handle it all. Oops. Look at the time. Break's over," he said, rolling back on top of me to resume his post-graduate studies.

Sure enough, when the evening came for the premiere of *Adam's Bone*, at the PMS Japanese Theater* on Hollywood Boulevard, there was no sign of F. Emmett Knight. He'd telegraphed me a week earlier that he was taking the train west and expected to be in Los Angeles the day before the premiere, but he never showed up. Louie offered to hire private detectives to try to locate my missing hubby, but I told him I preferred to procure my own dicks, although, as it happened, I was so busy, what with finishing up Morehead Heights, publicizing *Adam's Bone,* preparing for my next film—Sherman and I were going right into another picture, a sultry romance set in the Orient called *Fleshpot*—that I never quite got around to hiring those private detectives, though I told Louie, Milton Mare, and F. Emmett's mother I had, just so they wouldn't worry.

Morehead Heights was soon completed, and I had asked Arthur Deco, the studio's incredibly brilliant art director, to furnish and decorate it to match my matchless taste. I was down at the site daily, and Russell usually dropped by from wherever he was working during his lunch hour. Once Arthur Deco had put a huge bed into the master bedroom, Russell's visits became far less wearing on my furs.

Russell made a nice contrast to Sherman, blond to his dark hair; burly, with just the beginning of a beer gut to Sherm's sixpack abs; and their lovemaking techniques were radically different. Sherman was all tender gentleness, slowly, patiently driving his partner to cascading waves of ecstasy. Russell, on the other gland, had perfected his basic technique on the wrestling squad. He was raucous, wild, abandoned, given to pinning his partner immediately, and, if he didn't spend a lot of time on foreplay, he spent *hours* in the saddle. Energy and stamina were his way to a woman's heart. And my motto always has been, "Anything worth doing, is worth doing *rough!*" Most women would have sold

---

*A terribly outré movie palace, though, after thousands of complaints, Louie finally broke down and decided to sacrifice authenticity for comfort, taking out the mats and installing chairs.–Tallulah

their children into slavery for just Sherman Oakley, and I was having them both. But then, I've always felt that just because there's a steak at home is no reason not to stop and eat a hot dog if you're feeling peckish on the road. Or to put it another way, "Anything worth doing, is worth *over*doing."

In this blissful way the time passed until Morehead Heights was ready for me to move in. I decided to leave Sherman at The Garden of Kali. As a new movie-star-bachelor-around-town, he needed some privacy, and, as an established-movie-*Star*-bachelorette-at-large (well, nearly; my lawyer, Mason Dixon, had filed for divorce on grounds of desertion), I could use my privacy as well.

Once ensconced in Morehead Heights, I threw a housewarming party that is still spoken of in hushed tones of voice today. Everyone with PMS was there: Louie B. Thalberg; Sherman Oakley escorting Terry Cotta, a contract starlet that Sherm was sleeping with strictly for appearance's sake as I was still technically married; Cyril Von Millstone with Lois LaVerne, Lillian Gush, and Billy Bowlegs; Gilbert Rolaids, of course, unfortunately with Delores Delgado, who was rudely critical of Arthur's decorating choices; Bruce Camellia, Arthur Deco, and Lance Analvice, who all came stag, of course; adorable Norman Talmadge with perky Connie Lundquist; stalwart leading man Keith Kittridge with sultry Azure Welles, a newcomer from the Broadway theater that Louie had just signed who was to become one of my closest friends and make more films with me than anyone else; Vincent Lovecraft, with his longtime housemate C. Halibut Plugg (Plugg later worked at Warner's for years as Bette Davis's stunt double); feisty little Buster Hymen with Marjorie Barnswallow; James Dong Lowe with his wife, Fay Lo Sushi—all the gang.

But my guest list wasn't confined to just the folks with PMS. Winchester Buttress was the guest of honor, naturally, at this first public unveiling of his masterpiece. Pete Moss brought a phalanx of reporters, photographers, and architectural critics anxious to behold Buttress's achievement. Frank Lloyd Wright himself was there and made Winnie blush when he declared, "Only Edgar Allan Poe could adequately describe Morehead Heights!" What a flatterer!

There was other Hollywood royalty as well: Charlie Chaplin, who kept telling my waiters (lovely, well-set-up lads, all bare-chested, selected by Bruce Camellia) to break their chains of oppression; Dougie Fairbanks and Mary Pickford, obviously chagrined at the way my home's spectacular grandeur eclipsed their drab little shack; my old pal John Barrymore, a fellow social drinker who drank like a social fish, with his wife of the hour, What's-Her-Name Barrymore; adorable Lon Chaney; sweet Mary Philbin; giddy Buster Keaton; kinky Eric Von Stroheim, who didn't believe a word of my story about the truth behind *Grand Delusion*; diminutive Cecil B. DeMille escorting dreary, hopelessly homely little Gloria Swanson; and sprightly D. W. Griffith, who paid Morehead Heights the evening's most memorable compliment when he said it made his Babylon set from *Intolerance* "look modest by comparison."

And, just to show how completely egalitarian I am, I also invited Russell, who brought his scary little wife Talia to meet some movie stars. I privately suggested to Russell that perhaps, if Talia wanted the *full* Hollywood experience, I could ask Sherman to throw her a quick one* in one of the guest bedrooms later on, although oddly, Russell didn't take the suggestion very well. He responded rather rudely to my generous offer on her behalf. After all, by this time, several months after the release of *Adam's Bone* had exposed his talent to the world, Sherman had a waiting list. Hell, *I* had to make appointments with him these days, and we were about to start shooting *Fleshpot* together!

At one point I lured Cecil B. DeMille up to the master bedroom, determined to find out what his "B" stood for. He always claimed it stood for "Blount," but I ask you, have you ever heard of *anyone* named Blount? But once I got his jodhpurs off I saw the truth. Forever afterward to me he would be Cecil *Blunt* DeMille, which may be why we never worked together.

Although gourmet caterers prepared all the food, I myself had handmade a special fish entrée from a recipe I found in *The Memoirs of Lucrezia Borgia* just for Delores Delgado as a peace offering. (Once again I was the one trying to offer an olive branch, or, in this case, an olive loaf, while she remained the shrieking harpy.) After she ungraciously refused it three times, I got Billy Bowlegs to distract her with one of his hilarious slapstick gags, in this case shoving Charlie Chaplin out a third-story window,† while I slipped it onto her plate and covered it with potato salad. Gilbert told me later that she never stopped insulting my home all the way to the emergency room.

---

*Sherm's *quickest* took at least an hour.–Tallulah

†For some unknown reason, this was the only time these two great comic geniuses ever performed together, and we were the privileged few who were lucky enough to be there. What a shame, and what a terrible loss to the general public. They were hysterical together. What chemistry! We were all still laughing long after Chaplin had left in the same ambulance with Delores.–Tallulah

It's really a shame Delores had to leave early, as she would have loved the party's sensational conclusion. Around one A.M. I saw Talia wander out into the garden with Sherman. Knowing that unless Talia was an idiot or a lesbian, or both,* they'd be gone at least an hour, I felt safe in displaying my treasures to Russell in the master bedroom.

I was shocked from a state of ecstasy by a shrill scream! Suddenly the room was assaulted by intensely bright flashes of light and a loud hubbub! It seemed that Pete's photographers were snapping a bunch of photos of my bedroom, and that Russell and I, both by coincidence naked, were in the middle of these photos! Half of my guests were standing behind the photographers, while at the forefront of the excited, voyeuristic throng stood Talia, weeping noisily and pointing at us. "Talia, darling," I said, showing great compassion given the annoying circumstances, "do you mind? I'm trying to concentrate."

Talia ran out of the room and then the house, wailing: *"DADDY!"* Everyone else stood riveted to the spot.

Finally I said, "Well darlings, if you're all just going to stand there, could one of you at least pour me some champagne?"

---

*A *rare* combination, but then, Talia was a rare woman.–Tallulah

10

My Feet in Cement

The newspaper front pages the next day were all covered with sensational pictures of Russell and myself in delectable flagrante delecto. You couldn't recognize Russell in most of the photos unless you were intimately familiar with his rosy rear cheeks (which were well worth getting to know intimately), but I was unmistakable in all of them, and, fortunately, I looked exquisite. As *Grand Delusion* showed the world, I always looked ravishing being ravished.

I was lounging on my mammoth, family-size bed the morning after, thumbing through the various papers, picking out which shots to order prints of, when I heard the doorbell, followed maybe thirty seconds later by yet another shrill high-pitched scream, much higher and more feminine than scary little Talia's had been. It could only be Terrence, my newly hired houseboy and personal assistant, shrieking his little lungs out. Bruce Camellia had recommended Terrence, who had originally studied acting but was simply too effeminate for any conceivable male role.

I hurried downstairs to see what all the commotion was about. At the front door I found Terrence sobbing in terror and, sitting on my Welcome mat (Actually the mat says, "Time for Cocktails") was F. Emmett Knight, handcuffed, blindfolded, and gagged. An envelope was pinned to his lapel, and on it was written one word: "Tallulah."

I slapped Terrence, which brought him around (frankly, if I'd been a man, it would have turned him on), then removed F. Emmett's gag and blindfold. He was in a hysterical state, and I shortly had to slap him as well. Then Terrence got jealous and wanted to be slapped again. It would have been easier to just set the men slapping each other, but F. Emmett was still handcuffed behind his back, and all my handcuff keys were up in my nightstand, so I unpinned the envelope and opened it to read the note within as I returned to my bedroom to find the keys to my husband. The note read,

Dear Tallulah,

I'm sorry to have to return your husband to you earlier than you intended but, after last night, Don Damfino is no longer inclined to do you or me any favors. Which brings me to something I'm even sorrier to tell you, which is that I can't see you any more at all! Don Damfino made it very *clear that if I were ever caught anywhere near you again, my health would be severely endangered. I'm only still alive to tell you this because, mad as Talia was, she says she still loves me, and she told her dad that if he had me killed she'd pout for a month. Consequently, I will be fine, and the doctor says I don't really need toes to walk anyway. I will miss you, Tallulah. A guy always remembers his first piece of tail with special sentiment. You are an okay broad, Tallulah, but for now, I'm not even allowed to see your movies. Talia is pretty pissed at you, so, if I were you, I'd watch your back.*

Russell

How sweet of darling Russell to take time out of what was obviously a busy and trying day to pen me that touching little note, more treasured than any fan letter. I especially appreciated his parting compliment about my back. I remembered that he had always expressed a special fondness for my backside, which has never received the amounts of praise showered on my face. Even back in high school, on that first night with Billy, Mark, and him, according to his note, the night Russell lost his virginity he had enthusiastically volunteered to be the first to take a "backseat."

Once I got F. Emmett's handcuffs off, he calmed down some, though I had to throw a drink in Terrence's face to finally end his hysterics, and I *hate* wasting good alcohol, or even mediocre alcohol, or, for that matter, *godawful* alcohol, something my employees need to learn immediately if they expect to remain working for me long. Once Terrence had calmed down enough to sob quietly, I asked F. Emmett where the hell he'd been.

He had no idea. He said that when the train had arrived in Los Angeles, a large, burly Italian man had come on to him in the station men's room. Showing the common sense and self-restraint for which he was famous, he'd gotten in the man's car, where two other men and a lot of guns were waiting for him. He'd been blindfolded and taken somewhere. He'd spent the intervening months in a small, dark room, receiving his food through a slot in the door. He hadn't been beaten or sexually abused, even when he begged to be. Then, this morning, two large men wearing ski masks came into his room, handcuffed, gagged, and blindfolded him. Next he experienced a variety of sensations and sounds until I removed his blindfold here at Morehead Heights. I asked him if he'd ever heard anybody say anything about who ordered his abduction or why, but, unfortunately, he hadn't. It remains a mystery to this day.

When F. Emmett Knight saw the photos in the morning papers he hit the roof. "You were hogging this stud all to yourself!" he bellowed.

"Russell's not gay," I explained.

"You mean he hasn't found out he's gay yet."

"Trust me, I've known Russell for years. He's straight."

"That's what they all say."

"F, straight men *do* exist."

"Keep telling yourself that, Tallulah, when you're single again."

"What?"

"Well, I have to divorce you now. You've publicly humiliated me. Mother will insist. All America knows you've cheated on me."

"What do you care? You wouldn't sleep with me."

"That doesn't mean I want some other man wearing *my* beard on the front page of every newspaper in the country."

"Do you really think it made *every* paper in the country?"

At this point the phone rang. It was F. Emmett's mother calling from New York in a snit. I *had* made every paper in the country.

Louie was furious at first, claiming that America wouldn't pay to watch an adulteress act, but, as it happened, the grosses on *Adam's Bone* took a sharp leap upward as soon as the pictures hit the public. Two weeks later Louie rushed all my previous films back into release, and each did better than they had the first time around. Apparently America couldn't wait to pay to watch an adulteress act. I was hot again, and shortly thereafter, I was single again.

In the sort of bizarre twist that can only happen in Hollywood, at the same time F. Emmett was suing me for divorce on grounds of adultery, with me countersuing for annulment on the grounds that F. Emmett wouldn't even sleep with me unless he thought I was someone else, he was also negotiating *on my behalf* with Louie for a new contract based on my higher grosses. Thanks to my public disgrace, I was now PMS's most popular star. F. Emmett got me a colossal raise, which was fortunate because in the divorce he received one-third of my future earnings for seven years, from which he had to pay *himself* a ten-percent commission! Severing our matrimonial knot tied our finances into a Gordian knot. As I understood it, I was leasing myself from him. I believe I was paying *him* for depreciation of *me!* It would have been so much simpler if only he'd been willing to sleep with me, although perhaps Russell might have disagreed with that.

Shooting was going well on *Fleshpot*, at least. Set in the mysterious Orient, Sherman and I were wearing more than we had in the last picture, but we shed our costumes as often as possible. I was playing another temptress (it *was* my specialty!), trying, rather successfully I might add, to lure Sherm into sin. In the film's most talked about sequence I did the Dance of the No-Veils-At-All. It was a barn burner.

Off screen, however, my relationship with Sherm was hitting some bumps. He was just not the same, people-pleasing, get-along guy he'd been when we were doing *Adam's Bone*. I was lucky to spend one night a week with him, and when I complained about this he pointed out that there were only so many hours in a day, and I should be happy with one night a week. There were women, he pointed out, who sat on his waiting list for *months*.

Daffy Sid Grauman had instituted a bizarre celebrity ritual at a theater he owned less than a block from Louie's Japanese Theater. He was having all the big movie stars leave their footprints and autographs in slabs of cement in the theater's forecourt. I kept asking Pete Moss why I, as one of the biggest box office attractions in Hollywood, hadn't yet been invited to set my tootsies in concrete for the edification of future generations. My concern wasn't for me, you understand, it was for posterity. Pete promised to look into it.

Sure enough, as the premiere of *Fleshpot* drew near, I did receive an invitation to have my feet immortalized in cement. It was not going to occur at the premiere, of course, since that was being held at the PMS Japanese Theater, which had a rock garden instead of a forecourt, but neither was it being held at Grauman's Theater. Apparently they were initiating a similar celebrity tourist attraction on the Santa Monica Pier, as that is the locale to which I was invited. I was to be their first star attraction. The time chosen for the ceremony was unusual, I thought, as it was scheduled to take place at three in the morning on a Wednesday night. The representative of the Santa Monica Chamber of Commerce, a Guido "The Sadist" Damfino, who dropped by Morehead Heights to issue the invitation, explained to me as we were putting our clothes back on that the unusual time was so that the reporters and critics wouldn't have any scheduling conflicts. This seemed perfectly reasonable to me.

I gave all the details to Pete Moss so he could get the PMS publicity machine rolling. Pete said he'd never heard of a publicity event being held so late before, but I pointed out that its uniqueness would make it all the more newsworthy. He promised to look into it.

The problem with this sort of celebrity attraction is, I know from experience, that the fans like to have souvenirs they can take home and keep, autographed pictures or other mementos. Over the years I've given away thousands of autographed pictures to adoring and grateful fans. I didn't want my ardent devotees, especially ones devoted enough to show up at the pier at three A.M., to walk away disappointed. I wanted them to have something special to remember me by after I was gone.

I came up with the brilliant idea that the most appropriate souvenir for a cement footprint ceremony would be cement footprints! I decided I would bring a supply of preset autographed cement footprint slabs to hand out to the fans at the ceremony, at my own expense, I might add.

I laid out the molds in the backyard while Terrence mixed and poured the cement. Once they had started to firm up I stepped into them barefoot for a couple minutes each, while using a wooden dowel to autograph them. Once they had dried and hardened I had Terrence take them out of the molds and stack them in the trunk of my newly purchased limousine, the Moreheadmobile. The slabs were fairly large and weighed about twenty-five pounds each, so the car could only hold about twenty of them. I brought pictures for the other fans.

Promptly at three in the morning the Moreheadmobile rolled up to the Santa Monica Pier with Terrence at the wheel, and me waving from the backseat. There were barricades up bearing signs saying CLOSED FOR A SPECIAL EVENT. I got out of the car and strolled past the barricades and out onto the pier while Terrence unloaded the slabs that he was to carry and hand out to the fans.

I was surprised, as I neared the end of the pier, to see that there was no crowd of awestruck fans clamoring for me. There were just three men, all in trench coats and broad-brimmed hats. Two of them were tending a cement mixer, so I knew that I was in the right place. Seeing me coming, the largest of the men said, "Ah, Miss Morehead. Punctual as a professional. Right this way." He pointed toward a large washing basin with a nasty-looking gun.

"Where are all my fans, darling?" I asked.

"Why, we're all right here, Miss Tallulah," said the man again, brandishing the gun toward me in a manner I felt could be unsafe.

"I rather thought there would be more," I said, trying to conceal my disappointment. "The nice thing, though, is that everyone will get one of my autographed slabs."

"Miss Morehead, please," said the man with the gun. "Would you oblige us by stepping into this basin so we can get this ceremony under way."

"Certainly, darling. With my pumps on, or would you prefer barefoot? It's naughtier."

"Your option, my dear," said the gunman, the soul of courtesy. I noticed as I stepped into the basin, shoes off—pumps aren't free, after all—that the other men were drawing guns, too. As soon as I was standing in the basin the men started pouring the cement into it.

"You know, this is getting awfully deep for footprints," I mentioned helpfully as the cement rose to just below my knees.

"We know," said the first man. "Allow me to introduce myself to you, Miss Morehead. I am Don Lorenzo Damfino. It was my sweet little girl Talia that you humiliated by screwing her husband on the front page of every newspaper in America."

"Now just a darn minute, Don Damfino. Let me make two points. First, I was promised there would be cocktails. It's chilly out here. Where's my drink? Secondly, your daughter has only herself to blame for all that publicity. If she hadn't screamed her shrill little lungs out, the reporters and photographers wouldn't have come running and nobody would be any the wiser. Guido?" I asked, recognizing the young man who'd invited me here in the first place. "Is that you? Darling, could you get me a hot toddy? I'm freezing out here, and this icy cement isn't helping."

"I'm afraid my son will not be bringing you any booze. But don't worry. You'll have plenty to drink in just a few minutes."

"Excellent. But the sooner the better. The martinis I had in the car on the way over are wearing off. What are we drinking tonight, anyway?"

"Actually, you'll be drinking seawater, Miss Tallulah."

"Seawater? What the hell kind of drink is that? It sounds fishy to me."

"Let me clear things up for you, then. In a few minutes, when that concrete starts to harden, my boys here are going to toss it and you off this pier and into the Pacific Ocean."

"Did you clear this with Louie B. Thalberg? Because, quite frankly, this is about the most half-assed publicity stunt I've ever heard of. There's no press to cover it. There's no vodka. And now you propose a stunt that sounds unpleasant at best and downright dangerous at worst. Do you realize I could drown doing this?"

"That's the idea, Miss Tallulah. We're going to drown you."

"Well, who's stupid idea was that? If Pete Moss approved this I'll have him fired. Now, would one of you good fellows please get me a drink?"

"Miss Tallulah, try and understand. This isn't a publicity stunt. It's a murder."

"A murder? Good God, darling, that's illegal! Did you get a permit? We could all end up in jail. I might add that it's antisocial, and I am *not* an antisocial drinker! Who's being murdered by the way, darling?"

"You are!"

"Out of the question! Have you seen my schedule? I have thousands of publicity interviews to do for *Fleshpot*. I have script meetings for my next film, *Silent Echoes*. Costume fittings. Social engagements. I simply do not have the time to be murdered right now. Call my personal assistant, Terrence, and we'll see when we can pencil you in."

"You are very slow to catch on, Miss Tallulah, but you have shot your last film!"

"Nonsense! I'm still under contract."

"The only contract that matters right now is the one I've taken out on you."

"I never signed that. It will never stand up in court. Call my attorney, Mason Dixon, but first, haven't you at least got a hip flask? I refuse to be murdered sober!"

Just then Terrence stumbled into our little group, staggering under the weight of ten slabs of cement souvenirs. "Look out, Terrence," I hollered. "You'll drop those priceless collector's items!"

"What?" cried Terrence, who couldn't see very well around the tall stack of incredibly heavy cement. "I don't think I can hold these much longer."

"Drop the crap, faggot," Don Damfino snarled, rather rudely. I felt that, as an admitted murderer, he was hardly in a position to call other people names. Murder is not my definition of the moral high ground.

In any event, his order was unnecessary as Terrence simply couldn't hold the stack any longer and the pile slid out of his puny arms, sliding and smashing into Guido and the other man at the mixer, knocking both of them into the ocean. Don Damfino swung angrily around, although I don't know what *he* had to be mad about. *I* paid for the slabs Terrence had just shattered. Don Damfino pointed his gun directly at Terrence, who was already hysterical over his accidentally destroying half my stash of cement keepsakes. When Terrence saw the gun being pointed at him by a snarling Mafia hood, he fainted dead away. Some personal assistant. Just when I needed personal assistance most, he was out cold. I made a mental note to dock his pay for the evening.

Don Damfino, who was not making a good first impression on this girl, then turned back to me and said, "That's it, Tallulah. I've wasted enough time on you. This is for my little girl's broken heart." He raised the gun and pointed it directly at my face. I closed my eyes, wishing I had a straight scotch, or perhaps a Harvey Wallbanger.

I heard the shot, which seemed odd. I opened my eyes in time to see Don Damfino, with a small hole in his forehead, falling backward into the sea. I heard a familiar voice say, "Hold on, Tallulah, I'll be right there."

A masculine figure swooped down over Terrence's prostrate form, checking his pulse and breath. "He'll be okay." Then the figure stood and looked down into the water. The person then aimed his gun and fired twice more. "No point in leaving someone to seek vengeance. They were all murderers, anyway." Then the figure turned and grabbed me, yanking me out of the still damp concrete, crushing me in powerful arms, silencing my questions with an overwhelming kiss. When the kiss ended I was held back far enough to see the face of my rescuer. Once again my life had been saved by Illinois Smith, a.k.a. Major Babs! *What a man!*

"Tallulah, honey," she said, "you need a bodyguard."

"Major," I replied, "you're hired. Now let's get a drink!"

Major Barbara had to drive the Moreheadmobile back up the coast to Morehead Heights. Though we had managed to revive Terrence, after *my* ordeal *he* was in a *state!* Terrence shivered in the backseat with me as I poured brandy down his throat and vodka down mine. Terrence was whimpering, "Oh, Miss Tallulah, those awful men! Those awful *suits!* He pointed that big horrible gun at me! What if it had gone off? Oh my goodness! *Oh my goodness!*" I'm afraid Terrence put the "wimp" in "whimper."

"Terrence, darling," I said gently, displaying the compassion that marks the difference between a *great* actress and a merely incredibly beautiful one, "I realize that *my* brush with death has been very hard on *you,* but if you don't calm down and butch up I'm going to have to slap you again."

"Oh, Miss Tallulah, would you please?"

By the time we arrived back at Morehead Heights the sun was peeping over the Santa Monica Mountains and my morning copy of the *Christian Science Monitor** waiting on my porch. One glance at its smug headline and I did what I hadn't done facing death on the pier: I screamed and then fainted dead away.

The headline told the tale of the Worst Horror of the Twentieth Century. Satan, The King of Hell,[†] had signed *THE GREAT EVIL*[††] into law!

---

*I adored Mary Baker Eddy, a fabulous woman, and one of the *craziest* lesbians I've ever met. I have always been a *devout* Christian Scientist, except for that Going-to-Church-on-Sunday-Mornings thing, which is inconvenient, the No-Doctors thing, which I think dangerously inadvisable, and the No-Alcohol thing, which is *IN-SANE!*–Tallulah
[†]President Woodrow Wilson–Douglas
[††]The Volstead Act.–Douglas

11

The Worst Horror of the Twentieth Century!

I regained consciousness hoping that that monstrous headline had just been a nightmarish hallucination brought on by the stress of dealing with Terrence's hysterics, but alas, the horror was real. America, which, just two years earlier had defeated a power-crazed, would-be world dictator with excellent taste in women, who merely wanted to grind freedom under his boots while raping and pillaging Western Civilization, had now been conquered in a bloodless coup by the Forces of Hell operating through highly placed traitors in our own government! What had our boys fought and died for? Lucifer, Lord of the Flies, Potentate of the Pit, a.k.a. President Woodrow Satan, had betrayed every freedom-loving American. No wonder he was not reelected!

And then there was the *idiotic* tone of the *Monitor*'s coverage. They wrote about **THE GREAT EVIL** as though it was a *good thing!* Can you imagine? I cancelled my subscription immediately!

Thank heaven that Winchester Buttress had had the *genius* to prepare for *The Unthinkable* by building a distillery in Morehead Heights's spook-laden basement. I put the headless Indian brave to work manning the distillery. Since losing his head God knows how, God knows when, he had been wandering the hallways of Morehead Heights looking to replace his head by getting some one to give him some. His quest had so far proved fruitless as Terrence was terrified of him and I prefer, if at all possible, a man who can reciprocate.* Entrusting the headless Indian brave with this Sacred Duty seemed a good way to give his afterlife

---

*I've also always preferred, *whenever feasible,* to confine my romantic relations to the living, although, as I get ever older, I do find myself on the lookout for men who aren't so picky.–Tallulah

some *meaning!* Also, he seemed the perfect person to trust with my still as he had no mouth* and thus could not drink up the yield. The only drawback was that he could only materialize between dusk and dawn, so I needed someone to man it during the day. Terrence wouldn't set foot in the basement (nor would Terrence enter the as yet unused nursery Buttress had built *just in case* or the greenhouse or use the circular stairs in the library. The man was *timid!*) and Major Barbara, whom I had moved into the bedroom originally intended for F. Emmett Knight, which connected directly with mine (don't get the wrong idea; our relationship was *strictly platonic,* except, of course, for those evenings when I had no date) as my bodyguard, didn't like to let me out of her direct sight.† Pete Moss eventually found me a man at the studio, a failed actor named James Beam, to moonlight making my moonshine.

The next day the *other* papers trumpeted banner headlines about the bullet-ridden bodies of mobsters Don Lorenzo Damfino, Guido "The Sadist" Damfino, and Luca "The Sodomite" Cristillo washing up on shore in Santa Monica. Police were reported as suspecting a rival bootlegging gang of having eliminated the competition just as the bootlegging market was bursting wide open.††

Having taken Major Barbara on as my full-time bodyguard, I decided and she agreed, as a lark, that she should continue her masquerade identity of Illinois Smith. Many of my closest friends and associates, including Terrence and my next five or six husbands, never discovered her true gender. What a jackanapes!

The four of us—Terrence, Major Babs, the headless Indian brave, and myself—with James Beam during the days, made up a happy little household, even if Terrence never got over his terror of the headless Indian brave and refused to enter any room he was in. I tried to explain how he and his people had suffered, what with white invaders, losing his head (*had* to hurt!), body snatchers§ and other indignities, but

---

*Nor stomach, nor, in fact, any organs whatever. How I envy him. Dieting is a snap! The man weighs nothing at all!–Tallulah

†Which, frankly, got to be a real pain at times. Not *all* attacks are unwelcome. –Tallulah

††This was but the first libel of what were to be thirteen years of unjustified calumnies against bootleggers, those modern day, Zorro-like freedom fighters who dared to defy the evil men in power to protect the rights of the Social Drinker. God bless them for the wonderful work they did.–Tallulah

§I felt it inadvisable to mention to Terrence, or to the headless Indian brave, for that matter, that I had been one of the body snatchers who had stolen him. Why stir up trouble.–Tallulah

Terrence didn't care. He wasn't going anywhere near anyone who was headless or transparent, and the poor old headless Indian brave was both.

I felt it was odd for someone who was subjected to as much intolerance as Terrence was to be so intolerant toward someone else. But that is the dark side of human nature. Dead people have been shunned throughout history. In Colonial America dead people were forced to go about wearing scarlet "D"s sewn onto their clothes. Even today dead people are *legally* discriminated against in all fifty states! Think about it! The moment you die you lose all civil rights, you are stripped of your property, you are even forbidden to marry or have sex! It's barbaric! You probably think of death as something that only happens to *other* people. You thoughtlessly say hurtful things like, "I don't mind living near a cemetery, but I wouldn't want my sister to marry a dead guy." But just wait until someone you know dies, then you'll see the way they are oppressed. As I get ever older I become ever more concerned about our society's treatment of the dead, which is why I have always campaigned tirelessly for dead rights. In fact I was the Grand Marshall of the very first Dead Pride Parade at Forest Lawn's first annual Dead Pride Festival. Someday you'll wish you had done more, trust me. May I remind you that nearly *all* of the greatest men and women in history are dead? Remember, being dead doesn't make you a bad person, it just makes you smell bad.

And don't even get me started on the discrimination against transparent people, or about the horrible treatment given the Headless Community in our country. It's a national disgrace!

The Roaring Twenties, also known as The Jizz Age, was a sobering time for America. Fortunately, there were courageous bootleggers willing to defy President Beelzebub, Monarch of Hades, and keep America's Social Drinkers social. Nor was I antisocial at home, since, between James Beam and the headless Indian brave, I had a steady supply of vodka, gin, whisky, beer, and "Firewater."* As a result, Morehead Heights was a favorite Movieland playground and the site of many memorable parties about which I cannot remember a thing.

Oh, I remember a few flashes here and there: I remember a young starlet named Joan Crawford seducing Illinois Smith only to get the shock of her life. (I had to laugh!) I remember the night I walked into the sauna at the wrong moment and had to say, "Stan! Ollie! Please! Get a room!" and the time I said, "Fatty darling, stop! I'll never get the de-

---

*Apparently the headless Indian brave's own secret recipe.–Tallulah

posit back on that bottle now!" I remember the night I found Harold Lloyd dangling at the end of a vine a thousand feet above the massive boulders and crashing waves below Tumescent Tor, the result of one of Billy Bowlegs's droll slapstick gags. Billy had smeared the vine with grease to put the comic icing on the comedy cake. After we had rescued Harold, when he saw how we were all rolling on the ground with laughter, he got *ideas*. Billy Bowlegs went to his grave still complaining that "Harold stole *Safety Last* from me! If I hadn't tossed him off a cliff that putz wouldn't have *had* a career!"

I made many movies during this period, though only a few survive today. There was *Silent Echoes,* a stunning drama about something-or-other. I'll be damned if I can remember what it was about now. It's lost, so who knows?

By the time we shot *Silent Echoes* Sherman Oakley didn't have time for me in his personal life at all. In fact, he had hired a full-time, all-male staff just to "audition" and schedule his assignations. When I'd invite him to my dressing room to "go over the love scenes," all the little bastard would do was *rehearse!* Imagine! I had *made* stud boy, literally plucked him from among millions, and now he was too busy for me away from the cameras. I might add that, now that he didn't need them to advance his career anymore, Bruce Camellia and Lance Analvice were out in the cold as well. It turned out that left to his own devices, he was strictly heterosexual. How narrow-minded!

His women waited in line outside the stage with numbers pinned to their collars. Whenever Sherman had a break of more than half an hour he would call out a number and that girl would be brought to his dressing room. I understand the same conditions prevailed at his home, a large house in Bel Air called The Meat Rack. I don't know when, or if, he slept.

After *Silent Echoes* I was reteamed with Gilbert Rolaids in a stirring and deeply moving religious historical epic in which I played Joan of Ark. For those of you not familiar with the story, Joanie was a simple French farm girl who hears Divine Title Cards telling her to lead the French in battle against the English, who are invading their country to try to teach them some manners. For her efforts on behalf of her Blessed Title Cards, which only she and the audience can read, she is rewarded with martyrdom. Gilbert played her lover, a character we added to the story to give it some romantic appeal and a more "up" ending, when he leads the troops who rescue me from the stake just as my armor is starting to melt. The film, titled *A Burning Sensation,* was quite controversial and was actually banned in France, which only boosted its box office everywhere else.

Sherman and I then reteamed for *Ludicrous Lust,* a tale of love and treachery in which I had the very satisfying job of poisoning him. Frankly, the makeup men had to work on him a little longer each morning by then as his killing schedule of day and night assignations was beginning to take a toll on his perfect looks, not that Marcel Pouff, the head of PMS makeup, ever complained about having to spend extra time on him.

After *Ludicrous Lust* Louie borrowed Rudolph Valentino to do one film with me, the now legendary *Son of the Shriek,* a sand-and-camels epic shot out on location on the grueling Mojave Desert. Terrence insisted on being on the set every day and simply doted on Rudy, to the point that Rudy finally had to take out an injunction.* This was my first picture with Vincent Lovecraft, who played the lustful villain (his specialty) from whom Rudy saves me. It was the first picture in which Vincent uttered his famous catchphrase, then only a title card, "Love me or *die!*" The picture did well, and I got some amazing reviews. One critic wrote, "Tallulah out-blanks Vilma Blanky!" Who could ask for higher praise? Alas, this film is also lost.

After my teaming with Valentino turned out so well, Louie borrowed sexy Lon Chaney from Metro, and together we made *The Phantom of the Operetta,* about an amateur theatrical company trying to stage *The Student Prince* while plagued by murders committed by an insane disfigured person who wants to star in it. *Phantom* was recently voted by an international consortium of critics to be "the scariest silent movie ever made!" Even today audiences still scream with horror at the scene where Lon Chaney creeps up behind my innocent and unsuspecting self and rips off my mask!†

Terrence wouldn't come near the set during this film, which was just

---

*Incidentally, I don't believe those gay rumors about Rudy for one moment, despite the facts that (a) his wives were *all* lesbians and (b) I couldn't get into his pants with a crowbar! As for that one time I walked in on Terrence and Rudy *(before* the injunction), Terrence explained that Rudy had been bitten by a snake while answering nature's call and Good Samaritan Terrence was just sucking the venom out of the wound. This was a practiced skill of Terrence's. He often went out evenings to a remote section of Griffith Park where many reptiles lurked and spent *hours* on his knees sucking the venom out of snake after snake!–Tallulah

†The complex horror makeup I wore as The Phantom took Marcel Pouff over *ten minutes* to apply each morning, and required both base and eyeliner! I based my "Horror Face" look on Delores Delgado. How I suffered for my art.–Tallulah
Tallulah's normal glamor-beauty makeup usually took an hour to apply at this point in her career.–Douglas

as well after the Valentino incident, and Lon and I got on awfully well. I might add that I learned he wasn't just the Man of a Thousand *Faces!* Even today, some seventy years after his death, the memory of Lon Chaney still makes me moist.

Next Sherman Oakley and I made *Forbidden Fruit,* a sequel to *Adam's Bone.* The difference that six years made in Sherman's looks became instantly apparent when we got back in the old fig leaves. He still had the sixpack abs, but the worn look about the eyes betrays how much he's aged to anyone who sees the film. Rent it and see for yourself. I look fabulous, the result of my beauty regimen, including daily alcohol rubs, some even external, and of my affair with Gregg Boland, our cinematographer.

Then Gilbert Rolaids and I made a maritime melodrama called *Tramp Steamer,* a very popular little film, sadly lost today. I played the female skipper of a steamy little steamer-of-ill-repute, and Lois LaVerne, Azure Welles, and Terry Cotta played my crew. We sail from port to port, doing business doing the local sailors, until I get involved with Gilbert, who is a smuggler. Vincent Lovecraft played Gilbert's treacherous sidekick who betrays him to the feds and kidnaps me. "Love me or *die!*" once again, and once again I'm rescued, this time by Gilbert and the girls. The picture was great fun to make.

Socially, I was seen at all the best speakeasies around town, being escorted by the most glamorous men in Hollywood, and always trailed by "Illinois Smith," a.k.a. you-know-who. Somewhere during this period I was married to Louie B. Thalberg for a year or two, although I'm damned if I can remember exactly when or why.

The Jizz Age era of the silent movie was a grand time. Our very silence made us figures of mystery, idols who were larger than life. **THE GREAT EVIL** may have ravaged the country, but that only made the common people more hungry for the special escape we provided. However, it was an ephemeral period, and its unceremonious termination lurked just a few months ahead. The result would be an upheaval in Hollywood that would elevate some and leave others smashed. Guess which I was?

12

Smashed Idols

My next film was one of my strangest and most amazing pictures. What no one suspected at the time was that it would also be Sherman Oakley's last movie. The film, which is revered today by connoisseurs of fantasy motion pictures, was the brilliant science fiction masterpiece *Beyond Belief!*

The German science fiction treasure *Metropolis* had been *the* sensation of the year before. Louie, who believed the best original ideas were ones someone else had already shown to be successful, immediately set about planning his sci-fi epic. He imported the German expressionist master director Fritz Bumsen to write and direct this magnum opus and allotted a budget three times larger than he'd ever before spent on one film. He made only two conditions: the movie had to star Sherman Oakley and myself, and our costumes were to be as scanty as possible. Louie may not have known much about science fiction, but he knew what sold tickets for PMS.

The movie was set in the far-off, futuristic year of 1980, when interplanetary travel is commonplace. Sherman plays a human male, and I play a Martian woman. In the story a plague on Mars has wiped out all the Martian men, and so the women of Mars have gone to the other planets in search of men to repopulate their planet. Venus is a matriarchy, so the Venusian men are the most docile, while Jupiterian men are the *biggest,* if you take my meaning; therefore, Jupiter and Venus have attracted most of the Martian females, but I'm a rebel with a taste for earthmen. Typecast again.

I come to earth disguised as a human female (Marcel Pouff outdid himself—I looked *exactly* like a human!) searching for a mate and meet

Sherman, the hunkiest man in the solar system. Unfortunately, there are barriers to our love; he's a Catholic and I'm a Martian, so our love is forbidden! We become fugitives, pursued by the interplanetary sex police. Vincent Lovecraft plays the evil president of Earth and Delores Delgado was typecast as the wicked queen of Mars. I had myself recommended Delores to play the depraved alien monster, recognizing it as a perfect part for her as soon as Terrence summarized the script to me, something she would never have done in return. Finally Sherman and I escape from earth and live happily ever after together on the planet Mercury, where people will leave us alone.

The most remarkable aspect of this incredible picture is its portrayal of life on earth in 1980. At the movies, for instance, you not only saw the films in 3-D, but you could smell, taste, and feel the movies as well, though, of course, films were still silent and in black and white. After all, we didn't want to go *overboard* and have the film look *ridiculous!* In 1980 sex is so open that people wear only teensy little thongs (Louie's idea). Everybody has in-home entertainment with big, spectacular thirteen-inch radios that get their signals from cables wired right into each home. Further, everyone has machines that allow them to record their favorite radio shows on wax cylinders. People are so enamored of entertainment that the evil president of Earth played by Vincent is a former actor who is completely dominated by his even more evil harridan wife, who runs Earth through her husband based on the advice of her batty astrologer.* Dear Lillian Gush was cast against type as Vincent's awful wife, Nancy.

In the movie, by 1980 people have "atomic" ovens that can bake a potato in just *half an hour!* Everybody drives flying cars. Books have been eliminated entirely and replaced by home wax cylinders that read the stories to you. Civilization has also completely eliminated war, crime, disease, poverty, homosexuality, rain forests, live theater, and black people. It is a veritable *utopia!*

Beyond Belief! stunned audiences of its day with its unparalleled honesty and graphic frankness in dealing with the delicate and controversial subject of human-alien sexual relations, as well as astounding scientists with its spot-on and completely accurate forecast of humanity's future.

On the set, however, things weren't so rosy. Sherman was suffering from sexual exhaustion and was actually wearing more makeup than I was. Though only twenty-nine, he looked every day of forty-five. Fritz

*Yes, I know it's far-fetched, but that's science fiction for you.–Tallulah

Bumsen took to shooting him through filters, then to smearing Vaseline on the lens,* and finally to smearing it directly on Sherman.† Given that our scanty 1980-style costumes were actually smaller than the fig leaves we'd worn in *Adam's Bone* and *Forbidden Fruit,* the Vaseline had to be smeared on Sherm from head to foot. There was no shortage of volunteers for this job, though Marcel Pouff ended up winning the assignment by threatening a makeup strike.

Shooting was then held up when the incredibly greasy Mr. Oakley sat down a little too quickly and slid out of the chair and across the floor, wrenching his back. Sherm was unable to work for two weeks, and for the first week back, couldn't do anything strenuous, which is why, in the rocket ship in which we escape from earth, Sherm pilots the craft while lying down. The "G-Force Absorbing Space Chair" is actually just Sherm's traction rig with a lot of glitter sprayed on it.

Then there was the grotesque presence of the always unpleasant Delores Delgado. This was the first time Delores and I had ever worked together, and I will always regret recommending the thankless gorgon for the film, though she was *perfectly* cast as Cunterra, the hideous and wicked queen of Mars. The woman complained endlessly, especially about her elaborate Martian monster makeup, though it was the best she'd looked on film in years. Particularly, she griped about having to be green from head to foot, whining that, since the film was being shot in black and white she didn't actually need to be green. How typically unprofessional! I'd convinced Fritz that she wouldn't really photograph correctly if she *wasn't* green, and besides, the rest of us had to react to her as being green and that was much easier if she was green, not that she ever showed the slightest consideration for her fellow thespians. No trouper, she.††

The makeup stained Delores's skin, so she couldn't really wash it all off each day and thus went about with a greenish tint to her twenty-four hours a day throughout the twelve-week shoot. I thought it far more attractive than her usual sallow yellowish hue. Additionally, she felt that the tentacles made her look silly (as if anything could make her *not* look silly!), and she never completely mastered manipulating them.

Fortunately, there was a comic side to her makeup plight. The last

---

*Both Marcel Pouff and Lance Analvice happened to have large supplies of the lubricant in their professional supplies.–Tallulah
†Nor was he the first man to do this to the excessively active Mr. Oakley.–Tallulah
††I was also playing a Martian, but as my character is disguised as a human, I did not have to be green.–Tallulah

day of shooting she collapsed and had to be hospitalized. It turned out that the copper paste Marcel used to give her the green color had poisoned her. Who knew the makeup was toxic?* Delores almost died, but we all had a good laugh.

However, our merriment over Delores's illness was overshadowed by a terrible tragedy. Two weeks after shooting had been completed, Sherman didn't show up for a publicity interview. When no one answered his telephone, Pete Moss was dispatched out to The Meat Rack to try to locate Sherm. I was naturally concerned for my longtime friend and went along with Pete. What we found awaiting us was more horrifying than Delores naked. Sherman was home, but he was dead, just three weeks shy of his thirtieth birthday.

The police and the coroner later pieced together what happened, and Pete then ruthlessly suppressed the truth. Apparently, Sherman had fired one of his employees, and the disgruntled man had telephoned four hundred of Sherman's ex-assignations, telling each that she had been selected for a repeat session, and scheduling all four hundred for the same time. When the four hundred women arrived at The Meat Rack, things got out of hand quite quickly. The already severely sexually exhausted Sherman, with the last shreds of his old people-pleasing habits, had tried his best. The coroner listed the cause of death as "severe fluid depletion." He'd given his all to his art.

But once Sherman was dead, the remaining women who hadn't had their turns yet got ugly. What followed could only be described as a riot. The Meat Rack was completely trashed, and poor Sherman's body was violated in ways even mine has never been! The police never did find or recover the "souvenir" that one of those women snipped off Sherm's corpse. The "final resting place" of the most famous bit of Sherman's legendary anatomy remains a mystery to this day.

The funeral of Sherman Oakley was the largest ever held in Hollywood to that time. The streets outside the chapel were choked with hundreds of thousands of wailing women, most of whom with at least one "special memory" of meeting Sherm in the flesh. The grief was palpable. *Time* magazine called it "The Moan Heard 'Round the World." Sherman had never married, yet no less than six hundred different women put forth claims to be his widow.

A pall of sadness lay over PMS. Louie was inconsolable over

---

*Well, actually, *I* suspected that the copper was poison—remember, I was an honor chemistry student—but when I suggested using copper to Marcel, he hadn't objected, and I assumed that as a makeup professional, he knew his business.–Tallulah

Sherman's loss; not one of Sherm's films had ever lost money. Bruce Camellia, Lance Analvice, Marcel Pouff, and even Terrence were prostrate with grief. I was very miserable; not even the fact that Delores was still in critical condition could cheer me up. I felt a real need to get away, and I was not alone.

Louie came up with a brilliant idea: He sent Cyril Von Millstone, James Dong Lowe, Marcel Pouff, leading man Keith Kittridge, Vincent Lovecraft, and myself to Alaska to shoot a melodrama called *Eskimo Pie*, one of the most critically regarded of all my films. Keith and I played an Eskimo couple trying to make ends meet in the land of the Midnight Sun. Vincent Lovecraft plays the evil blubber merchant who threatens to foreclose on our igloo unless I submit to his lust ("Love me or *die*," as usual).

The discomfort of shooting a film wearing tiny fur bikinis (Louie's idea) in below-zero temperatures, and the fascination of working with a crew and supporting cast composed of real Eskimos, did wonders in turning our minds away from the tragedy of Sherman Oakley. I never knew what the Eskimos were saying, but certain things are the same in every culture, and I found that with Eskimo men, the roof may be made of ice, but there's a harpoon in the cellar.

When we returned to Hollywood we found a revolution in progress. Warner Brothers had released a dreadful piece of crap, some odd sort of minstrel show called *The Jazz Singer* with a gratuitous sound track, and it was enjoying a freak success. Everybody in Tinsel Town was going nuts converting to sound. Louie wisely wanted to wait while it blew over. He knew the difference between an innovation and a fad. "Talkies," he said, "that's a fad. Beautiful people nearly nude, *that's* a perennial!" He put Gilbert Rolaids and me immediately into another picture, a murder mystery titled *Blood on the Ceiling*, a now-lost film that became my last silent picture.

Eskimo Pie did poorly at the box office despite great reviews. The *Los Angeles Times* said, "*Eskimo Pie* is every bit as credible as *Beyond Belief!*" *Variety* praised the documentary aspects of the film: "*Eskimo Pie* gives 'authenticity' an entirely new meaning." The *San Francisco Chronicle* wrote, "Tallulah Morehead, in her fur bikinis, makes us believe she is freezing." But no amount of good press could get the audiences back to a silent movie.

Blood on the Ceiling suffered a similar fate. The critics were ecstatic. The *New York Times* praised the mystery plot: "It's been two days since I saw *Blood on the Ceiling* and I still haven't figured it out." Other critics tried to remind audiences of the wonderfulness of silent film. The

Chicago Tribune wrote, "When Miss Tallulah Morehead cuts loose in her big acting scenes, you'll rejoice that the movie is still silent!" But again, the audiences stayed away, preferring to listen to Jolson's nasal caterwauling periodically interrupted by his spewing dialogue while in whiteface.

Louie had no choice but to close down the studio for six months and retool for sound. Having six months off, and still reeling from the failure of two films in a row, as well as being still upset about . . . what? . . . what was it? . . . oh yes! Sherman's death, I decided to take my first real vacation. I packed up several trunks of clothes, Terrence, and Major Babs, and headed for Europe, where social drinking was legal! Little did I know that one of the greatest yet most tragic romances of my life waited for me in the Old World.

13

Countess Tallulah

Transylvania in the late twenties: has there ever been a more romantic setting? The forests, the mountains, the schlosses outlined against the sky in the moonlight, the bats, the wolves, the screams of the peasants, the streams of blood, the constant moaning in the background day and night—romance seems to waft through the air. And it was there, high in the idyllic Carpathians that I had the wildest romance of my very long life.

Lovely as London is, it held too many memories from two marriages back, so I gave it a miss this time out. For obvious reasons I also decided to skip Berlin, and indeed, Germany altogether. We sailed to France, where I was known as *La Sousé*. We landed at Le Havre, then river-cruised to Paris, lovely city, the wine so fine, the people so rude. Then we went by train to Cannes, then Nice—which was—then by ship again to Rome, where I was known as *La Lushio*. Oh, those Italian men were so forward! Poor Terrence's tush was black and blue. Finally, we motored deep into Romania, where my fame had never been penetrated, so I could finally be incognito, arriving at last in the small, unspoiled Transylvanian village of Klotsburg, taking rooms at the local inn: The Nosferatu.

The Nosferatu was a simple, picturesque place nestled against the towering Carpathians. Just outside, standing atop the mountain peak, was the awesome sight of Schloss Tepes, a crumbling medieval castle so positioned that from late afternoon to sunset The Nosferatu was literally in its shadow. I point this fact out to the reader so you will understand my puzzlement when I tell you that no one at the inn would acknowledge the existence of Schloss Tepes. I would ask, "What's the name of that castle, darling?"

"What castle?" the ones who spoke English would reply.

"The really big, crumbly one, just outside."

"There is no castle."

"That one, right there, dominating the landscape."

"Where?"

"The one you can plainly see through the window."

"I don't see any castle."

"Look, let me move this garlic out of the way, and you'll clearly see it."

"DON'T TOUCH THE GARLIC!"

"All right, darling, but look. See the castle? You can't really see anything else. Good God, look at the *size* of it!"

"I don't see any castle."

And so it went. No one would admit to its existence, even though it commanded the view. These people had less truck with reality than Pete Moss. But the people were friendly, religious folk. Every last one of them was wearing an enormous crucifix. One terribly sweet ancient crone came up to us the first afternoon, trying to press crucifixes on us. "No, no," I told her, "I don't want to buy any native crafts. But here, have one of my personally autographed pictures."

"No, no," the adorable, withered dowager replied. "Not for sale. A gift. For the lovely lady, the big man, and you."

A perceptive woman, she'd apparently seen right through Major Babs's drag, something Terrence had yet to do. I found her description of Terrence as a "big man" odd, though. He was actually very diminutive in height (shorter than Major Babs) and slight, almost delicate of build. In fact, he always wore shoulder pads in all his blouses to give himself more heft. I still demurred from accepting the precious hag's offerings. "You must understand, I'm a Christian Scientist, except for all the doctrines. We don't wear those things."

"Please, glamorous lady," the insistent, cherished biddy continued, "wear this for your mother's sake. It will protect you."

That was, of course, absolutely the wrong thing to say to get me to do anything. I turned to Terrence and said, "Give the hag an autographed picture for her trinkets and get rid of her."

The one thing that seemed to be missing from the idyllic existence in Klotsburg was any kind of nightlife. Everybody just seemed to want to hide away in their bedrooms the moment the sun set. It was only the gentle persuasiveness of Major Babs that induced the landlord to keep the barroom open after dusk so I could sample the charming local liquors. I was happily sampling a variety of interesting drinks when the main door suddenly banged open, though I had been positive that the landlord had bolted, barred, and barricaded it the instant the sun sank. Everyone in the room seemed to shrink back and grab hold of their crucifixes.

Then into the room strode the most magnetic man I'd ever seen. He was tall, clean-shaven except for a long white mustache, and clad in black, from head to foot, without a single speck of color about him anywhere. His face was a strong—very strong—aquiline, with high bridge of the thin nose and peculiarly arched nostrils; with lofty, domed forehead, and hair growing scantily 'round the temples but profusely elsewhere. His eyebrows were very massive, almost meeting over the nose, with bushy hair that seemed to curl in its own profusion. The mouth, so far as I could see it under the heavy mustache, was fixed and rather cruel-looking, with peculiarly sharp, white teeth; these protruded over the lips, whose remarkable ruddiness showed astonishing vitality in a man of his years. For the rest, his ears were pale and at the tops extremely pointed, the chin was broad and strong, and the cheeks firm though thin. The general effect was one of extraordinary pallor. His most striking feature was a pair of very bright eyes, which seemed to gleam red in the lamplight.

His eyes swept the room as the occupants shrank back from him. "Where is the American woman?" he asked in a commanding tone, with a rich, deep voice, colored by a tremendously sexy accent. "Ah, here you are, my dear."

When those bright red eyes fell on me, I felt a shiver run through my whole body. Drowning in those eyes, I felt an overwhelming desire to surrender to him completely. The man stretched out his hand toward me. Major Babs, who can sometimes be a little overzealous, stepped forward and grabbed the man's arm, saying, "Hold it right there, fella."

The man seemed merely to flick his wrist, but Major Babs went flying across the room to land in an unconscious heap on the floor. The man took my hand and kissed it. A ripple of intense excitement flooded me. I noticed, oddly, that he had hairy palms, not unlike my stepfather, Maxie. He said, "Allow me to introduce myself, dear lady. I am Count Vlad Tepes, the traditional feudal lord of these peasants. I live in lovely Schloss Tepes, which you must have been admiring through the windows all day. Welcome to my homeland. Enter freely, and of your own will."

"Why, thank you, Count darling," I replied. "You are most incredibly gracious. My name is Miss Tallulah Morehead."

"Not *the* Miss Tallulah Morehead, the great American motion picture diva?" he responded.

"Yes, darling," I answered. "I had no idea anyone had ever heard of me in this remote corner of the world."

"Oh yes. It's true," the count went on, "that there is no cinema in Klotsburg. But I have been known to visit the cosmopolitan metropolis of London periodically, in search of fresh blood, and I have seen several of your most remarkable films."

"Well, Count, allow me to introduce my companions. The gentleman you tossed across the room is my bodyguard, Illinois Smith. And this is Terrence, my personal assistant."

"A great lady of your international stature should not be staying in this hovel."

"Oh, I find this place quite charming and unspoiled. And besides, I'm traveling *incognito.*"

"How wise of you. But please, you must allow me to extend the hospitality of Schloss Tepes."

"Oh no, I couldn't," I lied. "I'm perfectly comfortable here."

"But I insist," the count went on. "You would be doing me the *highest* honor."

"Well, since you insist, Count darling. Terrence, pack our bags. We are decamping for Schloss Tepes!"

"I am delighted, my dear," the count replied, "I will return at once to my castle to prepare your rooms. My coach will call for you here in an hour." And with that the count was gone in a swirl of black cape. I looked out the window, but all I could see was the black hulk of Schloss Tepes looming in the moonlight and a lone bat flapping its way toward that lofty peak.

As I watched Terrence pack there came a knock at my door. It was the landlord. "Frau Morehead, *bitte,*" he begged, "do not go to the Schloss."

"Oh, so now you admit its existence."

"Yes, yes, but you must not go there!"

"Don't be concerned, my good man. I'll pay for the whole night. Really, this is not the way to compete."

"You don't understand," the man went on, apparently desperate to keep my business. After all, how many glamorous movie *Stars* do you suppose he saw each year? "The count, he is not a man."

"He looked like quite a well-set-up man to me, and I know a thing or two about men."

"But the count, he is a *monster!*"

"Is he really? Do you, by any chance mean he is a man of monstrous *proportions?* You whet my interest."

"No, I mean a *real* monster! A bloodthirsty berserker! Do you know what 'Tepes' means?"

"A big tipper?"

"No, it means 'The Impaler'!"

"Vlad the Impaler, you say? You whet my interest even more. I used to know a man named Sherman Oakley, and you could have called him 'The Impaler' as well. Count Tepes sounds fascinating!"

"If you go there you will die!"

"Nonsense! You have no way of knowing it, but I'm a screen *immortal!*"

"I mean it! The count, he will drain your blood!"

"I insist you stop maligning the count this way. I don't think he'd be pleased to hear the way you speak of him."

The landlord's eyes bulged with terror, an effect I've always enjoyed having on unattractive men. "Please, please, Frau Morehead, you will not tell him what I said? Please, I have a wife! I have a daughter! Please say nothing to the count of what I have told you."

"All right, darling. Now be a lamb, and help Terrence take these trunks downstairs."

True to his word, the count's coach, what they called a calèche, drawn by four coal-black horses, arrived spot-on an hour after the count's departure. The count's driver and personal assistant, a runty gentleman named Renfield, loaded my trunks, and then Terrence and I traveled in the calèche while Major Babs followed us driving the rented touring car.

As Schloss Tepes loomed ever closer I looked at it with wonder. It was obviously very old and not really in the best of repair. It was extremely massive, but its battlements were broken, and everywhere the stonework was crumbling. Not a single ray of light shone from any window. There was something about it, a haunted quality, that reminded me of dear old Morehead Heights, now so far away. I could almost picture the headless Indian brave wandering these corridors and feeling perfectly at home.

If I found Schloss Tepes homelike, Terrence had a very different reaction. The closer we got to it, the more Terrence shrank down in his seat, eventually starting to quietly whimper.

"Oh, Miss Tallulah," Terrence finally begged, "can't we please go back to the inn? You heard what the landlord said. He knows the man. He must know what he's talking about. I'm terrified! Look at this place. It's so . . . so *tacky!*" Terrence, I'm afraid, was a style snob.

"Terrence!" I commanded. "Butch up! And don't embarrass me in front of the count. Don't you think he's a fine figure of a man?"

"I think he's scary."

"So do I! Scary in a sexy way."

"No, scary in a terrifying way. He makes my blood run cold." This was unusual. Normally Terrence and I had very similar tastes in men.[*] But there was no time to compare notes further as we had rolled into the Schloss's roomy courtyard, with Major Babs and the car just behind.

The massive front door opened, and the count was standing there with a lamp, beckoning us in: "Welcome to my home. Come freely, go safely, and leave something of the happiness you bring."

"Thank you, darling." I said, laying a big kiss on our host. "Isn't this just too charming and Old World for words?" Indeed it was. The great entrance hall we were in didn't look to have been dusted or swept in centuries. There was a spider's web across the great staircase that must have been ten feet in diameter. Major Babs was looking about scowling while Terrence was trying to move about with his eyes closed.

"Sweet Heavens, darling, I'd fire the maid if I were you. She's not pulling her weight. That spider's web is *titanic!*"

"The little spider spinning his web," replied the count, although that spider looked to be a foot across to me, "to catch the unwary fly. The blood is the life, Miss Morehead."

"That's as may be, but a little housekeeping goes a long way."

"I have no maid, I'm afraid. Just my 'personal assistant' Renfield and myself, two single men living alone."

"Oh really?" asked Terrence, perking up for the first time. Opening his eyes made him reel. He put out his hand to steady himself, then saw what he was touching and screeched.

"Ah, two bachelors sharing a home," I said, ignoring Terrence's outburst as usual. "They're always a little messy, although this place has world-class rot going on. What you need here is a woman's touch. I'll have Terrence whip this place into shape in no time."

The resounding noise of wolves howling suddenly filled our ears, followed at once by Terrence's scream before he fainted dead away into Major Babs's arms. The count said, "Listen to them—children of the night. What music they make."

"Frankly, darling," I said, "I prefer a little Gershwin myself. So where are our rooms?"

The count conducted us, Major Babs carrying Terrence, into a suite

---

[*]That is, anything human with a penis.–Douglas

of rooms that were bright, clean, and cozy. A blazing fire was burning in each room's fireplace. And in one a feast had been laid out, including a collection of delicious-looking bottles of wine. The count, perfect host that he was, immediately poured me a goblet of wine. "This is very old wine," he said.

"Aren't you having any, Count darling?" I asked, noticing that he'd only filled one goblet. As a social drinker I never drink alone unless there are no other social drinkers around.

"I never drink wine," the count answered. Good God, a teetotaler! An abstainer! A freak! Maybe he *was* a monster! But no, a man who didn't drink, however odd that was, but who served his guests such excellent wine as I was having was obviously highly cultured and civilized. I was already half in love with him. As I heard him say, "I have a whole cellar full of hundreds of bottles of this wine," I fell all the way.

So began our strange, nocturnal existence at Schloss Tepes. The count was busy days but visited with us every evening. His native customs forbade him from eating with us, but Renfield prepared us delicious food, and there was a steady supply of the great wine.

After a rocky start, Terrence took quite a shine to Renfield. I didn't see what he saw in the man. Renfield wasn't too fastidious about his appearance or grooming, his posture was terrible, and then there was his diet. After Terrence told us what he ate, we were glad that he didn't eat with us, either.

The count was a perfect gentleman. This made me a little suspicious at first, remembering how F. Emmett Knight had been a perfect gentleman from the day we met until the day he'd called me "the Whore of Babylon"* in divorce court. As far as I'm concerned the term "perfect gentleman" is a euphemism for "boring date." Between the way the count never molested me and his roommate situation, I had my suspicions. Certainly Renfield was the merest whisper if ever there was one.

But it soon became apparent that the relationship between the count and Renfield was strictly that of master and servant, however much more Renfield might have liked. And the count's romantic pursuit of me seemed genuine as well. Believe it or not, he just respected me too much to sleep with me before marriage! Go figure.

"The local peasant women," he told me one day after we'd been there several weeks, "they are like my cattle. But you are fit to be my countess. Will you marry me, Miss Tallulah?"

Well, who could resist? The fact was, I'd been head over heels in love

---

*What slander! I've never been anywhere *near* Bablyon!–Tallulah with Vlad for some time and couldn't wait to be heels over head. I accepted at once and was delighted that he didn't favor a long engagement, either. We decided to be married the next night.

The following evening, in a stunning wedding gown I happened to have brought with me in my luggage, I became Countess Tallulah Morehead Knight Thalberg Tepes. The ceremony was performed by a crotchety old Romanian priest who appeared terrified. Major Babs was Vlad's best man while Terrence was maid of honor. Renfield was ring bearer.

My first husband had been the merest whisper of a homosexual and hadn't loved me. My second husband had been Louie B. Thalberg, and I can't imagine *what* I'd been thinking. Now I was married for the third time to a dashing, romantic, and mysterious Old World nobleman in what was a true love match. Alas, our flame burned too brightly, it could not last the night.

I can hardly bring myself to tell the tragic tale of our wedding night. At the wedding feast Vlad, as was his custom, neither ate nor drank, but I more than made up for it, social drinking for two, if you will. I was celebrating at last finding the right man, and the wine and champagne were flowing all evening. Renfield and Terrence were sobbing in each other's arms all through both the ceremony and the feast.

Eventually Vlad and I retired to my boudoir to finally make love for the first time. With a name like "The Impaler," I expected Vlad to be a very different sort of lover than he turned out to be. Rather than *impaling* me, Vlad made love not unlike a lesbian.* If I hadn't seen the evidence with my own eyes, I might have thought he was another male imposter like "Illinois Smith."

But *oh my God,* how that man could *KISS!* No man, before or since, has kissed me as deeply or as passionately. He didn't simply nibble at my neck for a moment or so. He kissed my throat with a penetrating deepness for what seemed like hours, leaving me feeling both drained and filled with ecstasy. The hickeys he was leaving, which I could clearly see in the mirror above my bed,† were not to be believed.

Finally, after what seemed like hours of ecstasy, Vlad rolled back off of me, seemingly satiated, his mouth smeared a bright red. "Vlad dar-

---

*I mean, of course, the way I *imagine* that lesbians make love. As the attentive reader knows, I have no first-tongue knowledge of such things.–Tallulah

†I could clearly see them because Vlad cast no reflection in the mirror to block my view of myself, yet another example of his modesty and consideration. Not being a narcissist he had no need to constantly view himself and simply refrained from casting a reflection.–Tallulah

ling, is that blood on your mouth?" I asked, careful not to sound judgmental.

"You're damn right it ish, Tallulah, old girl," Vlad slurred back.

"Have you been *drinking* my blood, Vlad, my love?" I asked, treading carefully, not wanting to offend him by belittling one of his native customs.

"You bet your shweet ash, Tallulah doll," Vlad garbled.

"How intensely kinky, my one true love."

"You ain't seen nothin' yet, Tallulah baby. Wash thish." Then Vlad spread his arms so he was lying spread-eagled, naked, on his back on the bed. "Eh? How about them applesh, lady?"

"You're lovely, my wild one, but what *are* you doing?"

"I'm turning into a bat." Vlad said, and then broke into a fit of giggles.

"Vlad darling, you're in such a good mood."

"You probably think I'm batty!" Vlad roared, while laughing his head off. "Wait, wait, wait. I really can turn into a bat. I can. I just have to remember how."

"Vlad, my dearest, if I hadn't been with you all evening and didn't know for a fact that you drank no wine or champagne tonight, I would suspect that you are drunk."

"Thash ridiculoush! I haven't drunk any alcohol in over four hundred yearsh! Five hundred if you don't count the crap we drank when I was alive. What did we call that crap? Oh yeah? Mead! Have you ever drunk mead?"

"No, I haven't had the pleasure."

"Pleashure! Ha! Stuff tastes like bullpissh."

"My dearest darling. You are looped."

"Nonsenshe! All I've drunk tonight has been your blood!"

"That's as may be, but I know drunk when I see it, and you are sloshed."

"Don't tell my daddy," Vlad senselessly replied, followed by another fit of the giggles. Almost immediately after the giggles he began crying: "You can't tell my daddy. My daddy's dead!"

"I'm sorry, Vlad darling."

"I don't want your pity!" Vlad screamed at me, then started crying again, "I killed my daddy a long time ago. I had to. He . . . he killed my mommy!"

"There, you see, Vlad, there is a *silver* lining."

"I loved my mommy!"

"Oh. How novel. I hope it didn't stunt your emotional growth."

"Shtunt my emotional growth? That'sh rich! Do you know how many people I tortured and murdered when I wash alive?"

"Aren't you alive now?"

"Over a hundred thousand people! I was mean. I wash the worsht bad ash in Transylvania! I kicked Turkish butt from here to Conshtantinople!"

"Well, I'm sure they deserved it."

"You're okay, Tallulah," Vlad said, turning weepy again. "You're really okay. You desherve a lot better than an evil old monshter like me. I'm shorry I ruined your life, Tallulah."

"Vlad darling, you're just a little inebriated. You'll feel better after you've slept it off. . . . Here, watch the dawn with me."

"The dawn!" Vlad screamed. *"Oh no! Your blood! Ish your God damn blood! I drank your blood and got drunk for the first time in four hundred years! Sho drunk I forgot to get back to my . . . NO, TALLULAH, DON'T OPEN THE CURTAINS!"*

I didn't think it was anything but drunken paranoia. I pulled open the drapes and the morning sun streamed into the room. What I didn't know was that my new husband had a rare skin condition. He was fatally allergic to sunlight! I heard him scream and turned back. At first I didn't see him. Then I realized that the smoldering pile of ashes smoking on the floor was shaped like my late husband. As I watched, a breeze swept in through the open window (the schloss was built before the invention of glass) and blew my husband's ashes away. Less than twelve hours after the wedding, I was a widow!

Oddly, there wasn't any trouble with the local authorities over the accidental death of Count Vlad Tepes. I didn't really feel up to handling any details, but Terrence, Major Babs and Renfield took care of everything.* Not only was there no inquest, but the villagers of Klotsburg seemed glad to be rid of him. Apparently Vlad wasn't very popular locally. When given the death certificate I noticed a peculiar mistake: They had listed Vlad's year of death as 1476. Not even close!

At the funeral a group of children sang a jolly song in their native language. The landlord of the Nosferatu translated it for me:

Ding dong, the Count is dead.
Which old Count,

---

*Strangely, the vivid and enormous love bites, or hickeys, as they call them now, that Vlad had inflicted on my neck in the heat of his burning passion, had disappeared within moments of his death.–Tallulah

The wicked Count,
Ding dong, the wicked Count is dead!

I didn't feel it was in the best of taste, but the children looked charming. I was given the Key to Klotsburg and declared their national heroine. I gave Schloss Tepes, which now belonged to me, to Renfield. It had been his home for so long, and I had Morehead Heights, after all. And it was to Morehead Heights I shortly returned, sadder but not wiser.

Ah, Count Vlad Tepes, others may revile you, but I will always cherish the memory of our oh-so-short time together. I will love you forever, my darling.

PART THREE

Miss Morehead Opens Her Mouth

1929–1947

14

Oral Acting

By the time I returned to Hollywood, Louie was ready to star me in my first sound film, the screwball comedy, *The Godawful Truth,* in which I played Penelope, the madcap heiress, and in which I sang for the first time.

Louie imported Broadway song-and-dance man Wilfred Wyndham to play my stodgy accountant boyfriend. I sweep him off his feet and take him on a whirlwind tour of reckless adventures through Manhattan, Paris, Nice, and Rome, teaching him to loosen up and enjoy life by having a drink, a laugh, and another drink.

The irony that the settings were the very cities I had visited on my journey to my ill-fated marriage to the late, beloved (except by people who knew him) Count Vlad Tepes could have been intensely painful. Fortunately, Louie's dinky budget and the technical challenges posed by making our first sound film, dictated that the film company never got any closer to Europe than the PMS back lot in Hollywood, creating locations about as authentic as a politician's vow of celibacy.

Art director Arthur Deco built a full-size replica of the Eiffel Tower out of wood on the back lot, where it stood for years. Visible for miles about, it became a major Hollywood landmark until it burned down in 1939.

The Godawful Truth was very successful and remains one of my most popular pictures. Bosley Crowther wrote, "Miss Tallulah Morehead can render a song senseless."

The enormous cash outlay required for the sound changeover, coupled with producing no films for six months, meant that Louie needed product churned out and churned out fast. My luxurious old schedule of one film a year, which I had maintained for fifteen years, except for

1925 when I'd been rushed into *Forbidden Fruit* just weeks after finishing *The Phantom of the Operetta,* was gone. They were still editing *The Godawful Truth* when I started shooting my next picture, the ill-fated romance, *An Affair to Forget,* with Gilbert Rolaids.

Had *An Affair to Forget* been a silent movie it probably would have been a hit, with the proven chemistry between Gilbert and I and a knockout plot about a precocious French schoolgirl (me, of course) and the older poet whom she cures of ennui until they are ripped apart by my parents who force me to marry a smelly wine merchant. (There are worse fates.)

Fifteen years had passed since *Heat Crazed!*, and Gilbert hadn't been a young man then. As far as audiences were concerned *I* hadn't aged a day since my debut, but Gilbert was fifteen years older, and now the age difference between us was all too obvious. We tried writing it into the plot, but it didn't help.

But even if we'd still looked like a believable couple there was still another problem: Gilbert's voice. Gilbert was tall, dark, robust, and Latin; people expected a deep, romantic voice. Unfortunately, Gilbert spoke with a very high, falsetto voice, sort of like Michael Jackson on helium with a Spanish accent. The fact that he was trying to speak with a French accent through his Spanish one didn't help matters any, either. Every time poor Gilbert opened his mouth in the film, audiences were reduced to gales of hysterical laughter.

The critics couldn't miss it, either. *Variety* wrote, "Gilbert Rolaids, it turns out, is Spain's Mickey Mouse." The brand-new trade paper, the *Hollywood Reporter,* was much kinder to Gilbert: "Gilbert Rolaids is every bit as believable as a romantic French poet as Miss Tallulah Morehead is as a schoolgirl." The *Los Angeles Times* also praised my performance, saying, "Those who fear that Miss Tallulah Morehead is a little long in the tooth to play a schoolgirl are presented with a graphic demonstration of the preserving effects of pickling." The *New York Times,* solidly in my corner as usual, said, "Miss Tallulah Morehead playing a schoolgirl at this advanced stage of her career should be a lesson to someone." Unfortunately, the *Post* spoke for most when it said, "*An Affair to Forget* is the most aptly titled picture in movie history." It was, I'm afraid, Gilbert's last movie. A sad farewell to one of the silent screen's greatest leading men.

Since *The Godawful Truth* had gone so well, the moment we were finished ruining Gilbert's career, Louie shoved Wilfred Wyndham and me into a full-fledged musical, set on a glamorous ocean liner, the delightful *Dancing in the Drink,* a film best remembered for its spectacular water ballet dance number, "The Incontinental." Vincent Lovecraft, Olivia Wildebeest, Azure Welles, and Paisley Tine made up our supporting cast, while comic relief was provided by my dear friend Billy Bowlegs,[*] reduced to supporting parts since sound had come in, and the always hilariously effeminate Franklin Nancyboy.

This was a happy experience. Certainly making a musical is the hardest work in motion pictures. You are in that rehearsal hall for many long hours, rehearsing the dance numbers over and over, until my poor little dance double's feet were bleeding.

But if the work was hard, we were a friendly company. Wilfred Wyndham was a workaholic perfectionist. While my poor dance double, Adela Rogers St. Croix, was being worked to death,[†] the rest of us were having a grand old time. Vincent Lovecraft is the very soul of wit. Olivia Wildebeest and Azure Welles were vivacious and fun-loving girls, sharing an apartment at the time and too wrapped up in their careers to date men. Franklin Nancyboy and his precious little wife, Agnes Nancyboy, who was not in the business, were devoted to each other. Agnes was on the set every day. She liked to keep Franklin on a short leash. But she always brought fresh-baked goodies with her: pies, cakes, turnovers, cookies, and they all went well with my martinis.

Billy Bowlegs, of course, was his irrepressible self. He had divorced Lillian Gush, whose career also crashed and burned with the coming of sound, and was on the loose romantically. He kept us all rolling with laughter with his constant slapstick gags, this time directed against Olivia, Azure, Adela, and all the girls in the chorus line. His masterpiece of japes came the day we were shooting the big "Man Overboard" production number. At the precise moment the kickline started the high kicks, all the stitching gave way on their costumes simultaneously, and the girls were high-kicking at the camera stark, staring naked. Billy was off to one side holding a single, very long thread and smirking. "Hey Tallulah!" he shouted. "How'd you like my beaver trap?" What a scamp!

Right around this time I received a package in the mail from Mildred Puett and Minerva Thatcher. They sent me a novel they had published that they felt would make a perfect motion picture, a story called *The Well of Loneliness* by someone named Radcliffe Hall. I read the summary Terrence prepared for me after he read the book, and I have sel-

[*]Tallulah and Billy's first film together.—Douglas
[†]Literally, as it turned out. If only we'd known about her poor heart murmur.
—Tallulah

dom been as deeply moved. I passed it along to Louie with my highest recommendations, but nothing came of it. Although there was to be no film of it then, I salted it away in my mind as a dream project for sometime in the future. It was to be nearly forty years before I finally got to make a film of Mr. Hall's remarkable book, and what happened then, well, that's a later chapter that we'll come to in due time.

The critics were enthusiastic about our shipboard songfest. The *Times* wrote, "Miss Tallulah Morehead is completely at sea in her new musical." while the *Post* wrote, "*Dancing in the Drink* makes the *Titanic* look like a mere maritime mishap." *Variety* wrote, "In *Dancing in the Drink* it's sing or swim. Swim, damn it, swim!" Thanks to its success I went on to appear in thirteen more musicals throughout the rest of my career.

Louie B. Thalberg, innovative film pioneer that he was, realized that in the rush to make films that were all talking, all singing, all noisy, we shouldn't lose sight of the basic cinematic values that audiences would always clamor for. Therefore, after *Dancing in the Drink* I made a stark drama, laying bare the deepest secrets of the human heart, called *The Naked Nudist*. Spencer Hooks, the award-winning Broadway Shakespearean actor, played opposite me. The film was banned outright in seventeen states and sold out everywhere else. The *Chronicle* wrote, "*The Naked Nudist* is the best thing to happen for clothes since the reign of Queen Victoria."

The whole cast of *Dancing in the Drink* were then reunited for *Broadway Bimbos,* along with brilliant director/choreographer Hermes Hyde. This delightful flick was the tale of three young Working Girls— Olivia, Azure, and myself—who come to New York and accidentally become Broadway stars.

Shortly after shooting began on *Broadway Bimbos,* on Valentine's Day, I attended the premiere of a new film from Universal called *Dracula,* about which I knew nothing. Twenty minutes into the film I fled the theater in tears. The opening reels of the film brought my marriage and tragic wedding night back so vividly that I couldn't bear it. And though Bela Lugosi looked nothing like my late, beloved (except by his victims and their survivors) husband, he dressed, and, more importantly, *sounded* exactly like Vlad! Terrence, who had accompanied Major Babs and myself to the film, was also moved to tears by the film's portrayal of Renfield. I had to remind Terrence that, unlike Vlad, Renfield wasn't dead. In fact, he and Terrence still corresponded.

Major Babs stayed behind and watched the rest of the film while Terrence and I drowned our sorrows in a nearby speakeasy. Afterward, when Major Babs described the plot of *Dracula* to me I was deeply offended! Though they had used an old family name of his rather than Tepes, there was no question whom they were portraying in the movie. It was nothing less than a massive slur on the good character of my late husband! When I saw Bela Lugosi coming out of the theater I'm afraid my temper got the better of me. I marched up to him. Lugosi, always courtly with women, was just saying, "Miss Tallulah, how delightful. I am a big fan . . ." when I cut him off.

"I'll have you know, Mr. Lugosi," I snapped icily, "that along with being Tallulah Morehead, I am also Countess Tallulah Tepes, the widow of the great man you maligned in your pornographic picture." I then hauled off and slapped him hard. "You'll be hearing from my attorney!" I said in parting.

The next day my lawyer, Mason Dixon, informed me that, legally, you cannot libel the dead. I was forced to simply ignore this celluloid calumny. The injustice of it made me steam at the time.

Ironically, a couple of years later I worked with Bela Lugosi when I appeared with him and Boris Karloff in Universal's production of Edgar Allan Poe's *The Black Pussy,* but fortunately, Lugosi held no grudge over our first meeting. He had other reasons for disliking me then.

Broadway Bimbos was another hit. The reviews speak for themselves: "I left humming a melody." –*Variety.* "I left, too." –*The Hollywood Reporter.* Talk about praise; the wonderful Broadway song-and-dance man James Cagney credited *Broadway Bimbos* as inspiring him to make gangster pictures when he came to Hollywood!

In the chorus of *Broadway Bimbos* was a talented young man named Ambrose Suderstrombork, who had leading man written all over him. Ambrose was tall, blond, blue-eyed, handsome, well-built. He had everything.

It was Vincent Lovecraft who first noticed something outstanding about Ambrose Suderstrombork. Vincent took an immediate shine to Ambrose and more or less took him under his wing, often inviting him back to his dressing room, where he would give the aspiring performer some pointers.* On weekends Vincent even had Ambrose over to the

---

*Vincent, essentially a generous man, was never too busy to give some young actor or another a pointer. Any Sunday afternoon in the thirties you would find a clutch of young actors gathered around Vincent's swimming pool. Since his retirement from motion pictures, he has devoted himself full-time to the cultivation of young male talent. He has spread himself wide for young talent. Why does he do it? Because, as he says, "I like to give back." And Vincent Lovecraft has given back to up-and-coming young talent all over Hollywood. In fact, he says that when they're

house in Bel Air, Rooster's Seat, that he shared with his longtime room-mate, C. Halibut Plugg, especially if C was away, for more intensive pointers.

By the time we'd finished *Broadway Bimbos* Vincent had brought Ambrose to Louie's attention, and Louie, shrewd judge of talent that he was, quickly plucked him from the chorus, rechristened him Rod Towers, and cast him in Gilbert Rolaid's old role opposite me in the super-spectacular sound remake of *Heat Crazed!* that was to be my next film.

The sound version of *Heat Crazed!* differs little from the silent version apart from the facts that (a) I am a more mature, seasoned actress; (b) instead of the leading man being a dark Latin man obviously older than I, he is a blond Nordic sort who is actually younger than I, though you couldn't tell that on film; (c) you could hear what we were saying; (d) when I vamped him, I sang the *Heat Crazed!* title song; and (e) we didn't even attempt the original, necrophilic ending.

I suggested Delores Delgado for Rod's wife, whom, you will recall, I murder in the climax. I felt that casting the hateful Delgado would get the audience's sympathy entirely on my side when I kill her, but Louie felt, as Delores was at least twenty years older than Rod, that this wouldn't really work, and cast another newcomer, perky Polly Morphus, as the doomed wife.

Heat Crazed! was an even bigger hit in sound than it was as a silent. Pete Moss came up with another great slogan for the posters: "She laughed when they called her 'Crazy'!"

There was no question that Rod Towers and I had real chemistry together on the screen, but I had trouble getting the chemistry going off-screen. When I tried to move our relationship beyond working and into more personal areas, like his pants, I got nowhere. At first I worried, oh no, another F. Emmett Knight, but then Rod explained that he'd left a girlfriend behind, back east, in his hometown of Long Beach, California, and that when he'd saved enough money for them to marry, he was going to send for her, bring her to Hollywood, and make her Mrs. Rod Towers.

"How terribly sweet," I said. "And what is the little darling's name?"

---

up and coming is the best time to give them back. Vincent teaches an acting work-shop these days called "Acting Like Crazy." If you're an up-and-coming young man yourself, you might think about taking his class. It's usually full, but if you're the sort of upstanding young man Vincent likes, he usually has an opening where he can just slip you in. If you're a talented young actor, believe me, Vincent Lovecraft wants to give back to you.–Tallulah

"I just told you, Mrs. Rod Towers," he replied.

"That isn't even really your name. I mean what is her name now?"

"Oh," he said. "Ah, gee . . . it's . . ." he glanced at the sandwich he was enjoying as we lunched on the set, "Barbara Ann. That's her name. Barbara Ann Langendorf."

"Barbara Ann Langendorf. How white. Well, she's a very lucky girl. But you know, we could still enjoy ourselves and she wouldn't have to know about it, ever."

"Miss Tallulah," Rod replied, shocked, "I couldn't. Brenda and I . . ."

"Barbara Ann."

"Right. Barbara Ann and I swore to be faithful to each other, and to wait for our wedding night."

"Isn't that unspoiled? Well, would you like to come over to Morehead Heights tonight, just for cocktails?"

"I'd like that very much, but actually, I already promised to come over to Rooster's Seat tonight for another pointer."

"I see."

After *Heat Crazed!*, I had a big change of pace, a slapstick comedy with the beloved comedy team Sturm and Drang, called *Stewed Prudes*. Fred Sturm and Frank Drang had, like me, come from vaudeville to silents to talkies. Unlike many silent comics (unfortunately, dear Billy Bowlegs was a prime example) whose careers foundered in sound, Sturm and Drang were only funnier when you could hear them bicker, and where they could exploit their various popular catchphrases: "Hey, Stupid!" "Do that again and I'll kill you!" and their most popular, "Kiss my ass!" which is still in use today.

Stewed Prudes, like all their films, really had no plot, just one hysterical comedy routine after another. We had pie fights, car chases, and a lengthy drunk scene. I hadn't played a drunk since high school, and, being strictly a social drinker, had never been inebriated myself. As has always been my custom, I held out for realism and insisted on consuming actual vodka stingers on camera for the drunk scene. The results speak for themselves in the finished film.

Frank and Fred were great fun to work with. No two takes were alike. They improvised so freely that no one even bothered to write a script at all! Oddly, I found this way of working easier than I expected. Memorizing a script has always been a tedious task that takes up valuable drinking time. Working with men who considered a script a hindrance was liberating. We just shot comedy routines until we had enough footage for a feature.

And off the set Sturm and Drang were even more fun. *Very* hetero-sexual boys they were, and once I got their baggy pants off of them, they taught me a new meaning for the word "teamwork"!

At the wrap party for *Stewed Prudes* the most wonderful news imag-inable was announced: *THE GREAT EVIL* had been repealed! The Home of the Brave had become the Land of the Free once more. Social drinking was legal again! The champagne flowed like water as I drank a toast to freedom, and then began to seriously celebrate.

15

The Bride of Frankenstein

When I awoke I was lying in my bed in Morehead Heights next to an unfamiliar man. When I looked closer, I realized I did recognize him, and when I did, I let out a scream. I was lying naked, next to the equally naked Scariest Man in the World, *Boris Karloff!*

Boris woke up, looked over at me with his hooded monster's eyes, and said, "Good morning, Tallulah dear." And then leaned over and kissed me.

"Mr. Karloff," I said, "aren't you being a bit forward?"

"Aren't we formal today, Mrs. Karloff?" Boris replied, and I went into shock.

What woman hasn't woken up after a particularly Social party and found herself married to a strange man? I'm sure that's happened to *all* my readers once or twice. But who else has woken up from a party and found herself married to Frankenstein's monster?

Not that I wish to malign dear Boris; he was actually a very nice, soft-spoken, polite Englishman, with an incomprehensible, boring obsession with cricket. In any event, finding myself married to Boris Karloff* was only one of the shocks I had waiting for me that morning.

Once I stirred up Terrence, he filled me in, and I had the largest series

*Despite Miss Tallulah's insistence that she was married to Boris Karloff in 1934 and 1935, I can find no evidence supporting this claim. Quite the contrary, all of Mr. Karloff's biographies, and the testimony of his daughter, Sara Jane Karloff, agree that although Mr. Karloff had five wives, not quite in Tallulah's league, Tallulah is never listed as one of them. In 1934 Karloff was married to his fourth wife, Dorothy Stine, the mother of Sara Jane, whom he married in 1930 and divorced in 1946. I can only redirect your attention to my introductory note where I warned you it wouldn't all add up or ring true.–Douglas

of surprises since the time Mildred Puett woke me up in Tijuana more than twenty years before. The big shock wasn't that I was Mrs. Pratt,* it was that it was 1934! My blackout had lasted just a little over a *year!* Honey, when I celebrate, I really cook!

Louie had been furious when I'd disappeared without a trace for more than six months. One production had to be cancelled, and another had been shot with *my* role being played by *Delores Delgado!* That was the lowest blow of all! I was on suspension.

Eventually I had been found in San Francisco working as a drag queen! Worse than that, I hadn't been too successful. When Terrence and Major Babs came to collect me, the owner of the club where I'd been performing said to them, "Tell your friend that if he wants to be a convincing woman, two words: Depilatory and Facelift. And if he must impersonate a celebrity, why not someone other than that washed-up old hag Morehead? Now, how about settling his bar bill?" What a rude monster! How sensible of loyal Major Babs to have broken his collarbone.

Once I'd been brought back to Los Angeles, a disgusted Louie loaned me out to Metro, where I was now halfway through shooting a film with Boris Karloff, a sequel to his *The Mask of Fu Manchu* called *Fu Manchu's Blessed Event!* I was playing Fu Manchu's white mistress (as with all the Fu Manchu movies, the film was wildly racist), who gives him a son.

Yes, you read that right. It wasn't bad enough that I'd lost an entire year in a Social Blackout, failed as an unconvincing drag queen, missed out on two films, been replaced by the *extremely* untalented *Delores Delgado* (thank God the film tanked at the box office), been suspended, been loaned out to Metro, was appearing in a racist piece of escapist claptrap (as opposed to the always high-class, quality films I made at PMS), and had married the Scariest Man in the World, but, worst of all, I was playing a **Mother!** Could I possibly sink any lower?

I learned the answer to that question when I arrived at Metro later that day and saw my costume.

Apparently Boris and I had had a whirlwind courtship and married three weeks into production. Further, I had been the aggressor in the relationship.

Oddly, considering that for most of the film I'm performing in a Social Stupor, I received some of the best reviews of my career, with

*Dear Boris's real name was William Henry Pratt. Thank heaven he changed it. –Tallulah

Variety calling Boris and me "the Lunt & Fontanne of horror movies." So immediate was my fan response among the Horror Community that both Universal, the Horror Headquarters of America, and RKO, which was trying to compete with Universal for the horror dollar, asked Louie for loanouts of me. Universal had the brilliant idea of teaming "Horror's Big Three," namely Boris, Bela Lugosi, and me, in a film that could charitably be described as "loosely adapted" from Edgar Allan Poe's *The Black Pussy.* RKO wanted to feature me in *HER!* Louie, still disgusted with my disappearance, agreed to both films, but with one proviso; they would have to wait until I first shot a super-spectacle for him at PMS.

Paramount had had a huge success that year with Cecil Blunt De-Mille's *Cleopatra,* starring Claudette Colbert.* Everyone expected them to turn out a sequel, but DeMille instead chose other projects, announcing that there could be no sequel to *Cleopatra.* How wrong he was.

Our legal department had discovered that Cleopatra, Marc Antony, Egypt, and the Roman Empire were *actual historical personages and places* and thus in the public domain. Paramount didn't own them. Anybody could make a movie about them. Thus Louie B. Thalberg, who never saw a bandwagon he couldn't jump on, decided that if DeMille wouldn't make a sequel, Von Millstone would. And so I came to play the title role in PMS's most expensive movie ever, *The Revenge of Cleopatra!*

I played Cleopatra, of course, and Rod Towers played Caesar Augustus. Despite being a natural platinum blonde, I played Cleopatra as a brunette, thus demonstrating the broad range of my legendary versatility. The film begins at the very moment that DeMille's picture ended. Cleopatra lies dying of snake bite beside the body of Marc Antony. My faithful friend Polidorus, played by the immensely tall (six foot seven) and strong character man Harry Rumpole, sucks the snake venom from my wound.† Over Antony's body I vow revenge on Octavius, who killed him and has become Emperor Caesar Augustus of Rome. With Polidorus's help I travel to Rome disguised as a Greek

*A lovely lady, and a charming lesbian, but hopelessly miscast as the Greek queen Cleopatra.–Tallulah
†Terrence, venom-sucking expert that he was, voluntarily spent many long hard hours demonstrating snake-sucking techniques to Harry Rumpole. So enthusiastic was Harry about the lessons he received that the coaching continued after the venom-sucking scene had been shot, and, in fact, even after the entire movie was completed. *That's* professionalism!–Tallulah

princess, intending to make Augustus fall in love with me so I can then kill him and take over his empire.

When I get to Rome all goes according to plan. I find Caesar Augustus is under the influence of his evil wife Livia, played to perfection by Delores Delgado, and her cruel son Tiberius, played by the always amusing Vincent Lovecraft. I seduce Augustus, and he falls for me hard. I'm about to kill him when we meet Jesus Christ (Spencer Hooks), when he comes to Rome with his disciples. I realize that I'm now in love with Augustus and we both convert to Christianity. With the help of Jesus and the disciples we foil the evil plans of Tiberius and Livia and kill them. Then the Roman Empire converts to Christianity, and Augustus becomes the first pope. Jesus himself gives the pope special permission to marry me, and we live happily ever after in the newly built Vatican.

As this brisk summary of what is, after all, a four-hour movie, shows, our film, unlike DeMille's pagan orgy of gratuitous sex and violence, was a moving and deeply religious epic about the power of Faith to change history.

Critics were stunned by this massive film, and their reviews reflected their bewilderment: The *Times* wrote, "In *The Revenge of Cleopatra* Miss Tallulah Morehead makes a spectacle of herself." *Variety* wrote, "In his Egyptian/Roman epic Cyril Von Millstone is unfettered by historical fact." The *Christian Science Monitor,* never my fan since I cancelled my subscription, gushed, "Miss Morehead's performance as Cleopatra is every bit as believable as the screenplay." The *London Times* wrote, "Watching a movie in which Cleopatra, Caesar Augustus, and Jesus Christ creep about a palace at night and stab Livia and Tiberius to death in their beds is to understand how far civilization can sink."

Though popular, the film was simply too expensive to turn a profit, and plans for a second sequel, *Cleopatra Saves Atlantis,* were scrapped despite the most powerful screenplay I'd ever had summarized for me, and I went off to Universal to work with my husband again, this time with Bela Lugosi as well, in Edgar Allan Poe's *The Black Pussy.*

I hear you out there, loyal reader darlings, saying, "Tallulah dear, I worship the stool you drink on, and *I believe every word* of this inspiring autobiography, but I've seen *The Black Cat* with Karloff and Lugosi, and you are not in it." I will explain.

I reported to work at Universal with Boris, Bela, some hopelessly plain-looking little actressette named Jacqueline Wells,* and darling

---

*I believe little Jacqueline Wells was mentally unbalanced. She later divorced Walter Brooks, whose mother was a *multimillionairess,* in order to marry *Lionel Atwill,*

David Manners, who was gorgeous and who I would have been all over me like *l'orange* on duck if it weren't for the facts that (1) my husband was in the film and on the set of a picture about a man who murders his faithless wife and her lover and (2) David was *just the merest whisper,* if you follow me. Presiding over us was the dark, fascinating master Edgar G. Ulmer.

The film made some slight changes in Poe's story, but basically I play Boris's wife, who is having an affair with Bela Lugosi. (I know—*insane!*) Boris finds out and walls us up alive in the cellar. When the police come and knock on the fresh brick wall, they hear what sounds like the wail of a bewildered kitty come from behind the partition. The police tear down the wall and find Bela and me behind it, still alive and using our last bits of oxygen to make passionate love as we die. (Well, what would *you* do in that situation?) The wails they heard were my passionate moans. Boris then goes completely crazy, laughing dementedly and saying over and over, "It was the pussy! It was that awful, disgusting, smelly black pussy! Ha! Ha! Ha! Ha! Ha! Ha! Ha!" Bela and I are rescued and live happily ever after.

Unfortunately, during my blackout celebrating the return of alcoholic freedom to America, Beelzebub's minions had conquered Liberty in another way. Lucifer's second-in-command[*] had inflicted Satan's Manifesto[†] on the motion picture industry, and the movie business had capitulated! The First Amendment was used for toilet paper for the next thirty years!

The Black Pussy was declared completely unacceptable for release, and Carl Laemmle Junior took the unprecedented steps of cutting me and my storyline out of the film altogether, instead building up a minor subplot about a devil cult that Boris runs as a hobby into the main show. The only glimpses of me in the released film that you saw were some shots of me lying in bed beside Boris, photographed through gauze netting. Another actress, a little nobody named Lucille Lund, replaced me in a few scenes as Boris's new wife, who is supposed to be Bela's daughter, who is killed off early. Jacqueline Wells's and David Manners's characters, extremely minor supporting parts in the original film, are built up into the hero and heroine. In short, the film was defaced beyond all recognition!

---

for Christ's sake, the orgy-throwing pervert who played the one-armed inspector in *Son of Frankenstein!* See what I mean? Certifiable!–Tallulah

[*]The Breen office.–Douglas

[†]The Motion Picture Production Code.–Douglas

The Breen office even objected to the *title!* Classic American literature apparently meant nothing to those barbaric cultural vandals. Hence
the name change to *The Black Cat,* and, just to strip the icing from the
cake, they even stuck a *cat* in the picture! Subtlety was completely lost
on the philistine Mr. Breen.*

By the time the ruined film was in release Boris and I were divorced.
Our marriage had been placid at best, dull at worst. Boris drank in moderation, ate in moderation, made love in moderation, he was, in fact,
just too English for words! But the worst thing was his inexplicable obsession with cricket! Every single weekend he attended cricket matches.
I didn't even know there *were* cricket matches in Los Angeles, but apparently a bunch of English misfit malcontents had some sort of cricket
club, and Boris never missed a game. I went with him exactly once! The
game is incomprehensible, The athlete's outfits are unsexy, and they
served *TEA!* I'd rather talk clothes with Terrence.

At Morehead Heights things were peaceful. Boris and Major Babs
(whom Boris knew only as Illinois Smith) shared an interest in military
history. Boris loved dogs and so took to Terrence's Yorkshire terrier,
Felicia, and the headless Indian brave was frightened of Boris and avoided
him.

The marriage might have worked out if Boris hadn't been so damned
curious. I had this one cupboard at Morehead Heights that I kept padlocked. Boris wouldn't leave it alone, and one day I was awakened from
a sound, restful stupor by the sound of a man shrieking in terror. Not
thinking clearly as I was shocked awake, I grabbed an immense butcher
knife and ran upstairs, followed closely by Major Babs. There we found
Boris standing before the padlocked cupboard, which he had pried open
with a crowbar. It so happened that this was the cupboard in which I
kept the jars containing the "keepsakes" I'd supposedly sliced off my
late husbands in *Bluebeard's Daughter,* which I kept locked up, as they
were valuable movie prop souvenirs.

As it happened, I'd never told Boris they were in there, so he didn't
know they were only props made by the brilliant artisans at PMS. Boris,
I'm afraid, thought they were real! Then he turned and saw me running
toward him brandishing that huge knife! Well, it was too much for poor
Boris. The Scariest Man in the World was terrified! He cupped his hands
over his crotch, screamed, "You won't get mine, Devil Woman!" and

*Good news for Tallulah fans: Concurrent with the publication of this book,
Universal is releasing, for the first time ever, the original, uncut, uncensored version of
The Black Pussy as part of the "Universal Monsters Classics Collection."–Douglas

turned and crashed through a second-floor window. Fortunately, Terrence happened to be outside and broke his fall, or Boris might have slipped right off the end of Tumescent Tor to certain death! As it was, both men spent four weeks in hospital.

Even after the misunderstanding was cleared up, Boris wouldn't come back. Some traumas just strike a man too deeply. We divorced on grounds of irreconcilable differences and went our separate ways. Four husbands down. Would I ever find true love?*

---

*Again, I must emphasize that the Karloff family and all historical documentation denies every word of this chapter. So far as we can establish it, Tallulah was *never* married to Boris Karloff. We can only assume that Tallulah's memories of making those two films with him while still recovering from her end-of-Prohibition bender have eroded over the years into a false memory. Fortunately, this is a Show Business Star Autobiography, so Truth isn't an issue.–Douglas

16

Empty Wombs

What woman, apart from my mother, doesn't long to have a child? However, after twenty years of PMS and four husbands, I was still childless, and the fact was, I wasn't getting any younger, as Bosley Crowther kept insisting on pointing out in his increasingly hostile reviews. If I was ever to be a mother I was going to have to take steps, and soon.

My mother was such a lousy example of motherhood you might have thought I'd have no interest in parenting myself, but I knew I could be a better mother than Mother. Hell, Terrence's Yorkie, Felicia, could have been a better mother than Mother, and, in fact, was.

Maxie had passed away during my marriage to dear Boris, although I believe his fatal heart attack was just his way of escaping Mother. I received a typically whining letter from Mother after Maxie's passing, bitching about how Maxie had left nothing but debts and she was being evicted from their bungalow, etc., etc., blah, blah, blah. Boiled down, it was her usual message: "Send money!"

I was just going to toss her letter in the incinerator as usual when Terrence pointed out that if the press got ahold of the story of my mother, a gigantic* alcoholic living in the gutter, they might miss the comical side†and twist it around and make it all *ugly!* Terrence pointed out that a four-hundred-pound woman lying in the gutter would be kind of hard to miss, and, despite my best efforts, it was widely known that she *was* my mother. I'd had my share of bad press before; I didn't need the papers blaming Mother's troubles on me.

---

*Tallulah's mother, by 1935, weighed a little over four hundred pounds.–Douglas
†Let's face it, my colossal, drunken mother lolling in the gutter, begging passersby for liquor, *is* a very funny image. It makes me smile even now.–Tallulah

In the end it was just safer to set Mother up in a little place of her own. She, of course, wanted to come out and live in Morehead Heights. I felt that bringing Mother into the severe southern California climate when she was accustomed to the milder winters on Long Island was simply too risky, not to mention that the cost of shipping her west was prohibitive. I found her a surprisingly inexpensive little place to call her own. Of course, I could have just paid off the debts on Mother's house and left her there, but, as Mother never got off the sofa at all anymore—in point of fact, *could* no longer get up unassisted—what point was there to her having all those other rooms? She couldn't keep herself clean, let alone a whole house.

I found a lovely little sort of "cabin" for Mother, (the realtor called it a "rundown plywood shack," but that description belied its rustic charm) a real fixer-upper, set off back away from the annoying noise of roads and towns and people in a lovely, unspoiled mountain woodland area. Since Mother couldn't get off the couch, she only needed the one room. This was before television, so she didn't need electricity, either, which was fortunate, since there wasn't any, nor a phone, which was just as well as some idiot at the studio always gave her my new number no matter how often I changed it. There *was* running water, in the form of a charming babbling brook just a few hundred yards outside the cabin for nine months of every year except when frozen solid, but a water heater would have involved having gas pipes laid in for the forty miles up the mountain from the nearest town, and before they could lay the pipes they would have first needed to build a road. It was just *way* too expensive! There was a wood-burning stove, an ax, and plenty of trees if she *needed* to heat water.

Obviously Mother couldn't survive out there on her own, but Terrence suggested I hire a full-time nurse to feed her, and hose her down once a week. Mildred Puett recommended a wonderful woman named Nurse Torquemada to give Mother the sort of loving care she deserved.

With Mother disposed of and my divorce in the works, I returned to work, this time at RKO where Merian C. Cooper, the genius behind *King Kong,* had borrowed me from Louie to play the title role in his fantasy adventure classic *HER!* I played a 3000-year-old pagan queen who rules a primitive tribe with an iron hand while waiting for the reincarnation of her murdered lover to return from the dead and live with her happily ever after. My costars were adorable Charles Farrell; burly, masculine English character man C. Aubrey Smith; and overly perky Zita Johann as the civilized trash that Farrell almost dumps me for. Fortunately, I sacrifice Zita to the god Zamboni during a big musical dance number, and Charles is then free to enter the Pool of Immortality with me—only the laugh is on me, since a second immersion in the Life Waters strips me of my immortality and causes me to age to 3000 years in just seconds.[*]

Charles Farrell was cute as the dickens, and in my newly single state I should have been all over him like mold on a Frenchman, but Charlie was *just the merest whisper;* in fact, Charlie always referred to his manliest part as "My Little Margie." He just wanted me to introduce him to Rod Towers. I painfully pointed out that Rod was not only straight, but engaged to sweet little Barbara Ann Langendorf, whom none of us had ever met as she was still way back east in Long Beach, California, but Charlie said, "That's all right. After all, *I'm married.* So what?" Apparently, Charlie was of the F. Emmett Knight School of Husbandry. On top of that, Charlie wore more makeup offscreen than I wore onscreen! Boris hadn't done that, even when playing the Frankenstein monster!

C. Aubrey Smith was another matter altogether, a man's man and a woman's delight. If you remember his magnificent face, then you remember his monumental proboscis. Well that wasn't the only organ on his body of unusually immense proportions. For the duration of *HER!* I was making love to Charlie onscreen and C. Aubrey off.

When *HER!* wrapped shooting, I returned to PMS to make *Scrimpy Endowment,* a lighthearted screwball comedy with Rod, Vincent, and Azure. Since I'd been gone from PMS so long on loanouts, the slogan Pete Moss came up with to advertise this movie was "Morehead for Rod again!"

During the filming of *Scrimpy Endowment* I began uncharacteristically putting on weight. I've always been bone thin, thanks to a rapid metabolism and a mostly liquid diet, but now, for some reason, I just started to swell up, and nothing seemed to work at reducing it. If you watch *Scrimpy Endowment,* you can notice how, for about a third of the picture, I'm photographed in close-ups, or standing behind furniture, or carrying large bundles, anything to conceal my alarming weight gain.

When the film was completed Louie ordered me to either lose weight or face character parts. Loretta Young told me of a wonderful weight-

---

[*]To achieve the horrifying effect of Tallulah's rotting on camera to the age of a mummy, they fixed Tallullah's head in place with a vice clamp and then did a series of "Invisible dissolves," while, between each shot, the makeup person removed more of Tallullah's glamor beauty makeup until, in the disgusting final 3000-years-old look, Tallullah appeared with no makeup on at all!–Douglas

loss clinic that catered to the rich and famous, where they were, above all, discreet. I checked in there for a few months, and though at first I just seemed to continue to expand, until I was as big as a bus and looked alarmingly like Mother, then suddenly, almost overnight it seemed, the excess weight seemed to just shoot out of me, and I was back to my old trim figure, though I needed to do some firming.

Doctor Lecter, my weight-loss guru, also ran an adoption service on the premises. Since his clients tended to be wealthy folk who could afford to give a child a good home, he kept a stock of unfortunate orphans for his clients who chose to adopt. The very day after my weight so suddenly returned to normal they brought a newborn baby girl in to show me. I must confess that, with my first glance at this baby's silky platinum blond hair and her enormous proboscis, I fell in love with her. Doctor Lecter told me that she needed a home. I felt almost as though my odd weight gain had occurred just in order for me to meet this little bundle of joy. We put the legal machinery in motion at once, and when I returned to Morehead Heights, I brought little Patty, my newly *adopted* daughter, with me.

Terrence had more than enough to do as my personal assistant, and Major Babs didn't have a maternal bone in, or near, her body, so I hired a lady, again recommended by Mildred Puett (who knew unmarried working women all over America), to be Patty's nanny. The woman, named Fanny Cleft, was wonderful with the child. I don't know what I'd have done without Nanny Fanny.

Terrence's duties as my personal assistant, coupled with his increasing age, made me decide to also hire a new houseboy, thus freeing up Terrence from the housework so as to concentrate on maintaining me. I found a young Japanese immigrant named Hisato and hired him. I'm tempted to describe Hisato as *the merest whisper,* except that he was more like a deafening shout. Hisato made Terrence look butch, and my *God,* how that man could sing! When I hired him, he was appearing in a first-rate amateur production of *Madama Butterfly,* in the title role!

As 1936 began, and I started shooting *The Thick Man,* a lighthearted comedy-murder mystery in which Rod Towers and I play Dick and Dora Williams, a married couple of detectives always on the lookout for clues and cocktails, my little household at Morehead Heights had grown quite a bit. There was myself, Terrence, Major Babs, Little Pattycakes, Nanny Fanny, Hisato, and the headless Indian brave, who took care of Little Pattycakes on Nanny Fanny's nights off. All that was missing was a husband. Not surprisingly, my next husband was already in sight.

17

Towering Ambitions

Little Patty Morehead was just the tonic gloomy old Morehead Heights needed. I spent so much time doting over my newborn daughter that acting just seemed like work. This is why I only made two films that year, the charming murder mystery *The Thick Man* and the romantic South Sea Island spectacle *Virgins of Krakatoa*, which was entirely shot on the faraway, exotic location of Santa Catalina Island. But most of my time was devoted to little Patty, or Pattycakes, as everyone called her.

Dear, loving Joan Crawford was so taken by little Pattycakes that she insisted on always being called to baby-sit. Other children had indifferent teenagers watch their children when they were out, but my Pattycakes had a great star and future Oscar winner keeping a sharp eye on her slightest movement. Watching Joan learning to nurture from baby-sitting my precious child was touching. I wasn't surprised that soon thereafter Joan followed in my footsteps and adopted her own daughter, although I've heard on the rumor vine that little Christina wasn't truly an *adoption* at all, if you catch my meaning. In any event, every time my entire household had to go out, Joan came tearing over to Morehead Heights, teaching little Pattycakes the meaning of "conditional love." And Pattycakes was equally crazy about Joan. Just the sight of Joan's world-famous face bending over her bassinet was enough to set little Pattycakes screaming her lungs out with delight.

Oddly, during this period, we noticed that little Pattycakes got a lot of bruises and welts. Since she only acquired these wounds when we were out and Joan was baby-sitting, there was only one possible conclusion to draw: there was something wrong with her blood, making it form causeless bruises.

Her Christian Science pediatrician (naturally I raised Pattycakes in my own semi-faith) said she was "manifesting a belief in bruises" and prescribed prayer. Without my knowledge Nanny Fanny took Patty-cakes to a *real* pediatrician, who ran blood tests. His diagnosis was even simpler: Pattycakes was drunk almost all of the time. I didn't understand how a baby who couldn't even crawl yet could get into the liquor cabinets. Then the source of the problem was identified and a treatment recommended: for the sake of my little girl's newly growing liver, I had to stop breast-feeding her. Fortunately, the doctor said I *only* had to stop breast-feeding the *baby!*

The shooting of *Virgins of Krakatoa* was like a vacation. Catalina Island was beautiful and unspoiled, at least when we arrived. I was playing Coozella, a native girl who is chosen to be the virgin sacrifice to the volcano god Mulatto because no one can get along with her. Rod Towers was the native boy Sashimi, who wants to disqualify me for the virgin sacrifice competition, and Vincent Lovecraft played the evil high priest Scatolo who intends to sacrifice me for spurning him. As you may have noticed, Vincent regularly degraded me in movie after movie. But Vincent, always gracious, used to say, "When I degraded Tallulah, I was only finishing what nature had begun."

One evening during the shoot, Vincent and Rod had returned to the mainland as they weren't in the scenes we were shooting, just me and the other virgin maidens doing our Dance of Chastity, some of which the Breen office ended up cutting as "excessively lewd." Unbeknownst to me, while we worked on the island, the police were raiding a party Terrence and Hisato were throwing, in my absence, at Morehead Heights! It sounded to me, when I learned of it later, like a harmless gathering. For one thing, it was all-male: people like Vincent and his longtime roommate C. Halibut Plugg, William Haines and his friend Jimmie Shields, James Whale and his friend David Lewis, George Cukor, Mitchell Leisen, Rod Towers, Cesar Romero, Cary Grant with Randolph Scott, Franklin Nancyboy on a rare night free of his watchdog wife, Charles Farrell, Nelson Eddy, Charles Laughton, Grady Sutton, as well as such behind the camera personnel as Bruce Camellia, Arthur Deco, Marcel Pouff, Lance Analvice, and, not surprisingly, F. Emmett Knight. There were also a number of unknown young would-be actors that Bruce had rounded up.*

As it happened, some of the boys were underage and a few of the guests were held on charges of unbelievable depravity. Pete Moss and

---

*Pattycakes, Nanny Fanny, and Major Babs were all in Avalon with me, and apparently the headless Indian brave either didn't attend or wasn't arrested.–Tallulah

his colleagues from the other studios had to work overtime hushing it up and getting charges dismissed. Fortunately, the Los Angeles DA's office and the police were completely corrupt in those days,* so it was just a matter of money.

But Louie B. Thalberg got a call from the gossip maven Hedda Parsons telling him that she had heard that *"supposedly* straight leading man" Rod Towers had been caught in flagrante delecto with a sixteen-year-old boy at a "homosexual orgy" in Hollywood. This was just plain ridiculous; Morehead Heights is almost *fifteen miles* from Hollywood! Louie managed to crush the story, then he summoned Rod to his office for a *serious* talk about his career.

None of this was known to me, isolated as I was out on the island, when Rod arrived on the set that afternoon and asked me to become his wife.

Since we weren't even dating, I was a little surprised. "What about your fiancée?" I asked.

"Who?" Rod replied, patently shocked that I hadn't just accepted him outright.

"Barbara Ann Langendorf, your fiancée back east in Long Beach, California."

"Oh yeah, her. Ah, she, ah, she's married someone else. I got a 'Dear Rod' letter from her."

"Rod darling, I'm so sorry. She must be a very shallow person. If she only knew all the temptations you've resisted out here. Why I know dozens of women besides myself who have thrown themselves at you, yet you've never touched any of us. What a foolish girl. But Rod darling, are you sure you're not just proposing to me on the rebound?"

"Absolutely not. I've been in love with you for years, but you were a big star and I was a nobody."

"True. Unimportant, but true."

"But now, I'm an even bigger star than you!"

"Not that it's important, but no, you're not."

"Louie says I am."

"Louie's wrong."

"The grosses on my films without you are up."

"Yes, but . . ."

"HER! tanked at the box office."

"It's a slow builder."

---

*Unlike now, when they're utterly honest and incorruptable!–Tallulah

"They pulled it from theaters after two weeks."

"It was too outré."

"They cut you out of *The Black Cat* altogether."

"Are you proposing or critiquing?"

"I'm just saying that unlike the public, I love you, and, since our films together gross more than our films apart, then our lives together should be more gross than apart."

"*The Black Pussy* was a much better movie than that tripe they released."

"I love you, Miss Morehead, and I want to be your husband and be a father to little Pattycakes."

"*HER!* will one day be revered as a fantasy classic!"

"Miss Morehead, please, will you marry me?"

"Well Rod darling, there's something we have to do before I can give you an informed answer."

"What's that?"

"Let me put it this way; you wouldn't buy a car without taking it out for a test drive first, would you?"

"What has buying a car got to do with . . . Oh! I see. Ah, is this point negotiable?"

"No!"

"Because I always thought that sex before marriage was a . . ."

"I married F. Emmett Knight without having sex with him first . . ."

"He told me."

". . . and it was a huge mistake. He turned out to be a *gay man* who just wanted to get married so people would think he was straight!"

"No! That's . . . that's execrable!"

"What?"

"Awful! That's awful! What deceit!"

"So I'm never making *that* mistake again! Anybody who wants to marry me had better be able to cut the mustard. Now, are you ready for your husbandly audition?"

"Ah, okay." And with that, Rod took a deep breath, gritted his teeth, and got the job done.

Louie was delighted with our plans to wed, which he said would be even better for the studio than it was for us, an odd sentiment, I thought, considering that he was one of my ex-husbands. Anyway, unlike with F. Emmett Knight, he saw no reason to wait. By the time we shot the spectacular conclusion of *Virgins of Krakatoa,* where the volcano erupts and Vincent dies in the lava and the island is destroyed, Rod and I were married. We were off on our honeymoon* by the time the Catalina Chamber of Commerce lodged its suit against PMS for the tremendous amount of damage done to their island while shooting the eruption.†

We had a little trouble deciding where to honeymoon. Rod wanted to go to Fire Island, New York, but I didn't feel like honeymooning in the same state with Mother. His second choice, San Francisco, just wasn't exotic enough for me. We finally went to Havana, which you could still do in those days.

Our sex life was odd but satisfactory for all, except for some grousing by Major Babs, who felt left out, on account of her being left out. Major Babs never really cared for any of my husbands, or boyfriends, or men friends, or girlfriends. She could be grumpy. Rod was an active, dutiful lover who could take orders, although he treated lovemaking more like a chore than a pleasure. He preferred sex at night, with all the lights off and his eyes tightly shut. If we made love during the day, for a kinky touch, he would wear my "Sleep Shades" blindfold, along with nose plugs for some reason.

Rod was a murmurer. As we made love he would, almost unconsciously, whisper in my ear, "Oh yeah, baby, take it. Take it, baby. Take it like a man." Except that where I've used the word "baby" Rod usually used proper names, and they were never mine. Now I know many women get ticked off when their husbands whisper someone else's name in an intimate moment, but I've always felt that as long as you're the one receiving the benefit, what does it matter who he's thinking of to help him get the job done? Do you imagine I was always thinking of Rod while I was with him? He was lucky I wasn't whispering back, "Oh yes, Kong baby. You're the king, Kong, you're the king!"†† So what did

---

* "We" being me, Rod, Pattycakes, Terrence, Major Babs, and Nanny Fanny. Hisato and the headless Indian brave stayed behind at Morehead Heights. After all, on a honeymoon, six is company and eight's a crowd.–Tallulah

† Santa Catalina Island is not a volcanic island, so Louie had spent a fortune having lava shipped there from Hawaii, reheated, and set loose for an amazingly realistic sequence. Unfortunately, cinematic verisimilitude clearly meant nothing to the residents of Avalon. It was a very popular movie, but between the cost of staging the eruption and the millions spent repairing the island, *Virgins of Krakatoa* couldn't have made a profit if every man, woman, and child in America had seen it three times.–Tallulah

†† I must admit I found *King Kong* to be *the* most erotic movie I ever saw! Even though Kong displayed no visible evidence of genitalia, despite spending the entire movie nude, I had no trouble vividly imagining his own colossal Empire State

I care when Rod called me Jean or Leslie or Clark or Cary or Humphrey or Jimmy or Fred or Harpo? He was taking care of business.

When we got back home from our divine honeymoon, Rod moved into my bedroom at Morehead Heights, and we shot the bolt on the connecting door to Major Babs's room. Rod was enchanted by baby Pattycakes and delighted in dressing her up in lots of charming little outfits. He also got along great with Terrence and Hisato, both of whom were devoted to him. Rod instituted a program of fire and air raid drills, and often, while I was out social drinking, Rod would stay home drilling Terrence and Hisato's brains out, though they never complained. In fact, the occasional argument broke out between Terrence and Hisato over who would get drilled first! That's the true spirit of Home Safety!

Life was blissful over the next two years while Rod and I made six films together in a row: Our first movie as a married couple was the charming prison musical *Babes Behind Bars,* Rod's first musical since *Broadway Bimbos.* Rod got along great with choreographer Hermes Hyde, spending many long, hard, sweaty afternoons locked in with him in the rehearsal hall, no visitors allowed, drilling away, even though Rod wasn't in any of the dance numbers. *That's* dedication! Wilfred Wyndham was also in this picture, which was my first with Ida Lupino.

Then there was the pirate adventure *Buccaneer Bride.* During the shooting of this film Vincent Lovecraft had to chain me to a post and flog me within an inch of my life, and then, you should have seen what he did to me in the *movie!* Vincent also had to torture Rod in this film, which was just silly to anyone who knew how deeply these two men loved each other, and how often. I remember seeing Rod stretched out on the rack in the torture chamber set, his magnificent physique glistening with sweat, and as Vincent's oiled black henchmen (hand-selected by Vincent) turned the wheel another couple notches, stretching Rod beyond the limits of human endurance, Vincent leaned over him, and the two of them harmonized a rendition of "Seems Like Old Times." It was almost a disappointment when the director and crew returned from

---

Building arising from his furry crotch with just the right prodding. Selfish old Merian C. Cooper refused to introduce me to Kong all the time we worked together on *HER!,* claiming that Kong was just a "special effect" (did he think I was *blind?*) and referring me to someone called Willis O'Brien, who I guess was Kong's trainer. Lucky Fay Wray! The beneficial effects of her passionate affair with Kong are undeniable; as of this writing she is 92, looking great and still going strong. Just imagine how fine she'll look when she reaches *my* age!–Tallulah

lunch and they took Rod down and put me up to shoot the scene in the script.

Then we made the film noir *Fatal Floozy,* in which I killed Vincent and Rod killed me. Bosley Crowther gave me one of his rare good notices here when he wrote, "Tallulah is so good as the corpse that one hopes she will be dead in all of her films from now on."

Then came the jungle adventure *Tarzan's Secret Shame.* Rod had a change of pace here and played a villain. Johnny Weissmuller, of course, played Tarzan, and homely Maureen O'Sullivan[*] played his drab mate Jane. I played the queen of a neighboring tribe of Amazons with whom Tarzan has a little fling. He was a swinger, after all. Rod played my pathologically jealous high priest who wants to sacrifice Tarzan, and Vincent played the white hunter who lusts for Jane in a completely unbelievable subplot, which I felt compromised the otherwise rigorous authenticity and credibility of the Tarzan series.

Next came the tuneful period musical *Alexander the Great's Ragtime Band.* You can have no idea how difficult it is to tap dance in a toga! This was followed by the noirish tale of forbidden love and sex, *Illicit Plaything.* At the same time I was loaned out to Disney to provide the voice of the Evil Witch in the enchanting animated classic *Seven Brides for Seven Drawfs.*

If I seem to have glossed over these last three films rather quickly it was because my mind at that time was elsewhere. Now that I had my own family and home life straightened out, one great acting role cried out to me. I wanted to play Scarlett O'Hara in the worst way! Even Vivian Leigh couldn't say that!

---

[*]Sweet little Maureen's screen persona was completely at odds with her real-life bull dyke personality. Her lengthy marriage and mothering of Mia Farrow fooled no one! After all, a *real* heterosexual woman, like me for a completely random example, would have been married *many* times. When a woman stays married to the same man for decades, it's a dead giveaway that the whole thing is a sham!–Tallulah

18

1939!

1939! All critics agree, it was the most Golden Year in the Golden Age of Movies! *The Adventures of Sherlock Holmes, Beau Geste, Dark Victory, Golden Boy, Goodbye Mr. Chips, Gulliver's Travels, Gunga Din, The Hound of the Baskervilles, The Hunchback of Notre Dame, The Man in the Iron Mask, Mr. Smith Goes to Washington, Ninotchka, Of Mice and Men, The Rains Came, Son of Frankenstein, Topper Takes a Trip, Union Pacific, The Women, Wuthering Heights, You Can't Cheat an Honest Man.* All these cinema classics have two things in common: (1) they were all released in 1939, and (2) I am not in any of them.

"Of course you weren't, Tallulah," I hear you saying (and you shouldn't keep talking when people are trying to read), "you were under exclusive contract to PMS, and none of those are PMS pictures." No longer true. F. Emmett Knight had renegotiated my contract with Louie to allow me to make one film a year for other studios if I could find one. Then F. Emmett began shopping me around to the other studios trying to line up pictures for me.

I screen-tested for *Of Mice and Men,* but the role ended up going to sweet little Creighton Chaney, who was delightful, but not nearly as To-Die-For Sexy as his late Dreamboat Dad, and not as good in bed either,[*] but a fine actor and a wonderful Social Drinking buddy.

F. Emmett put me up for *Dark Victory* as well, but Jack Warner reportedly said, "The audience isn't supposed to *envy* her blindness!"

---

[*]I was married to the divinely sexy Rod at this time and determined to make this marriage work. As Mother always said, "Five times the charm," but I wasn't a *nun,* for heaven's sake! The fact was, though not as incredibly appealing as his father, on full moons no one could top Creighton for raw animal sex!–Tallulah

I was offered a role in *Son of Frankenstein,* but my ex-husband, now happily remarried and about to be a father, flatly refused to work with me again, or indeed, to enter any room I was in. That poor man was *traumatized!* Bela Lugosi eventually took my role, though he glamorized it shamelessly.

Barbara Stanwyck landed the role I wanted in *Golden Boy,* though tremendously gorgeous little William Holden and I rehearsed the love scenes together at Morehead Heights for endless hours until Rod came home and caught us. Rather than being angry, Rod was so taken with young Bill that he offered to give the virile young actor some "pointers," though Bill wanted none of it. Bill went on to become a big, big star, but he was never too busy to stop by Morehead Heights for some heavy-weight Social Drinking.

Harry Cohn wanted me for *The Hunchback of Notre Dame,* saying something about "saving a fortune on makeup," but Charlie Laughton beat me out for the part by sleeping with Victor Hugo. Who ever heard of having sex with a *writer?*

MGM also nixed me from *The Women.* Joan Crawford replaced me in that picture, and that was the end of her baby-sitting gigs at Morehead Heights. F. Emmett told me, "Irving rejected you, Tallulah. He was rightfully afraid you'd outshine his wife, Norma."

"But Irving is dead," I pointed out helpfully.

"True Love never dies."

Darryl Zanuck offered me a role in *The Hound of the Baskervilles,* but I didn't think I could master running on all fours.

But above and beyond all those great movies that year, two tower over them all: *The Wizard of Oz* and *Gone with the Wind,* two movies which, though fairly good as they were, *could* have been masterpieces if only the men casting them had had a little more taste and vision.

I had wanted to play Dorothy Gale in *The Wizard of Oz* ever since the moment Terrence first read his summary of the treatment to me, a charming fable that seemed in every way to mirror my own life. Why, actually, if you think of the Scarecrow, the Tin Man, the Lion, the Wizard, and Professor Marvel as Dorothy's husbands, Glinda as Major Babs, Auntie Em and Uncle Henry as Mother and Maxie, the twister as Louie B. Thalberg, the Witch as Delores Delgado, Toto as Terrence (actually, Toto was a dead ringer for Felicia), and the Munchkins as my fans, the story was practically my biography, only without any sex or booze.

I offered to screen-test for the part, a major concession from someone who had been a movie star for nearly a quarter of a century, and I even showed up at Mervyn LeRoy's office in full makeup and costume as Dorothy on a rare day when I was free from the set of the picture I was doing for PMS at the time—a maritime melodrama called *Damaged Cargo*, which I starred in with Vincent, Harry Rumpole (much to Terrence's delight again), Spencer Hooks, and a new leading man named Justin Thyme.

Mervyn seemed a bit unprepared for my stunning appearance as Dorothy but came up with some lame excuse for not using me: "You see, Dorothy is supposed to be a little girl. We don't really think a woman past forty* is appropriate for the part."

I attempted to read the original novel, but it was just too dense to get through. Who wrote it? Tolstoy? All novelists should write their books in screenplay form so people can read them. But before I gave up and tossed it aside (Chapter 2), I did extract that the little girl in the book, judging from the illustrations, was about five years old, consequently, I was *shocked* when they cast matronly Judy Garland in the part. And they had the nerve to imply that *I* was too old! They had to strap down her enormous, bulbous breasts to even begin to *pretend* she was a child. They wouldn't have had that problem with me; by this time my breasts were sagging so low that in profile I appeared flat-chested unless I leaned forward.

Years later, when they remade *The Wizard of Oz* with an all-tinted ensemble, they cast Diana Ross as Dorothy, and I wish I had a drink for every year *she* was past forty.†

But even Dorothy, a role so close to me that many of you may have mistakenly thought you were reading *The Wizard of Oz* for the last hundred pages or so, paled next to the role of the century: Scarlett O'Hara!

There was no question that *Gone with the Wind* was *the* novel of the decade. Everyone who was anyone in Hollywood was having someone read it for them. Terrence read and summarized it for me; however, his summary was two hundred pages long, and so tear-smeared as to be illegible. I had Hisato read and summarize Terrence's summary, and Hisato got it down to fifty pages, unfortunately in Japanese. I had Major Babs, who was *extremely* skilled in tongues (I mean it! The woman was one hell of a cunning linguist, take it from me, just as I took it from her), read Hisato's summary and translate and summarize it for me. She got it down to ten pages. I then had Rod read Major Babs's summary of

---

*I have no idea *what* he meant by *that* crack!–Tallulah
†Oh look: I *do!* Cheers!–Tallulah

Hisato's summary of Terrence's summary, but he couldn't get through it. He apparently got distracted by a private fantasy involving the Tarleton twins and drifted off, locking himself in a bathroom with just page one. Finally, the headless Indian brave managed to boil Margaret Mitchell's endless, unreadable, self-indulgent tome down to one paragraph, which *I read myself!*

I was *consumed* by it! I couldn't put that paragraph down! For weeks people would call me up and invite me over for cocktails and I'd say, "I can't! I'm reading *Gone with the Wind!* I can't put it down!"

Rod would say, "It's late, Tallulah. Are you coming to bed?" and I would reply, "I can't! I'm too deeply engrossed in this third sentence. I must read a few more dependent clauses. I'll be up in a couple hours."

"Okay, fine, dear," Rod would answer, concealing his disappointment as he added, "Oh Terrence, would you come up here, please?" Then Terrence would go bounding up the stairs, grinning and stripping, while I started the incredible next sentence.

What an emotional roller-coaster that paragraph was! I *was* Scarlett O'Hara! The tempestuous teenager in sentence one: *me!* The foolish first marriage to a dork in sentence two: I wrote the book on that! (*This* book, as a matter of fact. See Chapters 7 through 10.) The lovers separated by war in sentence three: me and the kaiser! The multiple succeeding marriages in the fourth sentence: me, me, me, and again me! (In fact, I'd had even more husbands than Scarlett!) The plantation Tara: Morehead Heights! The devoted slaves: Terrence, Hisato, Major Babs, and the headless Indian brave. The misunderstood career woman: me! The endless pining for a married man who doesn't love her back: me and Cary Grant! The burning of Atlanta: our destruction of Avalon! Scarlett's father dies: my father was dead! Scarlett's mother dies: I *wished* my mother were dead! A story that goes on and on and on: *I* go on and on and on! And Rod Towers was *born* to play Rhett Butler! By the time I finished reading that paragraph, three months had just sped by while I was lost in a world that was gone with the wind. Oh! So that's . . . never mind.

Anyway, by the time I finished reading that paragraph, like reading my own diary, only far more legible, I knew that God, or at least Mary Baker Eddy,* intended me to play Scarlett O'Hara, which is more than I can say for that Vivien Leigh trollop!†

---

*No real qualitative difference between them. Just ask Mary.–Tallulah
†She and Larry Olivier were having a torrid affair even though both of them were married to other people! Have you ever heard anything so immoral? Yet they gave

F. Emmett got me a screen test for Scarlett, which was a sign that I was a very serious candidate for the part, as David O. Selznick didn't screen-test just anyone. He turned down Terrence, for instance, who, after reading the whole damn book, wanted to revive his long dead acting career by playing Scarlett in drag. But Scarlett is supposed to be a girl of eighteen at the beginning of the film, and Terrence had worked for me longer than that. True, I was also a year or two past eighteen, but on me the years were *undetectable,* and Vivien Leigh certainly hadn't been to her senior prom in living memory.

Seventy-five different people were working on the screenplay at the time, so no firm script was ready, but, as I had read the headless Indian brave's one-paragraph summation, I felt fully qualified to write my own screen test, reproduced here for you. Sadly, the film itself no longer exists. In fact, I understand that Selznick burned my test personally. The man needed to learn to delegate.

INTERIOR TARA. MAMMY AT THE WET BAR. SCARLETT ENTERS, CARRYING A *VERY* PREGNANT MELANIE, WHOM SHE DUMPS ON A DIVAN.

Scarlett

Take a load off, Melanie! Mammy darling! I've had to carry Mrs. Wilkes all the way from Atlanta, and she really should hit the gym. I certainly could have used a sidecar. Mix me one, will you Mammy darling! No wait! Make that a mint julep, with vodka. And an Irish coffee. I am Irish, after all.

Mammy

Yes, Missy Scarlett.

Scarlett

Oh, Mammy darling, don't be so formal. Call me Scar. And don't be so stingy with the vodka.

Mammy

There is no vodka, Missy Scar. The Union soldiers done take all the alcohol in the house.

Scarlett

What? Oh my God, Mammy darling! War is hell! Is there no alcohol at all?

---

that *slattern* the role of virginal Scarlett, a role that should have gone to a decently married woman like me. Larry was no better. I know for a fact that he was later cast in the title role in *Hamlet* solely because he was sleeping with the director!–Tallulah

> *Mammy*

All we gots is that sourmash moonshine Uncle Toby makes in his still out back, and that stuff blinded him.

> *Scarlett*

Well, frankly, my dear, what is there to look at around here? Pour me a moonshine and don't be parsimonious.

A YANKEE SOLDIER ENTERS. SCARLETT SHOOTS HIM DEAD IN HIS TRACKS.

> *Scarlett*

Mammy darling, drag that carcass out of here, and see if he's carrying any vodka.

> *Melanie*

Ow! Scarlett, I think the baby's coming.

> *Scarlett*

I should be so lucky!
SCARLETT YANKS A BABY OUT OF MELANIE AND TOSSES IT TO MAMMY.

> *Scarlett*

Mammy darling, have this washed and changed and give it a bottle of warm moonshine.
ASHLEY ENTERS IN A RAGGED CONFEDERATE OFFICER'S UNIFORM. HE RUSHES TO SCARLETT'S ARMS AND THEY KISS PASSIONATELY.

> *Ashley*

Scarlett, oh Scarlett, my darling. Can you ever forgive me? Oh, hi, Mel.

> *Melanie*

Ashley, I had our baby.

> *Ashley*

That's nice. Oh Scarlett, my one true love. I've been so blind, so very, very blind.

> *Scarlett*

Well then, you might as well have some of this moonshine. It's perky but a little insolent.
RHETT ENTERS, IN A RAGGED CONFEDERATE OFFICER'S UNIFORM. HE RUSHES TO SCARLETT'S ARMS AND THEY KISS PASSIONATELY.

> *Rhett*

Scarlett, my darling, I've come back for you. I can't live without you.

> *Scarlett*
> Of course you can't, darling. But what about the war?
> *Rhett*
> Frankly, my dear, I don't give a damn.
> *Scarlett*
> Language, darling! There's a baby around here somewhere.
> *Ashley*
> Scarlett, I love you!
> *Rhett*
> Scarlett, I love you!
> *Scarlett*
> As Mammy is my witness, I swear, I'll never be horny again!

As you can see, even from just reading this on paper without hearing my incomparable delivery, it was stirring and moving and, not surprisingly, had quite an effect on everyone present. The crew that filmed it was visibly moved, right out the door. Hattie McDaniel, who appeared in the test with me, invited me over for cocktails after the test.* Hattie, who was one of the *largest* lesbians I've ever met, and I became bosom buddies. I remember visiting her a couple of years later when she did things to me with her Oscar that I haven't even done with my husbands!†

But magnificent as I was, David O. ultimately gave the role to the English whore, probably as a result of his little known bipolar disorder. It was a grave disappointment. When the news reached me, on the set of *Mayfair Madness*, a comedy of manners I was making back at PMS with Rod and the sophisticated English comedian Brent Wood, I was so upset I had to go to a bar for the rest of the day.

The next afternoon I went charging into Louie's office, full of fire.†† Louie, although annoyed at being interrupted while plucking a young talent, nevertheless refastened his pants and listened to what I had to say.

It was simple: David O. Selznick didn't *own* the Civil War any more than Cecil B. DeMille had owned Egypt and Cleopatra. It was in the

---

*The idiots at Selznick International insisted that we use *fake* alcohol in the test. How shallow! No wonder the movies from there seem so phony. Nothing disgusts me more than Hollywood sham!–Tallulah

†How well I remember dear Hattie grunting over her Oscar. "It just ain't fittin'," she mumbled as she applied the elbow grease, "Tain't fittin'. Tain't fittin'!"–Tallulah

††More likely fire*water!*–Douglas

public domain. We could make our own Civil War movie, and we could use an *original* story rather than being tied to some overly long novel that no one in America had ever finished reading. Bette Davis,[*] whom Selznick had rightfully turned down for Scarlett early on, had her own antebellum rip-off, for which she'd just lifted a plot from the Bible,[†] in theaters so far ahead of Selznick's bloated production that she copped an Oscar for her belle a year ahead of the mentally unbalanced Miss Leigh. Why not us, too?

By the time *Mayfair Madness* had wrapped, the PMS's stable of writers[††] had knocked out a fantastic Civil War script for me, and mine was *original,* as opposed to Selznick's distended turkey, which was hopelessly bound to Miss Mitchell's barbell-disguised-as-a-book. There were roles for everybody—me, Rod, Vincent, Spencer Hooks, Harry Rumpole, Justin Thyme, Brent Wood, Terry Cotta, Delores Delgado (as the *insane* Mary Todd Lincoln, who creeps about the White House at night stabbing minor players), Azure Welles, Wilfred Wyndham, Billy Bowlegs, Jim Dandy, Torrence Del Amo, Buster Hymen, Connie Lundquist, Olivia DeHeffalump, and in their film debuts, the legendary black singer/actress Helena Handbasket and a newcomer from Broadway destined for stardom, the devilishly handsome Guy (pronounced "Ghee," as in Guy de Maupassant) Thanatos. The picture, as I'm sure you've already realized, was the great cinematic Technicolor magnum opus of a great romance endangered by a nation torn apart in Civil War, *East versus West!*

In *East versus West* I played the headstrong plantation heiress Wisteria McGillacuddy. Rod Towers played the noble-hearted scallywag Major Lance Domo. Vincent played the evil, lustful traitor Vermin McSnyde. Brent Wood, as my father, gives my hand, and the rest of me as well, to Vermin in marriage, even though I love the penniless scallywag Major Domo, and then dies of Terminal Plot Complications. Vermin treats me like garbage, and strip-mines our plantation. I'm about to run away with Major Domo when war breaks out between the states. He is drafted by the rebels, and I am swept into the Union WACS. We both have many adventures. At the end of the war, Vermin has framed

[*]A fabulous actress, and one of the *meanest* lesbians I've ever met, but all wrong to play a headstrong man-eater like Scarlett O'Hara.–Tallulah
[†]Terrence read me his three-page summary of the Bible, two pages for the Old Testament, one for the New, and while I found it *deeply* moving and inspirational, it frankly didn't strike me as boffo box office material, and it's all so *dated.*–Tallulah
[††]Not an expression or metaphor. Louie actually kept his writers in a stable out back.–Douglas

Major Domo for murder. He is about to be executed when he escapes. He hides out in a theater, where he can disguise himself. His cry of "Mister President, duck!" saves the life of Abraham Lincoln. President Lincoln pardons him, and Major Domo then frees the slaves, which had slipped Lincoln's mind. The newly freed slaves rise up and kill Vermin, so Major Domo and I can marry and live happily ever after. We raised many an eyebrow with our controversial final line of dialogue: Helena Handbasket, as Sissy, comes running in squealing, "Miss McGillacuddy, de slaves be killing Massa McSnyde!" to which I gave the famous reply, "Frankly, my dear, who gives a rat's ass?"

By far the most spectacular scene in *East versus West* was the thrilling conflagration when General Sherman burns Las Vegas on his march to the sea. Louie burned down everything on the back lot for this scene, including the full-size wooden replica of the Eiffel Tower that Arthur Deco had built back in 1930 for *The Godawful Truth* so we could shoot our Parisian scenes without having to put up with French people. The blaze built into a wild inferno, so fierce that I feared that the stunt doubles playing Rod and me wouldn't get out alive.* They did, though.

Griffith Park wasn't quite so fortunate. When the wooden Eiffel Tower collapsed, it accidentally ignited a brush fire that ended up blackening six hundred acres of the formerly pretty park. It wasn't a total disaster, however. Louie managed to get the blame for the holocaust shifted to a troop of Cub Scouts who were camping in the park at the time, and as they were all lost in the forest fire, they were unable to deny it, thus saving the studio millions in liabilities—money that would ultimately have come out of the pockets of you, the movie-going patron, in the form of higher ticket prices.

Critics were dumbfounded by our romantic historical epic. Bosley Crowther: "In *East versus West* all common sense is gone with the wind!" (Couldn't he have praised us without plugging Selznick's little wannabe movie?) Alexander Woolcott: "If you took all three Marx Brothers, rolled them into one, slapped them in drag and turned them loose on Margaret Mitchell's masterpiece, you'd have Tallulah Morehead in *East versus West*. I haven't laughed this hard in years." *Variety:* "Next to *East versus West*, Tallulah's *The Revenge of Cleopatra* could

---

*Vincent's longtime companion C. Halibut Plugg, who was usually Bette Davis's stunt double, played me in this scene. Olivia DeHeffalump and Helena Handbasket, being only supporting players, did their own stunt work. I'm afraid Olivia got a bit scorched.–Tallulah

stand as a piece of scholarly erudition." The *Hollywood Reporter:* "*East versus West* is, quite simply, the funniest motion picture ever made." *Ladies Home Journal:* "Bring five hankies to *East versus West* because you'll laugh yourself to tears." The *Los Angeles Times:* "It reminded me of entertainment." The *San Francisco Chronicle:* "*East versus West* is the best argument against the First Amendment ever made." The *New York Post:* "*East versus West* is the happiest bloodbath in history. By the end I was shouting with Tallulah, 'The West Shall Rise Again'!" The *Christian Science Monitor:* "*East versus West* is an hour and a half shorter than *Gone with the Wind*. It's also shorter on brains, logic, history, talent, and common sense, but it's long on laughs." With reviews like these, is it any wonder that *East versus West* was my biggest hit yet?

Of course, Selznick spread his money around like manure and got us shut out of the Oscar nominations, but posterity selected us. In 1980 *East versus West* was honored by the National Caucus of Black Film Critics as the First Major Integrated Hollywood Movie in Which the Black People Are Smarter Than the White People.

But the best notice of all came from little Pattycakes, who watched the film with me and announced, "Mommy funny." That was the accolade that closed the thirties on a high note for me. War may have been breaking out all over Europe, Rod may have been keeping a familiar secret from me, I may not have been getting any younger, and Mother may have been remaining relentlessly alive, but only one thing mattered: "Mommy funny."

And one other thing: "Mommy thirsty."

19

Throwing a Rod

Hillbilly Hijinks, my next film after *East versus West,* was a real change of pace for me, an agrarian slice of rural life in which Rod, Vincent, and I had a ball playing feuding hillbilly families.

Billy Bowlegs, who was not aging well, having become a heavy drinker since sound put an end to his stardom twelve years before (as opposed to merely Social Drinking like myself), played my irascible hillbilly father, despite being only four years older than I. It was to be his last motion picture. Though divorced from his third wife and a bit bitter, he never lost his legendary sense of humor. In fact, his death just before the film's release in an inexpensive Hollywood motel room, of what the coroner called "auto-asphyxiation," was actually one last slapstick jape, at least according to the young lady who was with him at the time, a Miss Peaches LaTushie, a "professional date" of no fixed address. According to Peaches, Billy was merely demonstrating the sexual-enhancement qualities of oxygen deprivation with a noose when a discarded banana peel provided one last pratfall, a gag that, ironically, involved actual gagging. Peaches was still wiping away her tears of laughter, and her fingerprints, when the police and the ambulance arrived.

Justin Thyme, Della Ware, Buster Hymen, Olivia DeHeffalump, and Torrence Del Amo were all in *Hillbilly Hijinks,* and contributed to the party atmosphere on the set. There was a good deal of location shooting out in the wilds of Reseda to give that authentic country look to the exteriors.

Nanny Fanny brought Pattycakes out to the location each afternoon so she could spend a little quality time with Mommy. She would be starting school in just a few months, and I wanted to see the little scamp whenever I could pencil her in.

The film dealt with two feuding mountain families, the Windsors and the Saxe-Coburgs, who have been killing each other off for decades for no other reason than Tradition. I played little Annie Windsor, and Rod played Cletus Saxe-Coburg. We fall in love but are forbidden to marry because we're not first cousins.* All the men in my family vow to kill Cletus, and all the women in Cletus's family vow to kill me. At the big county hoedown all the murder attempts go awry one after another. At the end of the movie Cletus and I are the only members of either family left alive and thus can marry and live happily ever after. In an epilogue set several years later Cletus and I share a rueful tear when we hear our sons vow to kill each other, and we realize that our precious family traditions will live on.

Inbreeding and genocide had never been used as the basis for a big studio romantic musical comedy before, but the reaction was a positive one. Richard Rogers later said that after seeing *Hillbilly Hijinks,* he and Oscar Hammerstein decided to "go ahead and write *Oklahoma!* anyway," and *Oklahoma!* is an acknowledged American classic!

My marriage to Rod had been a happy one so far. Rod was a dutiful lover, who did what he was told when he was told to do it, although he showed a certain lack of gung-ho enthusiasm. Rod was still beautiful (he had held on to his looks far better than the late Sherman Oakley had. Could it really already have been thirteen years since Sherman's death?) but he didn't seem to have much sex drive.

The one thing he *was* enthusiastic about was poker. Twice a week he attended all-male poker sessions out at Rooster's Seat with Vincent, C. Halibut Plugg, Bruce Camellia, Arthur Deco, Marcel Pouff, Lance Analvice, Cesar Romero, Guy Thanatos, James Whale, and others, often struggling young actors and dancers. I might have been worried about Rod gambling except that he always seemed to break even, arriving home with the same amount of money he left with, almost as if no bets had been made at all, but what else *could* they have been doing?

Women were strictly verboten. I suggested my dressing up in drag and coming along some week, but Rod turned pale and absolutely re-

---

*You may have noticed that I play someone "forbidden to marry" in a lot of my films. Given my marital track record I often wonder what my life would have been like if I had been forbidden to marry as often in real life as in the movies. Maybe there would have been fewer disasters like, well, the climax of this chapter. But with me divorce never sticks. I always marry again.–Tallulah

fused. These sessions were to get away from the wives,* to play a little cards, or some nude *Twister*,† and have some frank man talk. Sometimes Terrence or Hisato got to come along, so I thought they were stretching the boundaries of "all-male" pretty far, but Rod refused to smuggle me in.

Next I did a big color, show biz musical, *Everyone's Coming Up Rose's,* in which I played Rose, a New York "hostess" who helps struggling young actresses take a load off and put their feet up, making ends meet by making ends meet. Mae West had been offered the script first but had turned it down as "too smutty." I was able to bring it an air of class that glossed over the risqué elements. This was a musical *way* before its time.

I then played in two film noir murder stories in a row: *The Devil Wore Ermine,* in which I played a wealthy femme fatale who lures handsome Justin Thyme into infidelity and murder, followed by *The Mailman Always Comes Twice,* in which I play a waitress femme fatale who lures handsome drifter Rod Towers into murder, infidelity, and more murder. Witty Brent Wood was the victim in the first—Justin threw him off the Empire State Building—and Torrence Del Amo was killed in the second, when Rod and I poisoned his wardrobe, and then, later on, we drowned Buster Hymen, who played a private detective who was blackmailing us.

Following those films I was able to exercise my loanout clause and went to RKO again to make a horror movie, for legendary producer Val Lewton, my first since divorcing dear Boris. The picture we made, *The Curse of the Pussy People,* is highly regarded today for its subtle style of horror. Unlike Universal's more blatant approach, Val liked to suggest the horror indirectly rather than actually show it, achieved in this movie by the cinematographer never lighting my face.

Having worked for several months without Rod at RKO, I decided on the last day of shooting to skip the usual wrap party and headed straight for Morehead Heights, several hours earlier than expected. Pattycakes was in school, Nanny Fanny was asleep, and Major Babs was parking the car as I bounded upstairs, only to find Terrence and

---

*Though, oddly enough, as far as I know, Rod was the only married man there, except occasionally for Charles Farrell, Ernest Thesiger, or Charles Laughton. –Tallulah

†To the best of my researches, the game of *Twister* was not invented until some years later, but maybe they were indulging in some recreational activity that *looked* like *Twister*.–Douglas

Hisato sitting in the hallway outside my bedroom, holding numbers. They saw me, turned pale, and headed downstairs. When I opened my bedroom door, the sight that greeted me is one no wife should have to see.

There was my husband, Rod Towers, and my second ex-husband, Louie B. Thalberg. Neither was dressed, and they weren't having a script conference. In a surprise turnaround, Rod was plucking Louie for once.

There was an ice bucket on a stand beside the bed with an open bottle of champagne in it. I removed the bottle and then emptied the ice and slush all over my rutting spouses. This brought the festivities to a halt. Then I took the bottle downstairs with me for some serious Social Drinking.

So husband number five was yet another *merest whisper,* and apparently husband number two had fully switched teams as well. Was it me? Was it them? Was it me, or them? It's them, isn't it? Is it me? Rod had been able to fool me for five years, as F. Emmett Knight couldn't, because Rod was, at least functionally, a switch hitter, and he was strictly a pitcher, which is too many baseball metaphors to use about a man who hated sports.

Rod moved out that afternoon. Terrence and Hisato were ready to go with him, to the ends of the earth if need be,* but Rod told them to stay with me. Big of him.

After the divorce, I went on making movies with Rod for Louie; business was business. F. Emmett Knight, after all, was still my agent. Rod moved in with Louie. Ten years later, after I'd left PMS, when Louie finally retired, he and Rod moved to San Francisco and bought a house in The Castro together, which they called The Thalberg-Towers. I suppose it's a successful love story. I just wish I wasn't always the other woman, or, in this case, just *the woman.*

The evening of the afternoon I made the discovery, I was sitting downstairs Social Drinking alone while Terrence and Major Babs were out buying me a new mattress when Hisato came running into the room in tears: "Oh Missy Tallulah, it's just awful! Awful!"

"I know, Hisato. I'll miss him. But that's husbands for you. I guess straight men don't get married. Why would they?"

"No, no, Missy Tallulah, not that. Pearl Harbor! Pearl Harbor bombed!"

---

*You don't suppose that they, my loyal staff members, had . . . No! That's *Unthinkable!*–Tallulah

"That may be so, Hisato, but I didn't appear in *Pearl Harbor* so why should I care?"

"No, no. My English wrong. Pearl Harbor *is* bombed!"

"Who is Pearl Harbor, and why should I care if she's bombed? In case you haven't noticed, I'm pretty well bombed myself."

"No, no, Missy Tallulah, Pearl Harbor isn't a who, it's a where!"

"What?"

"Pearl Harbor in Hawaii. Japan, my Japan, has bombed Pearl Harbor!"

"What *are* you going on about, Hisato?"

"Japan has attacked America! We're at war!"

"Perfect, Hisato. The perfect end to the perfect day. Do we have any gin?"

20

War, War, War!

We're Privates on Display.
We're marching by,
Heads thrust up high,
Winking our eye.
We're Privates on Display
We penetrate,
To consummate,
A tete-a-tete.
So give yourself A major thrill.
Just take a seat, And watch us drill.
We're Privates on Display.

Lyrics to Privates on Display, by Ebb & Flo

December 7th, 1941, a day that will live in infamy: the day two of my now ex-husbands teamed up to betray me. By coincidence, it was also the start of a tiresome war. You may remember the war. It was in all the papers, and I think they made a movie about it.

Louie, now completely out of the closet and insisting on being called "Lydia," showed his/her sublime sense of humor by casting Rod and me immediately in another movie together. Ironically, the picture is perhaps the most popular film I ever made, the morale-boosting armed forces musical *Privates on Display.*

I'm sure all of you people reading this book have seen *Privates on Display* a least a few times. In fact, I'm hoping to see *Privates on Display* again myself, later this evening. There are certain cable channels that seem to show *Privates on Display* every night, although it's hell to try to watch through all that silly scrambling. Wherever I performed in cabaret over the last few years there was no question what everyone enjoyed seeing the most. "What do you want to see?" I'd ask, and they'd always yell back, "*Privates on Display!*" or words meaning the same thing.

I had another hit song in this picture, the score this time by the fabulously successful Broadway tunesmiths Bryan Ebb and Douglas Flo, the rousing march encouraging posture and deportment, *Stand Tall and Erect.*

Stand tall and erect,
And you'll command respect.
When on patrol or on the march,
Show the world you're full of starch.
I never would reject,
A man who is erect.

Lyrics to Stand Tall and Erect

Along with Rod, the cast also included Justin Thyme, Buster Hymen, Torrence Del Amo, and newcomers Chad Shivers, Max Donald, and Cal Olson as the aforementioned privates; Olivia DeHeffalump, Helena Handbasket, Ursula Majors, Rose Withers, and Connie Lundquist as the girls who love privates; Harry Rumpole as the gruff drill sergeant; Vincent Lovecraft as the evil and lustful base commander; and me as *myself!* This was the first time I ever played me, a role I felt really stretched my acting boundaries and showed my versatility. Indeed, I was a *tour-de-force* role for me!

The story concerned how the raw privates keep themselves up and at attention, anticipating the forthcoming visit of the great film star Tallulah Morehead to view the privates as they drill all over the parade grounds, reminding the boys of just what they're fighting for.

In the climactic parade grounds sequence, I sang my big morale-boosting number:

Stand tall and erect.
Just do as I direct.
For when your pride is in your hand,
You'll find a way to beat the band
Do not be circumspect,*
Just simply stand erect.

---

*Actually, there's nothing wrong with being circumspect, darling. Some of my best friends are Jewish.–Tallulah

Stand tall and erect,
And you can call collect.
And all your letters will be read,
If your pencil's full of lead.
You'll never know neglect,
If you're a man erect.

Stand tall and erect,
And I will genuflect.
Because I deeply love to see,
A man who can stand "up" to me.
If ever you're spot-checked,
Make sure that you're erect.

The men respond lustily and, for the big production number finale, march about the parade grounds, drilling like crazy, singing back to me:

We're Privates on Display,
Our potent smiles,
And rigid style,
Stick out a mile.
We're Privates on Display,
No chaperones,
In combat zones,
Just the bare bones.
We feel that we've got nothing to hide.
To show off makes us swell with pride.
We're Privates on Display,

Our loyalty's unswerving,
Our devotion's never forged.
It only takes one glance from you,
To keep our pride engorged.

We're Privates on Display,
Don't you agree,
We're great to see,
Or ask to tea?
In all your dreams we are the root,
Just cock our guns and watch us shoot
We're Privates on Display.

Then I made a stirring patriotic speech, finally ending with, "Hitler, Hirohito, Mussolini, can't we all just get along? No? Then eat American steel, fascist swine!"

This incredible patriotic display of two thousand privates, all marching about, tall and erect, in salute to me, singing lustily as they drill their brains out, led to such an overwhelming climax that it sent audiences sprinting from theaters directly into recruiting offices. FDR stated that I had done more to make men want to leave America for war zones than any other individual. When the movie was released, banner headlines proclaimed, "Watch out, Hitler! Here comes Tallulah!" while Pete Moss came up with one more inspired slogan before retiring: "They can kill you, but they can't kill a song!"

At Morehead Heights the war was a disrupting experience as well. Major Babs wanted to reenlist at once but, as she was well past seventy, no army was going to take her, no matter how male they thought she was. Babs went grouchily about the house for the next three and a half years, endlessly complaining that "people are killing each other all over the world and *I'm missing out on it!*"

Terrence was devastated. His beloved Yorkie, Felicia, had died in a fight with a neighborhood cat. I complained to the kitty's owner, but trying to convince a seven-year-old girl to put her vicious twelve-week-old kitten to sleep is a losing game. Finally, after the sociopathic little moppet had run to Daddy in tears, wailing that "the ugly witch from the scary house wants to kill Snowball!" her father told me to leave. I hopped on my bicycle (part of my new healthy exercise regimen) with the basket I'd tied on the back end to carry the little hellcat off to the pound, and pedaled away, hearing the father call after me, "Who's your role model? Margaret Hamilton?" I have no idea *what* he meant by that!

But it was my Japanese houseboy Hisato who suffered the worst outrage during the war. One of the most shameful pages in all of American history concerns our treatment of Japanese-Americans during World War II. Hisato, loyal and harmless, but born in Tokyo, was not spared. Not long after *Privates on Display* was released there came a knock at the door of Morehead Heights. They had come for my servant. I was at the studio, shooting a delightful screwball comedy called *The Lady Steve,* in which I disguised myself as a male, for the first time on film, for the brilliant comedic genius writer/director Preston Sturgeon. Poor Hisato was dragged off against his will, wailing, crying, and begging all the way, and taken to Metro-Goldwyn-Mayer, where he was held incommunicado until the summer of 1945 and forced to play villains in numerous patriotic war films. In fact, over the next three and a half years, Hisato appeared in more movies than *I* did! Oh, the inhuman horrors of war!

After *Privates on Display,* I made only two other movies in 1942: The aforementioned *The Lady Steve,* a screwball classic that started the rumors that persist, irrationally, to this day that I am actually a man in drag,* and then, on loanout to Selznick, the first of my two films with mega-genius Alfred Hitchcock, *Life Preserver.* The rest of my time was taken up with my war efforts, about which, more shortly.

Life Preserver was one of Hitch's fascinating experiments in suspense. The whole picture was shot in a tank out in Culver City. I played an heiress clinging to a single life preserver in the midst of the ocean after a German U-boat had torpedoed the luxury liner in which I was crossing the Atlantic. Also clinging to this single life preserver was a common coal stoker from our engine room who spouted communist jargon, played by hunky Patric Knowles, whom my character falls in love with; his sidekick, a gigantic retarded man of enormous strength played by Creighton Chaney, now using his father's name professionally; a sweet war widow who was nine months pregnant and gives birth at the climax of the movie; a black waiter who had graduated from Stanford with honors and knows more than any of the white people he has to take orders from;† a munitions manufacturer who was getting rich off the war, played by Lionel Barrymore;†† a pathetic war orphan played by darling little Roddy McDowell, whom I made a man of in his dressing room one afternoon while a leak was patched on the set;§ Adolph Hitler, pretending to be a Frenchman who had fallen overboard off his submarine when it torpedoed us; the ship's orchestra; and the Mormon

---

*I do not begin to understand this. Literally *thousands* of people have witnessed the incontrovertible evidence of my feminine gender with their own eyes, and other organs. Just my luck to have had lovers who were *excessively* discreet!–Tallulah

†Since this actor, named Dick Packer, like the rest of us, was soaking wet throughout the shoot, I can tell you that he was an actor of *tremendous dimensions.* Unfortunately, he was one of the sixty-three men in America who are wholly faithful to their wives. Bummer!–Tallulah

††*Not* the man his brother was. Sadly, dear brother John passed away during the shoot.–Tallulah

§For the rest of his life dear, unbelievably well-endowed Roddy (never did an actor have a more appropriate name) credited *me* with finalizing his gender preference! That's Star-Class gratitude for you, although, oddly, he never came back for seconds, apparently preferring to treasure the memory of our tender, frenzied, two minutes together unsullied by the risk of a less-than-perfect rematch. *Au revoir, mon enfant!*–Tallulah

Tabernacle Choir. Hitchcock made his obligatory cameo appearance as a corpse floating past us in the wreckage. This was the second movie I made in which I was wet throughout the entire picture.*

The reason I made only three films that year was that I was caught up in the war effort. At first I thought to join the Hollywood Canteen, until I learned that all we were supposed to do was *dance* with the heroic servicemen who were about to face death to make the world safe from German Expressionism. I knew, from my extensive experiences entertaining soldiers in the last big war, that a raw recruit facing battle really needs something more personal and satisfying.

I was almost despairing as to how to render my "special services" for our brave fighting men when who should reenter my life but Antoine, the one-time proprietor of Antoine's Night School, where I'd very nearly become a teacher twenty-seven years before, until fate, in the form of Lydia B. Thalberg, intervened and Motion Picture History became my major. Antoine, now in his fifties, but still a fine figure of a man, except for several facial scars—the results of "competitive business practices," as Antoine put it—was opening his own near-charity servicemen's entertainment center called Antoine's Canteen, and he invited me to become the official celebrity hostess, knowing that I was synonymous with happy soldiers.

Since Morehead Heights was on the coast, indeed penetrating deep into the moist Pacific, I felt that to keep Pattycakes safe from Japanese air attacks it was wisest to ship—I mean send—her off to boarding school inland. Pattycakes always loved horses so I enrolled her in Rodeo Rhetta's Boarding Ranch for Girls, where "No Cowgirl Ever Gets the Blues," in Arizona. Consequently, I was free to devote myself to America's fighting men. Nanny Fanny went on to other Hollywood children.

Antoine's Canteen was a movable feast. We would set up shop in rented quarters near a military base, entertain the boys for a few weeks, and then move on to another base. Army, Navy, Air Force, Marines, we didn't favor any branch over any other. Any enlisted man with a twinkle in his eye and a ten-spot in his pocket was welcome.

Of course, I wasn't as young as I'd been during the last war as some critics seemed to feel duty-bound to unnecessarily point out in review after review, but, in my defense, I'd like to point out that *no one else was, either!* Absolutely everyone still alive in 1942 that had been alive in

---

*Which was the first one, you ask? We're not telling, but send your best guesses to "Damp Tallulah Contest, c/o Morehead Heights, Los Angeles, CA." The first postmarked correct answer will win *Life After Death*.–Douglas

1918 was twenty-four years older than they had been, and I don't see why I should be singled out for criticism! I certainly wore my age better than most, thanks to my health and beauty regimen and Marcel Pouff.

Most of the girls who worked with me were far younger, yet there was no shortage of servicemen who preferred to be entertained by a seasoned and long-experienced entertainer such as myself who knew and had perfected ways of entertaining a man that the younger girls had not dreamt of in their wildest erotic nightmares. Throughout the whole of 1942 and 1943, whenever I wasn't shooting a picture, I entertained thousands of young conscripts, easing their fears, raising their morale, and taking their loads from them. The boys may have had pictures of Betty Grable in their lockers, may have seen Lucille Ball or Frances Langford on an improvised stage from a distance, but from Tallulah Morehead they got the kind of Hands-On treatment that put a smile on their face and a stain on their record.

In 1943 I made only three films, as I had the year before, to keep as much time as possible free for the more rewarding and fulfilling patriotic work of helping American servicemen rise to the occasion of defending basic freedoms, like free speech, Social Drinking, and promiscuous sex. And the defenders of Liberty voted me "Miss Take Liberties" of 1943.

The first of the movies I made that year was our follow-up to *Privates on Display*, the charming naval musical *Anchors Akimbo,* in which I sang the popular, jaunty sea-chanty known only as "The Sailor Song":

Some like a soldier from the infantry,
Some prefer an airman, that's their plea.
But though I'm proud of every vet,
I like a man who gets me wet.
Give me A Little Seaman,
That's for me.

Lyrics to *The Sailor Song*, by Ebb & Flo

Wilfred Wyndham, Justin Thyme, and Rod Towers played three sailors with shore leave, gobs discharged from their frigate, salty seamen spurting forth to flood New York City with their special essence. Olivia DeHeffalump, Ellafitz Willie,* and I play the women they meet who

---

*Primarily a world-class blues singer, Ellafitz Willie was a delight, and so perfectly named. I hate to tell tales out of school, but Ella fits in as many Willies as possible at every opportunity.–Tallulah

show them a good time before sending them off to war. My art was reflecting my life.

A Little Seaman can make me smile.
His inner demon, I'll try to rile.
If he's a he-man, I'll walk a mile.
For when a seaman has done a good job,
You'll know at last why they call him a "gob!"

Some will go to luncheon with the Cavalry,
And dine late with Marines who have some pull.
But here's one thing I must confess:
I like to eat in the sailor's mess.
Give me A Little Seaman,
And I'm full.

Preston Sturgeon directed *Anchors Akimbo,* and Hermes Hyde staged and directed the musical numbers. The popular musical performers Helena Handbasket, Taxi Thataway, Wolfgang Mozart,* and Fats Ellington and his White Guys That Sound Black all performed guest musical numbers. Franklin Nancyboy played the hilariously effeminate fellow that the sailors keep running into and beating up, climaxing in the charmingly merry and violent musical number, *Rolling Fairies in the Park,* recently declared the most offensive song ever written by GLAAD. Given that two of the men singing the number, the choreographer staging it, and the two men who wrote it were all themselves the *merest whisper,* it must stand as a sterling example of just how far some Hollywood people were willing to go in selling out their own people to pass. And let's not forget that the movie was produced by Lydia B. Thalberg.

A Little Seaman, a naval hunk.
He is the key man, if he's no monk.
He's just a free man, who's full of spunk.
Obtaining your seaman will not make you frown.
Just shiver his timber and blow the man down.

---

*I have *no* idea who or what Tallulah imagines by including this name in the cast, but I'm *certain* that Mozart had been dead for *a very long time* before movies were even invented! He is almost definitely *not* in *Anchors Akimbo.*–Douglas

So if you party on a base or landing strip,
Please don't invite me. I would rather rot!
The air force simply leaves me numb.
For navy men I'll always come,
To where a little seaman marks the spot.
He won't hold back his naval flow,
Like Moby Dick, he's sure to blow,
And give me A Little Seaman, . . . or a LOT!

After *Anchors Akimbo* and a couple of months touring with Antoine's Canteen, I returned to Selznick to make my second and last movie with Hitchcock. Critics had declared Hitch and me to be "the scariest combo since Karloff and Lugosi," and Hitch liked me. (I was blond, after all.) The film was the romantic psychological thriller *Amnesia*. I played a woman with no memory who doesn't know if she's murdered her husband or not. Gregory Peck played my doctor, who believes I'm innocent and is trying to unlock my memories. Jimmy Stewart is the detective who thinks I'm guilty and doesn't care if I remember or not, just so I fry for the crime. Of course, it turns out that all three of us have amnesia; I've forgotten that I'm innocent, Jimmy Stewart has forgotten that he's in love with me, and Gregory Peck has forgotten that he *is* my husband and hasn't been murdered at all. Peck then thinks that *he's* the murderer, even though there is no murderer, because he hasn't been murdered, so he becomes afraid that when I get my memory back I'll accuse him of murdering him, so he tries to murder me, and Jimmy has forgotten to try to save me. At the climax there's a big chase all over Washington, and I end up dangling from the top of the Washington Monument until everybody remembers that no crime was ever committed and that we're all just being silly.

The critics, who normally loved Hitch, weren't all that crazy about *Amnesia*. "Gives new meaning to 'pointless' " wrote *Variety*. "*Amnesia* is unforgettably forgettable." wrote the *Hollywood Reporter*, while the *Los Angeles Times* wrote, "A murder mystery with no murder and too much plot, *Amnesia* shows that even the great Alfred Hitchcock can go a little psycho sometimes. Watching the notorious Tallulah Morehead get so spellbound in her role as a woman who can't remember that there isn't anything to remember that it drives her into a frenzy, left me with vertigo. Audiences should give this turkey the birds."

My last 1943 movie was *Single Indemnity*, a film noir in which there *was* a murder. Rod and I commit the perfect murder when we kill Sam Francisco for the insurance money, only it turns out that he isn't dead, and he and Rod are trying to kill me for another insurance settlement. I let them think they've succeeded and collect the second settlement (apparently we were both insured against being murdered), then I murder both of them and take all the money, only to get killed by Justin Thyme as the insurance investigator, who then takes the money and skips to Rio.

Shortly after finishing shooting on *Single Indemnity* in April of 1943, the governor, still fearful of a Japanese attack on the California coast, declared a statewide blackout. Being a law-abiding Movie Star and Nearly Living Legend, I complied.

When I regained consciousness it was August of 1945, the war was in its last few moments, and I was in Fresno! It turned out that I'd been working the last six months as a girl's high school gym teacher in this arid, raisin-growing Hellhole.

They were happy to see me back at Morehead Heights, from which I'd been missing for just over two years. We immediately called little Pattycakes out at Rodeo Rhetta's (Though Pattycakes was nine years old by now, and growing like a weed, already taller than I) to let her know I was all right. Of the time between when I'd disappeared from Morehead Heights and when I started teaching girl's P.E. in Fresno, nothing was ever learned.

An odd thing has happened to me over the years since. Every once in a while, I will meet a total stranger who claims to have known me during the war. In and of itself this isn't all that strange. After all, I must have been *somewhere* during that lost period and almost undoubtedly was around other people. What is odd is they inevitably ask me about my "husband." Further, some of them remember my husband as being named Phil, others refer to him as Douglas,* while still others have asked me about a Brendan. The evidence clearly suggests that I was married again, at least once, possibly two, or even three times during this blackout. It was at this point in my life that I lost count of just how many times I've been married. I'm not being coy—though I do look *adorable* when I am being coy—I really don't know how many marriages I've had. Is that so unusual? I suppose you know how many times *you've* been married.

Which brings me to a plea to my older male readers out there: **PLEASE, IF YOU WERE EVER MARRIED TO ME AT ANYTIME, THOUGH ESPECIALLY DURING THE FINAL TWO YEARS OF WORLD WAR II, AND ARE NOT MENTIONED IN THIS BOOK,**

---

*Not me! I have a perfect alibi. I wasn't born until 1950.–Douglas

OR EVEN IF YOU ARE MENTIONED, BUT NOT AS ONE OF MY HUSBANDS, PLEASE CONTACT ME IMMEDIATELY AT MOREHEAD HEIGHTS, CALIFORNIA.

There was one very sad thing to learn when I returned to my life: during my blackout Mother had passed away. It was a sobering lesson to learn, which is the worst kind—to realize that because of my extended blackout my mother had died and *I wasn't there to enjoy it!* What a staggering disappointment! I had looked forward to Mother's inevitable demise for most of my life, the way a child anticipates Christmas, and I had missed out. In my absence, Major Babs had had Mother cremated and scattered at sea, so there wasn't even a grave on which I could dance. Curse these blackouts! In all my very long life, no doctor has ever been able to accurately diagnose the cause of them. They remain a mystery to this day.*

Amidst the joy of V-J Day was the special exultation of knowing that dear Hisato would soon return to his rightful place here at Morehead Heights, where he was sorely missed. Terrence, Major Babs, and the headless Indian brave had tried their best, but frankly, the house was a mess.

However, to my surprise and horror, it was not to be. Hisato, though released and free once more, refused to come back to the bosom of our little family, where he was loved, at least occasionally, especially if Rod visited. But now it seemed that, since he won that Oscar for Best Supporting Actor, he was *too good* to scrub my toilets! That's the kind of ingratitude one comes to expect in Hollywood!

I suppose it was just as well. Hisato used to use the leaf blower to dust. The fumes were so strong that even I could smell them, and the noise was enough to wake the dead. That isn't just hyperbole. When Hisato got that leaf blower going in the house, that was the only time I ever saw the headless Indian brave in the daytime, his hands clamped over his neck-stump.

But, for now, I was home, and ready to return to work at PMS. Little did I know that a major change of life lurked just ahead for me. My PMS period was about to end.

*Well, a few doctors *have* suggested a cause for my blackouts, but these men were so off-base as to be laughable. Every once in a while one of these quacks will insanely hypothesize that I suffer from *alcoholic blackouts!* Have you ever heard anything more absurd? How many times must I say it? I am *not* an alcoholic! I am merely a Social Drinker, no different than John Barrymore, Lillian Roth, W. C. Fields, or you, gentle reader! And, judging from the evidence of my blacked-out marriage or marriages, these were Social Blackouts.–Tallulah

21

No More PMS!

My first film back at PMS was the exciting desert romance *Sudan Sunset*. I played Melanoma, the simple Island Princess. ("Kiss? What means this strange word 'Kiss'?") The gorgeous young Indian actor who had made such a splash in Alexander Korda's exotic adventures, Tabu, was my adorable leading man, and I was absolutely delighted, and enormously impressed, when I found out what earned him his nickname "Elephant Boy."

Lydia B. Thalberg seemed to be economizing after the war. The gigantic, expensive PMS films I'd done in the teens, twenties, thirties, and forties were now a thing of the past. Yet *Sudan Sunset*, a silly blend of sand, scimitars, camels, turbans, and music, made on a shoestring, was one of my most popular movies.

In the most famous scene, I am seen leaning against a tent flap, singing plaintively to the moon, my voice rising to such a howl of anguish that dogs have been known to howl back blocks from the theater, a phenomenon that is still reported today by people playing *Sudan Sunset* on videocassette.

Sudan Sunset was such a success that there was immediate pressure to reteam Tabu and me in another exotic adventure at once, as we had tremendous romantic chemistry, despite the *slight* difference in our ages.* Unfortunately, Tabu was under exclusive contact to Universal, who had loaned him out in trade for Lydia loaning them Wilfred

---

*Tabu was born in India around the time Tallulah was shooting *Eskimo Pie* in Alaska, which makes him, at the time of his two films with Tallulah, a year younger than Tallulah was when she made her film debut thirty years before. This is what Tallulah calls a *slight* age difference.–Douglas

Wyndham to warble with the ever-oppressive Deanna Durbin in their musical-horror movie *Three Smart Mouths,* in which they both appeared with my former houseboy Hisato, who, now freed from playing sadistic villains, was free to demonstrate his remarkable singing voice, actually hitting notes a third higher than Miss Durbin could manage, which is why he made only the one film with her before being banished to working with Sonja Henie, which is punishment enough for *any* crime!

Lydia, as it turned out, was only too happy to loan me out to Universal, despite having only gotten one movie from me in over two years. Universal, who had underutilized me when I'd worked there ten years before, cutting me out of *Edgar Allen Poe's The Black Pussy* altogether, now decided to go in the other direction and overutilize me this time out, allowing me a personal tour de force by playing identical triplets, one good, one evil, and one wishy-washy, in the wild jungle adventure *Siren of the Congo.*

The cast of *Siren of the Congo,* along with Tabu and myself, included Turhan Bey, Maria Cortez, Douglas Dumbelle, Edgar Barricade, and my old costar Creighton Chaney, now known solely as Lon Chaney, Junior. The picture was written by the brilliant Curt Siodmak, who wrote the classic science fiction/horror novel *Donovan's Brain,* and its even scarier sequel, *Tallulah's Liver,* which he graciously dedicated to me. The film was directed by Curt's brother, Robert Siodmak, who directed such classics as *Son of Dracula, Cobra Woman, The Crimson Pirate,* and *The Spiral Staircase.*

Curt and Robert had both escaped from Germany, something I had done myself well before they had, but the experience had not bonded them together; these two had the worst case of sibling rivalry this side of Joan Fontaine and Olivia DeHavilland. Every day on the set they were bitch-slapping each other, as Robert rewrote Curt's script, and Curt gave backseat direction to the cast and crew.

Sadly, the picture was not a success despite a spectacular climax involving a volcanic eruption (utilizing stock footage from *Virgins of Krakatoa),* and the blame must be laid at Robert's door. He insisted Tabu wear a shirt for the first time in his career, and it concealed his talent. Plans to team Tabu and me a third time in *The Whores of Babylon* were scrapped, and Maria Cortez ended up making that picture with Turhan Bey.

Back at PMS, Lydia had a picture all ready to go before the cameras, the sequel to the incredibly popular *Privates on Display.* This movie was about the soldiers all coming home from the war and readjusting to civilian life. I played myself again, even more of a stretch than my Oscar-worthy turn as the triplets of *Siren of the Congo*, who personally welcomes the privates back and rewards each one for his outstanding heroism.

The film, as you've guessed by now, was *Privates in Public*, and lightning did not strike twice. *Variety* wrote, "*Privates in Public* is indecent exposure with songs. Tallulah Morehead fails to play herself convincingly. Apparently, she is now outside her own range." The public must have agreed, because the flick did no business.

The always fiery Ida Lupino and I teamed up next, as two tough broads kicking butt in the big city in the rough melodrama *Amok!* Ida was a woman after my own heart, a real professional whose potential reached far beyond what women were confined to in those days. In Ida's case, this would soon lead to directing, just as, in my case, it led to championship Social Drinking. The rumors that swept Hollywood of our having a torrid affair, however, are almost certainly mistaken. If I'd laid a finger on Ida at that point in time, Hattie McDaniel would have broken my arm. That woman was possessive! Even Major Babs, who was rapidly approaching eighty, was afraid of Hattie when she was "het up."

Amok! was also my last picture with my ex-husband Rod Towers, who was just five years away from retiring from acting, though the critics intimated that his performance suggested he already had.

Although *Amok!* had been a modest hit, Lydia seemed somehow disenchanted with me, more so even than when we divorced. My next two pictures were both loanouts, first to Twentieth Century Fox for the splashy Technicolor shipboard musical *The Gang's All Banged* with Don Ameche, Betty Grable, and Carmen Miranda,* then to Paramount, where I subbed for an ailing Dorothy Lamour with Bob Hope and Bing Crosby† in their laugh-packed comedy classic *The Road to Hell*.

I returned to PMS in the early spring of 1947 to make *An Ordeal to Remember,* a title that would better suit the next few months of my life. This grueling adventure melodrama was to be my last PMS picture. When the movie completed shooting I was summoned to Lydia's office.

"Tallulah, my darling, my one-time love, we've had a long run together, haven't we?"

"Well, Lydia," I replied warily, "that depends on what you mean by 'long.' "

---

*Yes, all the rumors you've heard about dear Carmen Miranda are true!–Tallulah
†Yes, all the rumors you've heard about Bob Hope and Bing Crosby are true! –Tallulah

"Well, in this case, Tallulah, by 'long' I mean thirty-two years, the thirty-two years since *The Lost Recess* and *Heat Crazed!*"

"It hasn't been that long."

"Yes, it has."

"All right, for *you* it's been thirty-two years. For me it's rather less time than that. After all, I shouldn't have to count the periods of black-out. And just look me in the eye and tell me I look even an hour older than I did when I started out."

Lydia looked me in the eye and said, "You don't look an hour older than when you started here. You look a *century* older!"

"I beg your pardon!"

"Then there are your aforementioned alcoholic blackouts, which are increasing in frequency and duration."

"I've never had an *alcoholic* blackout in my life! My last one was a Patriotic Blackout, ordered by the governor as part of the war civil defense effort."

"Tallulah, as your friend and ex-husband," Lydia went on, insanely, "I tell you that I believe you are suffering from alcoholism and need to seek help."

"Lydia, as your ex-wife and employee, I can assure you that I am strictly a Social Drinker. I do *not* suffer from alcoholism; in fact, I don't see how you could call that 'suffering' at all. If anything, I suffer from Socialism. I'm not an alcoholic, I'm a Socialist!"

"What you are not, Tallulah, is my employee any longer."

"What?"

"I'm dropping the option on your contract. I'm letting you go. In short, you don't work here anymore."

"You can't be serious! I'm your biggest star! I'm synonymous with PMS! This studio would be a bloody mess without me snugly in place!"

"No more. The simple fact is that I have no roles for a leading lady who is . . ."

Lydia finished his sentence but I can not pollute this page with the lie he spoke. Let us just say he mentioned what he believed my age to be. I won't repeat the ridiculous figure he mentioned, I'll just say it had a "5" in it. Somehow he had added together the eighteen I'd been when I made the original *Heat Crazed!* and the thirty-two years he mistakenly believed had passed since then, and come up with an extravagant, completely insane, wildly inaccurate age for me! And he was using this fiction, coupled with his delusions about my so-called drinking, as an excuse for letting me go. For the first time since high school I was un-employed, a free agent, at liberty, able to take up the dozens of imploring offers from the other studios that F. Emmett Knight had so far kept from me, as I'd been unavailable. Well, Tallulah Morehead was available now; in fact, I was downright easy.

Or I was until I stepped outside the studio gates for the last time. No sooner had I stepped past the guard's booth then I found myself abruptly handcuffed and manhandled into a waiting police car. I was under arrest! The next day the headlines on every newspaper in the country trumpeted the incredible, extremely unjustified charges that had been leveled against me. Since the charges against me, all completely bogus, are well known to all Americans and have been endlessly rehashed in every history of, and documentary on, the famous legal scandals of Hollywood, I will not further their spread by repeating them here. Certainly, all the slimy, lying details of the charges on which I was tried can be found in the published accounts of my trial, along with the trials of Fatty Arbuckle, Errol Flynn, Charlie Chaplin, Lana Turner's daughter, and O. J. Simpson, and, like all of them, I was innocent!

In Hollywood, however, every rumor is always true unless proved otherwise, everyone is guilty until proved innocent, and to prove myself innocent of the obscene charges against me, I was going to have to stand trial!

PART FOUR

Morehead for Everybody!
1947–1958

22

My Kampf!

The People of the State of California v. Miss Tallulah Morehead, the Nearly Living Legend was, without question, *the* most heavily publicized celebrity trial up to that time. Court Radio carried the entire trial live, gavel to gavel, on the air to a gigantic national audience attracted by the sensationalism of the lurid, and let me again add, totally unfounded, charges.

This was not my first appearance on radio, far from it. Radio was terribly easy "work." You went in, read the script out loud, received your check, and went home. It didn't matter how you looked, which cut my time in makeup from (by 1947) three hours to a mere ninety minutes. You could come in after a party or a romantic evening, or even during one, disheveled and hung over, and it didn't matter. Of course, they occasionally had studio audiences, but they were let in free so they deserved what they got. The hardest part usually was focusing my eyes enough to read the script. Even there, if I made a mistake reading the script, the other actors would "improvise," and we went on, often improving the scripts tremendously in the process.* The great thing about

---

*For instance, I played a woman named Desdemona in a nearly incomprehensible, musty radio script called *Othello* opposite Paul Robeson once. The dialogue was written in the most high-falutin', pretentious poetic garbage I've ever had to wade through, and it was *endless!* Robeson was awesome, of course, and also very good in the play, but what a yawner. I had to paraphrase most of my lines as I went along, as no one could ever follow this pseudo-English gobbledygook. I helped the play enormously, not only by simplifying my lines but by skipping whole unnecessary scenes. And then there was the ending! The hack who wrote this trash had written a terrible downer of an ending. I improved it, to the amazement of the rest of the cast, by ad-libbing a scene at the end where Desdemona wakes up. "Othello dar-

performing live was the complete absence of that do-it-over-until-we-get-it-right attitude that makes movies so tiresome to shoot.

There was, however, to be no script for my trial. It was to be completely improvised. I didn't really think this was wise, as the stakes were so extremely high, but my legal team said this was how it was done now. *Fully* scripted trials in Los Angeles were *almost* a thing of the past.

Mason Dixon, my lawyer of many years, was basically a civil lawyer, at least he was always very civil to me, but considering the enormity and the monstrousness of the absolutely untrue charges leveled against me, he felt I would need a top-flight criminal defense attorney if I was to escape the legal consequences staring me in the face. Clarence Darrow was retired or dead or something, anyway he was unavailable. Perry Mason, it turned out, was fictional. (Who knew?) I felt that this was hardly a large objection, as my defense was primarily fictional as well, but Dixon insisted that I have a living lawyer.*

My suggestion was that we hire Spencer Tracy or Ronald Coleman to play my lawyer, as they would be convincing, sound great on the radio, and the jury would love them. Who wouldn't believe Spencer Tracy or Ronald Coleman? But Mason Dixon, stick-in-the-mud that he

---

ling, I'm not dead at all. I knew you didn't mean it, you big hunk of hot jungle love. Cassio meant nothing to me. It was a momentary lapse. Come, make wild tribal love to me, you mountain of African Passion!" The director complained afterward that not only had I "ruined" the ending by returning to life, but I had confessed to an affair Desdemona hadn't had. "Desdemona never slept with Cassio." He claimed, "Iago made it up." "Well," I answered, "How the hell would I know that? The script isn't very clear. What's wrong with the woman? If she didn't even have an affair, then the whole play is *pointless!*" He railed back that some dead guy would be "shaking a spear" at me or something. I would merely point now to the rave reviews I received: "Tallulah Morehead's performance as Desdemona on *Dignified Radio Classics* last night, in what was undoubtedly the funniest *Othello* of all time, would probably make the Immortal Bard glad he's dead!" I would add, in conclusion, that without my improvements, that play would have been a *tragedy!* –Tallulah

*The fact is that fictional characters are discriminated against in our society almost as badly as dead people are. Having played many fictional characters in my long career, I feel very close to fictional people. Indeed, many of my closest friends are complete fictions. I have participated in myriad fictional benefits and charities, including *Fictional Relief,* the annual fictional fund-raiser organized by Sherlock Holmes, Princess Ozma, and Superman. Thanks to our efforts, fictional people are now allowed to own corporations and property, hold elective office, and, in Cook County, Illinois, to vote, a right we also secured for the dead. In recognition of my efforts on the behalf of fictional people I have been named an "Honorary Fictional Character." Or was the word "Honorable"? Well, no matter.–Tallulah

was, insisted on my using a *real* lawyer. Even after all this time, Mason didn't seem to understand how things worked in Hollywood.

Eventually I hired the famous criminal attorney Jerry Mander, a tall, charismatic man, whose professional motto was "I *Will* Get You Off!" So inspired was I by this man, his methods, and morals, that I have, ever since, adopted his motto as my own.

At Jerry's insistence I was wearing a modest and tasteful zebra-striped suit with a high neckline and matching turban in court. Jerry also insisted that my family, such as it was, be there every day, so Pattycakes, who, at thirteen was already six foot three, was yanked out of Rodeo Rhetta's to attend the trial along with Major Babs, who, now past eighty, had dropped her Illinois Smith persona for a general old-person, genderless androgyny, and Terrence, whose gender was also something of a guessing game to those meeting him for the first time.

The vicious prosecutor determined to rake me through the mud was a shyster named Hamilton Jefferson. We naturally immediately suggested simply dismissing all the trumped-up charges. I wouldn't print his reply, even if I could spell it.

The disgusting charges against me were, of course, front-page news in every newspaper in America for months, as well as analyzed in depth in Humphrey Brigand's best-selling account, *When Justice Was Glad to Be Blind: The Trial of Tallulah Morehead, The Nearly Living Legend*, published in 1950. They were also explored at length in the trial transcript, which was published soon after the trial ended and has gone through 114 printings. As both books are still in print, I see no need to tiresomely rehash that garbage on the pristine pages of my lovely book. There is really no point anyway, as I was completely exonerated and the charges were utterly disproven.*

The first issue to be dealt with was my constitutionally guaranteed right to a trial by a "jury of my peers." Jerry Mander successfully argued that not only was the usual jury mix of overweight housewives; semi-deaf, elderly, retired persons, and hard-core unemployables not my peer group, but they were people I wouldn't normally deign to speak to if I ran over them on the highway, beyond handing them an autographed picture. The judge, Justice Roy Legume, agreed, and the jury empaneled to consider my case consisted of Joan Crawford, Norma Shearer, Olivia DeHavilland, Tallulah Bankhead (that *copycat!*), Marlene Deitrich, Yvonne DeCarlo, Clark Gable, Jimmy Stewart, James Cagney, Robert Mitchum (a terrible distraction to have in the court-

---

*No, they weren't, and no, she wasn't.–Douglas

room, he's so dreamy), Brian Donlevy (not really my peer, he's more of a character actor, but I agreed to a little compromise there), and Cary Grant.

Then came the insulting opening statements. I refer to the record:

Jefferson: The prosecution will prove that Miss Tallulah Morehead, the so-called Nearly Living Legend . . .

Morehead: I object!

Legume: You can't object. That's your lawyer's job.

Morehead: So? Object!

Mander: To what?

Morehead: I am *not* a "so-called" Legend! I'm the real thing! I'm totally legendary!

Jefferson: Your honor, if I may continue?

Legume: Please.

Jefferson: As I was saying, we will prove that Miss Tallulah Morehead, beyond a shadow of a doubt . . .

Morehead: I object!

Legume: Miss Morehead, please, You can't object!

Morehead: But I wasn't even in *Shadow of a Doubt!* That was Teresa Wright. Of course, it's a perfectly natural mistake. We're practically twins, except that I'm blond, and she's so much *older* than I.

Jefferson: Your honor, this is most irregular.

Morehead: You and me both, darling. I think it was the salmon at lunch.

Legume: Order! Order in the court!

Morehead: About time, too. I'll have a vodka martini, heavy on the vodka. Jerry, what will you have?

Jefferson: Your honor, may I continue?

Legume: Frankly, I have no idea.

As you can see, Mr. Jefferson's obfuscation tactics had already bewildered the poor judge, who was only trying to be hospitable. But worse was coming. Members of my own household were called against me.

Jefferson: Now, Mister Terrence . . .

Terrence: Just call me Terrence. Everybody does.

Morehead: Terrence, don't flirt with the man.

Legume: Miss Morehead, please. You must remain silent.

Morehead: Where were you in 1928? We didn't need words. We had organ music!

Legume: Miss Morehead, remain silent.

Morehead: Thank you, Bosley Crowther.

Jefferson: Your honor, may I continue?

Legume: Please.

Jefferson: Terrence, how long have you worked for Miss Morehead?

Terrence: Twenty-seven years.

Morehead: I hired him when I was three!

Legume: Order!

Morehead: Order? The first set of drinks haven't arrived yet! The service in this courtroom is terrible! I'm seriously considering not leaving a tip.

Jefferson: Terrence, is it not true that at the housewarming party for Miss Morehead's home, she was found in bed with a member of the Damfino crime family?

Mander: Objection. Your honor, what does a sexual indiscretion more than a quarter of a century ago . . .

Morehead: When I was only three, and not legally responsible for my actions.

Mander: Tallulah, please, let me. Your honor, what has this ancient scandal have to do with the matter before the court today?

Jefferson: I'm trying to establish the defendant's longtime ties to organized crime.

Morehead: I did *not* kill Don Damfino!

Jefferson: No one said you did.

Morehead: I didn't say anyone said I did. I was just saying, I didn't kill him, or his son, or Luca "The Sodomite" Cristillo, either.

Jefferson: No one's accused you.

Morehead: Then I'm free to go?

Legume: Sit down, Miss Morehead.

Mander made mincemeat of the allegations on cross-examination.

Mander: Terrence, in all the years you've lived with the defendant, have you ever seen her commit an illegal act?

Terrence: Illegal everywhere, or just in Georgia?

Mander: Everywhere.

Terrence: Well, during Prohibition we operated a still . . .

Mander: Yes, well . . .

Terrence: And a brewery, and a speakeasy . . .

Mander: That's water under the bridge. I mean . . .

Terrence: Do artistic crimes count?

Mander: No.

Morehead: *Thank God!*

Legume: Order!

Morehead: Oh, please, you're no longer fooling anyone.

Mander: Have you ever known Miss Morehead to be violent?

Terrence: No, never. When she killed her fourth husband, it was a complete accident.

Jefferson: What?

Mander: Terrence . . .

Terrence: She had no idea he was fatally allergic to sunlight. They were newlyweds.

Morehead: Terrence, you traitor! How could you?

Jefferson: Your honor, we may wish to amend the charges.

Mander: Your honor, I move to strike the witness's comment concerning the defendant's fourth marriage from the record. It is irrelevant, unfounded, and prejudicial. Whatever may have happened between Miss Morehead and the late Count Tepes occurred in Romania and is outside the jurisdiction of this court. Not only has Miss Morehead not been convicted of this alleged crime, but the Romanian authorities have never charged the woman they still call Countess Tepes with any crime and, in fact, declared her a National Heroine.

Legume: Motion sustained.

Delivery Boy: Let me go! Let me go!

Legume: Order! What's going on back there? Bailiff?

Delivery Boy: Your honor, I'm from the Tenderloin Tavern across the street. I had a telephone order to deliver a pitcher of martinis to this courtroom.

Morehead: Here, boy. That's my order. What's the damage?

Legume: Miss Morehead, what is the meaning of this?

Morehead: Isn't it obvious, darling? I've been waiting all day for those drinks we ordered through you. Frankly, your service is abominable! So, during the last recess I called Tenderloin Tavern and placed a delivery order myself.

Jefferson: I object!

Morehead: Relax, Jefferson. I got enough for everybody. How rude do you think I am? Young man, serve the jury first. After me, I mean.

Legume: Order! Order! Bailiff, remove that man and his deliveries.
Morehead: Is this how low our system of justice has sunk?
Legume: Remove that alcohol!
Morehead: This will be overturned on appeal! Prohibition was re-pealed!
Legume: Alcohol is not allowed in the courtroom.
Morehead: What is this? Russia?

Well, you can see the kind of chaos the judge allowed, while I alone remained a voice of sanity. And worse was to come. Major Barbara was called against me. Loyalty was her middle name, at least in one of her many identities.

Jefferson: Please state your name for the record.
Ares: Barbara Ares, Major, serial number 000-00-0001.
Jefferson: Have you known the defendant long?
Ares: Barbara Ares, Major, serial number 000-00-0001.
Jefferson: Would you answer the question, please?
Ares: Barbara Ares, Major, serial number 000-00-0001.
Jefferson: Your honor, please instruct the witness to answer.
Legume: Miss Ares . . .
Ares: Major Ares.
Legume: Major Ares, you must answer Mister Jefferson's questions.
Ares: According to the Geneva conventions, I am only required to give my name, rank, and serial number.
Legume: That's for prisoners of war. This is a trial. You are required to answer the prosecutor's questions.
Ares: Very well. But I will be lodging a complaint with the United Nations.
Jefferson: Have you known the defendant long?
Ares: Since she was a small girl. We first met when she was a pupil at a girls school I used to have.
Jefferson: What became of that school?
Ares: I'm sorry, I'm not allowed to answer that question.
Jefferson: Why not?
Ares: Lilian Hellman has the entire story under copyright.
Jefferson: Are you employed by the defendant?
Ares: I am.
Jefferson: In what capacity?
Ares: I am her personal bodyguard.
Jefferson: Just how old are you, Major Ares?

Ares: I'm eighty-two.

Jefferson: Isn't that rather old to be an effective bodyguard?

Ares: I could still take you down with one hand, girly-man. I know seventeen ways to kill a man using only three fingers.

Jefferson: Yes, yes, I'm sure you think you could.

Ares: You want to try me, pussy-boy?

Jefferson: Your honor . . .

Ares: Come on, pussy-boy. I'll make it easy. Let's arm wrestle, right now!

Jefferson: Your honor . . .

Ares: Come on, pussy-boy! Right now! You chicken? Chicken, pussy-boy? Awk-bawk-bawk-bawk!

Jefferson: Your honor . . .

Legume: Major Ares, sit down this instant!

Ares: You want a piece of me, Judge?

Legume: Major Ares!

Ares: You think you can take me in that dress, Judge Pussy? Come on, go for me! I'll give you first shot!

Legume: Bailiff, restrain the witness.

Ares: Well, I'll get you anyway, pee-wee!

Bailiff: Oh God, help me! Arrrgghh . . .

Legume: Call for backup! Call for backup now!

Mander: Your honor, I move for a mistrial.

Legume: No mistrial—Aaaarrgghh! She's got me by the—AAAAH-HHHHHHH! *God, help me!*

As you can see, the court was no match for Major Babs. My lawyer didn't even bother to cross-examine her.

Other witnesses were more effective. The wet nurse testified that she felt the dwarves were at least as much to blame as I. After all, it was their wolverine. The owner of the tattoo parlor was a fairly hostile witness, of course, but he hadn't really seen much as he'd been too busy fighting the flames. The scoutmaster was an effective prosecution witness, but Mander completely blew him away on cross.

Mander: Mister Conklin, when was your first felony conviction?

Conklin: What?

Mander: Don't play innocent with me. Are you denying your numerous felonies?

Conklin: Yes!

Mander: So you admit you are a felon?

Conklin: No!

Mander: No? Yes? Which is it?

Jefferson: Objection, your honor. The witness has never been convicted of a felony.

Mander: So, you've successfully covered up your felonies?

Conklin: Yes—No!

Mander: You can't even keep track of your lies, can you?

Conklin: No!

Mander: So, you *can* keep track of your lies?

Conklin: Yes.

Mander: So, you admit you've been lying to the court?

Conklin: No!

Mander: So, you are still lying to the court?

Jefferson: Objection!

Legume: Sustained.

Mander: Mister Conklin, how many of your Boy Scouts will you admit to molesting?

Conklin: None of them.

Mander: So, you refuse to admit to your disgusting child molesting?

Conklin: Yes.

Mander: So, you *are* a child molester?

Conklin: No, you're twisting my words.

Mander: I think the jury can see who the twisted one is here.

Jefferson: Objection!

Mander: I'm through with this pervert!

As it turned out, Mister Conklin wasn't a child molester at all. It was a typo. Still, his lynching that afternoon helped to discredit his testimony in the eyes of the jury. These little misunderstandings arise in any trial.

Eventually, having exhausted the outer limits of slander, the prosecution rested. Now my defense was to have its day in court. But not without constant sabotage by the prosecution.

Mander: I call the Flying Wallendas to the stand.

Jefferson: Objection! Your honor, the defense is trying to make a circus of the court!

Mander: Your honor, prosecution witnesses have testified that my client executed a perfect flying quintuple somersault. As world-renowned aerialists, the Wallendas can testify that this is a physical impossibility.

Legume: Mister Mander, I will not have this courtroom used as a circus. Now call your next witness.

Mander: Very well, I call the Clyde Beatty elephants.

Jefferson: Objection!

Mander: Emmett Kelly.

Jefferson: Objection!

Mander: The Singer Midgets.

Jefferson: Objection!

You see how it went. How laughable to call it a fair trial when I was denied the very witnesses essential to my defense. Cyril Von Millstone was called next. Cyril had been retired now for more than a decade, but his mind was as sharp as ever.

Mander: Mister Von Millstone . . .

Millstone: I did not!

Mander: Excuse me?

Millstone: What?

Mander: Mister Von Millstone . . .

Millstone: Who is it?

Mander: Sir?

Millstone: Who are you?

Mander: I'm Miss Morehead's attorney.

Millstone: Who?

Mander: Miss Tallulah Morehead.

Millstone: Don't be ridiculous! Do I look like that old lush? I'm Cyril Von Millstone, the Greatest of Them All!

Mander: I know.

Millstone: There were four great directors, DeMille, Griffith, Von Stroheim, and me, and I was the greatest of them all!

Mander: I want to ask you about Miss Tallulah Morehead?

Millstone: Where am I?

Mander: Miss Tallulah Morehead?

Millstone: Tallulah? I discovered her! I directed her first movie, *Heat Crazed!,* back in 1915.

Morehead: He's confused. I wasn't even born yet.

Legume: Miss Morehead, please, sit down.

Millstone: She was such a pretty little thing back then, though you'd never know it now.

Morehead: I object!

Legume: You can't object. Besides, he's your own witness.

Morehead: Can't you see he's senile?

Millstone: I am not!

Mander: You are not what?

Millstone: What?

Mander: About Miss Tallulah?

Millstone: Miss Tallulah Morehead was the greatest star that ever lived!

Morehead: The man's a genius!

Millstone: I miss her. She's been dead a long time now.

Morehead: I object! I am not dead!

Legume: Overruled.

Morehead: But I'm not dead!

Millstone: Oh, you are too. Why fight it?

Mander: Mister Von Millstone.

Millstone: What?

Mander: *Mister Von Millstone!*

Millstone: You don't have to shout. I'm not deaf, you know.

Mander: Mister Von Millstone, Tallulah Morehead is not dead. She's on trial.

Millstone: What?

As you can see, no one could get anything incriminating, or even lucid, out of dear Cyril. Hamilton Jefferson was so cowed by the great man that he didn't even dare cross-examine him.

Finally the time came for me to set the record straight by testifying in my defense. I hadn't been an actress longer than I would admit being alive for nothing. If you have tears, prepare to shed them.

Mander: You are Miss Tallulah Morehead, the Nearly Living Legend?

Morehead: I'm innocent, I tell you, innocent! [Copious weeping]

Mander: Yes, yes, Miss Morehead. Do you need a moment?

Morehead: I need a drink.

Mander: You know why we're here?

Morehead: Yes, we're here to pillory an innocent woman! Is this the thanks I get for a lifetime devoted to helping others, never thinking of myself for a moment, only of others?

Mander: You know the charges against you?

Morehead: Lies, I tell you, lies! I'm innocent! Do you hear me? I'm innocent! [More weeping, exposing of leg to jury]

Mander: Could you just tell the court what happened, in your own words?

Morehead: Certainly darling. [Removes papers from purse and begins reading] It was a day like any other. I awoke in my bed at Morehead Heights, my beautiful movie-star mansion, when . . .

Legume: Miss Morehead, are you reading a script?

Morehead: Certainly not! I'm *performing* a script. You're a layman, so you can't be expected to know the difference.

Legume: Put that script away.

Morehead: All right. Terrence! Now then, It was a day like any other. I awoke . . .

Legume: Miss Morehead, what is your assistant doing back there with those cards?

Morehead: Those are my cue cards. He's holding them up so I can read them without using the script, like you asked. This is the way we do it in the movies.

Legume: Why are you reading your testimony?

Morehead: Well, the writers only just finished the final draft this morning. I certainly haven't had time to memorize it yet.

Legume: You're supposed to just say what happened in your own words.

Morehead: These are my own words.

Legume This script was written by professional writers.

Morehead: Damn right! When it's important, always use the best. You can't make a great trial out of a lousy script.

Legume: You're not supposed to use writers. Just use your own words.

Morehead: But these *are* my own words. I paid for them.

Legume: Put those cards away. Miss Morehead, please, just explain what happened in your own words.

Morehead: I'm innocent, I tell you, innocent! [More weeping]

How can you call it a fair trial when I'm denied the use of my professionally written testimony? Oh, justice in this country is truly tone-deaf. But the worst was yet to come, in the insulting cross-examination:

Jefferson: Miss Morehead.

Morehead: Mister Jefferson.

Jefferson: Now you claim to be completely innocent of these charges.

Morehead: As innocent as a newborn babe, suckling at his mother's wet bar.

Jefferson: Then how do you account for the testimony of Mister Conklin?

Morehead: The late child molester? I wouldn't raise myself to his level. If he's so honest, why can't he face me in open court?

Jefferson: He's dead.

Morehead: I heard testimony from Cyril Von Millstone that I am dead, but I haven't let that prevent me from attending court. Have you refuted Cyril's testimony? How can I have committed these offenses if I'm dead? Ha! Got you with that one.

Jefferson: What about the testimony of Nurse Sanguine?

Morehead: Deranged. She's probably under the influence of drugs.

Jefferson: What about Mister Dermagraph's testimony?

Morehead: He's jealous of my perfect skin.

Jefferson: What about the fifteen thousand eyewitnesses at the Hollywood Bowl?

Morehead: I ask you, whose word are you going to take, fifteen thousand nobodies, or one Great *Star?*

Jefferson: President Truman was among those witnesses.

Morehead: So? Frankly, I haven't heard his alibi for President's Roosevelt's death. Can we take the word of a suspected murderer?

Jefferson: What about Exhibit A, the film footage of you actually committing the crime?

Morehead: Oh, please, it's all special effects. Do you think King Kong and Fay Wray could really have a son? Nonsense. It's all done with stop-motion animation. Same with the footage of me. It's all animation. Willis O'Brien's hands can make me do anything.

Jefferson: So all the evidence and all the witnesses are wrong, and you are right?

Morehead: Now you've got it.

As you can see, I made mincemeat of the cross, expertly refuting all of Jefferson's silly charges and so-called "evidence." I felt acquittal was just around the corner, despite numerous grounds for appeal. You can imagine my shock, then, when the verdict came back "guilty!"

"Guilty! Are you insane? Weren't you paying attention?"

"Tallulah, please, be calm," said Jerry Mander.

"Be calm! I'm being crucified! I'll appeal! I'll fight it all the way to the Supreme Court!"

"Tallulah," said Jerry, "you'll never win it. The evidence is over-whelming."

"But . . . ?"

"Tallulah, just pay the two dollars."

So, on the lousy advice of my loser counsel, I paid the fine and had done with it. But to this day I maintain I was *innocent!* *

---

*It appears that even my ghostwriter, a man on *my* payroll, I must add, thinks that I was not exonerated, simply because I was found guilty by the jury, as if *their* opinions counted for anything. Therefore, let me be clearer. The recent Ramparts Division Police Corruption Scandal in Los Angeles *proves* my innocence beyond the merest whisper of a doubt! I was framed by those corrupt coppers, just like all those innocent drug dealers. I expect my conviction to be overturned at any moment. –Tallulah. (I'm afraid I have to add here that Tallulah's trial took place in 1947, before any of the officers involved in the Ramparts Division Police Corruption Scandal were born.–Douglas)

23

At Liberty

I was free, in every sense. At liberty. I was a seasoned actress, completely exonerated of the nasty charges brought against me by a jealous justice system and some very ungrateful parents of a boy who certainly *looked* eighteen, free of the contract that had bound me like an indentured servant to skinflinty old Lydia B. Thalberg, my ex-husband or wife (it gets confusing) and his studio, free to take any of the offers I was sure were flooding into F. Emmett's office (yet another ex-husband, or wife; it really is confusing) on an hourly basis. I was a woman of a "certain age," free, tight, and twenty-one plus change. Now that I was done with the court, I took my refunded bail and set off to celebrate my brains out.

When I next awoke, I was in my bed in Morehead Heights. A check of my bedside calendar (a precaution I'd had installed after the wartime blackout; Terrence had the duty of changing it every day so when I wake up I always know how many days I've been out) showed that only a week had passed since the last thing I could remember. Then, in another daily precaution, I checked the bed for strange men or stranger women. Sure enough, I found one. A handsome, clear-skinned Asian man of maybe twenty-five was snoozing away close beside me. I soon learned that he was Filipino, his name was Rudy, and he was my latest husband.

Unlike most of my earlier husbands (at least the ones I recall—I have no data on the man or men I may have married during my wartime blackout), Rudy had the kindness to inform me at once that he was the merest whisper of a homosexual. Apparently he was a friend of Terrence, whom I'd met at my trial victory party and had married as a forfeit during a party game. Why, I had to ask him, do men uninterested in women keep marrying me? So far, of all the, I no longer know how many, men I'd married, only dear Boris and Count Vlad Tepes were confirmed heterosexuals.* What did gay men see in me?

"The outfits?" Rudy suggested, running his fingers admiringly over the fabric of my zebra-print negligee.

"Well then, let's be more specific," I said. "Why did *you* marry me?"

"Green card," he succinctly replied. It seemed that Rudy's immigration status was in some question, and by marrying me he became a citizen.

I could have simply annulled Rudy, but that seemed churlish, and could have resulted in Rudy's deportation, which would not have been a very nice thing to do to the only honest man I'd ever married. It wasn't as if I had any other immediate husband aspirants pounding at Morehead Heights's sagging knockers, so we struck a deal. I would stay married to Rudy for ten years, barring one or the other of us falling madly in love with Mister Right, and Rudy would work at Morehead Heights as my houseboy.

We'd been badly in need of a houseboy ever since Hisato had been hauled off against his will to a thriving career. (He'd recently become the ninth Mister Moto, the first Japanese actor to play the role, and he spent his summers touring as *Madama Butterfly*.) Major Babs was really too old, and far too irritable for housework. Terrence did his best, but his duties as my personal assistant really kept him too busy for house upkeep. What if I needed him to dash down to The Liquor Barn for a bottle of vodka in an emergency and he was busy vacuuming? Rudy took over the household chores and the cooking (I *do* eat occasionally, despite rumors to the contrary) and was a tremendous success. Rudy continued running Morehead Heights even after we ended our marriage, right up until George Hamilton "borrowed" him for an evening in 1974 and never returned him. (George, if you're having this read for you, *I want Rudy back!* Frankly, this place has gone to hell without him!)

Rudy turned out to be a great gourmet chef and, more importantly, one hell of a mixologist. He could be trying at times, though. He tended

---

*And those two are problematical. As indicated earlier, all evidence refutes Tallulah's claim to have been married to Boris Karloff, and as for Vlad Tepes, historical evidence strongly suggests that he died in the fifteenth century. We can only refer the reader once again to the ghostwriter's note at the beginning of the book. It is my task to *record* Tallulah's reminiscences, not verify them. In other words, I am *not* documenting that Tallulah married Boris Karloff. She didn't. I am documenting that she *said* she married Boris Karloff. If you have a problem with that, go read something else. I can, however, verify that Karloff and Tepes were, in fact, confirmed heterosexuals.–Douglas to display outbursts of what they call "attitude" today, especially if he didn't like what someone was wearing. One evening he reduced sweet little Julie Andrews to tears at a Morehead Heights party simply because she arrived wearing the same gown she'd already worn while accepting her Oscar.*

Shortly after taking over running the house Rudy insisted vociferously that I purchase a washer and dryer. The headless Indian brave, always willing to pitch in and help, had been handling the laundry chores since Hisato's departure, and all he'd required were detergent, running water, and some large rocks (for my dry cleaning, he merely omitted the running water). Rudy, however, was unwilling to scale the treacherous crags of Tumescent Tor in order to beat my designer gowns against the two gigantic boulders that flank its rugged base and then rinse them in the always churning Pacific. Though I mocked Rudy's decadent, citified, washing ways, I did notice that, after Rudy took over, my clothes began to last longer. I had no idea that people routinely got more than two wearings out of their clothes. (Though more than two wearings of the same outfit around Rudy would put one in danger of a severe tongue-lashing, and not the fun kind, either.)

However, if I was going to make extravagant purchases like washing machines and dryers, or worse, pay my weekly liquor tab, I was going to need some cash flow. True, I had salted away millions, particularly back in the silent era, before the government felt free to help themselves to the few meager pennies I scratched out tilling the soil barefoot as a major movie star, and I was financially set for life, but much of that was tied up in investments: a winery here, a brewery there, a distillery or two. I could use some money coming in. I needed to get back to work. I needed to make a movie.

I called F. Emmett and, after spending twenty minutes on hold, told him to send over the best of the scripts the studios had sent him for me so Terrence could read them and I could select my first project as a free agent.

The next day a single script arrived. I called F. Emmett, who was in a meeting or something, so I asked his secretary where the other scripts were.

---

*Speaking of Oscars, my God, they give those silly trinkets to just *anyone!* Julie Andrews (a music hall singer, *not* an actress), Joan Crawford, Larry Olivier, *anyone!* I realized how valueless they were when Hisato won his. I mean, really, he wasn't an actor, he was *help!* This is why I have never lowered myself to be nominated.–Tallulah

"Who are you again?" the brain-damaged young woman asked.

"Tallulah Morehead, The Nearly Living Legend," I informed the ignorant child.

"Who?" she nasally whined down the wire.

"Miss Tallulah Morehead. I am Mr. Knight's oldest client."

"I don't know ... oh yeah," the unpleasant gorgon-in-training replied, "the ex-wife, the washed-up old lush, sure. He said you really were his *oldest* client, by at least a decade. Excuse me for asking, but what were you thinking, marrying him?"

"Not that it's any of your business, but I was a young woman in love."

"So was he, I bet." Then the vicious little harpy snorted in a disgusting manner, like a pig, or Judy Canova with a bad head cold.

"Is Mr. Knight in? I have urgent matters to discuss with him concerning the direction my career is to take." I told the mentally deficient future criminal, whom F. Emmett was obviously employing as a charitable action, giving work to the otherwise hard-core unemployable.

"Your career?" the nasty bit of vermin said. "I thought you were retired."

"Most certainly not! My fans would never forgive me if I deserted the screen."

"You still got a fan? Better make a film quick, before he dies."

"Of course I still have fans. Why, I receive charming fan letters all the time. I had one only last month. Or was it the month before? Well, it was definitely this year. It was from a young man who was mad about me, even though he kept misspelling my name as Olivia. He went on and on about how much he'd loved my performances in *The Adventures of Robin Hood* and *Gone with the Wind*."

"You weren't in either of those movies."

"No. But if I had been, I would have been brilliant! So his praise still counts."

"Sounds like he mixed you up with Olivia DeHavilland."

"Nonsense! I look nothing like that talentless cow! Is Mr. Knight in?"

"He said to tell you he's in a meeting until the fifties."

"But there's been some mistake. I asked him to send over the entire mountain of scripts the studios have sent him, clamoring for my glamor and brilliance, for the special *Magic* known the world over whenever people speak the single word 'Morehead,' but only one got here. I want the others."

"Yeah. I sent it over. There are no others. That was it."

"You can't be serious. I'm a *legend!*"

"So is the giant man-eating cyclops of Cyprus, and he hasn't got any script offers either. At least you've got two *eyes.*"

Well, there was no talking to the creature. She was obviously deranged. I asked her to tell F. Emmett to call me as soon as possible and hung up.

Two days later I received a letter from F. that read, in part,

> *Neither of us is getting any younger, Tallulah. I strongly feel that one of us should retire. Since you seem strangely determined not to, I shall. I suggest you seek representation elsewhere, if you are determined to unnaturally prolong what was once a stellar career. Good-bye, Tallulah. It was fun for a while, wasn't it?*
>
> F. Emmett Knight

And that was the end of that relationship. My first husband and agent for thirty-two years simply kissed me off and left to peddle antiques in New England. Perhaps he was right to retire. His letter didn't seem entirely rational to me. He was, after all, around sixty years old. Perhaps his mind had started to go. In any event, he was gone. The only good thing was that at least his revolting little secretary was out of a job. But then, so was I.

I took a look at the synopsis of the script Terrence had prepared for me, and I had to admit it had possibilities. It was called *I'm Not Crazy!*, and it was the tale of a sane woman wrongly committed to a hellish insane asylum, where she endures the tortures of the damned before she can get herself released. It was a tour-de-force role for a brilliant, seasoned actress like myself. It had Oscar written all over it. In fact, I had to insist Terrence erase all the "Oscars," so I could read the damned thing. But he was right. It was an Oscar-caliber role, not that I have ever cared about awards, which is why I've never received any. It's all about the craft.

I had Terrence call the producer, a Mr. Sid Lee, who, with his partner, Russell Zee, ran a small production company called S. Lee-Zee Films Inc, and inform them that the celebrated star Tallulah Morehead was interested in accepting their offer if terms could be agreed upon. I was given an appointment the next day with Russell Zee.

The S. Lee-Zee offices were upstairs above a liquor store on Hollywood Boulevard, between a massage parlor and a tattoo shop. I must admit to feeling trepidations as Terrence drove me into this unfamiliar end of town, but the liquor store relieved my misgivings. I always feel that a liquor store gives a neighborhood tone. The offices were not exactly plush. In fact, they were not exactly clean, and I don't think the walls had been painted since I'd been born, but the biggest shock came when Mr. Zee rose to his feet, roaring, "Tallulah, you old whore! Great to see you!" It was none other than my one-time paramour, high-school tutoring pupil, and swimming-pool gunniter, the son-in-law of the late Don Lorenzo Damfino, Russell, whom I hadn't set eyes on since the Morehead Heights housewarming party twenty-eight years before (when I was only three).

The years, which had washed over me leaving no trace, had been less kind to Russell. Always burly, he was now severely overweight. Frankly, if I hadn't vividly remembered the enormous appendage that lived in his stained slacks, I wouldn't have given him a second glance. "Russell darling," I said, perky as ever, "how nice to see so much of you. This is my personal assistant, Terrence, and my bodyguard, Major Barbara."

"Tallu doll, let me get a good look at you in the light," Russell bellowed enthusiastically as he yanked up his chipped, yellowed venetian blinds to allow the unfiltered sunlight to blaze into an office that had been white around the time the dinosaurs had become extinct. "Whoa!" he added, dropping the blinds back down again, and pulling down a shade that looked for all the world to be blood-splattered. "Maybe we shouldn't look that close after all. I can see you've never had any work done."

"No indeed, Russell darling. I'm as nature left me."

"How long ago did she leave?"

"Russell, old friend, what's this new last name? Why are you Russell Zee?"

"Oh that. Well, you remember all that trouble all those years ago with Talia and her father?"

"How is the shrill little banshee, anyway?"

"Christ, I have no idea. We've been divorced over twenty-five years now. I've been married three times since then. But anyway, back when there was all that commotion, and I was laid up for a bit with my foot problems, somebody rubbed out Don Lorenzo, his son Guido, and Luca Cristillo."

"The Sodomite," I blurted out involuntarily, glancing warily at Major Barbara, who stared straight ahead, icily. That woman's blood was colder than Loretta Young on a first date.

"Yeah, that's what they called him. Anyway, I figured, if someone was killing the whole Damfino family, then as his son-in-law and heir, now that Guido slept with the fishes—and anything else he got near—they'd be gunning for me next."

"Oh, I think you had nothing to worry about." I said. "Not that I know anything at all about the murders of the Damfino family, which I didn't witness firsthand from an icy bucket of cement."

"But, Miss Tallulah," Terrence began, too helpfully, "weren't they those men at the pier that time who tried . . ."

"Shut your dick trap, Terrence," Major Barbara wittily snapped.

"Major," I said, "why don't you and Terrence go get an ice cream, or a beer, or a tattoo, or a massage or something, while Russell and I catch up on old times?"

With the help out of the way, Russell resumed his story. "Well, since the Damfino murders were never solved, I thought I might be a target, so I went underground and assumed a new identity. I've been Russell Zee so long now, I sometimes forget I ever had another name."

"How did you end up in the movie business?"

"Well there, I gotta say, you inspired me. I figured if Tallulah Morehead can get rich in the movie business, *anybody* can."

"Now, now, Russell, no need for flattery among old friends."

"Speaking of old friends, if you peek around behind my desk you'll see another old friend of yours that would like to get reacquainted."

I stood up and peered over Russell's desk to see the little, well, actually very large, old friend he spoke of, giving its familiar salute. I confess to feeling weak-kneed at the sight. I seemed to swoon, but Russell caught me and helped me to my knees, from where I could help myself. By the time Terrence and Major Babs returned, sporting their fresh tattoos,* I had signed to star in my first Independent feature.

I ended up filming *I'm Not Crazy!* under conditions very different than I'd been used to back in my PMS period. Rather than deluxe sound stages, we were shooting in a warehouse in Van Nuys. Rather than a full union crew, we had a nonunion crew, if a director, actually Russell himself, under the name Dickson Bush, and a cameraman can be considered a "crew." Terrence did my makeup, and I wore my own clothes in my early scenes, while, after I was committed to the asylum, I wore a hospital gown. I was working for somewhat less than my former fee. In fact, the budget for the entire film was less than my customary fee, but, seeing as I was helping out an old friend, and no other projects were com-

---

*Terrence was still weeping from the severe pricking. Not usually the sort of thing he complained of.–Tallulah

peting for my time, I went ahead and reduced my price. And I was getting to take full advantage of the fringe benefit in Russell's pants.

This was to be S. Lee-Zee Films' first mainstream theatrical release. Their previous features had all been strikingly graphic love stories, which played in small, out-of-the-way theaters and smokers, with classic titles like *Sorority Initiation, Miss Juggs Pays the Milkman, Schoolgirls Cut Loose,* and *The Orgycats. I'm Not Crazy!* was to be their first film in regular theaters, with a big name, a running time of more than forty-five minutes, and in thirty-five millimeter. There was no budget for my customary enormous dressing room, but Russell allowed me full use of his office, and I allowed him full use of me. Best of all, Russell had no objection to my suggestion of a full wet bar on the set. Mind you, I am a professional. When I'm working on a film, I don't touch a drop of alcohol until the director says, "Cut!"

The actor who played the sympathetic psychiatrist who helps me was a marvelous young man whose professional name was Axel Spears. He had played the milkman in *Miss Juggs Pays the Milkman,* and, when Russell ran that striking piece of cinematic art for me, I was immediately impressed with his *enormous* talent, a talent almost too big for the screen. If only Cinemascope had been invented a few years earlier he might have gone on to a stellar career. That boy was made for the wide screen. Sadly, he made no other films after ours.

Since this was to be Axel's first role wearing clothes and speaking, he was naturally nervous, and it was inevitable that he would turn to an experienced and established star like myself, to teach him to be more at ease on camera. I asked Russell if he would mind my using his office to relax Axel and get him up for the shoot, and Russell said that was fine, as long as he could film it. Since the whole point was to get the boy (he was only eighteen) relaxed and at ease on camera, that seemed sensible. The resulting footage eventually saw a limited *(very* limited) release as one of the only two short subjects I ever made, under the title *Axel's Acting Lesson.*

About two thirds of the way through production the title was changed. Russell said that, given my performance, the title *I'm Not Crazy!* was no longer considered believable. The picture went into release as *The Snake Hole,* and it is generally considered my most astounding performance. The *Los Angeles Times* raved, "I wish with all my heart that I could praise Tallulah Morehead's energetic performance in *The Snake Hole,*" while *Variety* gushed, "Tallulah Morehead's performance in *The Snake Hole* must be seen to be disbelieved!" The *New York Times* wrote, "Tallulah Morehead gives a performance like no other I've ever seen, or ever want to again!" while The *San Francisco Chronicle* cheered, "Tallulah's mad scenes will make you flee the theater screaming!" With an avalanche of raves like that, and the word "Oscar" on everybody's lips,* I knew it would be only a matter of time before all of Hollywood was spread out before me again, and vice versa.

---

*If, that is, you understand "everybody" to mean Terrence, Major Babs, Rudy, and Russell, though I'm sure it would have been on the headless Indian brave's lips as well if only he'd *had* lips.–Tallulah

24

Oscar Wild

S. Lee-Zee Films Inc. only made one film at a time, so *The Snake Hole* received the studio's full attention. Thus, perhaps, I shouldn't have been surprised to learn that my film went into release exactly one week after we'd finished shooting it. The final film had a rough, unpolished, and, at times, underlit look to it. The cinematographer, a charming boy of twenty-two named Jerry, had only worked in eight and sixteen millimeter before, so he hadn't always realized just how much light thirty-five millimeter film required. Also, I confess, I had impressed the nicely built young man with just what a truly impressive performance I could give in the dark. And both Jerry and Russell agreed that the less light there was, the better I looked.

I was used to my films opening in every city in America, so I was a little surprised that *The Snake Hole* opened only in Alabama. Sid Lee was the business end of S. Lee-Zee Films while Russell handled the creative end. Sid explained to me that S. Lee-Zee Films never struck more than forty-five prints of a release. "Duping prints is our single largest expense in making a movie." Sid told me, which was certainly the first time I'd ever heard that. They released films "regionally," a week in one state, a week in another, mostly at drive-ins. I didn't really feel this release pattern was the best way to campaign for the Oscar I didn't want.*

It took over six months for *The Snake Hole* to open in Los Angeles, so by the time it reached LA, the Oscar campaign I was paying for (for

---

*Making actors compete against each other is offensive to my artistic sensibilities. It's treating actors like, well, athletes. Hence my refusal ever to be nominated. –Tallulah

the good of the film—I *spit* on Oscar myself) was in full swing, though I probably shouldn't have let Rudy proofread the ad copy. In the trade papers every day for the seven days that *The Snake Hole* played in Los Angeles, my ads ran, for which, overall, I shelled out more than I'd been paid to appear in the film. They showed a close-up of me I didn't consider flattering, but in which I was acting my brains out, with the copy "For Your Consideration, Tallulah Morehead IS *The Snake Hole!*"

"Rudy!" I complained, "That's supposed to say 'IN *The Snake Hole*' not 'IS'! What happened?"

"Typo," was Rudy's typically succinct reply.

To also help promote the film, for the week it played Los Angeles, I made personal appearances at the various drive-ins where it was playing. I was hoping to appear in Hollywood or Beverly Hills, to attract the Academy nominating committee members—strictly to help the film—but the drive-ins were in places like Inglewood, Downey, Arcadia, Granada Hills, San Pedro, and Watts, all communities I was visiting for the first time. "Why," I asked Russell, "didn't we play in any regular theaters?"

"Tallulah honey," Russell replied, "all you can do is make out in a regular theater. If you really want to nail your date, you have to go to a drive-in."

I couldn't argue with the logic, but I didn't really see how it was germane. In any event, the Academy evidently sensed my contempt for the whole awards circus, because I received no nomination for my stunning achievement in *The Snake Hole*. Indeed, my contempt for the paltry Oscar awards skyrocketed with the announcement of the Best Actress nominations for 1948. It wasn't so much my omission that shocked me as a certain insane inclusion; along with nominations for such serviceable journeymen actresses as Irene Dunne, Barbara Stanwyck, Jane Wyman, and the always unintelligible Ingrid Bergman, the Academy lost their minds completely and nominated the overwhelmingly untalented hag Delores Delgado for her wretchedly overacted "performance" in the unwatchable thrilless thriller *Busy Signal*. The only enjoyable scene in the whole film was the hilarious sequence in which Humphrey Bogart strangled her to death with a phone cord.

The secret of success is to give the public what it wants, and Delores's noisy murder was such a crowd pleaser that *Busy Signal* was a huge hit as well as a critical favorite. I really felt an Oscar nomination just for turning purple and gagging was an overreaction, although turning purple in a black and white movie isn't all that easy.

I had intended to simply ignore the Oscar ceremonies as usual, but to my horror, an invitation to actually present the Best Actress award was extended to me. Vincent Lovecraft told me privately that it had been Delores herself who had requested that I present the award. Between her ghastly acting and the undeserved sympathy she was receiving over the tragic recent death of dear Gilbert Rolaids at the too-young age of eighty-seven, the hammy old whore was certain she was a shoo-in and had told Vincent, "The Oscar will mean so much *more* if Tallulah has to hand it to me."

There weren't any other offers pouring in. Apparently, no one had read the trade paper articles about my departure from PMS, now some two years in the past, and just assumed I was still tied up to Lydia B. Minor. A little exposure to remind Hollywood that there was still a *real* actress in town might be a good idea. Besides, it wasn't as if Delores actually had a chance of winning, so I accepted the invitation.

The Motion Picture Academy Awards for 1948 are long forgotten now, and rightly so. The ceremony, hosted by cranky Robert Montgomery in March of 1949, was a fiasco from beginning to end. An incomprehensible foreign movie, aptly titled *Hamlet,* given Sir Laurence's overdone performance, took most of the awards, the only time the Best Picture Oscar has ever been given to a foreign-language movie. Why they didn't at least include subtitles, or better yet, dub the whole depressing mess into English, is beyond me.

Best Actress was one of the later awards, so I had nothing to do but drink for most of the endless ceremony. I managed to kill a little time by sneaking backstage to make hot, wild love with the smoldering Sex God William Bendix.

When I finally got onstage to make my presentation I was met with an ovation. My stunning, zebra-striped, off-the-shoulders gown brought gasps from the glamorous audience, caused perhaps at least in part because, in my haste to redress and get onstage after riding Bill Bendix to heaven, I had accidentally put it back on upside down.

I read the list of nominees, and then the man from Price-Waterhouse handed me the envelope. When I opened it I was overwhelmed with horror. To my disbelief, the name written there was *Delores Delgado!* Had they all lost their minds? It was bad enough to reward Larry Olivier, husband of that slut Vivien Leigh, for babbling gibberish for *hours* in a silly Scandinavian ghost story, but to *honor* that hateful bitch Delores was just *too much to bear!*

The whole audience was silent, hanging on any sound that came from my quivering, shocked lips, waiting to hear the unthinkable. The room seemed to swim about me. It made no sense. I reached out and took the arm of the nice man from Price-Waterhouse, to ask for some sort of explanation. Sadly, the man wasn't my darling Vincent, but his business partner, Mr. Waterhouse, and I didn't know his name, so I just stammered out the simple question, "Why, man?"

Before he could answer me the room erupted in applause. Jane Wyman was on her feet and *sprinting* for the stage. She ripped the Oscar from the poor little model holding it and began babbling an acceptance speech. The poor, deluded dear actually thought she had won for her performance as a deaf-mute in *Johnny Belinda*. How could she have? No one would have voted for that amateur acting job; she had never even bothered to memorize her lines!

The Waterhouse guy was ashen. He whispered in my ear, "What should we do? She didn't win."

"Do you want to tell that to a woman holding a gold-plated blunt instrument?" I asked. "Better leave well enough alone. Nobody but us need ever know."

The accountant glanced at the crazed look in Jane's eyes as she thanked everyone she'd ever met by name and said, "You may be right." Then he took the card with Delores's name on it and quietly ripped it into tiny pieces. "This is our little secret," he whispered. Two minutes later, he burned the pieces in an ashtray offstage.

And has Jane Wyman ever shown me the slightest *trace* of gratitude for giving her Delores Delgado's Oscar and saving her career? She has not! To my amazement, I was never invited to the White House even once during her eight years as First Lady! That's Hollywood ingratitude for you.[*]

Despite my breathtaking appearance at the Oscars, no new film offers were coming my way. I thought maybe I should put together a project for myself. I remembered that wonderful novel, *The Well of Loneliness*, by Radcliffe Hall, that the late Mildred Puett had sent me so many years before. I had Terrence reread it and re-summarize it for me. Then I had a brilliant idea.

Columbia was having an ongoing success with their delightful, low-budget *Blondie* movies. Sweet, but hopelessly plain little Rita Hayworth had had a great early career break in one of them, and I must admit I found Arthur Lake, who epitomized the virile American male as the robust, manly Dagwood Bumstead, to be a total dreamboat.

---

[*]You have to give Jane credit though. Throughout her years in the White House, she still found time to star in *Falcon Crest* every week. That drunken old dyke Eleanor Roosevelt never managed *that!*–Tallulah

I took Mr. Hall's novel and adapted it to fit the *Blondie* format, writing a wonderful part for myself. I called it *Blondie's Special Friend* and I sent it off to Harry Cohn at Columbia.

I won't print his off-color reply, but, in essence, he felt it was unproducable for unspecified reasons, though, he added, if Penny Singleton and I would be at all interested in enacting Scene 27 for him, live and in private, he would offer me a seven-year contract. I forwarded the script and Mr. Cohn's offer to Penny, whom I'd never met, but she wouldn't even discuss it. Frankly, that contract would have meant a lot to me at that time, but clearly, offering a generous helping hand to a fellow actress was not in Miss Singleton's repertoire. Alas, *Blondie's Special Friend* was not to be, although pirated copies of my script were enormously popular for years on the Hollywood underground circuit.*

I did finally find a new agent. Actually, it was Fred Sturm, formerly of the comedy team Sturm & Drang, with whom I had made *Stewed Prudes* back in 1932. Frank Drang had died heroically while entertaining the troops during World War II, having been found dead of a heart attack in a French brothel. Fred hadn't the heart to go on performing without his longtime partner, so he opened up the Sturm Agency, handling exclusively big stars who had been dropped by their studios. But even with Fred's help, no offers came my way in 1949.

Oh, I read for Margo Channing in *All About Eve,* but Joe Mankowitz realized that no one would ever believe plain little Anne Baxter could ever be a threat to me, and so settled for mild, shy little Bette Davis instead, a compromise that completely ruined the picture!

Cinematic genius Billy Wilder called up one day and asked if he could come over in conjunction with a movie he was preparing. Like any sensible actress, I jumped at the chance to work with this brilliant director. But when he arrived at Morehead Heights, it seemed he wanted to talk about anything but his next movie, whatever it was. Frankly, it was almost impossible to tell what the hell he was talking about. His accent was so thick I could only guess at what he was saying. He seemed content to listen to me babble on about my life, much as I'm doing now, while he sat and listened intently, taking notes. The next day he came

---

*Given the enduring underground popularity of my script, I later thought that the publication of it would be a profitable enterprise, as well as establishing my literary credentials prior to embarking on this project; however, tragically, the estate of Chic Young was adamant in its refusal to license it. Always I am thwarted by small minds!—Tallulah

back, and again just sat and listened to me talk about my life and adventures. I showed him around Morehead Heights, and he took snapshots of every room.

This went on day after day for two weeks. Finally he announced, through the translator I'd asked him to bring, that he was through.

"When do I report to the studio?" I asked.

"You don't," Mr. Wilder's translator replied.

"But, aren't you using me in your new film?"

"In a manner of speaking. Would it be all right if I brought Gloria Swanson over with me one afternoon?"

"Homely little Gloria? Whatever for?"

"To study you. She's starring in my new film."

"Gloria Swanson, that repulsive elderly has-been, is starring in your new movie? I thought I was your new star."

"No, no, no, no, no, no," Mr Wilder replied.

"All right," I said. "Though I think one 'No' would have sufficed."

"You won't be in the movie *directly,*" he cryptically answered, "but your influence will fill the picture."

"That doesn't buy the kitty any vodka, darling."

I eventually saw Mr. Wilder's bizarre exercise in star-bashing, and I'll be damned if I can see what influence I may have had on that awful bore. The only entertaining part of the picture was beautiful Billy Holden swimming.

As 1950 rolled around, Russell dropped by one afternoon. As he was pulling his pants back up, he mentioned he had a new script for me. It was called *Infraction,* and it was the tale of an ordinary woman (a stretch for me) whose arrest for jaywalking leads to a sordid life of crime. I had Terrence tear into it as soon as Russell opened my handcuffs. It was another tour-de-force role. Most of the picture took place in prison. I would get to talk tough, beat up other women, shoot people, and participate in two striking girl-on-girl rape scenes. I would be a fool to turn down such a great role. It would be worth it for the rehearsals alone. I said "Yes!" so fast, Russell barely had time to drop his pants again.

Much of *Infraction* was shot at a real prison, with real female inmates playing the inmates, so the picture had a startling level of realism, not to mention the wildest wrap party of my whole career. Jerry and Russell, the only men present, both said they wished they could have filmed the party. It would have been an underground classic. The inmate women were great. One couldn't help envying their carefree lifestyle. It was almost enough to make me wish I had been found guilty at my travesty of a trial.*

I took to hanging out weekends at a little seafront bar down in Laguna Beach, where I met a charming southern gentleman named Tom who said he was a writer. It turned out that he actually was and had written a charming play that was shortly to be filmed, and Tom kept saying that I was a "perfect Blanche." I eventually figured out that "Blanche" was a character in his play.

I had Terrence read the play, and he said it was beautiful, and that my character was a faded southern belle who was going mad and completely snaps after she is raped by an incredibly gorgeous hunk.

"Yes, but what makes her snap?" I asked.

Terrence answered, "I have absolutely no idea."

Tom introduced me to the young actor who was to play the hunk in the movie. His name was Marlon Brando, and the man was a *god!* It was very difficult to believe he would ever have to rape anyone, although I don't doubt that he's suffered many a sexual assault himself. Certainly I was all over him, like salt rimming a margarita, though Marlon had no qualms about returning that favor.

Tom had arranged for me to test for the producer, Charlie Feldman, and the director, Elia "The Rat" Kazan. Apparently my thirty-one years of movies, an amazing achievement given that I was only twenty-eight, wasn't audition enough. "Haven't they seen any of my many magnificent movies?" I asked Tom indignantly.

"Yes, they have." Tom replied. "But I've convinced them to consider you anyway."

"You know, my performance as a not-mad woman in *The Snake Hole* would have won me an Oscar except that I refused to be nominated."

"Hey, I'm already sold, Tallulah. Now to important matters. Who's buying the next round?"

He asked Marlon to do the test with me. "What will I need with Marlon, when I test for the part?" I asked Tom. "Are Feldman and Kazan *that way?*" I used the euphemism in case Tom didn't know about homosexuals. As it happened he did, but they weren't. It turned out that I was going to audition for the role in a novel fashion, by performing a scene from the play with Marlon. This certainly was never the way we did things at PMS! Obviously, Feldman and Kazan knew nothing about plucking talent.

---

*She was.–Douglas

I chose the rape scene for my audition, and Marlon and I rehearsed it under Tom's direction. I was worried about Marlon at first. Frankly, although he had real star quality for silent films, we were making a talkie (the silly talkie fad *refused* to die out!), and talking wasn't what Marl did best. He mumbled so indistinctly I had to guess when my lines came by when he had stopped talking. I was afraid he wasn't destined for a long movie career. His wretched diction just sank him no matter how much the camera, or the cameraman, loved him. True to my prediction, he dropped off the Hollywood radar after *Streetcar* and made no more movies that I know of. I understand he eventually gave up his hopeless pursuit of an acting career and went off to live on, or as, an island somewhere.

Marl's real talent only sprang up as we got into the violent action of the rape. It was going great when suddenly, for no reason, Marlon rolled off me, sat up, and lit a cigarette.

"What's the matter? Why did you stop! I was just getting warmed up!"

"Tallulah," said Tom, "that's where the scene ends. There is no more."

"That's no reason to stop a perfectly good rape!" I replied, outraged at this lack of professionalism. "How will you be convincing to the audience as raping me if you never have?"

"Jee mages a goo pout," Marlon said in his usual nasal gobbledygook.

"What did he say?"

"He said you make a good point," Tom answered.

"Damn right I do! Now get over here and show me how a *real* man rapes a woman! And make me believe it! I'll let you know when you're done!"

"Ooh gad id, babe," Marlon mumbled back. Then the boy demonstrated the talent that had set Broadway on fire every night, after the play.

Needless to say, Feldman and Kazan were stunned speechless by our audition scene, which I insisted on performing twice, and again in the limo on the way back to the house. The contracts were signed and the announcements were made. Tallulah Morehead would return to the screen[*] as Blanche Dubois in *A Streetcar Named Desire*. Tom and I decided that a celebration was in order, and we went out partying.

---

[*]There was a misconception going around Hollywood that I hadn't made a film in four years, since *An Ordeal to Remember* back at PMS. Somehow *The Snake Hole* and *Infraction* had slipped past their attention, although both films had turned a nice profit.–Tallulah

It was very warm when I awoke, but there was an odd odor permeating the air. "Terrence," I called out, "I don't think those eggs are fresh." Then I opened my eyes and let out a shriek.

I was lying on a rocky ledge above a bubbling and turbulent volcanic crater. Below me geysers of lava shot up in the air. The odor I was suffused with was sulfur. There was no one about. Slowly I began making my way down the steep slope of the volcano, hollering for a drink.

It turned out I was on the brink of Mauna Loa in Hawaii. I'd always wanted to visit this lovely vacation spot, though I was puzzled how I'd gotten there overnight.

Well, it wasn't exactly overnight, as it turned out. When I got back to civilization, I phoned Terrence back at Morehead Heights. "Terrence darling, I seem to be in Hawaii. Have the studio send a plane. I've got to get to the set."

"What set?" Terrence asked.

"*A Streetcar Named Desire,* of course. My stunning comeback film."

"It's done."

"What?"

"It's finished. It's released. It won Oscars."

"Which Oscars?"

"Best Director. Best Actress, Best . . ."

"*Best Actress! I won an Oscar! How wonderful! I must call a press conference!*"

"Not you."

"Not me? What do you mean not me? They couldn't have given it to that mousy little Hunter woman."

"No, no. She won Best Supporting Actress."

"That's more like it. So I *did* win the Oscar! I'll bet I was magnificent!"

"You're not in it."

"I must be in it. I signed contracts."

"Yes, but you disappeared. No one could find you. We've been looking for you for almost two years. Tallulah, it's May 1952."

"How time flies when you're blacked out."

"So, they couldn't wait. They filmed the movie with someone else."

"Some other, lesser actress played my role and won my Oscar?"

"Yes."

"Who was it?"

"You won't like it."

"What opportunistic bitch took advantage of my indisposition and stole my role and my Oscar? Who? Not Delores Delgado!"

"No, no. It was Vivien Leigh."

*"That crazy limey trollop stole my role and my Oscar **again?**"*

"I'm afraid so, Tallulah."

"I need a drink. Get your butt to Hawaii and bring me home."

In retrospect, it was probably a lucky thing I didn't do the picture. As you know, I have only contempt for awards. The fact that they gave a second Oscar to that untalented guttersnipe, who, to be perfectly frank, wasn't *acting* in her mad scenes at all, only proves yet again their utter worthlessness. If that homely, no-talent madwoman won an Oscar for that role, they probably would have given me *two*. One simply wouldn't have been enough, and I would have had to do the gracious thing and accept them, and be deluged with more film offers than I had time for. It would have been a terrible bother. Whereas this way I was able to go back to S. Lee-Zee Films and make the grueling female prisoners-of-war film, *Boot Camp Bitches,* which has been declared a "major camp classic," I assume because it's a classic about a camp.

But before those cameras rolled, I had a date with history, in the form of a summons from the House Un-American Activities Committee.

25

Seeing Red

Senator Joseph McCarthy was a rare type of man, one I didn't find at all appealing. He was downright rude, and he wasn't winning any friends in the motion picture industry with his silly anticommunist crusade, unless you count Walt Disney, Cecil Blunt DeMille, and Adolphe Menjou. Cecil I had had more than thirty years before (before I was born), so obviously it wasn't an experience I was in a hurry to repeat. Walt's pants were impossible to get into. He seemed to have something against sex, and as for Menjou, well, I would have thought Americans had learned their lesson about listening to the political opinions of people named Adolphe!

Apparently, back in the thirties, when I was just a little girl, I had gotten quite a reputation for painting the town red.[*] Senator Joe, not the brightest man ever to reach Washington, got this a little mixed up in his mind and thought it meant I was associating with "known Communists." Matters weren't helped any when that overboard radical Walt Disney told the House Un-American Activities Committee that I was a member of a Communist organization. HUAC didn't ask *which* Communist organization Walt meant. As it happened, Walt was referring to the Screen Actor's Guild. Mr. Disney wasn't very pro-labor.

I received a summons to appear before this dreaded congressional committee and name names of my Communist associates. My first instinct was to tear it to bits, but Terrence warned me that this would put me in contempt of Congress.

[*]Among other reputations she acquired, and earned.–Douglas

"I've been in contempt of Congress ever since they passed *THE GREAT EVIL,* back before I was born."

"Well, that was a different Congress, and remember, they have since repealed Prohibition."

"Don't use that vulgar word in front of a lady!"

"Maybe you should talk to your lawyer."

I called Jerry Mander, and he made the excellent point that, if I were jailed, I would be cut off from all alcohol supplies. It turns out that in real life, prison isn't near as much fun as it is in the movies. He promised to accompany me to Washington. "I believe I can get my own date," I told him.

"Not as your date, Tallulah. I'll be there to advise you legally, while you testify."

"Not really necessary. I was planning on taking Terrence, Rudy, and Major Babs."

"None of them have any legal experience."

"Nonsense! Have you any idea how many times Terrence has been arrested for lewd conduct? The LAPD had to hire a whole new under-cover task force because Terrence was on a first-name basis with all the old ones."

"I know, Tallulah. I get him off, remember?"

"You and half the navy."

"But he can't offer you legal counsel before Congress. You'll need me."

"Oh, all right."

Actually, I wasn't being completely honest when I said I could get my own date. The fact was that as I approached my thirtieth birthday, men weren't so easy to acquire as they had been. I began to wonder how other women in my position handled the terrible man shortage that ac-companied the Korean conflict.

I thought of asking Joan Crawford, who never met a pair of pants she couldn't get into, where she shopped for meat, but frankly, I'd never forgiven her for stealing my role in *The Women,* back when I was a lit-tle girl, and besides, Joan was so much older than I that her advice was really useless.

I remembered that silly movie Billy Wilder had made with Gloria Swanson. In that picture a semiretired film star meets a Sex God when the Sex God gets a flat tire and pulls into her garage. That seemed worth a shot, especially as Bill Holden wasn't dropping by any more.

I dropped a board with large nails sticking out of it on the highway that ran past Tumescent Tor. Results were immediate but disappointing. The first flat tire brought me an elderly woman who sat and told me about the joys of Mormonism while we waited for the auto club.

Next, it brought in a burly biker with more tattoos than I had shot glasses. He phoned a bunch of his friends, who came over to pick him up. While they were here, they gang-partied with me, which was great fun, but afterwards the house was such a shambles that even I noticed, and a number of items were missing. Also, it seems that a few of them, about six, while waiting for their turns with me, had decided to warm up on Terrence and Rudy, and, while neither Terrence nor Rudy complained, despite Rudy ending up in traction and Terrence getting three broken ribs, I felt I really needed men who could tell the difference between a Great Star and her help.

I decided this method was too random, so I positioned Terrence a hundred yards down the highway with a walkie-talkie to spot when an attractive man was coming and let me know which car he was in. Then I would hurl the board in front of the selected vehicle. This technique yielded better-looking men, but it turned out that most of them were perfectly capable of changing their own tires and tended to turn down my offers of a quick drink and an orgasm. Were there no gentlemen left?

One evening Terrence, Rudy, Major Babs, and I were attending a screening of a new Tarzan film, checking out the latest Tarzan, when Terrence mentioned that he'd lost track of just how many Tarzans there had been. They did seem to recast it every three months or so. Then I had a brilliant idea.

I placed ads in all the trade papers announcing that auditions for the role of Tarzan were being held every Saturday at Morehead Heights. As the star of *Tarzan's Secret Shame,* I felt I was fully qualified to select Tarzans. The ad said, "Arrive Undressed for Success."

I placed that ad in July of 1952 and have been running it ever since. It was a smashing success. Every week that I'm in town, on Saturday afternoon I can count on a handful of well-set-up young men showing up at my front door dressed in skivvies, bathing suits, or loincloths, ready to give their all for the chance to become the jungle's number one swinger. And when Terrence and I are traveling, Rudy handles them. I've met many wonderful young men this way, some of them even with acting talent.

I would have the men rehearse and perform with me an audition scene I had titled *Tarzan Sires a Son.* Each week one or two wouldn't want to do it and would leave. But there were always ambitious young men willing to do what it takes to become a star, and I've been unsurprised when some of them later popped up on daytime soap operas similarly attired. I might add that after more than forty years of playing Jane every week, I'm far better at the role than plain little Maureen O'Sullivan ever was.

Occasionally, men who weren't really a realistic choice for the part would show up, but I never turned a man away without a fair shot, or two if he was up to it. I will never forget the short, one-legged Englishman who showed up for the part one time in the early sixties. He may have been an offbeat choice, but he was eager to hop to it. I wonder whatever became of him?

Little Pattycakes was home from Rodeo Rhetta's that summer. The delightful little urchin was now six foot five, and half her body weight looked to be nose. She took to hanging about at Tarzan audition time until I sent her to her room.

Pattycakes had just turned sixteen, and people couldn't believe she was only ten years younger than I. But then, of course, she was adopted.

I threw her a lovely Sweet Sixteen birthday party. She invited a large number of teenage boys, but when I caught her kissing a boy in the hedge maze I was forced to send her to her room again and to post Major Babs there to make sure she stayed in. The boy was obviously guiltless. In fact, he had been clearly struggling like crazy to try to break loose from my boy-crazy daughter's iron embrace, so I allowed him to stay. I took over entertaining my daughter's young male guests myself, and every boy there went home happy, with a little surprise, and a few weeks of injections cleared that up as well.

I was shooting *Boot Camp Bitches* by this time, a terrifically popular film set in a woman's prisoner-of-war camp, focusing on the deep relationships that form between the lady prisoners and how they manage to survive emotionally by developing a passion for black leather footware. The movie was a violent one, featuring beatings, whippings, canings, spankings, slappings, paddlings, chafings, and Indian burns. At the climax the male Nazi officers arrive just as we prisoners rise up. We enslave the men, and the picture ends with the Nazi male hierarchy polishing our shiny new boots with their tongues.* In the years since its release I've had letters from hundreds of women from all over San Francisco

---

*I found out later that the men playing the Nazi officers weren't actors at all. Russell and Sid, always alert to unusual money-making ideas, had sold these roles to the highest bidders. The men in the German uniforms licking our boots and enduring swats with a leather switch had all paid hundreds of dollars each for the privilege. In fact, *Boot Camp Bitches* was the first film in movie history to turn a profit *before* it was even finished shooting! Show me another star who can claim *that!*–Tallulah

telling me how much this film meant to them growing up. I have made personal appearances in recent years at theaters playing revivals of this film and have been overwhelmed by the number of women who show up dressed in duplicates of our costumes in the picture. In an unusual move, Russell had hired my old pal Ida Lupino to direct, and her unique female perspective helped make this one of the few "women's films" to be equally popular with men and women alike.

No sooner had shooting wrapped than I was off to Washington to testify before Congress. I spent several days wandering around Spokane before Jerry Mander tracked me down and got me on a plane to Washington, D.C.

Appearing before the hated committee, I was asked to turn rat and name the names of people I knew to be Communists.

"All right," I said, "Joe Stalin, Lenin, Mao Tse Tung . . ."

"No, no, no," Senator McCarthy interrupted rudely. "We mean people in the movie business."

"Senator," I replied frostily, "didn't your mother ever teach you that it's rude to interrupt people? I know what you want. But I won't do it! I will not name names!"

"Miss Morehead, please," the odious man continued, "if you won't answer the committee's questions we'll be forced to find you in contempt of Congress."

"Then find me in contempt and be damned! But I will *not* name Lucille Ball! Why should John Garfield's career be blighted just because I saw him plotting the overthrow of democracy? You'll never drag that son-of-a-bitch Elia Kazan's name out of me! Nor will I mention the name of Emma Goldman, who was as charming a lesbian as I have ever met."

"Miss Morehead, you will answer our questions, or you will go to prison."

Jerry Mander talked to me quite severely back in my hotel room that evening. He explained that if I didn't testify, I could be cut off from all alcohol for quite some time. I prepared a list.

"Senator McCarthy," I said, when I'd been sworn in again the next day, "on the advice of my counsel, and over my strong personal objections, I have prepared a list of names for the committee."

"Excellent. Please read out the names of the traitors to America on your list."

I fished the list out of my purse and began to read the names I'd scrawled there, feeling like a rat every moment. "Jack Daniels, Johnny Walker, Jim Beam, Dewar's . . ."

"Miss Morehead, who are these people?"

"Johnny Walker Red? Sounds like a Communist to me." Jerry whispered in my ear for a moment, then I said, "I'm sorry. That was my shopping list. Apparently, I don't have the list I intended to bring."

"Well, can you remember any names, off the top of your head?"

Then I had an inspiration. "Yes, I can! I have tried to resist this committee, but I see you are too powerful for a simple woman like myself. In 1936, when I was just nine, I attended a meeting held by the American Communist Party. While there I saw one of America's greatest enemies at work, and I can no longer protect this viper in our bosom. The washed-up hag of a film actress Delores Delgado was engaged in a sexual three-way with Joseph Stalin and Karl Marx as they plotted the overthrow of the government of the United States of America. I'll swear to that on a stack of Bibles, and I speak as a non-practicing Christian Scientist. Now, how do I get a drink around here?"

That was the conclusion of my testimony. I was excused by Congress and returned to California, where Russell was ready to shoot a melodrama called *Grueling Fury* with me, while Pattycakes complained that I was preventing her from having any private life, and I faced alone the prospect of soon turning thirty.

One good thing that came out of all this mess was the end of Delores Delgado's career. She was over sixty, after all. For years afterwards she complained publicly that I was responsible for her being blackballed all over Hollywood. I don't know what the ungrateful woman was so upset about. I've been blackballed thousands of times, and I've always enjoyed the hell out of it!

26

Thirtysomething

After I shot *Grueling Fury*, a picture in which I was terribly upset about all sorts of things, S. Lee-Zee Films had another stark melodrama all ready for me, the frank crime-spree flick, *Scofflaw*. It was almost like being back at PMS again. Every picture I had made for S. Lee-Zee Films had turned a profit (though, to be frank, these films were made so economically that ten paid admissions usually put them in the black). I was now the reigning star of S. Lee-Zee Films, and Russell was writing my scripts for each while the preceding one was being shot. Fred Sturm had negotiated a back-end deal for me that was putting my life back on a paying basis, and I felt at last ready to accept the fact that in just a few short years I would be turning the dreaded age of thirty. I was ready for maturity, and ready for a drink.

I had been so successful as the sullen Helga in *Boot Camp Bitches*, which ran for a year without ever being projected indoors, that I was getting typecast as a mean, tough broad, a change from the temptresses I had played in the beginning of my career, back when I was a small child. In *Grueling Fury* I had played a wronged woman who took it out on anyone who got near her. Now, in *Scofflaw* I was playing a no-nonsense career criminal who goes on a wild cross-country crime spree, jaywalking, running stop signs, passing stopped school buses, ripping tags off mattresses, going through the nine-items-or-less checkout station with twelve items, and committing other antisocial activities until finally brought to justice by a crusading district attorney who happens to be my husband. During the touching final scene, when I bid goodbye to my husband, who has sent me up, and leave for my ninety days in the hoosegow, without the possibility of early parole, and beg him to wait for me, the audience reaction could hardly be contained. The honking and blaring of car horns usually completely drowned out my costar, Kent Clark, as he spoke the final line: "Speed it up, jailbird. I've got a date."

Hoosegow, coincidentally enough, was to have been the title of my next S. Lee-Zee Film, but somebody at Universal (then called "Universal-International," which struck me as redundant) had noticed that, rather than my being washed-up, my last five movies had all turned profits. Since Universal was in the business of making profits I was offered a two-picture deal for rather more money than Russell was paying me.

My first picture for Universal was a western called *Johnny Horndog.* I played a tough-talking, straight-shooting cattle rancher named Tombstone Tess who battles rustlers, Indians, and suitors. In that film I was the first to make Iron Eyes Cody cry. (Let's face it, the man was a waterworks. And now the headless Indian brave tells me he wasn't even a real Indian!) At the end I give up the outlaw Johnny Horndog, who has saved the ranch by killing all the bad guys and eradicating an entire tribe of Indians, and marry the sheriff who hangs him.

I spent most of the movie in the saddle, and often on horseback as well. The director later accused me of giving all the men in the cast saddle sores, or something like that. So silly. Easily half the men in that cast rode sidesaddle, if you catch my drift.

My next picture for Universal was *Abbott & Costello Meet She Who Must Be Obeyed,* a sort-of sequel to my film *HER!* made some twenty years before. The gigantic statue of myself as the ageless queen, which had been dominating the garden and hedge maze at Morehead Heights ever since, was moved temporarily to the back lot at Universal while we shot this amazing laugh riot.

In the picture, Abbott and Costello stumble into my lost city of Bor, where they become my sex slaves. It was something of a change of pace for the famous comedy team, not as kid-oriented as their previous pictures. I was warned that Bud and Lou liked to play endless games of poker on the set. I said this was fine with me, although as it turned out, all they ever did was play cards. Well, they weren't all that young anymore. I, on the other hand, hadn't aged a day. In fact, that was the whole point of the movie.

The critics noticed as well. The *Los Angeles Times* said, "Tallulah Morehead's return to the role of the eternal queen two long decades later robs the word 'ageless' of any meaning. It may be said with some degree of accuracy that she has finally grown into the role of a woman thousands of years old, although, for pure, hilarious comedy, the new film hardly compares with the wacky original."

Frankly, when the picture was done, I wasn't feeling all that peppy. I had, after all, made some sixty-five movies in the forty years since my debut back in *Heat Crazed!*, which is one hell of an accomplishment for a girl of twenty-eight.

But I decided to take some time off and just relax for a few months, to get my strength back. Unfortunately, my darling daughter, now nineteen years old, was a bigger handful every day. Six feet seven now, and socially backward, she was unbelievably forward with every man she met. Rudy and Terrence both complained of her annoying their gentleman callers. It seems she was not above pretending to be a drag queen if that was what it took to get into a man's pants. She fought with Major Babs, whom she referred to as Diesel, almost constantly, and by "fought" I mean fisticuffs. They went at each other like Rudy and Terrence sighting Tab Hunter.

By 1956, I was feeling well enough to go back to work, and signed with Amassed Artists for three movies. In the first I played the title role in the beloved science fiction classic *THAT!* I play a lady scientist called in to help Kenneth Tobey and Richard Carlson save the day when a rogue dose of radiation causes my normal housecat to grow to the size of the Smithsonian. Needless to say, my giant kitty regards mere humans as cat toys, and the city of Washington, D.C., is nearly shredded to bits. I come up with the brilliant plan to cover the Washington Monument with shag carpeting, turning it into a gigantic scratching post. All mankind seems to wilt when confronted by my giant pussy, but I stiffen their resolve to destroy the huge thing, which is using the National Mall as a massive litter box. Once treed on the Washington Monument, we bombed my overstretched pussy with a massive overdose of catnip. Effects mastermind Ray Harryhausen had the time of his career, bringing my enormous pussy to life.

In 1957, Morehead Heights became a star as well. *THAT!* had been a science fiction shocker. My second film for Amassed Artists was to be a supernatural shocker. Shockers were all Amassed Artists made. This film was to be a ghost story called *The Haunting of Horrible House*, in which I was to costar with suave Vincent Price. The director came out to Morehead Heights to discuss the picture with me, took a look around, and decided to shoot the entire movie right here in my home.

Well, this was fine with me. First, it meant I could sleep in, since all I had to do to go to work was come downstairs. Secondly, it meant the budget for sets, production design, and décor all went directly into my liquor budget, where it could do some good. The only real problem this entailed was getting Rudy to stop vacuuming during takes. How often, just as the director yelled "Action," did we hear the deafening roar of Rudy sucking away just off camera. "Rudy!" I would have to holler. "Knock it off!"

"All right," he would say, dripping his usual attitude, "I'll just have to do it later."

We eventually solved the problem by giving Rudy a small part in the film as Vincent's personal valet.

My house proved a big success as the haunted mansion. We kept the fact that it was my real home a secret, just to see if we could fool the critics. It worked. Reviewers later wrote, "The sets in this film seem to have truly been designed by a madman. Never has any home had a more apt name than Horrible House."

I invited Vinnie to stay at Morehead Heights—after all, why should I be the only one sleeping in? I installed Vincent in the husband's bedroom (although I was still married to Rudy, he stayed in the servant's wing). I assumed that Vinnie and I would get to know each other much better that way. Imagine my shock when he moved his *wife* in with him! What sort of a man wants his wife around when he's living with his costar? I guess the rumors about him are *true!*

As if bringing his wife in wasn't bad enough, Vincent covered the walls of his room with the most godawful, ugly, garish paintings. The man's taste in art was just ghastly. The paintings were so terrible I suggested using them in the movie. Why should they only frighten the servants? But neither Vincent nor the director took the suggestion well.

The headless Indian brave almost had his big break in this movie. Since the house in the film is filled with ghosts, I suggested using the headless Indian brave as one of the spooks, giving the movie an uncanny verisimilitude. The director was willing, and the producer was delighted, since the headless Indian brave would work for wampum. As he could only materialize after dark, we arranged a night shoot for his scenes, and I must say, he was a natural. Even Vincent, no stranger to horror movies, was scared of him. The director was ecstatic.

Unfortunately, when we viewed the dailies we were all in for a disappointment. It turned out that the headless Indian brave doesn't show up on film. The poor lamb went around for weeks so sad he could barely hold his neck-stump up.

The film turned out quite well, and is still popular today. The premiere coincided with Pattycakes's twenty-first birthday. We decided to let the premiere party double as her birthday party. Pattycakes complained that none of her friends could come, but I ask you, how many girls get to have birthday parties where they are surrounded by men like Rock Hudson, Tab Hunter, Cesar Romero, Clifton Webb, Nick Adams, Roddy McDowell, and Tony Perkins, not to mention Vincent Price presiding over all?

Speaking of Vincents, Vincent Lovecraft, my old PMS costar came, with his longtime roommate C. Halibut Plugg, and gave Pattycakes a sports car, which I thought was an excessively expensive gift for such an ill-behaved child.

Shortly thereafter I finally celebrated my thirtieth birthday. Pattycakes's present to me was to stay away for the weekend, something she did with greater frequency since getting that damn car. Vincent Lovecraft baked a cake on which he'd written "30 Again" in icing, though I have no idea *what* he meant by that! Dear Roddy McDowell stated sweetly that any day now he would be older than I, and I had to agree.

Rudy gave me the best present of all, a divorce. We'd been married now for ten blissful sex-free years, and he had his full citizenship papers, but he stayed on as my houseboy and made dear, anorexic little Audrey Hepburn flee in tears when he criticized the colors she was wearing. Ironically, my marriage to Rudy was the longest and most successful of my life. It's amazing what no sex will do for a couple.

As I looked back over thirty years of life, forty-two years in the movies, sixty-seven motion pictures, and nobody knows how many husbands, though at least six or seven, I realized how full and rich my life has been. Yet, I felt starved for a New Challenge. That New Challenge lay just ahead, for before I embarked on my next film, a touching, romantic shocker for Amassed Artists called *Bride of the Blob,* I was to make my first foray into the wonderful new world of television. The Vast Wasteland was about to get vaster.

27

Morehead from Coast to Coast

TV. Who could have known it would ever mean more than just men in frocks? I had originally inquired through Fred Sturm about appearing on live TV dramas, but then I learned that, unlike radio, you weren't allowed to hold your script, and, unlike the movies, you had to perform the whole thing all at once rather than in little bits and pieces. I decided to give it a pass. They expected me to memorize an entire script all at once, something I hadn't done since *The Lost Recess* back in 1915, before I was born! They were clearly insane! And I never work with madmen, unless the money is a hell of a lot better!

I was offered a guest spot on something called *I Love Lucy*, but I wasn't ready to play a lesbian on national television yet. Frankly, Lucille Ball had been very cold to me ever since I had listed her among the names I refused to name to HUAC. That's gratitude for you. I remember one evening when I'd had Mr. and Mrs. Ball over to Morehead Heights for a party that turned particularly ugly when Lucy barged into a private room—without knocking, I might add—and yanked Desi off me, screaming, "Stick it back in your pants, lover!" and then calling me all sorts of rude names. I'm not one to tell tales out of school about my fellow actresses, even shrewish bull dykes like Lucy, but, to be honest, I've heard rumors from very reliable sources that Lucy *wasn't* a natural redhead. Not only that, but she drank like Willy Wonka in the Chocolate Jacuzzi.

However, dear, rugged, sexy Groucho Marx, a total dreamboat whom I'm eighty-five percent sure I was almost never married to, was having an ongoing success hosting a TV game show called *You Bet Your Life,* and although I felt the stakes on his show were a little high, it was certainly popular, and it didn't involve memorizing anything. I spoke to Fred about setting up a pilot for me.

When a charming but shy young southern gentleman named Francis Gary Powers showed up at Morehead Heights, I realized, just as soon as he'd dressed and left again, that I was going to have to be clearer with Fred about what I meant by "set me up with a pilot."

Pattycakes was a terrible trial at this time. Some anonymous person had set up a trust fund for her shortly after she was born. I have no idea who the creator of the "C. Aubrey Fund" was, nor why he felt it necessary to leave my adopted daughter a trust fund, but since turning twenty-one, the girl had come into a large income and was using it to travel about in nasty, low places like Paris and Rome on her vacations away from UCLA, where she was squandering what little intellect she had studying something called premed. I wasn't fooled. It was just a way to meet boys.

Major Babs was now ninety-two, although she had the strength and vigor of a man three-quarters her age. Babs didn't approve of anything Pattycakes did, and the two quarreled and fought constantly. You would have thought Major Babs was jealous of Patty's claim on my attention, which was silly. I paid almost no attention to Patty as it was.

To be honest, Patty was starting to remind me way too much of her late grandmother, whom she strongly resembled despite their not actually being related, and Patty's gigantic nose.

Amassed Artists was preparing *Bride of the Blob* for me, in which I was to play the title role, but preproduction had hit a snag when Orson Welles turned down the role of the blob. I was at loose ends while the studio shopped about for a blob worthy of me.

Then Fred Sturm called. He had set up a TV production deal with the Seagram's people to sponsor a game show for me. It was a fabulous deal, with plenty of money and unlimited access to the sponsor's lovely product. They'd come up with a wonderful quiz game based on a game popular in taverns all over America. We shot a pilot episode, and the fledgling ABC network snapped it up for thirteen episodes.

The TV show was a breeze to do and occupied only one evening a week. During the days I was now shooting *Bride of the Blob,* the producers having decided that forty pounds of Cherry Jell-O was an adequate replacement for Orson Welles. It didn't speak as well, but it ate supporting cast members with just as much panache. The movie was loosely based on *Macbeth*, only instead of being king of Scotland, the main character was a gelatinous glop of goo from outer space; and instead of killing the king to take over the country, it just ate everyone who got near it; and instead of my encouraging it for my own ends, I just screamed and ran every time I saw it.

My big scene was my mad scene, based on Lady Macbeth's famous mad scene, where I get really, really mad, and shout, "Out, damned blob!" Many of my other speeches were also paraphrases from the overwritten original. For instance, in the play, when she learns of the prediction that her husband will be king, Lady Macbeth says, "Come, you spirits that tend on mortal thoughts, unsex me here, and fill me from the crown to the toe, top-full of direst cruelty. Make thick my blood. Stop up the access and passage to remorse, that no cumpunctous visitings of nature shall shake my fell purpose." In contrast, in the movie, when I learn that my husband has been infected by an alien organism and has mutated into a gooey blob of carnivorous ooze that no power on earth can prevent from eating every person in the world, I say, *"My God! The Blob! Aaaaaaahhhhh!"* which means practically the same thing, and was considerably easier to learn.

Similarly, in the play, after seeing her husband's crimes, Lady MacBeth says, "I have given suck, and know how tender 'tis to love the babe that milks me: I would, while it was smiling in my face, have pluck'd my nipple from his boneless gums, and dash'd the brains out, had I so sworn as you have done to this." In the movie, when I see my husband, the blob, eat an entire college basketball team,[*] I say, *"My God! The Blob! Aaaaaaahhhhh!"* though I pleaded with the director to at least let me say, "I have given suck," even going to some lengths to prove to him that I knew what I was talking about. On the last day of shooting, the entire crew showed up wearing tee-shirts that read "I've Been Given Suck by Morehead!" which was touching and true.

Meanwhile, every Friday evening I reported to the ABC studios on Vine Street in Hollywood to broadcast live my delightful and challenging quiz show, *Blotto!* The game was a simple one, based, as I said, on a popular barroom and fraternity game. Three contestants would compete each show. I would ask them trivia questions, and if they got the questions right, they won money. But if they got a question wrong, they had to drink a shot of that evening's featured hard liquor. The last contestant still standing at the end of the show went on to the big-money end-game, going head to head with me in the "White Lightning Round."

For the "White Lightning Round" we dispensed with the questions altogether. The contestant was usually far too drunk by this point to answer coherently even simple inquiries like, "What is your name?" We would do simultaneous shots of white lightning until one or the other of

[*]Something I have done myself in real life.–Tallulah. **Me too.–Douglas**

us passed out. If I passed out first, the contestant won the jackpot. If the contestant passed out first, all he got were his game winnings and a lifetime supply of Seagram's Seven, which, if he was driving himself home, often wasn't much. It was as simple as that. To keep it fair, I would do shots throughout the show along with the contestants so I wouldn't have a sober advantage in the end-game.

The show did extremely well in the ratings, and the home game, put out jointly by Milton Bradley and Seagram's, sold quite well also. I was praised by educators and bartenders for my signature sign-off line. Every week I ended the show saying, "Remember, kids, stay off drugs, and keep your bottoms up! Cheers!" However, after a few weeks the viewers, the network, and the sponsor all started to complain. For one thing, in the show, I encouraged the viewers to play along at home. We were on at seven-thirty on Friday evenings, and by the time we went off the air, a large portion of the home audience had passed out, and those that hadn't were generally too drunk to comprehend the commercials on the rest of the evening's programs.

But the primary problem was that I never lost the end-game. In the first eight shows we never gave away the jackpot. I thought the sponsor would be pleased by the money I was saving them, but they said the audience liked to see a contestant win once in a while. I'll never understand that attitude if I live to be a hundred.[*] The contestants were *nobodies!* I am a *Star!* Of *course* the audience prefers to see *me* win!

I consented to an adjustment. My shots became double the strength of the ones served to the contestants. Still no winners. In the eleventh show they tried putting up a panel of hard-core alcoholics. Again, no winners. For the twelfth show, they tried bringing winos in right off the street. Still there was no winner, and it looked rather suspicious that I was on a first-name basis with all the contestants.

For the thirteenth show the producers, desperate to give the jackpot away, quadrupled the strength of my shots while giving the contestants colored water. This finally produced the desired result. I passed out live on national TV, and a local street wino walked away with ten thousand dollars, although he didn't get too far.

I woke up in a hospital room with all sorts of tubes sticking out of me. Apparently, I'd been in a coma for five weeks. *Blotto!* was permanently off the air, and a man who introduced himself to me as Doctor Stein informed me that I was in need of a liver transplant!

---

[*]Actually, Tallulah hit one hundred back in 1997.–Douglas

28

Cry Me a Liver

What person facing a serious illness hasn't asked himself the question, "Why me?" Certainly this was how I felt. Why should I, of all people, suddenly have my liver go on the fritz, *for no reason at all?* Why do bad things happen to good movie stars? I had been at pains to take meticulous care of my health all my life, never eating to excess and getting plenty of good, healthy sexual exercise, yet now, from out of the blue, my liver had gone ballistic.

There had been no warning whatever, unless it had come during one of my social blackouts, and I hadn't had one of those that lasted longer than a day or two since missing out on *A Streetcar Named Desire* seven years earlier. It was true that I hadn't really felt my best for a couple years now, but I attributed that to the natural slowing down with age that accompanies turning thirty. But now, out of nowhere, cirrhosis. Go figure.

My family rallied to my side—though by my family, I mean only Terrence and Rudy. Major Babs seldom left the house anymore, and Pattycakes was in Mexico, hiding, she said, from the shame of my TV show, although I don't see what was so embarrassing about your mother being a national TV star who had proven she could drink anyone under the table. A donor liver, I was informed, was immediately available, which was fortunate, since I apparently had a very rare, almost peculiar blood type. I was to go under the knife at once. I pleaded to be allowed to have sex one last time, just in case, but the doctor turned me down, while Rudy chimed in, "Don't look at me, lady." Dear Terrence managed to round up a compliant orderly for me.

When I asked Dr. Stein for a drink before the operation he was even more adamantly unreasonable and mumbled some insanity about my not ever being allowed to drink again. I began to worry about being operated on by a man so clearly deranged, but he gave me a shot of something wonderful, and I no longer had objections to anything.

Need I say the operation was a success? If it hadn't been, you would have been reading something else for the last twenty-seven chapters. Fortunately for you, I lived, yet my health didn't snap back. I went home after a few days but was back in the hospital again in a week. More tests, and my doctor came in to give me the bad news. Pattycakes was back by then, and she, Major Babs, Terrence, and Rudy were all gathered by my bedside while the headless Indian brave listened in from home on the phone.

"What is it, Frank?" I asked Dr. Stein. "Tell me the worst. No, wait. Maybe a martini first, to cushion the blow."

"No!" Dr. Stein bellowed, rudely. "No alcohol! How many times must I tell you?"

"What's the trouble, Frank? What's wrong with me?"

"Don't get me started," Rudy put in, unnecessarily.

"It's your new liver . . ." Dr. Stein began.

"What's wrong with it? Is it defective?"

"No, it's perfectly healthy. In fact, it's too healthy."

"What do you mean?"

"Well, the problem is rejection."

"My God, my body is rejecting my new liver?"

"Not exactly. Actually, your new liver is rejecting you."

"What?"

"Well, basically, your new liver has taken a look around its new surroundings, and is now screaming 'Get me out of here!' "

"That's the way I feel whenever I look at the house."

"Quiet, Rudy. So Doctor, what do we do?"

"Well, we should replace the liver again, as soon as possible, and hope for a closer match."

"What do you mean by a closer match?" Major Babs asked.

"Well, it's not enough just to match the blood type. What would be ideal would be a blood relative, where you have a close genetic match. But you don't have any blood relatives that you know of, do you?"

"No, my daughter is *adopted!* As it happens, she does have the exact same, extremely rare blood type as mine, but that's just a *coincidence,* I tell you. After all, I wasn't married at the time, although I did marry

Rod Towers shortly thereafter, and we did have sex, no matter how repulsive he found it.

"What are you talking about?" Dr. Stein asked, having evidently drifted off while I spoke, a not uncommon phenomenon. Rudy did it all the time.

"I was just saying that my daughter is adopted; we're not actually related. Movie Star's Honor."

"But if Patricia were actually Tallulah's daughter, then you could use her liver?" Major Babs asked.

"Well, no, of course not. It would kill her."

"Yes, I realize it would kill her. I'm just asking if, given that they have the same rare blood type, if they were really related and something *awful* happened to Patricia, like if she drove that smarty-pants car of hers off a cliff, for instance, her liver would be a better match for Tallulah?"

"Well, theoretically yes, she would then be a much better match. But Patty isn't a blood relative, and isn't dead."

"I wish everyone would stop talking about me as if I weren't even here!" my daughter interrupted in her usual whiny tone.*

"Honestly, Pattycakes," I explained as patiently as possible, "no one was talking about you. We were discussing me, and my health. Forgive my self-centered daughter, Doctor; like all teenagers, she thinks it's always all about her."

"I'm not a teenager. I'm nearly twenty-two."

"Dear, no one is talking about you at all. Do you mind if the subject is me for a change?"

"What change? When do you ever talk about anything but yourself?"

"Please forgive her, Doctor, she's upset with worry for me. Babs, why don't you take Patty home?"

"I was just going to suggest that very thing, Tallulah," Major Babs said. "Leave everything to me."

With that, Major Babs and Patty left. If I'd known then that I was never to see my darling little girl again, I wouldn't have parted so an-

---

*Though, in Pattycakes's defense, I should point out that with her enormous nose, it was very hard for her not to sound whiny. She was doomed to a nasal voice. It's funny, my costar in *HER!*, back some eight or nine months before Patty was born, C. Aubrey Smith, had a very similarly huge nose, yet his voice wasn't at all nasal. —Tallulah

grily from her, but none of us can see the future. Sometimes just focusing on the room around us is damned hard.

Fortune smiled on me that night. Against all odds, another liver that matched perfectly with me became available just a few hours later. An accident victim whose head was missing, so her identity was never established, was brought in, and her liver was installed in me, where it percolates on to this day. I'm told it was from an otherwise healthy (except for being headless) young woman in her early twenties.

When I regained consciousness after the operation, all my family was there except for dear little Pattycakes. Since I still had a tube down my throat (which I found strangely pleasant), I had to write out my questions on a pad of paper. I scribbled out my first question.

"Nope," replied Major Babs, as in charge as she'd been back before World War One. "The doctor said absolutely no alcohol."

"Don't worry, Tallulah pet," said Rudy. "I'm right on top of it," as he switched bags on my IV, replacing the saline with a martini drip. Dear Rudy, always prepared.

Having dealt with important matters, I next scribbled out, "Where's Patty?"

"She left," Babs answered. "She said she'd had enough of sickrooms and hopped in that car of hers and took off. I don't know where she went, and I can prove it."

"I'm sure she'll be back by the time you get out of the hospital," said Terrence.

"You want to put a little money where your mouth is, Terry?" Major Babs asked.

It may have been a cynical attitude, but it was on the mark. I have never seen or heard from my daughter since. She must have lost her head, because she drove off that day and never looked back. I don't know how or where she lives. She never even made another withdrawal from her trust fund. I can perhaps understand her turning her back on me, but why cut herself off from her own money? It's a puzzlement, and her absence leaves an empty spot in my heart to this day. I hope she's had a happy life.

Darling Pattycakes, if you're out there reading this book, please call me, write, anything. I love you, my only child. Please come home. Most is forgiven, and Major Babs is long dead.

Yet it was Major Babs who comforted me with this thought, spoken one day as she changed the dressing on my incision: "Tallulah, as long as you live a bit of Patty will live on in you." How right she was.

MY LUSH LIFE   225

Meanwhile, to heal my broken heart and speed my recovery from my operations, I decided to travel. Leaving Major Babs and the headless Indian brave behind to watch over Morehead Heights and keep a candle burning for my prodigal daughter, Terrence, Rudy, and I embarked for England, on the first leg of what turned out to be a long, leisurely, complete global circumnavigation, even though none of us is Jewish.

PART FIVE

Morehead Around the World!
1959–1961

29

Hammer Me!

England, that Spectered Isle, that chunk of chalk, that land of warm beer, bad food and worse teeth! It had been forty-one years since I had been there on my first honeymoon, and now, at the mature age of thirty-two, I barely remembered the place, the obscure language, or why I had ever married F. Emmett Knight in the first place. What had I been thinking? That's what comes of marrying too young—in my case, before I was even born.[*] This is why I have always felt that no one should be allowed to marry until *after* birth![†] I do not approve of Womb Robbers.

But now I was back in London as a fully mature adult, in the company of two men who would do nothing to interfere with my fun as long as I did nothing to interfere with theirs. The city had only grown larger. Nelson's Column was still an awesome sight, once I'd tracked Nelson down,[††] and Big Ben was just as big, although I could have done without his constantly chiming in.

One evening Rudy and Terrence took me to a theatre in the West End, which is located on the east side of London. The movie was a comedy that was full of fairies. That's what I get for letting Rudy and Terrence pick the film. It was called *A Midsummer Night's Dream,* and

---

[*]I know it sounds insane, but mathematics is a science, like Christian Science, and forty-one from thirty-one leaves minus ten, which must have been my age when I married F. Emmett, no matter how much I may have looked twenty. After all, *numbers* can't lie!–Tallulah

[†]Though it would appear these days that my advice has been misread as, "No one should marry until *giving* birth."–Tallulah

[††]Since Jeanette MacDonald had retired nine years before, Nelson was touring nightclubs with Gale Sherwood and Edgar Bergen. The bizarre things some people find entertaining!–Tallulah

it was evidently some sort of fairytale for gay children, like *The Wizard of Oz,* where it all turns out to be a dream, although, instead of singing and dancing with midgets, in this picture all they did was talk, talk, talk.

My old pal Charlie Laughton was in this picture, playing Bottom, although both Terrence and Rudy said they'd seen him play Bottom before, at intimate parties. In a plot development stolen directly from Walt Disney's stark coming-of-age drama *Pinocchio,* Charlie grows donkey ears. A Fairy Queen, mistaking Charlie for an ass, falls madly in love with his first glimpse of this Man-Bottom, like every Fairy Queen I've ever known, and I've known quite a few, although I didn't marry *all* of them.

Toward the end Charlie plays Pyramus in a touching film-within-a-film about tragic lovers. Frankly, Charlie completely exploded his overblown acting reputation in this part. For years people had spoken of Charlie as some sort of great actor, though I couldn't see it. He didn't have the raw talent of a Sherman Oakley or a Rod Towers. Well, his performance as the tragic Pyramus put the lie to that reputation once and for all. He was ghastly! Instead of weeping, the audience was laughing their heads off. I was just glad he wasn't there to hear his disgrace.

The oddest thing about this movie was its unusual technique. The director had shot the whole thing in endless long shots. There wasn't a single close-up, or even a medium shot, in the entire movie. To compensate for this visually static camera, the film had been shot in the most amazing 3-D process I had ever seen. It was incredible. It looked for all the world as if there were no screen at all, just a big platform full of living actors, right there in the room with you. In one mind-boggling effect, the fairies seemed to run right up the theater aisles and mingle with the audience. I could have sworn I saw Rudy slip one his phone number.

I later discovered that this unique 3-D process, which had been patented under the technical name "Live Theatre," was very popular in London. There were films shot in this unusual style playing in theatres all over the West End, with some very big stars. I found it a striking innovation, but once the novelty had worn off, I missed the immediacy of huge close-ups. Not surprisingly, this so-called "Live Theatre" process has never caught on in Hollywood. A gimmick like that can never replace the excitement and freshness of editing and close-ups.

By the wildest coincidence in the world, shortly after the movie ended, we ran into Charlie on the street outside the theatre. The poor man looked exhausted. Worried that he might have stuck his head into the theatre and heard the audience rudely laughing at his pathetic Bottom, I invited him to come for a drink, but he just wanted to get home to his little spitfire wife Elsa and jump her bones. The palpable sexual energy between these two hot lovers was always radiating from them. They could barely keep their hands off each other in public. Now there was a real marriage, a true merging of bodies and souls, unlike all the sham travesties of marriage I'd been in. After spending ten years married to Rudy, it was refreshing to see two people like Charlie and Elsa who were madly in love and wildly banging each other's brains out day and night. Ah, *l'amour.*

As we headed back to the townhouse I'd taken in lovely Bloomsbury I heard a voice call out, "Tallulah, doll-baby!" I turned and saw an unfamiliar elderly man approaching me.

"I'm sorry, sir, you have the advantage on me. Naturally, as a world-renowned *Star* and Nearly Living Legend, everybody recognizes me, but I don't know you, darling," I breezed, always approachable, even with men old enough to be my late father.

"Tallulah, my God, it's been over forty years, but I'd know you anywhere."

"Impossible, sir. I am barely thirty-two."

"Oh please! It's me, Mark, from high school!"

"Mark? Can it be? My second-favorite tutoring pupil?"

"In the flesh. Well, not in the flesh yet, but I can be quickly. You got a place around here?"

"But, Mark, darling, you're an old man. What happened to you?"

"The twentieth century, same as you. Hey, babe, I loved you in *The Haunting of Horrible House.*"

"Thank you, darling. You know, that was shot in my own fabulous movie star mansion Morehead Heights, mounted firmly atop priapic old Tumescent Tor overlooking the churning Pacific. Where have you been? Why haven't you ever been to see me?"

"Tallulah, doll-face, I haven't been back to the states since 1917."

"Then how did we meet? I wasn't even born in 1917."

"Oh, drop the act, Tallulah. I was drilling your lights out back in high school, remember?"

"Vividly. But, you were a handsome young buck. Now, you've got no hair, and lots of stomach."

"The years leave their mark."

"Not on me. I'm *ageless!*"

"Well, I'm sixty-two, however old you say you are. You got a place we can go? I'd take you to my place, but the trouble and strife would pitch a fit."

"Excuse me? I'm sorry. I don't speak the language."

"I mean my wife doesn't allow me to bring women home. Where are you staying, and why are the two fruitcakes hanging around?"

"This is Terrence, my personal assistant, and Rudy, my latest ex-husband and traveling companion. As for where I'm staying, all I've got is a room in Bloomsbury."

"Just a room, that will do for you and me," Mark replied, breaking into a song. "One room's enough for us, though it's on the top floor. Life may be rough for us, but it's trouble we'll ignore."

"Before we break into a dance number I have to tell you, it's an entire townhouse, and Terrence and Rudy are staying there, too."

"They have their own bedrooms?"

"Of course."

"Then why are we standing around here?"

Soon we were tucked away cozily at my place. After reminiscing, we started to catch up on old times while Mark redressed. And I'm glad to report that Mark's best feature hadn't aged at all. Mark, of course, was familiar with my career. The whole world loved my movies.

"I must admit," he said, as he hunted for the remains of his underwear, "you threw me when you said Rudy was your ex-husband, but then I remembered that first husband of yours, what was his name?"

"F. Emmett Knight."

"Right. I bet I know what the 'F' stood for. I guess you always had a habit of marrying the gay boys."

"Not a lot of choice. Straight men don't need to marry."

"Hell, I'm as straight as they come, and I've been married for over thirty-five years. My wife is Lady Harridan. Distant Royal Cousin."

"You've made a life over here, then?"

"I had no choice. I couldn't very well go home again. When I got over to France during the war and got a look at what was going on, I realized I had to get out of there. It was *dangerous!* I developed an allergic reaction to being shot at, and came down with a severe case of Goldbrickitis. When they wouldn't ship me home I, ah, quit. Yes, that's what I did. I quit, and came back here. I've been here ever since."

"What did you do for a living, darling? Gigolo?"

"Hardly. You inspired me. I said to myself, if Tallulah Morehead makes a living acting, how hard can it be?"

"Thank you, darling. Were you any good?"

"Not really, but I was genuinely American. I worked steadily, playing Americans, for years."

"What films were you in, darling?"

"Only a few. Mostly the stage."

"What's that?"

"Tallulah, still a kidder. Anyway, about ten years ago, I quit acting and became an agent, like that first husband of yours. At my age, and with my looks gone, there's more sex for an agent. Hey, you looking for work?"

"Well, I have a Hollywood agent, of course. But I'm over here, recovering from surgery, and haven't thought about working."

"What surgery? Obviously not a facelift."

"Thank you, darling. How sweet. I might be interested in making a picture or two while I'm seeing the world."

"You know, I might have just the project for you. You did that spook show with Vincent Price. Done any other horror movies?"

"According to Bosley Crowther, I've done nothing else. But yes, I did several. *Fu Manchu's Blessed Event, Curse of the Pussy People*. I worked with Bela Lugosi, both Lon Chaneys. Hell, I was married to Boris Karloff briefly."

"Old movies and has-beens. I mean any recent horror movies, like the one with Vincent Price?"

"Yes. I did THAT! And *Bride of the Blob*. They were both shockers!"

"Great! I gotta get you in to see Mike Carreras over at Hammer."

"What is 'Hammer'?"

"'What is Hammer?' Tallulah, baby, Hammer Films is the hottest studio in England. Their horror movies are raking in cash all over the world. You're perfect. Who could be scarier than you?"

As it turned out, Hammer Films was a little company making movies in a large country mansion they were pretending was a film studio. Two years earlier they had made a Technicolor remake of *Frankenstein* starring two men I'd never heard of, Peter Cushing and Christopher Lee. The picture had been a huge success the world over. They had followed it with a *Dracula* remake, again libeling my dearly departed third husband (from back in the days when I could still keep count), and a *Frankenstein* sequel, and both had been even bigger successes. Now the studio was cranking out horror movies faster than Rudy cranked out martinis.

Mark took us to see Hammer's *Dracula*, and, while it once again portrayed my late beloved—except by his minions—husband as a feral, blood-drinking, undead fiend, the dreamy Christopher Lee did capture my darling Vlad's wild sexual charisma. Additionally, the film movingly dramatized his tragic sun allergy, creating sympathy for the sufferers of this rare condition the world over by quite accurately depicting his horrible, unnecessary death in a scene that reduced me to tears, while shifting the blame from me to Peter Cushing, who played the villainous Van Helsing.* After the movie I was sobbing so hard I couldn't even help search for Terrence, who was found cowering under a chair in the back row. I noticed that after we saw the picture, Rudy took to leaving his bedroom window open at night and hanging a sign from it that said GARLIC FREE ZONE.

I couldn't wait to have Christopher sinking his fangs in my throat and solid, dependable Peter pounding his way into me.

As it happened, the Hammer team had a vampire picture in casting right then.† Anthony Nelson-Keys, the producer, was delighted to have a big American star to give it a little more stateside marquee heft. Soon I was working with Chris and Peter and being directed by darling Terry Fisher in the Hammer horror classic *Bats in My Belfry*. In an attempt to vary the formula a little, in this picture Peter played the sexy vampire always nibbling at my neck, and suave Christopher was the nasty vampire hunter always ruining our fun.

To give the picture further novelty, instead of having me play the imperiled virgin whom the vampire visits at night, they gave that role to some buxom newcomer named Amber Something, while I played the vampire's even more evil mother-in-law. In a wonderfully erotic scene, Chris Lee took out his enormous stake and hammered the hell out of me!

But the rumors I'd heard about all Englishmen being gay turned out apparently to be true. Although Terry and Peter were both married, and Chris later also married, I couldn't get into any of their pants to save my life. Even Jimmy Sangster, who wrote the picture and who was also married, wouldn't give me a tumble, and it's a measure of how desperate I was that I'd even *consider* having sex with a *writer!*

I first grew suspicious at the casting interview with Tony Nelson-Keys and Terry Fisher when I started to undress and they *stopped* me. This had never happened before in all my years in the movies! Even Russell had had sex with me before officially casting me in movies he'd written specifically for me.

On the set, things got worse. When I suggested rehearsing, all Peter and Chris would do was *rehearse!* How unprofessional! Everybody treated me with the respect and deference more properly due to an *old lady!*

---

*Though firm, upstanding Peter was playing the evil vampire murderer, frankly, he could pound his stake into me any time he liked!–Tallulah

†To be fair, Hammer Films generally had a vampire film in casting from 1958 to 1974.–Douglas

Hammer was famous for having buxom starlets running about in low-cut, flimsy, see-through nightgowns. Not me. In the costumes provided for me, I was just a head sticking out of the top of a teepee. I kept expecting Apaches to take up residence in my petticoats.

Terrence had another theory. He suggested that maybe the British were just too polite for sex. I took his suggestion, and the next day, at Bray Studios—the name given the drafty old house where we shot the picture—I said to Chris Lee, "I say, Chris old bean, would you be so very kind as to shag my brains out?" Lee roared with laughter and then repeated my "witticism" to everyone on the set.

But the worst disappointment came the first afternoon, when we broke for Afternoon Tea and these fanatics actually served *tea!* How can you expect anyone to act after choking down that vile swill? After the first day, Terrence began bringing along my own private "tea," prepared at home by Rudy.

All in all, working in England was placid but dull. Everyone seemed to find the idea of a woman past thirty wanting a little shagging, or, better yet, a *lot* of shagging, hilariously funny. I'm afraid I didn't see the joke myself.

By the time *Bats in My Belfry* had wrapped, Mark had lined up another picture for me, a Roman Spectacular to be shot in Italy. I also received an invitation to attend a festival of my films in Paris. Since the festival was to take place before the film was to start shooting, I decided to accept and visit Paris, where I'd heard the men *liked* sex with women and no one would serve tea while a drop of wine remained on earth.

30

Paris When It Swizzles

I love Paris in the springtime. I love Paris in the fall. Why, oh why, do I love Paris? I'd tell you, but my publisher advises me that if I say anymore I'll owe the Porter estate a royalty, like they need more money.

Illinois Smith and I had flown over Paris in 1918 during our escape from the kaiser, but that had been at night, and during the war they always referred to as "The Big One," so it was obvious *they* hadn't had sex with the kaiser. A decade later I had visited Paris briefly on my way to Transylvania and my darling Vlad. But now I was arriving for a two-week festival retrospective of my career by the French Academy of Cinema Art, at the climax of which I was to be given the title *Commandeutrix des Arts et Lettres,* recognizing me as a Genius every bit the equal of Jerry Lewis.

As it happens, I speak French like a native.* Terrence and Rudy were both fluent in French. Indeed, it was all either of them could do to keep their tongues in their own mouths. Communicating with the gallant French would be no problem.

After breezing across the channel from Folkestone to Boulogne, we took a train to the glorious City of Light. After a couple hours on the train we pulled into a station. I asked the conductor if we were in Paris. He mumbled some indecipherable gobbledygook that Terrence translated as, "Shut your stupid mouth, American pig," so we knew we were in glamorous Paris!

The conductor then added what Terrence translated as, "Get your God damn asses off my train," so we disembarked onto the platform of

*A native of Idaho, that is.–Douglas

Gare de Nord. There, as we were jostled and shoved about by people snarling what Terrence translated as, "Out of the way, American swine," we heard a voice calling *"Mademoiselle Morehead, s'il vous plait!* Over here." Looking about, we spotted a devastatingly handsome man of maybe fifty waving to us.

This man handed me his card, which read, M. JACQUES FROMAGE, CURATOR, FRENCH NATIONAL CINEMATEQUE. He was in charge of my retrospective, titled *Tallulah Morehead: Le Miserable Actress,* and had come to welcome and escort us to our hotel, a luxurious establishment in the Marais district called Le American Couchon.

(I assumed that the *M* stood for *Monsieur,* but Jacques later explained that it was merely the initial of his first name, Monterey.)

The program for my retrospective was a large one: twelve double features and the opening and closing nights at which I would appear in conjunction with a single film. The opening night they were presenting *The Revenge of Cleopatra.* The next twelve nights they ran *Dancing in the Drink* and *Broadway Bimbos, The Godawful Truth* and *The Lady Steve, Life Preserver* and *Amnesia, Adam's Bone* and *Forbidden Fruit, Fatal Floozy* and *The Devil Wore Ermine, Virgins of Krakatoa* and *Sudan Sunset, HER!* and *Abbott & Costello Meet She Who Must Be Obeyed, Alexander the Great's Ragtime Band* and *The Gang's All Banged, Privates on Display* and *Privates in Public, East versus West* and *The Mailman Always Comes Twice, Fu Manchu's Blessed Event* and *Curse of the Pussy People,* and *Beyond Belief!* and *Amok!* The closing night would feature my investiture, preceded by a rare screening of the uncut, original European version of my debut film, the silent *Heat Crazed!.*

Since I was only required to appear the two evenings, and I had seen all the films they were running, I had the rest of my time free to sightsee and go nightclubbing about this most enchanting of cities. Jacques Fromage insisted on personally squiring Terrence and me about, while Rudy preferred to go out evenings on his own.

Unlike most French people, Jacques was politeness and gallantry itself. He went on and on about my *miserable* acting. His willingness to ruthlessly praise my work, and his fearlessness in calling me a genius and the greatest actress in the world, was winning my heart again as surely as it had when F. Emmett Knight was so brutally frank with me over forty years before. I was soon falling in love with the handsome curator, who, after all, *had* to be straight. He was *French!*

My first morning in Paris, as I was enjoying my eggs with a light breakfast wine, a note was slipped under my hotel room door. When Terrence fetched me the note, it proved to be a typical French fan letter, except for being written in English. It read,

> *American Whore, If you value your worthless life, take a friendly word of advice, and go home now!*
>
> The Phantom!

Terrence, who wasn't used to French fandom, was instantly terrorized by the anonymous mash note. "Don't panic so easily," I told him. "I've been getting letters like this from Bosley Crowther and Frank Nugent for years. Just ignore it."

That day Jacques took us to the Eiffel Tower, perhaps the most beautiful and inspiring structure in the world. "Just imagine," said Rudy, who came along on our day trips, "going to the top and sitting there during an earthquake. That would be *hot!*" There was no arguing with him.

That afternoon, back at the hotel, I was in the bar when I was hit with the need to visit the ladies room. I asked the desk clerk for directions to "the Loo." To my surprise, they didn't have a public one on the premises, but rather, he gave me complicated directions to an enormous, almost palatial facility nearly a mile away, at the east end of the Champs Ulysses, or something like that. This turned out to be well worth the long trip, for it was, without doubt, the largest, and most lavishly decorated ladies room I'd ever seen in my entire life. I suspected that I was in the wrong place, but when I asked an attendant if this was indeed the Loo, he replied, with typical Gallic savoir-faire, "Yes, you stupid American ass! Of course it's the Loo!"

"Well, where do I go to relieve myself?"

"Anywhere you like, you overbathed, colonial pissbag. The entire Loo is equally relaxing and inspiring, not that a cretinous American asswipe would know great art from my father's scrotum!"

"Actually, I've always been an ardent devotee of scrotal art."

"You have obviously mistaken *moi* for someone who gives a *merde.*"

"Thank you, darling," I replied, always happy to find a more-polite-than-most Parisian. I wandered the gigantic hallways, their walls covered in magnificent, enormous paintings and their floors littered with elderly statuary, looking for a sufficiently private place for my ablutions. This Loo followed the common continental custom of being unisex. Indeed, there were crowds of people of all ages and genders all over, enjoying the tremendous plethora of artwork. I finally found what seemed like a private enough spot behind a lovely statue of a bare-breasted woman from which some vandal had broken off the arms. I had hiked up my skirt, squatted down, and had barely begun the business at hand when all hell broke loose and I found myself hauled off to a French jail by a couple of rough but attractive *gendarmes,* who stubbornly refused to treat me with gratuitous brutality.

Jacques Fromage was only too glad to come to my rescue and bail me out of the hideous Bastille. Apparently there had been some sort of tragic mixup, caused no doubt by the various different ignorant French persons' failures to master English.

When we got back to the hotel there was another note under my door. This one said,

American Bitch, You have not heeded my warning. Leave Paris.
Flee for your life. If you accept the ludicrous French honor, you
will not live long enough to regret it. I tell you this as a friend.
                                                              The Phantom.

Jacques was much concerned when he read the anonymous fan letter, albeit one slightly less than usually gushing, in the customary French style. He then said that at the Academy the day before they had received a similar note, which had read, in French, of course,

My Friends, if you persist in honoring the talentless, drunken
American slut, a disaster beyond your imagination will occur!.
                                                              The Phantom.

"How bizarre," I said. "Have you any idea who the note refers to?"

"None whatever." Jacques replied. "But now that I see the one you received, it occurs to me that the one we received might be referring to you."

"Which part?" asked Rudy. "The disaster beyond your imagination or the talentless American slut?"

"Difficult to say," Jacques replied. "We need more data. If this Phantom writes again, save the notes for the police."

"Whatever you say, darling. Now, it's time for your reward. Make love to me."

"Madame Morehead, please. I mustn't take advantage of my position."

"We can use any position you like."

"I will see you in the morning, *ma cherie*. But I urge you to take this threat seriously."

"Threat? What threat?"

"This note."

"You think it's a threat? It sounds like the usual French fan letter to me."

"I think this person may be very dangerous."

"Oh please. If the last war taught us anything, it's that the French are no danger to anyone."

"That may be, but there is nothing to indicate that The Phantom is French."

This was certainly a sobering thought, so I forgot it as quickly as possible.

Over the next few days, Jacques took us to the Arc d'Triomphe, the palace at Versailles (nice, in an understated way, but certainly no Morehead Heights), the Pantheon, the Jardin des Tuileries, Montmartre, the Hotel de Ville, and cruising on the Seine. One day Jacques tried to take us to see Notre Dame, but the pretentious woman never showed up, despite our waiting around all day in a drafty old church on a small island. However, while we waited we were served sacramental wine by the homeliest man I have ever set eyes on, with absolutely disgraceful posture.*

Evenings were even better. Jacques would introduce that evening's double feature to the audience of tasteful, discriminating art lovers, then he would swing by Le American Couchon and collect Terrence and me for an evening in the gay nightspots of Paris, as well as some of the straight ones: the Moulin Rouge, the Trocadero, even the Folies Bergére, although Terrence got nauseous there and had to leave. Gallant escort that he was, Jacques insisted on taking Terrence back to the hotel himself, leaving me to enjoy the show, the drinks, and the girls by myself.

Each morning I found a new note under my door and Jacques found a new one on his desk. The general message was always the same. I was not to appear at the closing ceremonies or accept the honor being conferred upon me, or some terrible event would occur. Each was signed "The Phantom."

---

*I mean it! Quasi was so extremely unattractive that when he showed me around the bell tower while Jacques and Terrence were inspecting the nave, I *almost* didn't have sex with him! I might add, in the throws of passion, when most men would call out my name or cry, "Oh God! Oh God!" Quasi kept shouting "Sanctuary! Sanctuary!"–Tallulah

No one had a clue as to the identity of this Phantom. I assumed that it was some man so obsessed with my undying beauty that he wanted me all to himself. The police theory was that it was just an average Parisian, disgusted at the idea of honoring an American.

Jacques arranged for armed bodyguards to accompany me at all times, as there was no way to ship Major Babs over here in time. Besides, at ninety-four, just how much protection could she offer? The unfortunate side effect of this precaution was that just as things between Jacques and me were heating up, we were never permitted to be alone together. Every day Jacques grew more passionately devoted to me, yet if he even laid a finger on my arm, the guards would wrestle him to the ground. I wouldn't have minded so much if the guards had been willing to take up the slack. But I couldn't get them to wrestle *me* to the ground. Here I was, in the most romantic city on earth, having a romance with a true gentleman, and I couldn't get a tumble, except for impetuous Quasi, who really knew how to ring my bell.

I began to wish The Phantom would materialize. At least I could get some action. No such luck.

The morning before the next-to-last evening Jacques received a note that read,

Mon Ami, you have persisted in ignoring my friendly warnings. To make sure you do not make the mistake of dismissing me as a crank, tonight I will make a small demonstration of my power. Heed my warnings, or innocent people will suffer. Don't make me kill!

The Phantom.

The program that night was an oddly matched double feature: they were to run my 1946 melodrama *Amok!* preceded by my silent science fiction adventure *Beyond Belief!* Sadly, all that was to run amok that evening was the audience.

Vincent Lovecraft, who was in both pictures, had come all the way from Hollywood, accompanied, as always, by his longtime roommate, C. Halibut Plugg, for a question-and-answer session with the audience following the screening.

That day Vincent and C. Halibut had gone along with Jacques, Terrence, and me on our Parisian rounds. Vincent suggested visiting the Musée de Louvre, but I was legally enjoined against revisiting that particular landmark.

Vincent never got to his question-and-answer session. During the screening that evening of *Beyond Belief!*, at the very moment that the deplorable Delores Delgado first appeared onscreen in her toxic green makeup as Cunterra, Queen of Mars, an explosion ripped through the movie screen, shredding it to ribbons. At the same moment another explosion in the projection booth destroyed the Academy's projectors as well as the prints of *Beyond Belief!* and *Amok!* A hideous voice rang out over the noise and smoke, crying, "I warned you! This is but a sample of my power. If you honor the American Whore tomorrow night, an even greater disaster will occur!" The audience, in a complete state of panic, sprang to their feet and stampeded to the bar.

Vincent and C. Halibut were nervous wrecks as they told me the dramatic events of the evening, although my stalwart Jacques was completely cool under the pressure. I questioned them closely about the important details of the disaster.

"Was the bar damaged?"

"Not so far as we could tell."

"What about when the audience stampeded the bar?"

"No, they didn't damage the bar."

"Were the bartenders able to cope with the tremendous rush for post-disaster libations?"

"Not really. They worked as fast as possible, but three bartenders can hardly be expected to handle seven hundred French people demanding drinks. Many people couldn't be served at all, and had to leave for other taverns."

"Oh my God, the humanity!" I confess my weakness. I sobbed over the senseless tragedy. Obviously this Phantom was no respecter of cocktails. *The Fiend!*

The Academy was in no shape for the final night's ceremonies. The closing festivities were moved to Garnier's grandiose Opéra, the infamous opera house where, with typical French logic, they performed only ballet.

One more note was under my door that morning. I got only a brief glance at it before it was snatched up by the gendarmes, who were now very determined to catch this nasty Phantom, who had so overworked three noble bartenders. Further, in addition to the bartenders and the damage to the National Cinema Academy, a film critic had suffered a sprained ankle in the melee. That *really* meant **WAR** to the French!

The note read,

Evil American Bitch From Hell, this is your Last Warning! If you enter the Opéra tonight, then the carnage that will occur will be on YOUR *head! Beware! Beware!*

The Phantom.

I was a bit annoyed when the gendarmes confiscated it, as I wanted to paste it in my scrapbook with the rest of my beloved fan mail.

Terrence tried to talk me out of going that night, but I am nothing, if not a trouper, and I'd been promised free drinks all evening, not to mention the far from inconsequential stipend. Terrence stayed behind at the hotel, while Rudy, Jacques, Vincent, C. Halibut, and I went on to the show.

Garnier's Opéra House is a wildly grand theater, fully worthy of me. The centerpiece is the incredible seven-ton chandelier that dangles above a strangely unconcerned audience. The wine, I must add, is excellent.

The evening started well. There were police everywhere. The huge auditorium was packed. When I was introduced, I tottered out onto the stage with a freshly filled champagne flute, and the roar of the standing ovation was deafening. Cheers filled the air. You'd have thought the predominately French audience didn't know I was an American. Fortunately, the movie was the silent version of *Heat Crazed!*, so it wasn't necessary to wait for the audience to quiet down to begin the picture.

Suddenly there I was up on the screen, as I'd looked nearly forty-five years earlier, long before I was born. The audience gasped at the flagrant proof that my looks hadn't changed an iota in all those years. I think Rudy put it best when he looked up at the hastily erected screen and said, "Who the hell is that?"

And there was the late, great Gilbert Rolaids, swaggering in his prime. The audience hung on every frame as I teased and vamped Gilbert into a homicidal frenzy. In the dark, my darling Jacques took my hand and whispered ecstatically in my ear, "My God, Tallulah darling, you used to be *beautiful!*"

"Thank you, darling," I whispered back.

The amazing, original climax, where dear Gilbert makes violent love to my corpse, hadn't been seen by audiences since before nearly everyone present, myself included, had been born, and has never been seen again since. The stunned audience sublimated their palpable shock with roaring gales of hysterical, nervous laughter.

After the picture finished Jacques and I returned to the stage to cries of, *"Le floune alcoholic!"* which I needed no translator to tell me meant,

"The brilliant tragedienne." The screen flew up into the catwalks, and I stepped up to center stage. As I opened my mouth to thank the audience, the world turned suddenly upside down.

Loud explosions went off on both sides of the stage, releasing great clouds of smoke. The lights went out, and the stage dropped away beneath my feet. Apparently I had been standing on a trapdoor, and it opened the moment the room went dark. I plummeted into an abyss. I landed in a heap on something soft, only to be immediately seized from behind by a rough, strong pair of hands. A cloth was clamped over my face and I breathed in acrid fumes. My head began spinning, and all went black!

31

In Seine!

When I regained consciousness, I heard the thunderous sounds of a large pipe organ being played furiously, which is, frankly, not my favorite large organ. I opened my eyes to see a terrifying sight—no alcohol anywhere in the room! What was in the room was the aforementioned pipe organ being played like crazy by a menacing figure dressed from head to foot in black.* One might have thought that the enormous hooded black cloak would be the most striking article of apparel the figure was wearing, but it was not so. One's attention was immediately drawn to the grotesque, deep blue mask the creature wore. Only a misshapen mouth showed beneath the mask, while a pair of satanic red eyes glowered deep within its sinister eyeslits.

The room was built of stone and constructed of gothic arches. There were no windows. The door arches were barred like a cell. There was an enormous lever protruding from one wall, and beside it a sign saying, "DANGER! DO *NOT* PULL THIS LEVER FOR *ANY REASON WHATEVER!*" On another wall a large ring of keys hung on a peg. The floor slanted to a grilled drain in the center. I was lying on a small bed, to which, it turned out, my left ankle was attached by a short chain. Could it be that the kaiser was still alive after all these years and had recaptured me? It didn't seem likely, but mine was a face few forgot, no matter how hard they tried.

"I say, Phantom darling," I called out, "Phantom, Fanny. Hey! How about a drink for a lady over here?"

The music stopped. The Phantom turned and glared at me. When he spoke, it was in a harsh, sinister whisper. "So, bitch. You have awoken

---

*Wise choice. Black is so slimming.–Tallulah

at last. You failed to heed my warnings, you talentless, ugly whore! Now, you will die for it!"

"You know, for a Frenchman, you speak English with no accent at all. How about a martini?"

"That is because I am not French."

"Really? Because your choice of terms seems so French. Any wine around this cellar?"

"This is deeper than any cellar. We are in my Phantom Lair, far beneath the river Seine, in the famous sewers of Paris. A fitting place for a sewer rat like you to die."

"Then we should celebrate, darling. Any champagne?"

"Indeed there is!" said The Phantom, as he pulled an ice bucket from behind the organ console. A bottle of champagne was chilling in it, but I noticed only one flute.

"Aren't you having any, Fanny?" I asked politely. As a social drinker, I never like to drink alone unless there's no other choice.

"Oh, I'm having it all. You see this bottle? It was bottled in 1897, the year the world was cursed with your birth."

"Nonsense, darling. I'm only thirty-two, and I don't look that."

"You certainly don't."

"Thank you, darling. So pour me a flute and let's celebrate this occasion."

"This occasion is your death. I'm going to drink this rare and expensive champagne myself, in front of you. And then, you will die."

"While that is unspeakably rude, I don't think it will actually kill me."

"Of course not, you moron!"

"Are you *sure* you're not French?"

"You still haven't recognized me, have you, you stupid whore?"

"You certainly sound French. And how could I recognize you? You're wearing a mask."

"Well, Tallulah, I've waited years for this moment. It's time to cast the mask aside and show you the last face you will ever see."

With that The Phantom threw off the hood, cast off the cape, and tore off the mask. I screamed in horror at the repulsive visage that stood revealed. Twisted and scarred though it was, there was no mistaking the hateful countenance underneath as anything but the ghastly face of *Delores Delgado!*

"Delores darling, please, put the mask back on. What happened to your face?"

"What happened? What happened? *You happened!* For almost forty-five years, since the day you first sashayed your slutty behind into PMS and seduced my husband!"

"But, what did I ever do to you?"

"What did you ever do to me? You have to ask? You carried on an affair with my husband right in front of the whole world!"

"Well, I think that was Gilbert's choice."

"And he has paid. I poisoned him with arsenic so slowly they never suspected murder."

"Well, then, we're even. Now, let's share a flute of that fine champagne and then I'll be on my way."

"*Even? You call that even?* Screwing my husband was only the start! You poisoned me at your housewarming!"

"Nonsense. The belladonna was, perhaps, a little ripe . . ."

"You insisted Marcel Pouff . . ."

"Dear Marcel. How I miss him."

". . . use that toxic copper makeup on me in *Beyond Belief!* Which is why I blew up that movie at my first entrance last night!"

"And now you've nearly killed me. Like I said, we're even. Now let's have a drink."

"You've sabotaged and slandered me for decades! While my career spiraled downward, thanks wholly to your poisoning Louie Thalberg against me, you made one wretched, embarrassing movie after another without ever displaying the slightest *trace* of talent! Then, one year, thanks to one great role, I had a chance at a real career resurrection, and you gave *my* Oscar to *Jane Wyman!*"

"She won."

"*NO SHE DIDN'T!* Do you think I didn't understand the meaning of that look that crossed your face when you opened the envelope? That bastard Waterhouse, chained right there where you are now, told me everything before he died."

"Well, you have to admit, it was a good joke. Jane certainly fell for it. Let's have a drink and then we'll call Jane and tell her the bad news."

"I'll be taking my Oscar back from her personally, when she dies in here next month."

"Then it's all straightened out. Well, if you're finished, how about some bourbon and branch water?"

"*I'm not finished!*"

"All right, just straight bourbon."

"As if giving my Oscar to that woman wasn't enough, you had the *gall* to tell the House Un-American Activities Committee that I was a Communist!"

"You told me yourself that you were raised in a Burlingstoke commune."

"I grew up in Burlingstoke *Common!* It's a *town* in England, you ignorant fool! I was blacklisted from the industry. I tried having plastic surgery to change my appearance, to escape the hounding and the harassment, and the butcher did this to my face! When I heard that you were to receive this ludicrous, undeserved honor from these tasteless French fools, it was the *Last Reel!* You've hounded my existence and ruined my life for too long, and now you will *die!*"

"Well, Delores darling, it's been great fun reminiscing old memories with you. Good Times, eh? But now, I really have to go. You retired persons may have all the time in the world to just sit around and gab, but I'm due on a film set in Rome in three days."

"The next time you are photographed, it will be in the Paris morgue!"

"Nonsense. The lighting there is most unflattering. Are you going to open that champagne or not? I'm getting parched by all this chatter."

"Yes. It's time for me to open it, drink it, and then club you to death with the bottle!"

"You'll never get the deposit back that way."

Just then another voice cut through the room. It was the voice of my beloved, the handsome Monterey Jacques Fromage: "Don't panic, Tallulah, we'll save you."

I looked behind me and there, behind the barred arch, were Jacques, Terrence, and Rudy.

Terrence was crying as he said, "Has she hurt you, Tallulah?"

"She's wounded me deeply. She said I was a lousy actress."

"Mon Dieu!" cried the devoted Jacques. "You are a goddess of the screen! Your acting will live forever."

"Which is more than she will," Delores interrupted with her customary rudeness, "because she is about to die, and there is *nothing* you can do to prevent it. But I will permit you to stand and watch."

"You can't kill Tallulah," Jacques yelled supportively, "she's a screen *immortal!*"

"He has a point, Delores. I am immortal."

"What does he know? Fromage, you cheesy fool, you wouldn't know talent if it was rammed up your ass! Tallulah couldn't act her way out of a paper script, and Jerry Lewis has no talent, either!"

In a small, quiet voice that was terrible to hear, Jacques said, "What did you say?"

Delores almost spat in his face through the bars as she replied, "I said

Jerry Lewis is a talentless buffoon whose movies would make a baboon look like Charlie Chaplin. Dean Martin carried him for years. Jerry Lewis is an unfunny bore who amuses only the witless and the clueless."

Jacques loosed a great, bellowing *"NON!"* Then we heard a strange grinding noise. It was the steel bars that were keeping my rescuers at bay. Jacques, in the massive adrenaline rush which accompanied his hearing Jerry Lewis trashed to his face, was bending the bars apart without even realizing he was doing it. Delores, her eyes widening in shock, backed away from him, but she was too late. In a rush of rage such as I have never seen before or since, Jacques was through those bars and sprang on Delores like a madman, throttling her wattled throat. Terrence was next through the bent bars. He sprang over to the peg and grabbed the ring of keys, then ran over to unlock my shackle. Rudy strolled through the bars last, and the three of us stood placidly, watching Jacques passionately strangling Delores.

"Don't you think we should try and stop him?" Terrence asked.

"Why, darling?"

"Well, he's killing her."

"What's your point?"

"Say," Rudy put in, "what's this lever for?"

"I have no idea."

"I think we should separate them." Terrence put in. "Jacques could get hurt."

"I don't see how, Terrence. And Delores is turning a remarkably flattering shade of purple. It's the best she's looked in years."

"I have to know," said Rudy, who then yanked down on the large lever.

Immediately a great panel in the ceiling slid away, and a colossal torrent of water came thundering down into the room, directly onto Jacques and Delores.

"Oh, I see," said Rudy. "It diverts the Seine through this room. I wonder why."

"Rudy, you imbecile!" I shouted. "This is a new dress!"

At that moment, Jacques washed up at our feet. As Rudy and Terrence helped him to stand, I suggested our departure, as the room was quite rapidly filling with river. We fought the current back to the bent bars and out onto a stone stairway leading up just beyond.

"What about Delores?" cried Terrence, always concerned with irrelevancies. "She'll drown."

I turned back, saw Delores thrashing helplessly, and dove into the violent water.

"No, Tallulah!" Jacques cried. "You can't save her! You'll drown, too!"

A few moments later I emerged from the raging waters and scrambled up beside them, brandishing the bottle of champagne. "This could have been lost thanks to your carelessness, Rudy. Think before you act."

An hour later we were all back in my suite at Le American Couchon, finishing off the sixty-two-year-old champagne. Whatever her faults, Delores had great taste in wine. I saw a look pass between Jacques and Terrence, after which Terrence took Rudy and left Jacques and me alone.

"I see we are alone at last, my darling rescuer," I said.

"Yes, Tallulah. I asked Terrence to take Rudy and give us some time alone together."

"How wise, my darling," I said, pouring us two more flutes full of bubbly. "So, sweetheart, how did you find me?"

"That was Rudy. He's been cruising the sewers for weeks."

"I've always suspected as much. That explains the men he brings home."

"He was looking for The Phantom."

"Why did he think to look there? Force of habit?"

"Rudy figured that since The Phantom seemed to materialize at will in any Parisian building, he, I mean she, chose, they must be connected through tunnels. That led him to our world-famous system of sewers. After you were kidnapped, he came and got Terrence and me, and we followed the organ music."

"How fabulous, my darling. Now, haven't you something you want to ask me?"

"I see I cannot hide my heart from you. You've seen that I'm in love."

"I knew. A woman always does."

"I know it's a lot to ask on such a short acquaintance, but then, at my age, time grows precious."

" 'Your age,' piffle! What are you? Fifty?"

"*Oui.*"

"So, you're a few years older than me. What does that matter?"

"It doesn't matter at all. It's not even relevant. It just means that I've waited a very long time to find true love. I could hardly mistake it when I found it."

"Of course. As you know, I've been married a few times, so I know a thing or two about love."

"Then your answer is . . . ?"

"Oui! Oui! A thousand times *oui!"*

"Thank you, my dear. You've made Terrence and me the happiest men in France."

"What?"

"Now, I know you're upset about losing an efficient assistant. I know he's been with you for forty years. . . ."

"I'm only thirty."

"But Terrence is seventy now, and he's ready to retire. He wants to settle down here in Paris with me, and I want him to as well. He was afraid to tell you himself, so he asked me to ask you if you'd mind terribly if he left your employ. I knew a great woman like you would understand."

"I don't understand."

"If only you could stay for our wedding, but we know you have to get to Rome for your next great movie."

So that was it. After a mere forty years, Terrence just upped and abandoned me in the middle of The European Wilderness at a moment's notice, after stealing the heart of the one who was to have been my next husband. Imagine! Only Terrence could turn a Frenchman gay!

The next day Terrence and Jacques were there, unnecessarily holding hands like schoolkids, at Gare de Lyon to see Rudy and me off on the train to Rome. That same morning, Delores Delgado's body washed up in a fisherman's net a few miles downstream from the city. Like any wise fisherman, he threw her back.

32

A Roman Spectacle

Rome, the Eternal City, like my career. I little suspected I would find love there, but Roma, dear Roma, was where I found Paolo, the love of my life, except for all the others.

But before the pleasant discovery of Paolo came the unpleasant discovery awaiting me at my hotel, the La Dolcé Villa. It was a book, a book by my darling, missing child Pattycakes, the infamous international sensation, *Mummy Darling*.

The newly published book had been sent over by Major Babs. I immediately called the publishers to see if they knew where my darling girl was, but they were as bewildered as I, hard as that is to imagine. It turned out that Pattycakes had completed the manuscript secretly, shortly before her disappearance. The publishers wanted to know if I knew where to find her. They hadn't heard from her since she ran off, either, and they had royalty checks for her. I told them to forward the checks to Morehead Heights, where I would know just what to do with them. As for where Patty was, I had a gut feeling she was very near, closer than my clothes, which are often as hard to relocate as Patty has been.

With Terrence gone and Rudy out busily cruising all seven hills, I was forced to read Patty's book myself. Those of you reading this book will know just how tedious a chore reading a book can be. And this one was a pip, though, in a strange way, it made her running off more understandable. *Mummy Darling* was clearly the work of a severely deranged mind. Her mental state must have been deteriorating long before she finally snapped, under the pressure of my illness, and fled. Somehow I had missed the warning signs of the madness that clearly flowed through the book's wildly unhinged pages.

As if the title weren't bad enough, making me sound like something moldering under a pyramid, the description of me and my life within was weird, to say the least. Patty, in the grip of her delusional state, portrayed me as some sort of alcoholic bisexual nymphomaniac who was constantly boozing when she wasn't jumping into bed with anyone that slowed down long enough. Have you ever heard anything so absurd? Me? A nymphomaniac? An alcoholic? I needed a drink!

I read some of these ridiculous charges to Mario, the twenty-year-old bellhop who had restocked my depleted wet bar, as we redressed after I gave him his tip, but apparently the boy spoke no English, although he had other oral skills.

And me, a bisexual? How ridiculous! I've *never* had a lesbian relationship with *any* of the women I've slept with! I explained this to the maid after she finished making the bed and me, but she didn't really grasp English all that well, either. Or maybe I just wasn't speaking clearly enough with my voice *muff*led.

And as for me being an *alcoholic,* well, gentle reader, you can say it along with me by now: I'm *strictly* a *social drinker!* But it seems I had an antisocial daughter.

But the description of my life as one endless, alcohol-lubricated journey from crotch to crotch, while starring in a string of unwatchable kitch-fests (apparently the opinions of the French meant *nothing!* Next she'd be saying that Jerry Lewis wasn't a genius, *either!*) paled next to the pathetic parenting fantasies the book was awash in. In a state of deep denial that is probably common in adopted children, Pattycakes had worked out an elaborate fantasy, which she presented as fact, in which she was not my *adopted* daughter at all. She claimed, get this, that I was her *actual,* biological mother. According to her bizarre, irrational ramblings, I had *somehow* gotten pregnant *out of wedlock,* as though that were even possible, and had been passing off my real daughter as my adopted child. Have you heard anything so *insane?* She'd clearly been spending too much time around Loretta Young. And what evidence did she offer, besides her obstinate refusal to accept reality? Her resemblance to my mother, our matching, extremely rare blood types, the identical martini-glass-shaped birthmarks we both had on our left inner thighs, and other similar, flimsy "proofs."

Wildest of all was her belief that her father was Gary Cooper. Let me make this clear: I can state here with absolutely no fear of contradiction that Gary Cooper was *not* Pattycakes's father! My affair with Coop was *years* earlier!

Actually, if you have someone count back nine months from Patty's birth for you, you'd find me in the midst of the filming of *HER!*, and my leading man in that film was Charles Farrell, whose wife would certainly have objected if he'd cheated on his boyfriends with me, not to mention the fact that I was spending all my offscreen time then with C. Aubrey Smith, that extremely tall, distinguished British character man with the impressive, oversized snout. And you know what they say about a man with a large proboscis: they can let fly with one hell of a sneeze. But did my freakishly tall daughter ever point her colossal nose in that direction? No! Not that she had a reason to, since she was, I repeat, *adopted*. Only Dr. Lecter knows who her birth parents were, and he had long ago gone to his reward, a lovely home in Pensacola.

I'm afraid *Mummy Darling* is nothing more than the paranoid ravings of a sick child. It may read like an attack on my character and parenting skills, but it was really a cry for help, a flight from reality in print that was closely followed by the real thing. If only I'd seen the signs, or the manuscript, I might have been able to prevent her final breakdown, or at least its publication and subsequent international bestsellerdom, the forty-seven paperback reprints, and that *ridiculous* movie in which Meryl Streep gave such a laughable performance as me. That Oscar was *wholly* undeserved!*

Besides, what did Pattycakes know about my character or my parenting skills? The girl spent most of her life in boarding schools. We were barely acquainted. She was not merely insane, she was presumptuous, just like her grandmother, to whom she wasn't related.

Meanwhile, as this pathetic tissue of baseless lies, three-quarter-truths, and innuendoes was climbing the best-seller lists in America and Europe, I was at work on that magnificent multimillion-dollar spectacle of ancient Rome, *Caligulee, Caligula!*

The star of *Caligulee, Caligula!* was the fascinating Italian superstar Steve Reeves.† If the pathetic sham which is the Oscars needs further discrediting, I need only point out that Steverino (his name in Italian), a Mediterranean Olivier, was, like me, never even nominated for that hollow facade of an award. As we started work together, all Italy was still reeling in shock at the recent Academy Awards debacle in which not only had Steverino's awesome and deeply moving performance in *Her-*

---

*Is it any wonder I have only derision for the Oscars when that untalented hag, who can't even make up her mind what her natural accent is, wins one for playacting the role of *me* in one laughably deranged movie, while *I've* been playing me for *decades,* in almost *ninety* laughably deranged movies?–Tallulah

†Actually, the late, great Steve Reeves was from Montana and spent most of his life living in San Diego.–Douglas

cules Unchained, the single greatest male performance ever captured on film, been overlooked, but the award had actually gone to that ghastly lump of talentless flesh *Charlton Heston,* for a performance that was nothing more nor less than a feeble *parody* of Steverino's colossus of an accomplishment! What can they have been thinking? *Ben Hur,* done him!

Steverino, who was modest to a fault, and chaste to the point of rudeness, was masking his disappointment remarkably well on the set. He was playing a heroic Trojan warrior named Phallus Maximus. On a sea voyage, a storm blows him off course, a waterspout actually picking up his ship and flying it through the air until it crashes to earth on the island of Minos, where it smashes down on a horrible monster called the Minotaur, whom it crushes flat.

The Minutians, a race of tiny people, celebrate their liberation and offer Phallus Maximus their crown, begging him to become the king of Minutianland, but all Phallus wants is to return home to Troy. None of the Minutians know where Troy is. They've obviously never seen or used a Trojan before. They advise him to consult the Oracle of Dephi. The Oracle directs Phallus to go to the Eternal City (Rome) and ask the Great and Terrible Emperor Caligula for directions home. When Phallus asks the Oracle which way to go to get to there, she tells him, "Follow the Appian Way. Follow the Appian Way. Follow, follow, follow, follow, follow the Appian Way."

"But what if I lose the Appian Way?" Phallus thrusts inquiringly.

"Well, then," the Oracle continues, "just follow any old road, since all roads lead to Rome."

Phallus journeys to Rome, along the way acquiring three traveling companions, an almost equally hunky slave named Spurtacus, who wants to ask Caligula for his freedom, and a pair of gorgeous conjoined identical brothers, the Testicles Twins, who want to ask Caligula to separate them.

At Rome they meet Caligula, but he turns out to be a not very nice person who makes them compete as gladiators in the arena, saying he will grant their requests only if they slay Commodious, a wicked Cyclops from Uniopteria, an island to the west.

I, of course, expected to play Steverino's lovely leading lady, only to my amazement, there was none. The producer told me that their marketing research showed that Steverino's primary audience didn't care if there were any women in his movies at all, as long as he wore those fetching, off-the-shoulder togas and sweated a lot. Bulging pectorals, male bonding, and gladiator-on-gladiator action was what they wanted.

I was cast against type as Caligula's evil grandmother (at *my* age! Imagine!) Livia, ironically the same evil character that Delores Delgado had played back in *The Revenge of Cleopatra,* whom Augustus, Jesus, and I had sensibly murdered. Needless to say I gave a performance far superior to the late, unlamented Miss Delgado. As Livia I give Caligula bad advice and plot against everybody until Phallus slays Commodious and demands that Caligula keep his promises.

Caligula instead declares himself a god, makes his horse a senator, and kills me and six hundred other people. Finally, Phallus thrusts his huge weapon into him, killing him as well. The new Emperor Claudius shows Spurtacus that he really is free as long as his mind is free. He shows the Testicles Twins that they are stronger together than they are apart, and shows Phallus that the pattern stitched in his cloak is really a map back to Troy. Soon Phallus Maximus is back where he belongs, packed into the Trojans, making people happy.

My role was more of a supporting character part than the sort of starring roles I'd always played in the past, but such is often the fate of leading women past thirty in Hollywood, even in Rome. I obviously wasn't working every day. In fact, although the picture shot over three months, I actually worked for only fifteen days. Since Steverino was too busy appearing in almost every scene to have the customary affair with me, I was truly at loose ends. This left me with plenty of time to see the sights of Rome.

Since the pope had so rudely snubbed F. Emmett Knight and me by refusing to come over and perform my first, simple wedding ceremony, I decided to return the insult and pass on visiting the Vatican.[*]

But with Terrence gone and Rudy preoccupied, I was at loose ends most of the time. That is, until I met Paolo. He tightened my ends up something fierce.

I was dining at a sidewalk café one afternoon, enjoying the sun of a Mediterranean June, and a little light wine to wash down my lunchtime boilermakers, when a young man caught my eye. Paolo was just twenty-two, but with the sophistication and worldly experience of men half his age. Paolo was extremely handsome and clear-eyed, with curly black hair on his head, chest, arms, legs, and all other exposed body parts.

---

[*]Actually, the pope who refused to marry Tallulah and F. Emmett was Pope Benedict XV, while the pontiff at the time of Tallulah's Roman stay was Pope John XXIII, though, as a lifelong Christian Scientist (a contradiction in terms if ever there was one), Tallulah can be forgiven for not keeping current on the ongoing pontiff turnover, or popover.–Douglas

Even his chin exhibited curly black stubble if it had been more than an hour and a half since his last shave. He wore pants so tight they were nearly subcutaneous, and, although he had mastered English, he'd apparently never learned how to button his shirt, which was fine with me.

His English came out in the sexiest accent imaginable. "Tour-a guide?" he asked me when he came up to my table. "American-a Missy, you wanna tour-a guide?"

"Actually, darling," I said, warm and approachable with my public, as always, "I wouldn't mind a guided tour of you." To help bridge the language barrier, I reached over and touched him in a spot universally recognized as meaning, "Hello, Sailor."

Paolo's adorable face lit up with understanding. He grinned with an innocent lust and said, "One hundred-a lira," which is Italian for, "I want you."

Twenty minutes later we were back in my suite at La Dolcé Villa, where Paolo preceded to teach me the meaning of "stamina." Four hours later, when we took a break for cocktails and oxygen, I suggested that Paolo move into La Dolcé Villa with me. Paolo broke into his charming grin and said, "One thousand-a lira, per week! And Tues-a-days off," which is the Italian phrase for "Yes."

It turned out that Paolo was a war orphan who'd been supporting himself on the streets by offering his talents to wealthy foreign female visitors. Living gland-to-mouth as he had, he might easily have fallen into vice and disreputable occupations, but, fortunately, he met me, and I resolved to save this boy for myself.

When Rudy got a look at Paolo, his reaction was, "How much? And how soon?"

"No, no," Paolo said hurriedly. "Not-a men. I'm-a just for the ladies."

"Don't worry, Paolo," I said in front of Rudy, admiring Paolo's unusual but appreciated restriction, "Rudy won't bother you, because he knows if I catch him annoying you, he'll be unemployed immediately."

"All right with me, lady," Rudy replied with his usual charm. "I don't need to rent anyway."

With Terrence gone, I had need of a personal assistant, so I put Paolo on salary immediately, to fill my gap. It soon became apparent that although Paolo's services were far more personal than Terrence's ever were, he wasn't really much assistance in organizing my life. I realized that when I got home to America, I was going to have to hire someone else to take on Terrence's old chores. However, Paolo's unmatched ability to give my body a workout such as it had seldom known* soon suggested a different position. (Actually, Paolo suggested multiple positions, and they were all suggestions well worth taking!) I put Paolo on staff as my personal trainer and masseur and have never looked back, except when ordered to. After all, when a woman passes thirty, a certain amount of effort is required to keep Uncle Time at bay. My never-aging appearance throughout the sixties in large part owed its spooky permanence to the tireless efforts of perky Paolo, who always rose to the occasion whenever required.

This might, I suppose, be a good spot to share one of my beauty secrets with you readers. One of the antiaging treatments I began with Paolo was my famous alcohol rub. This is unsurpassed for maintaining a youthful glow. There are five simple steps to an effective alcohol rub. They are

1. Hire a masseur. Personal tastes may vary, but this one hint is very important: When going through their ads, always avoid any masseur whose ad includes the giveaway warning phrase "strictly legit."
2. Use alcohol, internally.
3. Undress—the masseur.
4. Rub the masseur vigorously, paying special attention to any particular stiffness that pops up. And finally,
5. Apply resulting protein shake, either externally or internally, as desired.

By following these simple steps you'll feel better in no time, and feeling better is the real secret to looking younger.

Paolo also showed me a trick that took years off my face in just moments. Paolo took to accompanying me to the set, primarily to "rehearse" in my dressing room between takes, since little Steverino spoke little or no English. (I don't wish to shock his fans, but Steverino's voice in the English-release versions of his films was always dubbed, believe it or not.)† Before putting on the wig I wore as Livia, Paolo would apply a little youthenizing procedure of his own, involving a staplegun, and I

*If you've never had a twenty-two-year-old Italian man make violent love to you for hour after hour, darling, you're a virgin!–Tallulah
†As noted earlier, Steve Reeves was from Montana, and spoke English perfectly, though his voice *is* generally dubbed in the American-release prints of his films. –Douglas

would emerge looking twenty, as befit the queen of Rome, Caligula's terribly youthful grandmother, Livia.

This worked quite well until one unfortunate afternoon. I was playing an intimate scene with lovely Steverino in which I was trying to seduce the gorgeous gladiator. I was nose to stunning Roman nose with the former Mr. Universe, heading for a longed-for liplock, when the staples under my wig gave way suddenly. The resulting slap of overstressed face sent burly Steve Reeves flying across the set. I sometimes have this effect on men, more and more as the years rush past.

By the time my part in *Caligulee, Caligula!* wrapped shooting, Mark, back in London, had lined up another film for me, a biblical epic to shoot in mysterious Egypt. I packed up my clothes, my bottles, and Paolo; and he, Rudy, and I headed for Cairo, to barge down the Nile.

33

I Remember Mummy

Egypt, Ancient Land of Mystery, Jewel of the Nile, Inventor of Alcohol. It was here that Rudy, Paolo, and I traveled to film my next triumph as a truly International Star at last, and let me tell you; that hellhole is hotter than Bette Davis under the collar the night *Mildred Pierce* won Best Actress!

Paolo and Rudy both suggested hiring an Egyptian guide, so it was necessary for me to remind them that although I'd never set foot in Africa before, I *had,* after all, been the queen of Egypt back in *The Revenge of Cleopatra,* so, of course, I had Cleopatra's intimate knowledge of the streets of Cairo.

However, the acquisition of a chauffeur seemed a reasonable idea. As Erich Segal never said, being a Movie Star means never having to drive yourself. Hiring didn't seem to be a problem. Anytime I stepped outside my hotel, The Crumbling Casbah, I was besieged by Egyptians of all ages making offers of all kinds. I grabbed one, more or less at random, and asked him if he knew where a lady could get a drink. He did, though he wouldn't have one with me. To my shock and horror, I learned that Muslims are prohibited from drinking alcohol! No wonder that obscure religion has never caught on.[*]

I asked the gentleman, as we strolled to the American Bar, if he could drive. The man, whose name was Akbar, said he could. Any name with "Bar" in it inspires confidence, and a teetotaler is generally a good

---

[*]Actually, as a devout Christian Scientist, I was also forbidden to consume alcohol, only I was never stupid enough to pay any attention to the mad ravings of my church, or, indeed, to have ever set foot in it. If I'd followed every insane stricture Mrs. Eddy laid down in her morphine-induced delusional states, I'd be minus a liver, which would certainly have brought me nearer, my God, to Thee.–Tallulah

choice for a designated driver, however otherwise insane they are, so I hired him on the spot to be my chauffeur and guide while I remained in Egypt. (It turned out that Cairo had changed *drastically* in the few, brief years that had flitted by since Cleopatra had lived there. I could barely find my dressing room.)

When I introduced Akbar to Rudy and Paolo, both seemed a bit wary. "What-a do you know about the man?" Paolo asked.

"What did I know about you?" I answered. "I don't have any long-time acquaintances in Egypt to choose from.

"He's wearing a fitted sheet. J.C. Penney's," sniffed Rudy about Akbar. The man knew linen.

Frankly, I think Paolo may have been a little jealous. It probably won't shock you to learn that Paolo had been sharing my bed since back in Rome (purely for reasons of thrift; Paolo was cheaper to own than to rent) and had probably fallen a little bit in love with me.* He no doubt worried that since Akbar was closer to my own age (actually, at forty-two, Akbar was a good deal *older* that I), I might be planning on sup-planting Paolo in my bed with him. I made it clear to Paolo that Akbar was there to *augment,* not replace him. And once Paolo got the hang of the fun that could be had in an overcrowded bed, he eased up on his ob-jections.

However, I have to say that security at The Crumbling Casbah was definitely subpar. I have never been a jewelry-horse. I do wear rings on each of my fingers (Rudy refers to them as my "gold knuckles"), but these are *all* wedding rings. The damn things do accumulate. (I've re-cently had to have the two oldest resized to fit my thumbs, as I had run out of fingers.)

But I've never been one for draping myself in expensive jewels. For one thing, they would be very hard to see under my omnipresent mink and sable coats (which, I might add, got unbelievably uncomfortable under the Egyptian sun! You can't believe the sacrifices and suffering one endures to maintain the proper Movie Star Image, which I do solely for the benefit of You, the Motion Picture Fan). Further, I prefer to in-vest my money in more practical, income-producing ways, like distil-leries and breweries, and the odd winery. Still, it was inevitable, over the

---

*This sort of thing happens to me constantly. I have wild, hot, filthy, degrading ani-mal sex with a man night after night, and afternoons as well, for a few months, and inevitably, they fall madly in love with me. It's my fate as one of this century's Great Love Goddesses. In general, the only dependable way I have ever found to prevent a man falling in love with me is to marry him, and I never made *that* mistake with Paolo.–Tallulah

many years of my career, that a few glittering little baubles came my way, generally gifts from admirers or husbands.[*]

Soon after Akbar moved into my suite with us (again, I was sharing Paolo and my bed for purely *economic* reasons, making me the meat in one hell of a Mediterranean Manwich!), some of the few, trivial trinkets I had amassed over the years started turning up missing. First some earrings were misplaced. Then a diamond stickpin disappeared. Then my tiara, which came originally from the Russian Crown Jewels, went walkabout. Finally, a lovely little necklace, containing the world-famous No-Hope Diamond, a gem Marie Antoinette had worn to the guillotine (have you any idea how hard bloodstains are to get out of jewelry?) and which had changed hands through violence over three hundred times, apparently evaporated.

The hotel detectives could uncover no clue. The suite hadn't been broken into. Neither Paolo nor Akbar, who had recently taken to wearing a better grade of bedsheets, pure silk, had heard or seen anything. The Cairo police naturally suspected Rudy and Paolo, since they were foreigners, but I pointed out that Paolo could have stolen them back in Rome, where he'd know people to fence them, while Rudy had had years of opportunities to pilfer and hadn't bothered.

"Me?" said Rudy, understandably offended. "Take *that* vulgar trash? I wouldn't wear those on Halloween."

So it was a complete mystery. No one had any idea what could have happened to my jewels. The hotel manager insisted I keep my remaining ornaments in the hotel safe, but if they couldn't protect them in my own room, I certainly wasn't going to trust them to the hotel's full-time keeping. Since Akbar was a native, I assigned him the task of nosing about Cairo and seeing if he could divine where my jewels had gone, but his mission never bore fruit.

The movie I was shooting was a biblical spectacle about Moses, originally titled *The Ten Plagues of Egypt,* although before release the name was changed. There was concern that the title might get confused with a similar, but inferior, picture made by the late Cecil Blunt DeMille. I was so furious at Blunt for blatantly plagiarizing my movie, trying crudely to conceal his theft by shooting his knockoff version four years earlier, that I never spoke to him again!

The movie went into release as, and can be found at your local video outlet under the title of, *Torah! Torah! Torah!* Steve Reeves was teamed with me again. Steverino played Moses, once more outshining his petty

---

[*]Two mutually exclusive classes of people!–Tallulah

rival, the pathetic Charlton Heston, or as we took to calling him, "Cheston."

Instead of doing the obvious thing and having me play Moses' girl-friend/pharaoh's wife, the queen of Egypt—Cleopatra—once again, or casting me against type as Moses' dowdier shepherdess wife, Bo-Peep, I was peculiarly cast as Moses' Egyptian mother, the sister of the old pharaoh, who finds the infant Moses among the bulrushes and raises him as a Single Mother. Frankly, calling a man who was at least a year or two older than myself "Son" took all the acting I could muster. There were so many other things I would have preferred calling him. "Daddy," for one.

Steverino again unprofessionally insisted on maintaining a profes-sional relationship with me, and all my attempts to get under his tunic failed. I tried to explain to him that, as a Method Actress, I needed to re-ally make love to him if I was going to be convincing in our love scenes.

"We don't have any love scenes," he said in his pidgin English, fla-vored by his sexy Italian twang.* "You're playing my mother."

"Look, Steverino . . ." I said, patiently.

"Stop calling me that."

"Right here, on page thirty-six, my line reads, 'Moses, you wacky jackanapes, I love you.' "

"Yes, but it's not a love scene. My next line is, 'Have faith in me yet a little while, my mother, I love you as well.' "

"Sounds like a love scene to me."

"It's just a child's love for his mother."

"Don't be ridiculous! Whoever heard of a child loving her mother?"

"Didn't you love your mother?"

"Don't be macabre!"

"What about your daughter?"

"What about her? Did you read her insane book? Look, Steve. I'm an artist. I can't play an *imaginary* emotion, like Filial Affection. I need to play something real, like Lust."

Though my logic was irrefutable, Steve wouldn't come around. Yet, through my efforts alone, our love scenes were the talk of the picture. Pauline Kael, in her review a year later, appreciated the psychological depths I dragged this movie down to, when she wrote, "Tallulah Morehead's performance as Moses' Egyptian mother is unforgettable. She turns Moses' life in Egypt into an Oedipal nightmare so intense, any boy would part an ocean to escape." At least the critics understood.

---

*That, of course, would be a Montana twang.–Douglas

Since my role was essentially a Star Cameo, I had plenty of time for sightseeing with Akbar. One week we spent floating down the Nile to Thebes. We visited the Temple of Luxor and the Valley of Kings. Frankly, the Egyptians didn't really take very good care of their tourist attractions. The most highly touted places were in a deplorable state of disrepair, and looked older than Estelle Winwood. A fresh coat of paint and some refurbishing and replastering would have done wonders. God knows, getting replastered always works for me! And that Sphinx needed a nose job more than Nanette Fabray

On the final day of shooting we were doing the orgy scenes at the foot of Mount Sinai, where the Israelites party hardy, while waiting for Steve to bring the tablets down from the mountain. The director, an Italian man whose name held more vowels than the alphabet but was unpronounceable, and I disagreed violently about my character in this scene. I felt that, as the Mother of the Host, she would be in the full swing of things, having wildly abandoned sex with her Nubian bearers directly in front of the Golden Cow (my affectionate nickname for the overpaid and overpraised Italian starlet playing Moses' rustic wife). The director had this nonsensical notion that she would sit around weeping and praying like a party pooper.

I had been rehearsing the scene I had in mind with the four splendid Nubian musclemen who played my bearers for the better part of a week. In fact, I can safely say, it was the *best* part of the week. The boys and I had our act down, or I should say "acts," as there were a number of different feats we had rehearsed and perfected and were ready to trot out for the cameras, but the director was adamant in his refusal to shoot it my way. Finally, at the insistence of the producer, we shot it both ways. The producer eventually overruled the director and used my version in the final cut, saying it was "better box office."

The wrap party was held on the set, as it was already prepared for an orgy anyway. The wine flowed like the flooding of the Nile. After a few hours, some of us decided to move on to the private home of one of the crew members for a more intimate revel. Rudy had made a friend and already left. Paolo was tired and wanted to go back to the hotel and nap. Akbar, as my chauffeur, agreed to drive me over to the party locale. My memory, however, doesn't extend that far.

When I awoke, I was in the most uncomfortable bed I'd ever been in. My head throbbed something fierce. I needed a little hair of the dog, or in this case, jackal. I glanced about under my lashes, since opening my eyes more than a slit sent another stab of pain through my head. What a party!

We must have been in some sort of car accident. As I glanced about I could see, even through only slightly opened eyes, that I was swathed from head to toe in bandages. The horror of being in a foreign hospital, tended by God-only-knows-what kind of doctors, was only intensified when I noticed the filthy, rotting condition of the bandages I was wrapped in.

I could see a crowd of people gathered in front of my bed, held back by a velvet rope suspended between four-foot chrome poles. It must have been a teaching hospital, as along with many adults there were numerous small children crowded nearby, peering over the velvet rope at me. A man in a suit was reading aloud from what looked like an elderly scroll, which I assumed was my medical chart, in a language I didn't understand. The medical students, some looking as young as six or seven, seemed to hang on his every word.

Quite frankly, I was thirsty. Rudy must not have been by yet, as there was no martini drip. In fact, there was no IV drip at all. What kind of third-world Hell House was I in? I realized immediately that, no matter how much my head ached, if I could walk, I needed to get out of this primitive Egyptian hospital immediately!

I opened my eyes all the way. Several of the children squealed and pointed at me, chattering in some strange tongue. The parents all smiled, laughed, and patted their little heads.

The only pain I could feel was the throbbing in my skull, although, heaven knows, that was enough, but nothing felt broken, or even bruised, and I desperately needed a drink. I wasn't just sober and hungover, I was actually parched, a condition I've seldom experienced. So I reached out to the sides of my odd, boxlike bed and started slowly to haul myself to my feet.

The reaction from the crowd was instantaneous, though not what a patient looks for in her doctors when exhibiting signs of recovery. Almost everyone in the room screamed. The sound cut through my head like a white-hot swizzle stick and literally knocked me flat again. I tried a second time to pull myself to my feet and this time the scream was louder. However, I kept at it. Moving was difficult. I was bandaged so tightly, my joints were stiff instead of me. I eventually made it to my feet and clambered out of the odd, boxish bed. The people around me went berserk at this point, grabbing their young medical students and running in various directions. I have no idea what engendered this outlandish panic, but terror was sending everyone running away. I looked over my shoulder to see if some unspeakable monster was creeping up behind me, but all I saw was the rest of my hospital room, which, I might add, was somewhat overdecorated, in a typical Egyptian style, looking not unlike our Palace-of-the-Pharaoh set in the film. There were golden statues, cases full of scrolls, tablets, and musty old jewelry, and the walls were lined with colorful hieroglyphics and pictoglyphs.

The doctor who had been reading from my chart had dropped to his knees and was apparently offering his prayers to Allah, as he had his arms extended above his head and kept bending over and touching his forehead to the floor while babbling wildly in my direction.

"I'm terribly sorry, Doctor darling." I said, in my usual warm, friendly fashion. The reaction wasn't what I expected. The man seemingly spoke no English, and whatever he thought I said, it only made him more subservient. I continued, "As I say, I'm sorry, darling. No offense intended, but I can't stay here. I'm a Christian Scientist, and I can't accept medical help from whoever you are. I'll just be on my way. Send my bill to Morehead Heights at Tumescent Tor, California."

Apparently I was wrong about the man not knowing English. Since I had plainly spoken to him in English, he now began answering me in English, babbling out, "Punish me not, oh Great One. I am an insect, a worm, but I am your slave! Command me, Ancient One."

"Well, darling," I replied, beginning to find him attractive, as men crawling on their bellies, begging my favors, have always tickled my fancy, "for one thing, stop calling me 'Ancient One.' I don't really care for the ring of that moniker. And could you get me a drink? Maybe a vodka martini, or a stinger, or a manhattan, or a box car, or a Harvey Wallbanger. Hell, I don't care. Anything. I'm drier than Cat Woman's litter box."

"Command me. Command me," the little man kept repeating.

"I have," I said. "Now find me a libation."

The man continued babbling in an attractively self-abasing style but showed no signs of actually getting me a drink, so, trailing rotting bandages, I shuffled off in search of one myself.

As soon as I stepped into the hallway, more people began screaming and running. Nobody would slow down or come near me, let alone answer a question. Finding a large glass door to the outside, I decided to leave while I could, head back to the hotel, and order up.

Once outside, I found the people on the streets in just as hysterical a state as the ones inside. The folks in front of me would scream and flee, while behind me an ever growing throng of torch-bearing people followed, jeering and shouting but not daring to approach nearer. All told, it was the weirdest public appearance I've ever made.

As it happened, I was only a few blocks from my hotel. When I shuffled up to the front desk at The Crumbling Casbah, the desk clerk just screamed and fainted dead away. I had to fetch my room key from the cubbyhole myself. The mob held back, outside the hotel doors, but as the elevator doors were closing I saw them streaming in.

Back in my room I found both Rudy and Paolo. "Where have-a you been, mia darling?" Paolo blurted out, rushing up to hug me.

"And what on earth are you wearing?" Rudy added.

"I have no idea," I replied. "But could you please cut me out of it?"

"Let me get my pinking shears," Rudy said, striding over to his sewing basket.

"Where's Akbar?" I asked.

"No one-a knows. No one's a-seen him, a-you or the car since-a you left the party a week ago," Paolo said. "I've been-a so worried."

"How sweet, darling. I need a . . ."

". . . martini?" said Rudy, placing one in my hand.

"Thank you, darling. Now, what's this about Akbar being missing?"

"Simple, sweetie," said Rudy, as he began cutting me out of the bandages. "Akbar drove off with you a week ago, and we haven't seen you, him, or the car since."

"How bizarre. Well, I've had enough of this godforsaken desert. Who wants to go skiing?"

"How can you go skiing in Egypt?" Rudy asked.

"You can't. I say we head for Switzerland."

"I like-a it," said Paolo.

"Works for me, honey," said Rudy. "I'll start packing up whatever Akbar hasn't stolen."

"Rudy!" I snapped. "I won't have Akbar maligned like that when he isn't here to defend himself."

"Oh, get real, Tallulah. Who do you think swiped all your jewelry? King Tut? The man has stolen your car, for Christ's sake."

"It's the studio's car, and he may have been waylaid by marauders."

"And I may marry Elizabeth Taylor."

"Oh, Rudy, I'm so happy for you."

"Tallulah," said Paolo, "even-a I know he's-a being sarcastic."

The next day, on the plane to Geneva, Rudy handed me the English-language Cairo newspaper, saying, "Isn't that Akbar?"

The man in the photo, who certainly *looked* like Akbar, was accepting a check from a man in a suit beside an open sarcophagus, with some moldering mummy lying within, but the caption identified him as Ardeth Bey, an Egyptologist, who was selling the Cairo Museum a recently unearthed mummy.

The picture was on page 10 as part of an article that was "continued from page 1." I turned back to the front page, where I was confronted by the headline, **"MUMMY COMES TO LIFE IN CAIRO MUSEUM! Hundreds Flee from Stalking Horror!"**

"Good Heavens, Rudy, did you read this article?"

"Tallulah, you know I only read the fashion section."

The article was blood-chilling. Only a week before, this Ardeth Bey person had sold the Cairo Museum the mummy of Queen Necrotitties, a 3500-year-old corpse recently unearthed in the Valley of Kings. Yesterday afternoon, at the unveiling of the Necrotitties exhibit, as the curator read from the Sacred Scroll of Thoth, which Isis allegedly used to raise Osirus from the dead, whoever the hell *they* were, before the astonished and horrified faces of the assembled patrons the mummy of Queen Necrotitties came shudderingly back to life and clambered out of its sarcophagus. The shambling, ancient horror chased and terrorized the populace, and it was only by pure luck that no one had been throttled to death by her withered, eldritch, dead hands. A courageous mob, bent on destroying the blasphemous abomination, followed her path of devastation through the streets of Cairo, right into The Crumbling Casbah Hotel, where she was still believed to be hiding, lost somewhere in the upper floors. Police were looking for Ardeth Bey, who had also disappeared, with the museum's money.

"Good God, darlings!" I exclaimed with relieved terror. "We got out of that hotel just in time! This hideous creature from centuries past is apparently lurking about our hotel. We're lucky this undead thing didn't murder us in our sleep! I've had more than enough of Egypt for this century!"

The front page also had a large photograph of the exposed face of the repugnant primordial monstrosity, and, while she may once have been beautiful in the dim recesses of antediluvian prehistory, she was now desperately in need of a good moisturizer, and some blush wouldn't be a bad idea, either. She had dry, wrinkled, sagging dead flesh hanging off features to make you scream. She was all the ugly atrocities that age and death can ravish mankind with in one ghastly, lurid nightmare countenance that made Rondo Hatton look like Marilyn Monroe.

"Look at this!" I said, brandishing the paper before Rudy and Paolo's revolted eyes. "Have you ever in your life seen anything so repulsive?"

"Mamma mia!" cried Paolo in dismay, though I don't think his mother would have been flattered.

"She looks familiar," said Rudy, casually.

"Some grisly voodoo effigy from your pagan island youth?"

"Voodoo is on Haiti. I'm from the Philippines. And weren't you in *Pagan Island Youth?*"

"Not me, Rudy darling. That was Delores Delgado." There was a pause. Then Rudy and I faced each other and said in unison, *"That's who she looks like!"* although in retrospect I must say that that was a *terrible* and uncaring thing to say about a perfectly respectable and innocent mummy.

"Good God, Rudy darling," I said, shivering with gooseflesh. "The thought of Delores Delgado coming crawling back from her grave, now *that's* scary! And *so* like her."

Two weeks later, while vacationing in lovely Zermatt, at the base of the *other* Matterhorn (a perfect oversized replica of the famous one in Anaheim), Mark called from London, telling me to report to Madrid in the spring to begin shooting another movie, this time in Sunny Hispania!

34

Spanish Fliers

Christmas 1960 we spent in lovely, snowy Zermatt. Along with Rudy and Paolo, Terrence and Jacques came from Paris to spend the holidays with us. We invited Major Babs to fly over, but she apparently didn't feel up to it, and didn't even reply to the invitation. Vincent Lovecraft and C. Halibut Plugg were there as well, and although he is condemned to spend eternity haunting Tumescent Tor, and probably wasn't even a Christian, the headless Indian brave was with us in spirit as well.

Rudy, Terrence, and Jacques had pooled resources and bought me a facelift for my holiday present. Though, at a mere thirty-plus, I had no real need for one, I went through with it early in the New Year anyway, just to please them, and it did eliminate Paolo's staple gun treatments, which, if I wasn't drunk enough, could sting a mite.

Before I checked into the Youth in Asia* Clinic in Geneva for my minor facial tightening, Rudy, Paolo, and I returned to Rome briefly to attend the world premiere of *Caligulee, Caligula*. Seeing my face projected on the enormous Cinemascope screen prompted Rudy to whisper in my ear, "Looks like you're getting that lift *just in time!*" I acknowledged his sweet comment by affectionately stamping my spiked heel into his loafer.

I confess I was a little worried that returning to Rome would spawn an attack of homesickness in Paolo and he might want to leave me and return to his former life on the exotic streets of *Roma*. As it happened,

---

*The clinic financially supported those famous children who you always hear are starving in China, hence the clinic's name. That it was a good cause was even more reason to go through with the *entirely unnecessary and gratuitous* procedure.
–Tallulah

Paolo didn't want to be in Rome again, even though he *was* wanted in Rome. It was amazing how a mere year of first-class hotels and movie-star pampering had soured him on his previous existence of providing distraction and healthy physical workouts to wealthy female tourists.

Dear, handsome Steve Reeves was still obstinately refusing to give me a welcome-back tumble. I figured I'd wear him down during our next film together, since we had worked out so well in our last two pictures and our chemistry together on the screen in *Caligulee, Caligula* was so unmistakable. However, as it happened, Steve, for reasons I cannot fathom, had had a clause written into his contract barring me from appearing in any more of his films. I guess Steve was more insecure about his looks than he needed to be.

But perhaps his fears were justified. It was true that he virtually disappeared when photographed next to me. Whenever I appeared on the screen at the *Caligulee, Caligula* premiere, I could hear excited whispers all over the theater, making comments that Paolo translated as, "My God, is she for real?" "What the Hell is that?" "What on earth is she wearing?"[*] and, "I hear it's really Marcello Mastroianni in an unbilled cameo!" I can only assume from that meaningless last one that Paolo's mastery of Italian wasn't as great as he liked to pretend. After all, he'd only lived in Italy since birth and had learned the language when still a very small boy. How much do *you* remember of things you were taught when you were two?[†]

In Italy I was still worshipped as *La Lushio*. I was mobbed everywhere I went by people who, though thronging to get close and jostle me personally, were nonetheless too polite, in the way of all Europeans except the French, to actually acknowledge their recognition of me or bother me to pose for pictures or sign autographs. In fact, they often ignored me completely, or shoved me violently to one side in order to pinch Paolo's behind.

Once back in lovely Switzerland, I checked into the Youth in Asia Clinic in Geneva, where a team of four surgeons, working for a mere twelve hours, performed the few tiny tucks and minor facial tightening that refreshed my always youthful face. Rudy pointed out that when I recovered from the surgery, I *looked* like a Youth in Asia, as the tightening of my face not only made me look younger but had stretched my eyes into an Oriental appearance. When Mark stopped by my Zermatt

---

[*]Actually, that was Rudy, and it was in English.–Tallulah
[†]I, for one, in recent years, have often completely forgotten all that early, complicated, toilet training.–Tallulah

chalet for a brief business visit, he said he thought my new "Madame Fu Manchu" look could work to my advantage, and he immediately began contacting studios in Hong Kong and Japan to line up a picture for me in the exotic East. Soon I was signed to make a musical in Tokyo after I completed my Spanish feature.

By the time Rudy, Paolo, and I reached Madrid in April, my new face was set, and I was raring to go. This picture was a period piece. In fact, the period was so important, that it was used for the movie's title, *1,000,000 Years Ago*. Hammer Films of England was producing it, but as the picture was set before the invention of rooms, the entire film was to be shot on exterior locations in Spain. Ray Harryhausen, who had stretched my ravenous pussy to the size of a national monument in *THAT!*, was again providing the special effects.

Scientific experts had been consulted to make this a one-hundred-percent authentic and scientifically accurate portrayal of what life was really like back in the days when humans shared the planet with dinosaurs. The historical accounts written by cavemen had been studied, and as a result, this movie left paleontologists and anthropologists the world over in a state of stunned silence.

Records of the period had provided the designs of the genuine, bona fide fur bikinis the women of the period wore. I had extensive experience wearing fur bikinis, having first popularized them back in *Eskimo Pie*, over thirty years before, when I was a toddler, so I was surprised when I was told I wouldn't be wearing one. Rather, I was given a floor-length fur robe to wear, which was no picnic under the hot Spanish sun. It seems someone had noticed that my recent surgical work hadn't extended below the neck and that there were incisions from my two liver transplants. Indeed, I hadn't been asked to do any nudity, or near nudity, since 1938, even when called for artistically, or when enthusiastically volunteered for by me. Movie standards in the sixties had become so much more puritanical and repressive than they had been during the more liberated thirties.

I played Yuk, the queen of the Blonde Tribe, which was perennially at war with the hated Brunette Tribe, while dodging herds of tyrannosaurs and hunting that most delicious of delicacies, brontosaurs.

The plot concerned two youngsters, a Blonde cave boy named Bob and a Brunette cave girl named Skreek, who fall in love even though their tribes hate each other. They carry on behind everybody's back until Bob interferes in a battle between his cousin Drek and Skreek's brother Achoo. Achoo slays Drek, and Bob, in a fit of anger, feeds Achoo to a family of velociraptors. This really puts Bob and Skreek's romance on the skids, so they decide to run away and start their own tribe. To keep the tribal elders from pursuing them, Skreek schemes to fake her own death by making it appear that she's been eaten by a tyrannosaur. Unfortunately, she is unable to tell Bob of her plan, since language hasn't been invented yet. Bob thinks Skreek has actually been eaten, so he prepares to jump in the neighborhood volcano.

Before Bob can leap into the lava, however, the volcano erupts. Bob and Skreek find each other amidst the ashes and make sweet love. I catch them in the act and am outraged by both the illegal practice of inter-hair-color sex, and by their perverted use of the forbidden missionary position instead of the approved doggie-style. I am about to execute both of them when I am carried off by a pterodactyl. The two tribes line up on either side, trying to decide whether or not to kill each other, when a flotilla of rafts arrive, carrying a tribe of Redheads. This leads the Blonde and Brunette Tribes to realize how stupid and blind they've been, and they put aside their differences and join together to kill all the redheads.

As you can see, this movie, though set many weeks in the past, held a timely message of tolerance for people of different hair colors, except redheads, that is as true today as it was in prehistoric times. In addition, I'm told it was closely based on a true incident that actually happened, although the real events may have occurred only 999,999 years ago.

While shooting it, I became the toast of the Madrid art scene. Pablo Picasso declared my famous, though newly renovated, face to be "cubism personified," while Salvador Dali told the world that I was "truly surreal!"

Both men insisted I sit for portraits and, once I discovered that I was welcome to drink while I sat, I was up for it.

Pablo and I ended up making wildly abandoned, kinky love right there on the floor of his studio when he finished my picture, getting covered in paint, although Pablo began cursing me passionately once I'd untied him.

I can't say that I really cared for any of the resulting paintings. In Picasso's portrait I looked not so much like a Movie Star as a bookcase, and one made by a seriously disturbed carpenter, I might add. That picture now hangs in the Chicago Art Institute, where I hope they take care of it, as I'm told that if it's ever destroyed I'll start looking like it.

Salvador did two paintings of me. In Salvador's portraits I was at least recognizable, and he'd made the more conventional choice of leaving my nose on my face rather than relocating it to my right knee as Pablo had done. But Sali, as I took to calling him, had taken the unusual approach of painting me as I would appear if I didn't possess a skeleton. In one, titled *Gene Pool,* I was not so much a person as a puddle. The other, a study titled *The Persistence of Morehead,* which Sali presented to me as a gift, had me draped like a sheet over the barren limbs of a twisted tree. This picture disturbed and haunted visitors to Morehead Heights for almost forty years, until I sold it, two years ago, for seventeen million dollars. Honey, that buys a hell of a lot of vodka!

A beautiful young Jamaican actress named Martine Beswick made her screen debut in this film as the star-crossed Skreek, and then went on to fame as a Bond girl and Hammer horror queen. There was no question but that I was a role model for the shy, retiring newcomer. My old flame, or was it "Flamer," Tab Hunter, was brought over from America to play Bob. Lady Joan Plowright, in a wig Rudy stole at the end of production, played Grag, the Queen of the Brunettes. (The movie was set before the invention of Male Domination, and so presented precivilization as a matriarchy, which is why the bone of contention between the tribes is hair color instead of spear length.)

Sir Laurence Olivier was a constant visitor on the set, as was Danny Kaye, although only on days when Joan wasn't working, and we were all asked not to tell Joan that Danny was in Madrid. God only knows why. Maybe she found Mr. Kaye as insufferably annoying as I did. Joan and I got on together just fine. Any woman who would steal a man away from that crazy trollop and role-thief Vivien Leigh is okay in my book. And, as this *is* my book, Joan's a Saint, and, if you ask me, *she's* the one who should be knighted!

Larry, of course, was coaching everybody on exactly how to act like a caveman. He gave elocution lessons in grunting, and even, heavily disguised, made an unbilled cameo appearance as the guy who gets eaten by a tyrannosaur in the first hunt scene.

While the cast all appreciated Larry's coaching, especially Tab, whose Shakespearean work ever since has shown Larry's influence, Ray Harryhausen, who was hand-animating the dinosaurs (this was before computers, when special effects were required to look fake), didn't seem to welcome Larry's unsolicited advice on how the dinosaurs acted. I guess Larry just rubbed him the wrong way, as Ray certainly wasn't above soliciting suggestions. Indeed, on several occasions he asked me if I remembered just exactly how a tyrannosaur walked, or whether a triceratops could run, or what a brontosaur sounded like. Being a team player, I gladly shared my expertise.

The shooting was marred by only one terrible incident. It happened the day we were to shoot the scene of me being snatched up by a pterodactyl that then flies off with me. My snatch performed perfectly, as always, but the flying-away shots were a disaster. Two full-size pterodactyl claws were suspended from the bottom of a helicopter. I was to be strapped into these, and the helicopter was then to lift me off the ground and fly me over the nearby ridge. Once out of camera range I was to be gently lowered to the arms of the waiting crew, who would then unstrap and free me from the copter's clutches. Later, at the studio back in London, Ray would place a flapping pterodactyl over the helicopter. A stunt woman was engaged to do it, but I insisted on filming the stunt myself. After all, who had more experience at acting while incredibly high than me? The insurance company calculated how much I was worth, and then said it would be financially riskier to use the stunt woman. I was on.

The helicopter shot also seemed to go perfectly, right up to the moment we cleared camera range and were supposed to begin descending. Instead of gently lowering me to the crew below, the helicopter gained altitude, picked up speed, and sped off toward the south, trailing me underneath.

What nobody knew at the time was that our helicopter pilots weren't in the helicopter. They were back at the Madrid helipad, tied up and gagged in a closet. The men flying the helicopter were escaped terrorists who had subdued the real pilots and snuck out of Madrid in their place. Now they were heading for Africa, with a Glamorous International Treasure (me) dangling beneath as their hostage!

I, of course, had no idea what the hell was going on. Being unable to do anything but ride along, I made myself as comfortable as one could get when strapped into primordial reptile talons while being whizzed through an increasingly thinning atmosphere by crazed terrorists. Fortunately, I had long ago learned the hard way that when flying you never know what may happen, how long you'll be stacked (which is true in general for women, let me tell you) over LaGuardia, or what they will serve while you are, so you had better come prepared. I had done just exactly that. Stuffed inside the capacious inner pockets of my regal fur robe were two enormous thermoses which Rudy had filled with martinis before I left for work that morning. Mind you, I had a wet bar in my trailer at the remote location. The thermoses were in case of emergencies, and this did seem like an emergency, at least until I had consumed most of the first thermos.

Eventually jet fighters from the Spanish Air Force (no, I'm not joking) caught up with us. We were flying over a forest at the time. The terrorists radioed the planes to back off or they would take steps to prove they were serious. Suddenly we began losing altitude. I found myself being slapped by the tips of trees. "I say, pilot darling," I hollered as loudly as I could, "do you think you could take it up a bit? I like a little bush as much as the next guy, but this is ridiculous! Damn! I've sloshed my drink."

Of course, they couldn't hear a word I was babbling, and besides, swinging me through the trees was the point. The Spanish Air Force, seeing a Nearly Living Legend in immediate peril of becoming a Non-Living Legend, flew off.

After several hours we shot out over water, having reached the Mediterranean Sea. To avoid radar tracking, the helicopter dipped low, and I found myself skimming the waves. This hardly seemed the time to take up Talon Surfing, but my opinion wasn't being asked. As the waves slapped at me, I found out how spongelike fur could be. By now, both thermoses were empty, and it didn't look like my abductors were planning to stop long enough for me to refuel. I decided I needed to take action. As I was only a couple feet above the surface of the sea, in fact, at times not *above* the sea at all, I decided it was time to exit this flight. I took off my fur robe, which I wore over the strap to conceal it, and then I unstrapped myself, took a deep breath, and let go of the talons. Once I hit the water, I lost consciousness.

I woke up in a Spanish hospital. I had a broken leg and two fractured ribs. A fishing boat had seen me fall and rescued me. The Spanish Air Force, seeing me abandon the flight, had then blown the helicopter to atoms, completely ruining two perfectly good pterodactyl claws. After a short recuperation period, I was off to Japan, where I was in for some rude surprises.

35

Dis-Oriented!

Japan, Land of the Rising Sun. I had never visited the Mysterious East before, so I was avid to meet a whole new race of men. Since my new film was to be a Japanese musical, I decided to do a little research first. While on a quick trip to London, mostly to overdub grunts for *1,000,000 Years Ago,* where my guttural noises had been completely rewritten by Noel Coward, I attended a performance of a traditional Japanese kabuki play called *The Mikado* so I would have some idea what I was in for.

My leg was mostly healed. I had a slight limp, but I was always able to use liquor as a crutch. My newly revamped face almost looked the age I claimed. Preliminary reviews were calling my performance in *1,000,000 Years Ago* "authentically primitive." Paolo was keeping me satisfied, and the Spanish government had declared me a National Heroine. I was on an emotional upswing, little suspecting the unpleasant surprises that lay ahead in the sinister Orient.

The movie is one you've probably never seen, for very good reasons that I'll get to in time. It was the bizarre Japanese musical *A World of Woozy Song,* written by the famous team of Yamashiro and Hammerstein. My new, Asian looks had first brought me to the producer's attention, and then my singing voice was declared "ideal" for Japanese music.

The first of the rude shocks that awaited me in Tokyo was learning of the second-class status accorded women in Japan. I was used, like most women, I imagine, to being treated like a goddess. Little did I suspect that in Japan women were considered second rate, to put it mildly. I was expected to walk *behind* my houseboy/ex-husband and my Italian masseur, both of whom were on *my* payroll! Chivalry wasn't just dead in Japan, it never existed in the first place!

In stores, restaurants, and other public places, men whose job was catering to the public would ignore me until Rudy or Paolo placed an order or asked a question. The usual response whenever I said anything was a shouted, "Women do not talk!"

This from a culture that had given the world that great invention, saki. I must say, I developed a real taste for saki, although the peculiar Japanese insisted on serving the stuff overheated, and usually went berserk when I poured mine on the rocks. First the English with their weird warm beer, next the Japanese with their hot saki. What was next? Seething-hot Irish coffee?

But an even worse shock was waiting for me when I interviewed with the movie's producer. Although I had signed contracts to make the movie, Mr. Nakagouchi assured me that a woman's signature on a contract was considered worthless in Japan, and I wasn't truly signed for the film until he personally approved me. With that, he dropped his pants to his knees and told me to kneel down for my audition.

At last, someone who understood the proper way to do things in Hollywood. It was with a sense of relief that I prepared to perform my usual audition, which has made me what I am today, but I was about to come face to face with the shameful secret of Japan.

"Well?" grumbled Mr. Nakagouchi. "What are you waiting for? My massive, mighty manhood strains for you! Get on with it!"

"I would," I replied, "only I can't find it." This was quite literally true. Calling Mr. Nakagouchi's equipment "massive, mighty manhood" was making a mountain out of a mosquito bite. Eventually, deep within his silky pubic hair, I found a microscopic bump that made him groan when I touched it, so I figured that was his G spot, and I went to work.

Before the contracts were considered iron-clad, I had to do the same with the director and the cinematographer, as well as my usual policy of including the editor. To my horror, I found the same shocking lack of dimension in all of them. How the hell did Japan ever get overpopulated? The primary difference between Japanese men and women appeared to be that the men lacked vaginas, though they did seem to possess clitorises. At last World War II made some sense. The nasty, warlike, aggressive tendencies of the Japanese were nothing more than a national case of overcompensation! No wonder they insisted on treating women as inferiors. Many of their women were better hung than the men!

But an even bigger and nastier shock awaited me on the set. My costar was to be *Hisato,* my former *houseboy!* This was humiliation on a grand scale! I was expected to costar with the help!

And on top of everything else, they made me wear these hideous kimonos, all yellow, a color which doesn't flatter me, and a makeup job that made Bozo the Clown look understated.

I telephoned Mark in London and Fred Sturm in Los Angeles, trying to get them to break my contract, noting that it would be critically damaging to my professional reputation for me to share billing with a man who used to scrub my toilets. There was a very nice-looking fellow in the cast named Sum Yung Guy who would have been a vastly more appropriate costar for me. Unfortunately, it was pointed out by both men that, first off, a woman's opinion was considered worthless in Japan, and secondly, it would be hard to make a convincing case that my career would be damaged by my sharing billing with an Oscar-winning actor. Would no one but me ever see the worthlessness of those pitiful trinkets?

The upshot of it all was that I was stuck singing and acting with a man who used to rinse out my underwear. True, Rudy was my houseboy, and I had been married to him, but that was different. He wasn't in show business, and we'd never played a love scene.

Hisato, two-faced as always, pretended to be delighted to see me, kissing me, hugging me, fussing over me, calling me "Missy Tallu," and generally according me the respect no other man in Tokyo bothered with. But how do you accept as an equal colleague someone who has mopped up your vomit?

One man who was right at home in Japan was Oscar Hammerstein. The attitudes and ideas he'd been expressing in lyrics all his life were perfectly at home in Japan. For me he wrote the following big solo:

He beats me and he kicks me,
And he socks me in the nose.
He tramples on my kneecaps,
And he runs my pantyhose.
They say that I should leave him,
But what nobody knows,
Is I'm his,
I love him,
'Cause he owns me!

He's broken both my arms and,
He has gouged out my left eye.

He says if I report him,
That he'll laugh and watch me die.
He ate my mother's liver,
Just to see If I would cry.
I don't care.
I love him,
'Cause he owns me.

He smells bad, he's ugly.
He's terrible in bed.
But if I couldn't have him,
I'd much rather be dead.

So though he's left me crippled,
And disfigured half my face.
And though he's knocked my teeth out,
To hang them around his place.
I know that if he left me,
I would be a basket case.
I don't care.
I love him,
'Cause he owns me.

Hearing me sing this number brought tears of joy to the eyes of Oscar and all the Japanese men. They agreed that Oscar had truly captured the essential nature of a woman's true love and devotion. For my part, I was amazed at how the man could write a parade of hit musicals with his head lodged so very *far* up his butt.

There was still the problem of how to prevent America from seeing me playing a subservient role to my servant. As the end of shooting drew near an idea occurred to me.

Taking Paolo with me, I cornered Mr. Nakagouchi in his office. Before Nakagouchi's astounded eyes, I undressed and stimulated Paolo into his full attack mode. When Nakagouchi had a good eyeful of the enormous Italian sausage Paolo was burdened with, I laid out my ultimatum. Either *A World of Woozy Song* was prohibited, *in print,* from ever being released in the United States, in perpetuity, or I would introduce Paolo to Mrs. Nakagouchi, and as many other Japanese women as he could manage. I would further see to it that photographs showing just what a *real* man looked like would be circulated throughout Japan.

The myth of Japanese male adequacy would be destroyed for a generation.

And how did Mr. Nakagouchi react to this threat? Well, let me put it this way; have you ever seen *A World of Woozy Song?* I rest my case.

Before leaving Japan, I had time for one quick business enterprise. I had an idea for an invention specifically "tailored" to the Japanese. I got together with a patents lawyer and made the arrangements and investments necessary for the manufacture, distribution, and promotion of what I called "Power Pants." They were basically long, thick tubes of cloth stuffed with cotton and attached to the crotches of pairs of men's briefs. When worn, it gave the average Japanese man the very convincing illusion of having a penis. In the years since, "Power Pants" have made me more money than my film career.

Mark had more film offers for me back in Europe, but I'd been away from home for almost three full years now, and I was anxious to get back to Morehead Heights and my weekly Tarzan auditions. We decided to continue on home, traveling eastward.

There was some question as to Paolo's immigration status, and as I didn't want to screw up a good relationship by marrying him, I eventually brought him back to the states, listed on my customs form as a "souvenir."

I felt we all deserved a little vacation and decided to stop over at our newest state, Hawaii, en route home. I had been to the big island before, when I missed out on *A Streetcar Named Desire,* not a pleasant memory, so we decided to stay on one of the smaller, lesser-known islands. I was able to book accommodations at a very reasonable rate on an island called Molokai.

We ended up only staying one night, however. Frankly, the residents of Molokai were, without question, the homeliest folks I ever saw grouped in one place. I mean jaw-droppingly repulsive. In fact, they could literally drop their jaws on the ground. Shaking hands was to be avoided, since you never knew what might break off in your hand.

Eventually the day came when we arrived back at Morehead Heights, out on friendly old Tumescent Tor. A sad surprise awaited us there. The house was suffused with a smell worse than Rin Tin Tin's backyard. The source brought grief to us all, except Paolo. Major Babs had passed away, probably at least a year earlier according to the coroner, and only the headless Indian brave had found the body. My loyal companion and educator of many years, my rescuer from perils and fearless protector was gone. I had the house thoroughly aired out, cleaned, and freshened before giving her room to Paolo. It did, after all, connect with mine.

But now I was back and ready to resume my legendary Hollywood career.

PART SIX

Last Call
1962–1969

36

Back in My Saddle Again

My world-spanning junket had taken three years. Rudy had his work cut out for him, once the odor left behind by a year of Major Babs moldering upstairs had been disposed of. I sponsored Paolo for his green card, employing him as my personal trainer. I hired a new personal assistant, this time a perky young woman named Iris, who took command of my personal schedule. And I immediately reinstituted the weekly Saturday Tarzan auditions, that being Paolo's new day off.

My first order of business was another visit to the plastic surgeon, this time a respectable Beverly Hills doctor whose clientele was mostly Hollywood stars, to have my unfortunate Oriental look restored to a more American appearance. Once I had my old face back, it was time to get back to work.

My Hammer vampire flick, *Bats in My Belfry,* had been a huge hit stateside in a double bill with Hammer's *Frankenstein's Biggest Blunder,* which also starred Peter Cushing, and American-International Pictures was clamoring for my services. AIP, as American-International Pictures was generally known, was having a major success with their ongoing series of movies based on the stories of Edgar Allan Poe, all starring Vincent Price and all directed by a young man named Roger Corman.

A British actress named Hazel Court had done a few Hammer films and then come over to America and been successful in several of the Price-Poe pictures, so when Roger Corman heard I was back in Los Angeles, he was knocking at Fred Sturm's door with an offer for me to costar again with Vinnie Price, this time on real sets!

I eventually appeared with Vincent, Peter Lorre, little Debra Paget, and a very young Jack Nicholson in *Edgar Allan Poe's The Premature Climax.* Poe had apparently been a very neurotic gentleman, and this story, considered by literary critics to be his Most Frightening, explored the deepest terrors a man can know. The film we made from it was a terrifying exploration of the most horrific aspects of human sexuality, especially when practiced while buried alive. I played the chilling female specter that Vincent summoned up every time he made love to Debra (as if anyone would want that drab little mouse of a girl when I was around) in order to attempt to ward off the titular horror.*

The biggest problem with the picture was trying to make a feature film out of a five-page short story. Poe's original tale came to a sudden, messy end just as it seemed to be getting started. At the very point where it began to really penetrate its subject deeply, it was all over. We had to be sure that our movie of *The Premature Climax* didn't end too quickly also, leaving the audience unsatisfied. Roger Corman and his screenwriter, Richard Matheson, solved the problem by grafting the plot of *Les Miserables* into the Poe story. This expanded the running time from ten minutes to four hours, so, ironically, they ended up having to make radical cuts in the picture to bring *The Premature Climax* to a head more quickly.

In the picture, honeymooning Vincent and Debra had to keep the lovemaking short, so that Inspector Javert, played by Peter Lorre, didn't catch up with Vincent. My character had been Vincent's first wife, who had never ceased complaining about Vincent's sexual inadequacy until Vincent had her buried alive. Then my ghost haunts Vincent whenever he has sex. The irony is that my attempts to terrify him actually cure him of the problem I was upset with him for in the first place. Unfortunately, most of what got cut were my best scenes. All the material that explained who the hell I was, was gone, so, in the final picture, I'm really just a minor role, playing a howling ghost that materializes for no explained reason in all the love/horror scenes.

The picture made a hefty profit in spite of the butchery. Part of the reason was Roger's notoriously economic approach to filmmaking. He didn't waste time. We shot most of the picture before lunch. A few location shots required a day on the cliffs of Palos Verdes, acting around paintings of castles, but the whole movie took only a week to shoot. With Roger, there was no such thing as, "Take two."

The critics even seemed to enjoy the picture, despite the narrative

---

*Nor was this the first time I had been called a "Titular Horror." My poor puppies had been drooping a bit of late. I had asked my doctor to explain the small bruises I was getting on the underside of my breasts, and he said they were toe marks. Apparently I had been kicking them as I walked.–Tallulah

holes, and I received some of my best notices in years. The *New York Times* raved, "Tallulah Morehead is also in this movie," while *Variety* gushed, "Others in the cast include Tallulah Morehead." Needless to say, I was flying high with reviews like that. It was as though I had been rediscovered. In France I was a genius. In America I was "also in the cast." At last I was getting the kind of recognition I deserved.

But *Edgar Allan Poe's The Premature Climax* was the only film I made in 1962. In 1963, on a trip to New York, I met a fascinating and creepy young artist named Andy Warhol, who declared me to be "officially fabulous," which tipped me off at once that he wasn't husband material.

Little Andy, who was the blondest man I ever met, insisted that we make an Art Film together. As I am always on the cutting edge of motion picture trends, I was ready and raring to go. All I needed to know was who would my leading man be, and how quickly could he get his pants off.

To my amazement, I was to have no leading man at all. Indeed, I was to be the entire cast. This was truly the world of the avant-garde! We shot the whole movie in a single afternoon, in Andy's warehouse, which he called The Factory. I was asked to disrobe on camera for the first time in many years, so I knew I was in the hands of a *genius!*

The finished film, my only film in 3-D, by the way, was titled, rather accurately, *My Left Breast.* My face wasn't even in the film. Andy just kept a camera focused on my left breast, while he asked me questions about my breast and its adventures, what famous people had kissed and/or caressed it, what my relationship with it was, and how it differed from my right breast. Meanwhile, the camera followed my breast around as I sat, walked, chatted, and enjoyed a number of cocktails.

To my amazement, the picture received a good deal of attention in avant-garde film circles, and a number of highbrow critics reviewed it quite seriously. Even Hugh Hefner, the glamorous publisher of *Playboy* magazine, weighed in, calling it "the most heartbreaking and horrifying film I have ever seen."

Ironically, while playing the titular horror in a popular horror movie hadn't led to any more work, playing the titular tit in a limited, art house release did bring in the work offers. In 1964, I appeared in three movies in the one year for the first time since 1946.

The first was a wild, black and white horror movie called *Who the Hell Killed Baby Jane?,* in which I was reunited with Lillian Gush, with whom I'd made my screen debut in the silent *Heat Crazed!* forty-nine years before, in a previous life. Lillian had retired from the screen when sound came in but had recently made a comeback playing mean old ladies, at which she was very good.

Lillian and I were cast as sisters who had been movie stars and who now hated each other and are always trying to kill each other. Such a character role, playing an elderly, former movie star, was such an unusual stretch for me that I really didn't think I could bring it off. It took two hours to remove all the layers of grotesque makeup from my face before I was ready for the cameras each morning. Since I had killed Lillian back in *Heat Crazed!*, it was only fair that Lillian killed me in this picture.

The scariest moment came while chatting with the director one afternoon, when he casually mentioned that he had wanted to get Delores Delgado for Lillian's role but hadn't been able to locate her. Once I swallowed the horror of the idea of playing this film with the hateful Delores, I had the gleeful joy of telling him that Delores had drowned in Paris, finally giving her public what it wanted.

Who the Hell Killed Baby Jane? was a huge hit, actually the most financially successful film I ever made. I was shooting *Wet, Wild and Willing*, a musical about white-water rafting starring a singer named Elvis Presley, if I remember his peculiar name correctly, when *Baby Jane* opened and was immediately a smash hit. I received great reviews that actually mentioned my performance. I had, of course, been playing a character *decades* older than myself! The character I played in the picture had supposedly been a child star in vaudeville way back around the time I was a child star in vaudeville, and that was *long* before I was born. Perhaps the general knowledge that I was slowly approaching forty had made people start thinking "character actress" and casting me in these elderly roles.

Anyway, *Baby Jane* was a cultural phenomenon. I was asked to appear on a variety of TV shows to talk about it: *The Tonight Show, Merv Griffin, The Red Skelton Show, Engineer Bill's Cartoon Express, Romper Room*. Bob Hope played me in a wig on one of his so-called "comedy" specials, though the television critics rightly pointed out that Hope wasn't nearly as funny in the part as I had been.

Once the Elvis picture was done (and went on to make quite a tidy profit as well, further proof that I was hot, since that poor hillbilly singer couldn't act at all and garbled his words when he sang to the point of unintelligibility, so it *can't* have been *him* people were paying to see), Disney popped me into a leading role in a children's fantasy musical called *Mary Poppers*. I played a magical nanny who takes a whiff and goes flying. I sailed into the lives of a proper English sexually dysfunctional family and used my musical magical poppers to straighten out their screwed-up sex lives. It was sort of a change of pace for Disney, which didn't even have a wet bar on the set.

After the New Year, I launched 1965 by playing a nun (talk about a *stretch*) in the biggest musical of the year, Rogers and Hammerstein's bewilderingly popular mix of singing nuns, adorable children, and mawkish sentimentality, the hideous and beloved *It Sounds Like Music*, a musical so sugary it has killed diabetics on three continents. And although I have never been drunk enough to sit through the whole thing, it was the movie where I met Ernie.

37

My Marriage to Ernest Borgnine

I remember *nothing* of my marriage to Ernest Borgnine!*

---

*Possibly because it never happened, but try telling *her* that. See the Ghostwriter's Note at the beginning of the book.–Douglas

38

Whoopsi-Daisy

After my divorce from Ernest Borgnine in mid-1965, to capitalize on the monumental success of *Who the Hell Killed Baby Jane?*, I went on to do three more horror movies that year. First I was reteamed with Lillian Gush, and another old PMS costar, Olivia DeHeffalump, as well as Cousin Agnes[*] (our only appearance together), in the southern gothic ax murder spree picture, *Shut Your Damn Mouth, Stupid Sylvia!* in which I played Sylvia, as well as singing the touching title song,[†] one of the few horror films to even *have* a title song.

Robert Allman, who had directed *Baby Jane,* also directed this follow-up. As it was an independent film, eventually released, like *Baby Jane,* by Warner Brothers, it had several different people investing money in it. One of these investors was Al Bronze, the president, chairman of the board, and CEO of Whoopsi-Cola, a beverage I'd never heard of before but which he was quick to tell me was one of the biggest selling "soft drinks," whatever the hell *they* were, in the country. Eventually Rudy explained to me that Whoopsi-Cola was the nonalcoholic ingredient in a rum & coke.

"I see," I said to Al on the set. "You manufacture a mixer. How noble."

"It's not just a mixer, Miss Morehead. People drink it straight also."

"What on earth for?"

---

[*]Her brilliant talent showed our shared genetic heritage. Sadly, my legendary looks weren't shared as well, as Aggie was one of the *plainest* lesbians I ever met, and I knew Marjorie Main!–Tallulah

[†]Actually, Tallulah sang the song within the film, Patti Page sang it over the opening credits.–Douglas

"It tastes good."

"You can't be serious."

"No really. People buy millions of gallons of it every year, and only a small percentage of that is used as a mixer."

Though I was to become very attached to Al, I'm afraid I never acquired a taste for the hideous brew his fortune was based on.

By the time I started shooting my next film, *Demented!,* in which I played yet another ax murderess, Al and I were an "item," going steady, and having sleepovers. As Al was running a huge corporation, I saw no reason to unnecessarily burden him with boring details from my daily life, like the full extent of Paolo's duties or the exact nature of the Tarzan auditions. Al was almost sixty, and though many pointed out the large age difference between us,* I didn't care. I'd found a simple, gentle, gallant, charming, and affectionate billionaire to call my own, and I was in love. And if the sex wasn't all that great, well, that was why Paolo stayed on salary.

My final film of 1965 was the thrilling color gore-fest *Doctor Scary,* which starred my old friend Guy (pronounced "Ghee") Thanatos. Guy and I had last appeared together in my Civil War epic *East versus West,* back in 1939, and since then, Guy had become a major horror star, every bit the equal of Vincent Price, Christopher Lee, and Peter Cushing. At the conclusion of shooting, Al Bronze and I were married.

At long, *long* last, I was in a true love match, married to a genuine heterosexual. Al had even been married twice before, so I knew he was honestly attracted to women. I could have done without his constantly going on about how much he had enjoyed my movies back when he was in high school, and I put my foot down the day he mentioned that I had been his mother's favorite actress all her life.

True, Al wasn't the best-looking man I'd ever married, though he looked better than Lydia Thalberg had. He was short, plump, and bald, but he wore those five-thousand-dollar Italian suits so extremely well. He had only a small house on the West Coast; his primary residences were his gigantic estate, the Bronze Acres, out on Long Island, and his Manhattan townhouse, near Whoopsi-Cola's corporate headquarters. He sold the California house and moved into Morehead Heights while out here, while I took over his New York residences when we were back there. Being married to a New York business wizard turned me bicoastal, which was the first time I had ever been accused of that!

---

*Al was almost exactly ten years younger than Tallulah, though he may never have known this.–Douglas

Thanks to Al, my refrigerator was always stocked with Whoopsi-Cola. In fact, most of the bottles he loaded it up with back in 1966 are still there. I'm afraid I never developed a taste for the bubbly swill. It's not as sickening as milk, but that's the best thing I can say about it.

If I never could stand the stuff, I couldn't say that publicly then. As soon as I became Mrs. Al Bronze, I became *the* celebrity spokeswoman for Whoopsi-Cola. I made personal appearances promoting it. I am seen drinking the stuff (or at least what *looks* like the stuff, and is poured out of Whoopsi-Cola bottles, though I'd spiked it with rum to make it palatable) in all of the rest of my movies that weren't period pieces. I appeared in all their commercials, starting with the famous "For those who think they're young" campaign.

The only time in 1966 I was publicly seen drinking something more wholesome than my husband's vile brew was during a TV guest appearance on *Batman*. Everyone who was anyone was guesting on the *Batman* TV show as wild comic book villains, some drawn from the comic book, others created for the show, around the personality of the star.

Mine was the latter. On *Batman* I challenged the Dynamic Duo for supremacy in the Gotham City crime scene as The Drunkard, an always inebriated Super Criminal, who renders her foes unconscious with her deadly alcohol breath. Even here, my husband's product found its way into the show, Batman cleverly switching my real drink (which, for realism's sake, *was* a real drink; no need to treat the show like a comic strip) with Al's revolting product, which rendered The Drunkard helpless.

Looking for a New York–based film to be in so I could spend more time with Al, whose work required his presence in Manhattan most of the time, led me back to my old social drinking buddy Tom Williams, whose play about a streetcar I'd nearly saved the movie of fifteen years before. This time, Tom had turned out his only film musical with songs by my old team of Ebb & Flo. The film was called *Fiddler on a Hot Tin Roof* and was about a faded southern belle living in Russia who learns her husband is gay and then has to emigrate to America when the cossacks come for all the gay people. In light of my horror reputation at the time, the critics called it the scariest musical ever made. Tom loved it, but Tom was always drunk, and I should know, because I was drinking with him.

When I finished work on *Fiddler*, I returned to California to make another horror movie, this one an original for AIP titled *Guess What's Coming to Dinner*. Al was stuck in New York and could only come out for weekends. Unfortunately, his second weekend back at Morehead

Heights he got up in the middle of the night, as elderly men do, and was wandering the halls in the dimness when he suddenly came face-to-stump with the headless Indian brave.

I'm afraid I hadn't told Al about the headless Indian brave. How do you tell the man you love that you've been living for forty-six years with a man who is (a) a different race, (b) dead, and (c) headless? My sanity gets questioned enough as it is.

Anyway, Al was unprepared for the shock, and his poor heart, whose precarious condition I was unaware of, just gave out. The poor, dear man just dropped dead on the spot. The headless Indian brave was beside himself, which only made him look even eerier, with upset, and apologized in sign language again and again. I tried my best to comfort the dispirited spirit as I went over Al's will.

Actually, what I was going over wasn't Al's will quite yet. I had had this draft made, knowing that he intended to change his will. In the old will, most of the money, and a controlling interest in Whoopsi-Cola, was left to his rude, ungrateful son Thad, by a previous, less holy and blessed union. My stepson Thad had refused to come to the wedding, and had been freezingly rude to me whenever I stayed out at Bronze Acres, where he lived, always referring to me as "the lush" or "the old whore," and sometimes even being openly insulting.

I knew Al intended to disinherit Thad, as I made him tell me he planned to before I would have oral sex with him. But Al was so busy, he had neglected to sign the new will I'd had drawn up for him. Rather than allow Al's last wishes to be thwarted by his unexpected, premature demise, I decided to just go ahead with the new will. Rudy signed the new document for Al, with a remarkably accurate facsimile of Al's signature that I'd had him practicing for months, just in case of the unthinkable. Paolo witnessed it. As it happened, codicils in the new will made each of them millionaires, but that was a mere coincidence.

Thad got the Long Island estate, Bronze Acres, for which I had no use, his trust fund, and ten million dollars, but no Whoopsi-Cola stock, and if he contested the will he was to get nothing.

The remainder of the estate, amounting in all to roughly thirty billion dollars, and sixty-five percent of Whoopsi-Cola went to me, though it was small compensation for the irreparable loss of a living, loving old man. Paolo was such a comfort to me in this trying time. And I received a very sweet note from Terrence in Paris, inviting me to come mourn my loss with them.

This seemed like a good idea, so once I had finished up work on

Guess What's Coming to Dinner, I packed up Paolo, Iris, and Rudy, and headed for France.

I stopped in New York on the way for a meeting with the Whoopsi-Cola board of directors. Being the new owner, I was able to improve the product tremendously. To the classic formula Al had worked out decades earlier, I added two vital ingredients that had been missing up until now: rum and vermouth. The board blustered that it could no longer be sold as a soft drink to kids, and I said, "Only if you tell everybody." And then took off, to assuage my grief being comforted by Paolo in Paris. By the time I returned to America, a year and a half later, the stupid mishandling of the vastly improved product by my disloyal staff had driven Whoopsi-Cola into bankruptcy. I might have taken a major loss, if I hadn't, in a burst of fence-mending generosity, sold out all my interests in the company back to Thad for sixty cents on the dollar. Poor Thad. He ended up losing the estate.

As for me, I was prostrate with grief, in luxury, in Europe.

39

Plastered in Paris

My marriage to Al Bronze had lasted only eleven months. From when we first met until his too soon death was barely a full two years. Even the steady stream of alcohol, the constant ministrations of Paolo, and the thirty billion dollars couldn't heal the ache in my heart. It seemed I was fated never to live long in wedded bliss. Thank God for unwedded bliss!

After a couple months of grieving in Paris, during which I consumed a good deal of the new, improved Whoopsi-Cola, Jacques Fromage had to attend the film festival in Cannes and invited us to go along. The French Riviera seemed as good a place to grieve as any, so we went.

I could barely bring myself to face the public, so I hid my tears behind sunglasses while Paolo and I sunbathed on the Cote d'Azur and forced ourselves to attend parties, screenings, receptions, orgies, and wine tastings. It was *awful,* but I managed to get through it.

After the festival ended, my grief drove me on to Nice, where I purchased a modest thirty-room house overlooking the harbor, and hid from the world with Paolo, Rudy, and Iris, while Terrence and Jacques returned to Paris. One day Mark, my European agent, dropped by to comfort me, although a man every day of seventy years old isn't all that much comfort compared with Paolo, but old habits are hard to break. While dressing afterward, he mentioned a couple film offers.

"No, no, no," I said. "I'm an old widow woman. I'll never work again."

"You're not old. You're ageless."

"True, but facts must be faced. I'm frankly forty now. Who would want to see me in a movie?"

"Hammer films. They've offered you a two-picture deal."

"Of course. More horror. That's what I'm good for now. Scaring children. Pour me another martini, darling."

"One is a sequel to your dinosaur film."

"I died in the first one. How can I be in the sequel? No olive, onion."

"You're playing your own, revenge-crazed twin."

"Seeking revenge on a pterodactyl?"

"On the Brunettes."

"That is a good idea, I must admit. Stir, darling. Shaking bruises the gin. What's the other one?"

"A Frankenstein picture with Peter Cushing."

"Dear Peter Cushing. How I love Peter. All my life, I have loved Peter. But no. I'm a grieving widow. Leave me here in my loneliness."

"Do you think Al Bronze would want you to shut yourself away from the world like this? No! He wanted you to go on sharing yourself with the world, just as you've always done."

"No, no. I'm too sad. Too melancholy. Just out of curiosity, what are they paying?"

"A million dollars for the two films."

"I'll do it. But only because I can't allow my grief to deprive my legions of fans."

So I shot *When Dinosaurs Ruled the Block* in Spain in late 1967, and *Frankenstein's Reason for Living* in England in early 1968. While I was in England, I also shot a short, antismoking public-service film to be run in British schools that was titled *Against All Fags*.

When Dinosaurs Ruled the Block was just a run-of-the-mill, slice-of-prehistoric-life picture, but *Frankenstein's Reason for Living* was a remarkable and stunning movie, the most romantic of all Peter Cushing's many Frankenstein films.

In the movie Peter, as Baron Frankenstein, is walking through London one evening while discussing the importance of heredity versus environment with his science pal, Charles Darwin. Darwin turns out to be a social Darwinist, who believes that class is inborn and bred. They find the lifeless remains of a victim of Jack the Ripper. Baron Frankenstein bets Darwin that he can take this lifeless corpse of an old whore, reanimate her, and, in six months pass her off as a lady at a royal ball. Being gentlemen, they only bet one pound, which is what a dollar weighs in England.

Baron Frankenstein brings the corpse back to life, but Darwin, wanting to win his bet, has cheated. The whore's brain had spoiled lying around that Whitechapel alley, so Frankenstein plans to put in the brain of his niece, whom he kills, he thinks temporarily, to bring back to life in the new body. Unknown to Frankenstein, Darwin has switched brains on him, so the brain he puts into the dead whore is that of Jack the Ripper himself.

I played the "monster" Frankenstein brings to life; the old, murdered whore, with the brain of a male serial killer. The makeup artist, Roy Ashton, spent about ten minutes each morning covering up some of my larger plastic surgery scars so I wouldn't be *too* horrifying.

As Baron Frankenstein is teaching me to be a lady, he falls in love with me. In one big scene, we dance about wildly after I learn to say correctly, "The pain in my brain has all gone down the drain."

What he doesn't know is that at night I've been going out and murdering a string of starlets, and then, in the version released in Europe and the Orient, having sex with their lifeless bodies. During the movie I kill the lovely Hammer horror queens Martine Beswicke, Veronica Carlson, and Stephanie Beacham.

At the climactic royal ball, I've fooled everyone into thinking I'm a real lady, until I suddenly go berserk and kill Queen Victoria. A howling mob then chases me all over London and rips my body to pieces. Baron Frankenstein, heartbroken, says, "I've grown accustomed to her face" and slips my severed head into his satchel as a souvenir. Then he pays Darwin his ill-earned pound and leaves town, to start all over again somewhere else in the next movie.

As you can see, along with the lurid thrills, the movie was a stirring plea for tolerance for homicidal, lesbian necrophiliacs who have been resurrected from the dead everywhere. For me, there was the challenge of playing a man, albeit a necrophile serial killer, trapped in a woman's body. To research the part, I had a padlock installed on my dressing room's inner door and then trapped as many men inside my body, one or two at a time, as I could manage. I must have struck a chord as, in the years since its release, I've received several letters from homicidal, lesbian necrophiliacs, at least one of whom claimed to have been raised from the dead, thanking me for my compassionate performance. These letters always moved me very deeply before I turned them over to the police.

But, though these films kept me busy, my heart just wasn't in movie acting anymore. I'd been in eighty-eight movies over the last fifty-three years, and what other forty-year-old woman could say that? But I was tired and sad. So I returned to Nice to drink and make love to Paolo. Nothing else made any sense.

Then, in December 1968 the Alabaman actress Tallulah Bankhead died. Needless to say, the similarity of our names had caused us both much confusion over the years, but this time it was too much. My death was widely misreported all over America. I eventually packed up my family, sold the Nice house, and returned once more to Morehead Heights, where I held a press conference to make it clear that I was not dead, no matter how I looked.

Fred Sturm had a film offer for me, but only one. It seemed, even with the huge success I'd had in horror movies barely five years before, there just weren't many roles for an actress over forty. I began to think seriously about retiring. I had left a large legacy of film work and I was a billionairess, so I didn't need to work. I took the offered film but told Fred that would be it.

The picture was yet another dinosaur film, but as this one was being made by MGM instead of Hammer, it was being shot in Hawaii instead of Spain. You could hardly argue with being paid to visit Hawaii. The picture was titled *Jurassic Tart*, and in it I played the very first prostitute in history. It was probably the best of my dinosaur trilogy, but the truth was, I just didn't care anymore.

However I still had one great project I'd never gotten to do. For almost forty years I'd had *The Well of Loneliness* sitting around as a dream project. It was simply too advanced for Hollywood in the thirties, or the forties, or the fifties, but now it was 1969. Film censorship had become a thing of the past. The time was come for me to share my vision of a romantic love story with no men. *The Boys in the Band* had been a hit in New York and was being filmed. Why not a female answer? And, after eighty-nine films, who was more qualified to direct this project from my heart than me?

S. Lee-Zee films had long gone out of business, and Russell had died of a heart blockage years before, but his son, Tyrone Zee, was following in his father's mattress stains, running a small, independent film company that specialized in risky subject matter called Cocksure Movies. When I pitched my idea for a film of Radcliffe Hall's groundbreaking novel, unlike the rebuffs I'd received in the past from Lydia Thalberg and Harry Cohn, Tyrone Zee's response was, "A Lesbo sex film? That is *so* hot! I'm in!"

So I had one more movie to make, my most personal statement yet.

40

Bush Whacked!

For almost fifty years I had treasured the deeply moving summaries of *The Well of Loneliness* that Terrence had written for me. I had lovingly imagined how each scene would be played and shot. Now, with Cocksure Movies solidly standing up behind me, the time had come for me to write the greatest screenplay of all time. I sat down, right here in this room at Morehead Heights, in this chair, on this stain, and began dictating the script to Iris.

I haven't told you much about Iris. She was now in her early thirties. Unlike Terrence, who lived at Morehead Heights, and who was basically at my service twenty-four hours a day for forty years, Iris lived in her own apartment in Santa Monica and insisted on having a life of her own, which I thought was terribly selfish of her. However, she was extremely efficient, which made one of us. She had recently married what I assumed was a nice young man. I never met him, as Iris, as a condition of the marriage, had gotten an injunction enjoining her husband from coming within a mile of me. I guess she didn't trust him.

Working as many as two hours a day, we knocked out the screenplay fairly quickly, and Iris delivered the five-hundred-page document to Tyrone Zee. Tyrone called the next day.

"Tallulah baby, I *loved* the first six pages of your script."

"What about the remaining four hundred ninety-four pages? Several of them are very good. Refill this, won't you please, Rudy? And Iris's spelling is *excellent!*"

"Tallu, doll, I've never read an entire script in my life, even ones I wrote. I don't know why people write more than six pages. If the script is done right, at page six you should be able to just write 'And so forth' for the rest."

"I'll bear that in mind in future literary endeavors."

"Anyway, I loved it, and I think we can even use bits of it. I've sent it on to the rewrite boys, and we should have a shooting script for you in a month."

"I sent you a shooting script. Thank you, Rudy."

"No, Tallulah, you sent me a first draft."

"I've been writing that in my heart for half a century."

"Which is why it's so polished for a first draft; but, Tallulah, you're not a professional writer. You're a Great *Star.*"

"True. Refill this again, would you, Rudy?"

"You've shown us what's in your heart. Now my pro boys just need to polish and edit it a bit to get it ready for the cameras."

"Edit?"

"It's five hundred pages long. *Gone with the Wind* had a shorter screenplay."

"That was pulp trash. This is *art!*"

"But it's too long. The movie would run eight hours. We want to run ninety minutes, an hour forty-five tops."

"I won't have it butchered!"

"No butchery. Just a light trim of four hundred pages or so."

"What about the scene at the marketplace?"

"Better than *Hamlet.* Gotta run. Love you, Tallulah baby."

The man had charm. I wondered why he was still waiting to have sex with me, since his late father never held back a moment, but Tyrone never showed any sexual interest in me personally. Maybe he was *that way,* although I never married him.

A month later I received a ninety-five-page script from Tyrone Zee. I had titled mine, *The Well That Never Runs Dry.* The script that came back was titled *The Carpetmunchers.* It was the story of an airline stewardess and a cheerleader who are roommates. After having quite graphically described lovemaking sessions with their brutish boyfriends, both of whom break up with them after sex, they fall into each other's arms for a cry and discover the love that dares not speak its name. They begin seducing other young women right and left, until, in a spectacular finale, all the other cheerleaders and the other stewardesses get together for an enormous, girl-on-girl orgy. It bore no resemblence to my script whatsoever, although it still said "Written by Tallulah Morehead" on the cover. After Iris finished reading it to me, I took an ice-cold shower and then phoned Tyrone.

"Tyrone darling."

"Tallulah. Did you love your script?"

"This isn't my script."

"We had to make a few changes."

"It's an entirely different story. A manhattan please, Rudy."

"Yeah, well, it turned out yours was based on a book, and we would have had to buy the rights. So, we made a few cosmetic changes and, presto, an original!"

"An original what? It's wall-to-wall lesbian sex."

"Except the opening scenes, where their boyfriends pork 'em and then throw them out. That's the *motivation.*"

"But there's no character, no plot, almost no dialogue. Just lots of all-girl sex."

"Yeah! Isn't it just incredibly hot? Best screenplay I've ever seen."

"Who wrote it? Thank you, Rudy darling."

"You did."

"This isn't what I wrote."

"No. I had a professional writer tweak it slightly."

"Who?"

"He prefers to remain anonymous. He wants you to take all the credit."

"Or blame. I can't shoot this. Why, it's nothing but soft-core pornography."

"Trust me, Tallulah. By the time this hits theaters, no one will call it *soft-core* pornography."

Time proved Tyrone correct. The casting sessions were something else. Tyrone kept a camera rolling at them, and a number of the auditions, years later, were released on home video under the title *Fox Hunt.* As the astute reader will have noticed by now, it was not uncommon in the movies for a certain amount of sexual activity to take place at auditions, generally between the auditionee and the director and/or the producer and/or the cameraman and/or the food services guy, but at the auditions for *The Carpetmunchers,* all the sex, and there was one hell of a lot of it, was between the actresses auditioning. Eventually, choosing between these nearly identical actresses was impossible, and I let Tyrone choose whom he wanted.

I played a cameo part in the picture as the cheerleaders' stern mistress, but I wasn't in any of the love scenes. Every time I tried rewriting the love scenes to add my character, Tyrone took me back out again. "Tallulah," he said, "you're too big a star. Leave the audience wanting to see more of you."

I shot the numerous love scenes as tastefully as possible. Tyrone kept suggesting I shoot more frankly. I refused. I found long days on the set quite tiring, so Tyrone often took over for me in shooting the love scenes, letting me go home early while he shot the last few pickups,* though promising to shoot them *exactly* as I'd laid them out.

I found directing to be tremendously fulfilling. I'd sit in a chair all day and give orders, and everybody did everything just as I wanted it done. Best of all, I could enjoy a cocktail as I worked. I should have switched to directing *years* ago.

When it came time to edit the picture, I prepared to have my customary affair with the editor, only he turned me down. "Don't be silly, Madam Morehead," he said, showing me a little too much respect. "You're the director. Of course we'll do it your way."

"But, even so. Wouldn't you like a little extra motivation?"

"No, ma'am. But I do want to tell you what an honor it is working with you."

"Thank you, darling."

"My grandmother used to talk about how you were her favorite actress back when she was a little girl, before she died of extreme old age about ten years ago."

"Just cut the damn movie, motor mouth."

I was happy with my "Director's Cut," and Tyrone said he was also. I went home to audition Tarzans while Tyrone arranged for the premiere and release. I had suggested at least returning to my title, but Tyrone said, "Look, we don't own the rights to that dyke book you read, so our lawyer advised us to avoid any use of the word 'well.' Anyway, *The Carpetmunchers* tested great with our target audience."

"Art house critics and literary lesbians?"

"Yeah. Them."

The premiere was held at a theater I wasn't previously familiar with. It was called The Pussycat Theater and was on Santa Monica Boulevard in West Hollywood (it's still there I believe, although its name has changed). The posters outside the theater were promising. They read "Cocksure Movies Presents a Morehead Film! When you want fun, cry 'Morehead!' *The Carpetmunchers!* They frolicked in the bush and yodeled in the canyon!"

As I was going in, Tyrone took me to one side and said, "Tallulah, I thought I should tell you, I have re-edited the picture."

---

*Normally the term "pickups" referred to miscellaneous insert shots. Here, I'm afraid, it refers to the performers.–Douglas

"What? You've tampered with my masterpiece? How could you?"

"Check your contract. I have final cut. And all I've done is tweak the footage a little. Your vision is still intact. I've just focused it a little better."

"If you say so. Where's the bar?"

The movie was actually not all that different from what I'd made. All Tyrone had done was to add footage to the love scenes, footage he'd shot when I wasn't there. The new footage was of a remarkable frankness. It also changed the rating from R to XXX. And it proudly proclaimed, "Conceived, Written, and Directed by Tallulah Morehead." For once, I almost wished I hadn't gotten such substantial billing.

The film wasn't reviewed by any real critics, but the Pussycat people played it at their chain of theaters in big cities all across the country, and Tyrone reported back that it made huge profits. The audience I intended it for, let us say, women of a certain mindset, never found it, but it apparently entertained men by the tens of thousands. I don't know if Radcliffe Hall ever saw it, but if he did, I doubt he'd have recognized his book as the source material.

Tyrone was happy to work with me again, but, looking at the silly mess that was *The Carpetmunchers*, I thought to myself, "That's it. I *can* still sink lower, but I see no reason to." I called Fred Sturm and told him I had officially retired. I let Iris go, went home to Morehead Heights, and poured myself a drink.

PART SEVEN

My Reclining Years
1970–1999

41

The Seventies

42

Where the Hell Am I?

"Where the hell am I?" I cried out upon awakening. There was no answer. I was alone. I soon realized I was in my bedroom at Morehead Heights, but where was Rudy? Where was Paolo? Where the hell was anybody?

At noon someone let themself in the front door. I almost leapt out of my skin,* and went running up, starting to say "Rudy, where the hell have you been?" when I saw it was a middle-aged, plump black woman, so reminiscent of my dear Hattie McDaniel, who was letting herself into my house.

"Who the hell are you?" I asked.

The woman rolled her eyes skyward and said, "Not again. Miss Tallulah. I have to tell you every week. I'm Mona. I'm your cook."

"Where's Rudy?"

"You loaned Rudy to George Hamilton six years ago. He never came back."

"Six years ago? What year is it?"

"Nineteen eighty."

"What happened to the seventies?"

"Don't ask. You might want to get dressed. Your doctor will be here in an hour."

"My doctor? What do I need with a doctor?"

"Honeylamb, you're eighty-three years old and you still drink like a fish. A little medical maintenance is a good idea."

---

*Not an exaggeration. My skin had loosened up considerably by this point. –Tallulah

It was true. I had missed an entire decade. I hope nothing interesting happened.

My staff now consisted of Mona, my cook; Hazel, the maid; and Felipe, the gardener. None of them lived in, and none of them had any idea what had become of Paolo, though apparently he had left, even before Rudy. Isn't that always the way? Give a man a million dollars and suddenly he's *too good* to get paid to have sex with a withered old lady. When I met that ungrateful boy he was just a street hustler in Rome. What can I say? Friends are like booze: they make you feel good for a while, but they always run out eventually. The headless Indian brave was the closest thing to a familiar face around, and he doesn't even *have* a face.[*]

It was pleasing, at least, to learn I wasn't fully forgotten, except by myself. Many of my old movies still ran on television, now in color. In fact some ran on TV in color despite having been *made* in black and white! Someone had been set loose with crayons. Either that, or my eyes or my memory weren't all they had been.[†] My life was placid, uneventful, dull. Actually, it was a lot like being dead, except people spoke to me, I could still drink, and I smelled better most of the time.

The worst thing was, I could find no evidence to indicate that I'd had sex in ten years. Except for the alcohol, life now was *worse* than death! I needed to get out more. In fact, I don't know that I'd been off of Tumescent Tor in years.

It's a traumatic thing to go off for a drink in your forties and wake up ten years later in your eighties. There's nothing like no sex to really age you.

A glance in the mirror showed that the facelift I'd had almost twenty years before had definitely worn off, and if my breasts had had bones, they could have been classified as additional arms. I wondered if I could titillate any men with my newfound ability to tie them in a knot, but after experimenting with that trick at that week's Tarzan auditions (at least *some* traditions had continued unabated, whether I remembered them or not), I decided that the novelty didn't compensate for the looks of horror, or the *wilting* effect it produced in the increasingly smaller

---

[*]The dear headless Indian brave is now my longest surviving companion, if one can use the term "surviving" about someone who has been dead for centuries. But dead or not, he is a credit to deceased, cranially impaired Native Americans everywhere.–Tallulah

[†]Actually, all three apply.–Douglas

number of men that could be persuaded to go through with a *full-force* Tarzan audition.*

One day I got a call from a young man who identified himself as a film historian, who had been going through obituary files and couldn't find a date for my death. Could I please inform him just exactly when had Tallulah Morehead died.

I explained that I hadn't selected a death date yet, but that I was open to suggestion. "Oh my God!" the man squealed. "You don't mean you are actually Tallulah Morehead and you're still alive?"

"I'm pretty sure the answer is 'Yes' on both counts."

"Oh my God, *my God!*" the man continued squealing in a manner that put me in mind of the late F. Emmett Knight. Why is it that so many men who are the *merest whisper* are so damned loud? "I've got to interview you! *I've got to interview you!* Everybody thinks you're dead!"

"Everybody thought Vivien Leigh could act."

"Oooooooh! You're *too funny!* I must interview you before you die. You have so much to share about the old, *old* days."

"I'll try to squeeze you in."

When this young man showed up, he made the late Terrence look butch, so I knew sex was out of the question. He was full of questions, mostly about my horror movies and my clothes, and of course, who was gay in old Hollywood. "That's easy," I said. "Everybody except Bogart, Gable, and C. Aubrey Smith."

"Who's Sea Aubrey Smith?" the ignorant young dolt asked.

"Leave my house," I replied.

When his article, titled *Morehead Back from the Dead,* which I felt was a slight exaggeration, appeared in *Hideous Monsters Magazine,* I began to get calls. One was from an agent. Was I interested in working again? No, no. I was retired. I was disinclined. What kind of money were we talking?

His name was Kevin Edwards, and he put me in touch with an Englishman named Sir Webster Lloyd Webfoot, who wrote Broadway musicals. He came out to meet me, and announced his intention to write a musical about me in which I could play myself, as I was now, on Broadway! The resulting musical was called *Pacific Coast Highway,* that being the name of the street that runs past Tumescent Tor.

---

*Probably the sight of my breasts tied in a square or, how unfortunately appropriate, a *granny* knot, was not all that erotic, but I thought the effect when I tied them in a nice, pretty bow was quite pleasing. The men these days, however, just didn't seem to have strong stomachs.–Tallulah

Sir Webster had me come to New York, where it turned out I still owned Al Bronze's townhouse, as he insisted on doing his Broadway musical in Manhattan even though it was set in California and would have benefited from location shooting.

The story was about me meeting a young, handsome screenwriter who helps me write a comeback feature. " 'Comeback'? I hate that word! It's a Pathetic Bid For Attention!" I wail at the screenwriter.

I fall madly in love with the writer, which, right off, shows how muddleheaded this piece of ficton was. Imagine a big star like me falling in love with a *writer?* Insane! I may have married my houseboy while drunk, but I *never* fell in love with a writer! Only a writer could write something that idiotic!

As if that wasn't stupid enough, the writer then spurns me for his girlfriend! Can you imagine such drivel? What writer would be stupid enough to spurn a *Big Movie Star* for some secretary? What planet was this Sir Webster from, anyway? Then I remembered. England.*

My big number was my song about how we didn't need words to act in silent movies. It used rather a lot of words to say I could communicate anything without words.

With one stare
I don't need to talk.
With one glare
I can stop your clock.
I can make your mirrors break.
With one stare you'll know
That you'd better go.

With one stare
I can train your mutt.
If you're bare,
I can grope your butt.
When I act it's with my head.
And what's more I'm not dead.

I can't recall
A thing I did last fall

---

*The English have always had a grossly oversized amount of misplaced respect for writers, hence their dopey devotion to that talentless, overwriting hack they call "the Beard of Avon." So he married a shy lesbian named Avon? So what? Does that make him Neil Simon?–Tallulah

But in '22,
I went to a zoo.
Or was that me?
Or Myrna Loy, oh gee.
Oh yes, now I know,
I did Clara Bow.

With one look
I do all I can.
With my Hook,
I'll kill Peter Pan.
Silent music starts to play.
Silent tunes, my dear,
Awfully hard to hear.

With one stare
I've returned today
Did you care
That I'd been away?
Wait! My mind's starting to fog.
Daddy, where is my dog?

Silent music starts to play
I don't have a clue.
Who the hell are you?

With one stare
My brain's in a haze.
In my hair
I'll ignite a blaze.
They'll say Morehead's back, Oh God!
This time I am staying.
I'm staying for good.
I'll be back
Where I'll have a few nips.
With one stare,
Read my lips!

See what I mean? In the second act I had an idiotic song about the
Whispered Conversations we used to have on the stages while filming

our silent epics. "But, Sir Webster," I tried to protest, "we didn't have to whisper. They were *silent* movies, remember?"

"Tallulah darling. You're just a face and a voice. *I'm* a *genius!* Leave the creative stuff to me."

"Well, then," I added, "what about the lyric in the title song about the wagon trains bringing settlers to Los Angeles during the Gold Rush?"

"What about it?"

"I don't know what they taught you in British schools, but the Gold Rush was in *Northern* California! It brought people to San Francisco. And *no one* came to Los Angeles in a covered wagon. It's surrounded by mountains. It just never happened!"

"Don't worry about it. Go rehearse Act One." By which, I might add, he merely meant I should run over the scene with the other actors and the director. No one seemed to remember the true meaning of 're-hearse' anymore.

Moviemaking had changed a great deal in the years I'd been out of it. Live television techniques had corrupted it. Instead of shooting on different locations over a period of weeks, we were expected to shoot the whole thing in one evening, performing it live onstage, in front of a live audience, like a high school play! I considered it a childish way to work. We weren't even supposed to stop and go back and retake something if we made a mistake. "Just go on," was the order.

We played two weeks of preview performances at the spooky old Allsop Theater on West 45th Street, just off Times Square, to get used to the novelty of an audience, and then came The Big Night.

Everybody was very kissy-face. My leading man, who had stayed in character by resisting my seductions offstage as well as on, preferring to have an affair with one of the cuter guys in the dance line, was all over me like flashbulbs on a philandering Royal Family Member. Frankly, at now eighty-four, I found doing the whole show all at once *very* tiring. I didn't need to expend extra energy running around from dressing room to dressing room squealing. It was hard enough to play a sex-starved old lady without someone at least throwing me a quick one backstage to help me focus better.

In the weirdest change from the old way of doing things yet, the critics had been invited to the performance. I felt they should wait for the release of the film, but I was assured that this was how things were done on Broadway.

Well, the show went all right. I rose to the occasion and gave a brilliant performance, every once in a while even doing parts of the same script the rest of the cast was doing. I was cheered and showered with flowers after the performance, which is no way to get clean.

I was simply too tired for the party and asked Sir Webster if anybody minded if I skipped the festivity.

"No, no," he replied. "Everybody understands you're no longer young. To have given a performance like that at your age is triumph enough."

"Enough with the insults. I need some sleep."

"Just go on home. We'll talk tomorrow."

With that I was off to the airport and was soon snoozing away in my first-class seat on the red-eye flight back to Morehead Heights.

Early the next evening the phone rang. It was Sir Webster in a state of consternation. "This is Sir Webster Lloyd Webfoot. Has anybody there heard from Tallulah?"

"This is Tallulah, darling. How are you? How do the rushes look?"

"What are you doing in California?"

"I live here."

"But you're supposed to be here!"

"You told me to go home."

"I didn't mean California!"

"What's the problem, darling?"

"What's the problem? What about tonight's performance?"

"What are you talking about?"

"The performance tonight! There's an audience sitting in the theater waiting to see you!"

"But I already *did* the show, last night. Why should I do it again tonight? Didn't you get it all shot? Do you need retakes?"

"What are you talking about? This isn't a movie! You have to do the show every night, live!"

"Don't be silly, darling. Doing the same show night after night? That would get old in a hurry. Now go cut the film and leave this old lady alone."

"There is no film! This isn't a movie! It's live Broadway theater! You have to do the show every night! Now get back to New York City right now!"

"Don't be silly. What is this? High school? Now, Webster, I'd love to discuss this further, but it's time for *Matlock*. Drop in next time you're in Los Angeles." And then I hung up.

How the hell was I supposed to know that they had preserved this bizarre ritual in New York of hiring actors to perform movies live onstage, night after tedious night? Who in their right mind would want to do that?

Pacific Coast Highway closed for three weeks, then reopened with Faye Dunaway playing me. The critics had said that when I sang, the show lost all claim to being a musical. Miss Dunaway, they said, continued my proud tradition. The show ran a week. I told them they should have filmed it.

43

Gilligan's Streetcar

As it happened, this insane craze for live actors doing movies live on-stage had caught on all over the country. Frankly, the appeal is lost on me. Where are the close-ups, which are the *essence* of Great Acting?

Still, this craze did allow me to finally give the performance America had been deprived of a few, brief* years before. A strange, never explained, blackout had deprived the world of my Blanche Dubois back in the fifties, the poor old world having had to *make do* with Vivien Leigh's embarrassing "performance," which had been given my Oscar, only because everyone was afraid that if they'd told her how terrible she'd been, she would have another of her "episodes." Poor little Sir Larry. How he put up with her all those years, I'll never know. Thank Heaven for Joan Plowright—and Danny, of course.

There was nothing I could do about *Gone with the Wind*. Vivien's ghastly, charmless performance had sunk that film like Natalie Wood on a moonlight swim. Again, moviegoers had attended the film only because of their fear of what Vivien might do if they didn't go, and for the raw, animal sex appeal of hunky, all-man Leslie Howard.†

But *A Streetcar Named Desire* I could still save, onstage! A theatrical producer who has begged me to keep his name out of this book (Bill Overlander) arranged, in 1985, for me to tour as Blanche Dubois opposite that Great American Actor Bob Denver as Stanley Kowalski.

We played Chicago, Denver, Kansas City, Cleveland, Toronto, Buf-

*Believe me, there's *nothing* briefer than a year you can't remember.–Tallulah
†Leslie Howard's brutal, sweaty, raw animal sexuality as Ashley Wilkes was so intense that for a few years after the release of *Gone with the Wind* Ashley and Leslie became the most popular names in America for newborn baby girls.–Tallulah

falo, Albany, Atlanta, St. Petersburg, Miami, New Orleans, Austin, Dallas, Albuquerque, San Diego, San Francisco, and Las Vegas, sometimes as many as three performances in a city. The reviews were unanimous.

I did particularly well. In one review, titled *Streetcar Derails, Williams Killed,* the critic wrote, "Crazy as Tallulah seems, right from her first entrance, you still expect Bob's Stanley to crack first. The rape scene may be the funniest piece of staged slapstick I have ever seen," while another critic simply wrote, "Who is raping whom?" Another critic suggested, "Perhaps this time, the last line should be, 'I have always depended on the *blindness* of strangers.' "

Bob Denver was a Stanley for the ages. Oh, Marlon Brando had been very good in the movie, in an obvious sort of way, but for sheer, lustful, ram-me-like-a-jackhammer-baby, hot, sizzling sex, Bob Denver was not to be topped! Marlon Brando, Bob Denver; when it comes to acting or sex, there's simply *no* comparison!

Vegas was a fun sort of town, the sort of town where an eighty-eight-year-old woman could still get an active young man for the night with one phone call. My old hillbilly singer costar, Elvis Presley had apparently had a freak success with a Vegas lounge act. I realized that if that untalented nobody could do it, I could. I decided to put an act together for myself for the lounges.

I hired a batch of gorgeous musclemen to appear with me. Keeping them close to me was a problem, so when I was sewn into my skintight costume each evening,[*] I simply had the boys sewn into the outfit with me.

I sang songs from my films, as well as popular rock songs of the day. My rendition of *Bohemian Rhapsody,* as a solo number, was unsurpassed, as was my lovely rendition of *Satisfaction.* Both are on the pop album I did a few years later, *Tallulah Morehead Rocks Her Brains Out.*[†]

The act was a huge success the first night. The lounge was packed with people laughing their hearts out. But that was it. It was half-full second night. Five people came to the show the third night. The fourth night it was completely empty, and the fifth night, the musclemen didn't

[*]No mean trick itself, considering how extremely loose my skin was.–Tallulah
[†]The album is still available, from me here at Morehead Heights, as it didn't really sell all that well. The other cuts included such gems as *Boogie People, The Name Game, Twistin' the Night Away, Yesterday, Day Tripper, Let It Please Be Him, Hotel California, Karma Chameleon, Hound Dog, The Hustle,* and *Cop Killer.*–Tallulah

show up, either. Oh well, I gave it a shot. The same thing happened to Sir Noel Coward.*

Then it was back to Morehead Heights. This time, I thought, I'm really retired.

I was drinking one evening, at a West Hollywood bar called The Eagle when I met Trevor. As always, I was treated like a goddess by the Eagle boys, but Trevor was something else. He asked me, in the course of casual conversation, about the money I had inherited from Al Bronze. Since Trevor had been maybe two years old when I married Al Bronze, I thought it enterprising of him to even know about it. I mentioned that, yes, I was still a billionairess. Even I can't drink up thirty billion dollars in a mere twenty-two years, no matter how hard I try. And I was never stupid enough to invest in any of my own projects.

The moment I mentioned being financially *comfortable,* Trevor lost all interest in the handsome young man he'd been kissing on the dance floor and turned all his attention on me.

That night a man went to bed with me without being paid to for the first time in I don't remember how many years. Admittedly, I had to give him a certain amount of basic instruction. He, quite frankly, wasn't completely sure where it went.

"I'm sorry," he said, so adorably, in that darling little lisp of his, "but, you're my first woman."

I didn't even know they still made virgins. Turned out Trevor had been born a virgin, but I didn't hold it against him.

To the best of my knowledge, I hadn't been married since Al Bronze died,[†] but I've never been known for breaking habits. In May 1990 I became Mrs. Trevor Berman. He may have been my ninth or tenth or eleventh husband, but I was certainly his only wife.[††]

There was a small difference in our ages. I was ninety-three, he was twenty-five, but we knew those years would shrink as time went by. After all, as he said, "When you're one hundred, I'll be thirty-two."

He wasn't the most skillful lover I had ever had. No one would mis-

---

*Except, of course, that Coward had a gigantic success in Las Vegas, and he didn't use musclemen, at least on stage.–Douglas

[†]It's *possible* that I was married one or more times during the seventies, but there's no evidence supporting it, and none of my staff remember any husbands during that period.–Tallulah

[††]Tallulah may have been Trevor's only wife, but there is every reason to believe he had even more husbands than she did, only they weren't *his* husbands.–Douglas

take him for Paolo or Sherman Oakley or Major Babs. But, then, quite frankly, I wasn't really up for the more rigorous sexual escapades of my youth. With my shaky pelvic cradle, there was always the danger of reducing my pelvis to powder.

On the plus side, Trevor said there was nothing on earth like oral sex from a woman who could remove her teeth first. Unfortunately, Trevor couldn't return the favor. His every attempt at cunnilingus had ended the same way, with a violent nausea attack. I guess he'd been frightened by a bush when a child.

Trevor took over as my manager, which was nice, since I'd never had one before. Next thing I knew, I was doing commercials for adult diapers. You may remember them.

"Hello, I'm Tallulah Morehead, darling. You know, you can't buy vodka, you can only rent it. And these days, I'm lucky to rent it by the hour. In fact, I've gone twice just since we've started talking. In one end and out the other, which is why I depend on Sop 'Ems, the adult personal security system. It brings families back together. Just strap on a Sop 'Ems and your daughter-in-law will let you back on her good sofa again. Bottoms up, darling!"

I didn't think this was the most dignified job I could have, and it was giving the public the seventy-five-percent wrong impression that I was incontinent. But when I mentioned this, Trevor got all huffy. "What? You think you're too good for piss-rag ads? Hey, children in China would kill to sell Sop 'Ems!"

"Then let them. I really don't need the money. And the work isn't exactly fulfilling."

"You, you, you. It's always all about you! What about *me?* Providing your services to sponsors is my profession. I'm trying to establish an independent income, so I'm not living off of you, and you thwart me! Are you trying to ruin me? You hate me, don't you?

"Nonsense, darling."

"Yes, you do. It's because I used to be gay, isn't it? I know your other gay husbands hurt you, but I'm not them! When do I stop paying for their sins?"

"I'm sorry, Trevor darling. How can I make it up to you?"

"Buy me a Porsche."

"All right." It was like having Pattycakes back again.

Trevor booked me on talk shows, and had me making public appearances at store openings on behalf of Sop 'Ems. I ran into Vincent Lovecraft at one of them.

"Tallulah, what the hell are you doing those stupid diaper commercials for? They have no class at all. You *can't* need the money. Honey, remember your image. We're a couple of the last survivors of a glorious, golden era in movies. Don't cheapen it with this crap."

"Vincent darling, it's Trevor. I do them for him."

"Tallulah, are you going to keep making the same mistake *all* your life?"

"I can't imagine what you mean, darling."

Then Trevor decided to become an actor. His first suggestion was that I tour in *Streetcar* again, this time with him as Stanley. Although Trevor as Stanley *would* make Bob Denver come across like Marlon Brando, the fact was that at ninety-four I wasn't really appropriate casting for Blanche anymore, even if I had the energy for it.

His next suggestion was a stage adaptation of something called *Harold & Maude*. "Trevor, darling, I simply don't have the energy to do a stage play. I don't have the energy to do the commercials."

"You're so selfish! I hate you! I wish I was dead! How will I ever become a star if my wife won't pitch in and help? You selfish bitch!"

"I'm sorry, dear. Is there any way to make it up to you?"

"Buy me a yacht?"

"Well . . ."

"I knew it! You hate me!"

"All right. You can have a yacht."

"Thank you, honey. Now, about the play."

And so it went. I might have actually ended up doing that *Harold & Maude* thing he was set on if Vincent hadn't dropped by Morehead Heights one evening a month later while Trevor was out at his lodge meeting.

"Get in the car, Tallulah," Vincent said, with an attractive brusqueness.

"Where are we going?" I asked.

"Your husband's so-called 'lodge.' "

It turned out that Trevor wasn't at a lodge hall at all. He was at a private home in West Hollywood. I don't know if he was an Elk or a Moose or what, but he was some sort of horny animal, and it was certainly rutting season, judging by the vigorous, all-male orgy he was in the middle of when Vincent and I walked in.

Vincent, it turned out, had hired a private detective to investigate Trevor after our conversation. Not only was Trevor cheating *on* me, he was cheating me directly. He was having my commercial fees paid directly to him, and had been liberally helping himself to my bank accounts, to the tune of fifteen million dollars.

At the divorce Trevor actually had the gall to ask for alimony. The judge was laughing heartily as he threw the little pissant out.

Good Lord, I was ninety-five years old. Would I *never* find True Love?

44

Afterlife Is a Cabaret

Gilmore. You remember Gilmore, from the introduction, so many pages ago? Well, at very long last, we've come full circle and back to Gilmore again, and the final chapter of my adventures to date, as those of you who read the table of contents are no doubt aware.

I met Gilmore at a Has-Been Convention, excuse me, I mean an Autograph Collector's Show, where formerly famous people sit at long tables signing ancient photographs for five bucks a pop. This one was held at a lovely hotel in Studio City owned by Beverly Garland, a fabulous actress I never got to work with, although I have had sex on her premises a number of times.

I was seated at a table along with the girls from *Petticoat Junction,* Woody Strode, Gary Lockwood, my own dear Steve Reeves, the annoyingly shrill woman who was the voice of Snow White, half a dozen ex-Munchkins, Alan Young, Jackie Joseph, Tommy Kirk, the surviving cast of *Bewitched,* three former Tarzans, and Ronald Reagan. Since I didn't need the money, I wasn't charging for my autographed pictures, which made my line a little longer, though Reagan called it a "Cheap Stunt," and he'd know.

Gilmore arrived already equipped with a stack of photos of me, and other memorabilia, and began inundating me with his worshipful fandom. Once I made certain that he wasn't the least bit interested in marrying me, I let him wash over me.

I visited his apartment and found it was really a small, private museum entirely devoted to my career.

As I said in my introduction, I soon hired Gilmore as my new personal assistant. He happily moved into Morehead Heights, taking up residence in Terrence's old room. It was almost like having old Terrence back again, except that Gilmore was somewhat more butch than Terrence, but then, so was Mary Tyler Moore.

As I also said in my introduction, it was Gilmore who had the idea of my entering cabaret. He introduced me to Bryan Miller, a talented musician who entertains at gay piano bars, a wonderful innovation that allows piano lovers to drink while enjoying live piano music, and if there's anything I enjoy as much as drinking, it's a talented pianist. Bryan, in turn, introduced me to Douglas McEwan, a bitter, would-be actor and comedy writer, scratching out a living on the fringes of show business when not cruising squalid, slimy dives for sleazy gay sex with any grubby low-life pervert he can find.* In short, my type of man.

Bryan, Douglas, and I began putting my cabaret act together. Since I was ninety-five years old, it was decided to forgo the big, athletic dance numbers that Gilmore suggested. We worked out an act that consisted of me performing a few numbers I'd made famous during my career: "Heat Crazed!," "Stand Tall and Erect," "Sudan Sunset," "With One Stare," and so forth, along with a couple more contemporary numbers, like "Let It Please Be Him," and "Unforgettable," at least on the rare evenings when I could remember its lyrics,† interspersed with stories about my career, humorous anecdotes and jokes, all carefully crafted by myself, Bryan, and Douglas. Bryan would work onstage as my accompanist and straight man (a real stretch for him, though he brought it off with all the panache of Rod Towers), feeding me lines and playing my music. Gilmore and Douglas often appeared as well, doing sets within my show, Gilmore singing with Bryan about his worship of me while Douglas did his always popular, amusing, filthy sex songs.

At my first major engagement, at a club called The Velvet Room, which was much nicer than my tryout club, The Rubber Room (they wouldn't let me leave; they *loved* me!), Hisato came out of retirement to sing a couple of numbers as well. Vincent Lovecraft even made one appearance with me, though he seemed more interested in cruising the audience for late-night company than performing.

I caught on. I played clubs in Los Angeles, New York, San Francisco, and Chicago. I emceed evenings of talent when I presented "protégés"— generally struggling, half-talented, vulgar standup comics and lovely

---

*I am *not* bitter.–Douglas

†How does it go again? *"Unforgettable, something, something, something. Unforgettable, la da de da. That's why, darling, dum de de de dee. That some one so, something or other. Blah de blah de blah, unforgettable, too."* Yeah, that's it. –Tallulah

lady singers. I had a gift for fingering talent, and set more than one youngster on the roller-coaster ride to show-business obscurity.

Not surprisingly, at this point in my life, I was most popular with gays, but at least, I'd stopped marrying them. Younger stars adored me, like that darling Bernadette Peters. As anyone who knows me well will tell you, I have always loved Peters. I played benefits and smokers, and found a whole new generation of fans.

I was briefly offered a movie comeback role in a picture to be called *The Black Stallion,* with O. J. Simpson in the title role, but he withdrew from the film suddenly for some reason, and the project collapsed. At present I am considering a comeback this year in something called *The Blurry Witch Project.* We'll see.

But, successful as I've been, once you get past one hundred, performing becomes a tad fatiguing. I needed to save my energy for drinking and, hopefully, a little more sex.

All of which, in turn, led me to this book, one last way of sharing myself with my millions of adoring fans. Since Douglas was literate and available ("idle" is what the Republicans call it), he seemed the right person to sit here for the last year and listen to me rattle off these memoirs, which have finally brought me, for the second time, to the turn of a century. Who knows what the next one will bring?

EPILOGUE

Morehead Revisited

"Miss Morehead, *please,* we want *more!*"

I hear you, gentle reader, but no, this is it, darlings. Isn't this enough? An entire century of reminiscences should satisfy anybody. Thank you for coming this far with me. I love each and every one of you, and if you drop by Morehead Heights, I'm prepared to prove it.

What has this year of mud wrestling with my personal demons taught me?

Never wear glasses. It will make you look better, and make the men look better too. Clarity is overrated.

Never marry a man who won't have sex with you.

Always tip your waiter generously. He handles your drinks. And overtip the bartender; he's doing God's Work.

Never mix, never worry.

In fact, I'll shorten that advice.

Never worry.

After all, you could spend that time drinking.

Cheers, darlings.

APPENDIX

Tallulah's Complete Filmography

All unattributed films are PMS's.

1915   Heat Crazed! (silent version)
1916   The Human Woman
1917   Bluebeard's Daughter
1918   Grand Delusion
1919   Adam's Bone
1920   Fleshpot
1921   Silent Echoes
1922   A Burning Sensation
1923   Ludicrous Lust
1924   Son of the Shriek
1925   The Phantom of the Operetta
1925   Forbidden Fruit
1926   Tramp Steamer
1927   Beyond Belief!
1928   Eskimo Pie
1929   Blood on the Ceiling (Tallulah's last silent movie)
1930   The Godawful Truth (Tallulah's first talkie)
1930   An Affair to Forget
1931   Dancing in the Drink
1931   The Naked Nudist
1932   Broadway Bimbos
1932   Heat Crazed! (sound version)
1932   Stewed Prudes
1934   Fu Manchu's Blessed Event (MGM)
1934   The Revenge of Cleopatra

1935	*Edgar Allan Poe's The Black Pussy* (Universal)
1935	*HER!* (RKO)
1935	*Scrimpy Endowment*
1936	*The Thick Man*
1936	*Virgins of Krakatoa*
1937	*Babes Behind Bars*
1937	*Buccaneer Bride*
1937	*Fatal Floozy*
1938	*Tarzan's Secret Shame*
1938	*Alexander the Great's Ragtime Band*
1938	*Illicit Plaything*
1939	*Seven Brides for Seven Dwarfs* (animated feature, Disney)
1939	*Damaged Cargo*
1939	*Mayfair Madness*
1939	*East versus West*
1940	*Hillbilly Hijinks*
1940	*Everyone's Coming Up Rose's*
1940	*The Devil Wore Ermine*
1941	*The Mailman Always Comes Twice*
1941	*Curse of the Pussy People* (RKO)
1942	*Privates on Display*
1942	*The Lady Steve*
1942	*Life Preserver* (Hitchcock and Selznick)
1943	*Anchors Akimbo*
1943	*Amnesia* (Hitchcock and Selznick)
1943	*Single Indemnity*
1945	*Sudan Sunset*
1945	*The Siren of the Congo* (Universal)
1946	*Privates in Public*
1946	*Amok!*
1946	*The Gang's All Banged* (Twentieth Century Fox)
1947	*The Road to Hell* (Hope and Crosby, Paramount)
1947	*An Ordeal to Remember* (last PMS Picture)
1948	*The Snake Hole* (S. Lee-Zee Films)
1948	*Axel's Acting Lesson* (16mm short, *very* limited release, S. Lee-Zee Films)
1950	*Infraction* (S. Lee-Zee Films)
1952	*Boot Camp Bitches* (S. Lee-Zee Films)
1952	*Grueling Fury* (S. Lee-Zee Films)
1953	*ScoffLaw* (S. Lee-Zee Films)
1954	*Johnny Horndog* (Universal)

1955   *Abbott & Costello Meet She Who Must Be Obeyed* (Universal)

1956   *THAT!* (Amassed Artists)

1957   *The Haunting of Horrible House* (shot at Hungfair, Amassed Artists)

1958   *Bride of the Blob* (Amassed Artists)

1959   *Bats in My Belfry* (Hammer, England)

1960   *Caligulee, Caligula!* (Pastafazool Films, Italy)

1960   *Torah, Torah, Torah* (Pastafazool Films, Egypt)

1961   *1,000,000 Years Ago (Hammer, Spain)*

1961   *A World of Woozy Song* (Toho Studios, Japan; never released in the USA)

1962   *Edgar Allan Poe's The Premature Climax* (AIP)

1963   *My Left Breast* (Andy Warhol in 3-D)

1964   *Who the Hell Killed Baby Jane?* (Warner Brothers)

1964   *Wet, Wild, and Willing* (Paramount)

1964   *Mary Poppers* (Disney)

1965   *It Sounds Like Music* (Twentieth Century Fox)

1965   *Shut Your Damn Mouth, Stupid Sylvia* (Warner Brothers)

1965   *Demented!* (Warner Brothers)

1965   *Doctor Scary* (American Pictures Enterprises)

1966   *Fiddler on a Hot Tin Roof* (Twentieth Century Fox)

1966   *Guess What's Coming to Dinner?* (Warner Brothers)

1967   *When Dinosaurs Ruled the Block* (Hammer, Spain)

1968   *Frankenstein's Reason for Living* (Hammer, England)

1968   *Against All Fags* (English public-service antismoking film)

1969   *Jurassic Tart* (MGM, Hawaii)

1969   *The Carpetmunchers* (Cocksure Movies. Tallulah's last film, which she also wrote and directed)

1994   *The Black Stallion* (unmade, with O.J.)

2000   *The Blurry Witch Project* (future project)

Acknowledgments

Many years ago my friend, the actress and comedienne Christy Kanen, created a sketch character she called Miss Olga Hungova, a washed-up, alcoholic, Norma Desmondish ex-movie star. In the beginning, Olga was but one of Christy's large retinue of hilarious characters, but Olga seemed to have a life of her own, and soon overshadowed her fictional sisters.

In 1986, I began writing for Olga, joining Christy and Bryan Miller. One of the first pieces I worked on for Olga was a TV appearance in which she was plugging her autobiography, which I had titled *My Life . . . I Think*. For the next ten years the three of us wrote jokes and songs for Miss Olga, as her popularity in various Los Angeles gay clubs grew. Then Christy chose to retire from performing, and, in particular, to kill off Miss Olga, from whom the joy of performing had long drained away.

But Olga's fans still loved her. I was often running into people who asked when Miss Olga would come back. When I began this project in 1999, my intention was to co-write Miss Olga's life with Christy. However, after reading the early chapters, Christy decided that she did not want to perpetuate Miss Olga's existence any longer. "Olga is dead!" she firmly stated.

But I was aware that I was doing the best writing of my life, and I was loathe to just burn it. So Miss Olga died, Christy's jokes came out, and Tallulah was born. I quickly found that being liberated from Olga's established history freed me to fire up the wilder aspects of my imagination, and took the story into places Olga had never gone. The remaining Olga fans reading this book will recognize much of Olga's personality, as well as *Privates on Display*, but they will be meeting Pattycakes, Major Babs, Sherman Oakley and so many others new.

But not one word of this book would ever have been written without Christy being there first. Her retirement from performing is a sad loss to comedy.

Bryan Miller, our other Olga collaborator, has been an enthusiastic booster of this project from day one. Many of his jokes and suggestions adorn these pages. He has put up with listening to fresh chapters read aloud, often at two in the morning, and made many helpful suggestions, as well as allowing himself to become a fictional character. To give only one example from dozens, it was Bryan who suggested the phrase "I'm only a Social Drinker" to my ear. Further, the various song lyrics scattered throughout all have melodies, and most of those melodies were composed by Bryan.

Bryan's Life Partner, Gilmore Rizzo, has also been an enthusiastic booster, has put up with being fictionalized (that the fictional Gilmore is about eight years younger than the real man helped), and made the single most useful suggestion that anybody contributed. When I was looking for a new name for the character, it was Gilmore who casually said, "You ought to call her Tallulah Morehead."

Michael Berman gave me both the computer I began the book on and the sofa I lay on while thinking up Tallulah's adventures. Thanks to Michael, this project went from being an idea, to being a real thing.

My brother, Barry Young, gave me the computer on which I finished the book, and has also given me a lifetime of brotherly love.

The lovely and talented Jayne Hamil took time away from making more famous people on TV appear funnier than they are, to listen to immense amounts of this work over the telephone, offering always on-target suggestions, as well as also giving me many decades of love and support.

My friends James Diederich and Dick Whittington both read the finished first draft, and their suggestions and enthusiastic support kept me on track. Further, it was Dick many years ago, who first clued me in that I was funny, and taught me much of what I know about comedy and writing.

My longtime friend Lee Nordling, a first-rate comics editor, took time to read my grossly overwritten book synopsis and show me how to ruthlessly chop a third of it away. Thanks to his editing skills, it turned into the lean sales tool needed to market the manuscript. Great gift. Thanks, Lee.

My sister, Gretchen Lloyd, came through with much-needed cash at a crucial juncture in the marketing process, and I've always said, the best expressions of affection can be deposited or spent.

My agent, Melanie Mills, read it, got it, and sold it. Without her, I'd be doing something else that I like a lot less. It's never easy taking a chance on an unknown.

John Scognamiglio changed my life one day, by buying this book for publication. No thanks are adequate for that. He then proceeded to edit it gently, which, for a first-time author with a tendency to split his infinitives and who doesn't know a subjunctive clause from a hole in the ozone, is such a relief. Being edited is never fun, but John kept it free of gratuitous pain.

Glen Hanson, using some extraordinary superpower of ESP magic, from three thousand miles away, reached into my brain and plucked out Tallulah's image for the magnificent cover illustrations, which made me laugh out loud. Believe me, gentle reader, that is *exactly* how Tallulah looks, and may even be how I look, though I would never wear those shoes. Glen's pictures are the delicious icing on the cake that is this book, and they are perfect! My only regret is that there isn't one of his hilarious sketches in every chapter. Who needs Chris Alexander when they have Glen Hanson?

Lastly, I would be disingenuous at best if I didn't invoke the magic name of Patrick Dennis, actually Edward Everett Tanner III, who was certainly there first. I've been reading Dennis since I was ten, and his influence is screamingly obvious on every page of this story. My well-thumbed first edition of *Little Me* was never farther than two feet away from my computer throughout the writing of this book, if only to ensure that nothing in my tale duplicated anything in his. It was at once the example I was trying to equal and the pitfall I was trying to avoid. The *Around the World* section of this book, written in conscious imitation of the structure of Dennis's *Around the World With Auntie Mame,* is a deliberate homage, my way of acknowledging my debt to Dennis within the text itself.

My thanks to all, and, as Tallulah would say, cheers darlings.

The Wit and Wisdom of Tallulah Morehead, Living Legend

Tallulah on Family

"I never knew my father. Unfortunately, I can't say the same about my mother."

Tallulah on the Critics

"When we made the film noir *Fatal Floozy*, Bosley Crowther gave me one of his rare good notices when he wrote: 'Tallulah is so good as the corpse that one hopes she will be dead in all of her films from now on.' "

Tallulah on the Big Roles

"I had wanted to play Dorothy in *The Wizard of Oz* ever since Terrence first read his summary of the treatment to me. The story was practically my biography, only without any sex or booze."

Tallulah on Imbibing

"I suppose I should comment here on the subject of alcohol. I'm only going to say this once and then I shall drop the entire subject. I am strictly a *social drinker*! Just because you're alone is no reason to be anti-social."

Tallulah on Men

"The silly story that all my husbands were gay still persists, to the point that at my last wedding the band played *Here Comes the Beard*."

Tallulah on Being a Lady

"It is not a lady's function to fill her own gaps, except in prison, of course."

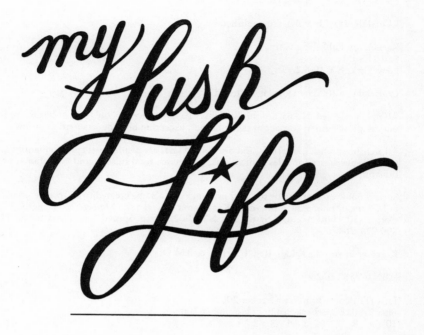

Douglas McEwan

KENSINGTON BOOKS
http://www.kensingtonbooks.com

KENSINGTON BOOKS are published by

Kensington Publishing Corp.
850 Third Avenue
New York, NY 10022

All Kensington titles, imprints, and distributed lines are available at special quantity discounts for bulk purchases for sales promotions, premiums, fund-raising, and educational or institutional use.

Special book excerpts or customized printings can also be created to fit specific needs. For details, write or phone the office of the Kensington Special Sales Manager: Kensington Publishing Corp., 850 Third Avenue, New York, NY 10022. Attn. Special Sales Department, Phone: 1-800-221-2647.

Kensington and the K logo Reg. U.S. Pat. & TM Off.

ISBN 0-7582-0223-7

First Hardcover Printing: October 2002
First Trade Paperback Printing: November 2003
10 9 8 7 6 5 4 3 2 1

Printed in the United States of America